HOT UNDER THE COLLAR

THE DOGMOTHERS - BOOK ONE

roxanne st. claire

Hot Under the Collar
THE DOGMOTHERS BOOK ONE

ISBN Print: 978-1-7339121-2-9
ISBN Ebook: 978-1-7339121-1-2

COVER ART: Keri Knutson (designer)
and Dawn C. Whitty (photographer)
INTERIOR FORMATTING: Author EMS

Critical Reviews of
Roxanne St. Claire Novels

"Non-stop action, sweet and sexy romance, lively characters, and a celebration of family and forgiveness."
— *Publishers Weekly*

"Plenty of heat, humor, and heart!"
— *USA Today* (Happy Ever After blog)

"Beautifully written, deeply emotional, often humorous, and always heartwarming!"
— *The Romance Dish*

"Roxanne St. Claire is the kind of author that will leave you breathless with tears, laughter, and longing as she brings two people together, whether it is their first true love or a second love to last for all time."
— *Romance Witch Reviews*

"Roxanne St. Claire writes an utterly swoon-worthy romance with a tender, sentimental HEA worth every emotional struggle her readers will endure. Grab your tissues and get ready for some ugly crying. These books rip my heart apart and then piece it back together with the hope, joy and indomitable loving force that is the Kilcannon clan."
— *Harlequin Junkies*

"As always, Ms. St. Claire's writing is perfection…I am unable to put the book down until that final pawprint the end. Oh the feels!"
— *Between My BookEndz*

Dear Reader:

After the success and support I received for the nine-book Dogfather series, I'm thrilled to launch this "spin-off" series. The Kilcannon kids have found love, and so has "The Dogfather" who set all those romances in action, but there are still the "Mahoney cousins" and now the Santorini stepkids. Enter Gramma Finnie and Yiayia... The Dogmothers! One grandmother has the steel spine of a Greek warrior, the other has the heart of an Irish poet. With the help of some very special puppers, these two are on a matchmaking mission to make sure all of their grandchildren are hooked, hitched, and happy. I am so excited to write this new series and I sure hope you'll come along for the ride.

Like all of the books in the previous series, the covers of The Dogmothers books were all photographed at Alaqua Animal Refuge (www.alaqua.org) in my home state of Florida using rescue dogs and local heroes. And, as I did with The Dogfather Series, a portion of the first month's sales (digital and print) is donated to that amazing organization dedicated to helping animals survive, thrive, and find forever homes. (One of my own is an Alaqua rescue!)

As always, I have to acknowledge the incredibly talented team of professionals that keep me sane and happy, and allow me to focus on writing books for you. Love and gratitude to my developmental editor, Kristi Yanta; my copyeditor, Joyce Lamb; my proofreaders, Marlene Engle and Chris Kridler; and my most beloved assistant, Maria Connor. Behind the scenes, there is a husband who cannot be matched, two (grown) kids that still cheer every book like it's the first, and two dogs who own my heart and soul.

xoxo, Rocki

Before
The Dogmothers...
there was

Sit...Stay...Beg (Book 1)
New Leash on Life (Book 2)
Leader of the Pack (Book 3)
Santa Paws is Coming to Town (Book 4 – a Holiday novella)
Bad to the Bone (Book 5)
Ruff Around the Edges (Book 6)
Double Dog Dare (Book 7)
Bark! The Herald Angels Sing – (Book 8 – a Holiday novella)
Old Dog New Tricks (Book 9)

Find information and buy links for all these books here:
http://www.roxannestclaire.com/dogfather-series

For a complete list, buy links, and reading order of *all* my books, visit www.roxannestclaire.com. Be sure to sign up for my newsletter on my website to find out when the next book is released! And join the private Dogfather Facebook group for inside info on all the books and characters, sneak peeks, and a place to share the love of tails and tales!

www.facebook.com/groups/roxannestclairereaders/

Dedication

This book is dedicated the original "Dogmothers" –
the super fans who make up a private Facebook reader
group where we gather to celebrate "tails and tales."
I would be lost without this community of
pawsitivity…and I hope these special readers know
how much their love and support means to me.

Prologue

"The attitude that you embrace
will change the reality that you face."
— Gramma Finnie (*embroidered on a pillow*)

"FAKE IT TILL YOU MAKE IT."
— Agnes Santorini (*screamed into a pillow*)

gnes Santorini stepped out of the Bitter Bark
Bed & Breakfast into the sunshine with one
simple thought: Life was good.

Okay, *okay*. Life was mostly crap. But it sure beat
the alternative. And no one knew that better than a
woman who had experienced both.

Taking a deep breath like she'd learned in yoga,
Agnes took a moment to get her bearings, panning the
view of quaint brick buildings, flowered window
boxes, and a vast park bursting with green at the
center of it all. Familiar, comforting, and genuine, the
town of Bitter Bark was not at all unlike Chestnut
Creek, just a little over an hour away, where she'd

lived almost her entire adult life until her husband died ten years ago.

She missed the small-town North Carolina life, she thought as she began to walk. But, after making sure her grandchildren were ready to take over the family restaurant, Agnes had done what any widow her age was supposed to do—she retired to Florida.

Blue skies, palm trees, and endless talk about arthritis and grandkids had suited her well enough in the sea of Spanish tile and retention ponds they called Jacaranda Lakes. She'd settled into an inexpensive condo, made a few somewhat tolerable friends, got unbeatable at canasta, and acquired two ridiculously cute dachshunds and one was-probably-cute-once boyfriend.

Pygmalion and Galatea were the lights of her life. Ted, however, bought the farm. Literally. He won a million dollars in a Florida Lottery Scratch-Off game, bought his grandson a farm in Iowa, then went there to live, and Agnes hadn't heard from him since.

But eight months ago, her simple retired life changed in a heartbeat. Well, the *loss* of a heartbeat. During the six and a half minutes that her heart *didn't* beat, Agnes experienced something called "circulatory death."

And then she circled right back to life.

Having defied the odds, she knew her very existence had suddenly become more precious and meaningful than ever. That's when Agnes set out to live her life over again, as a different woman, to accomplish whatever it was she'd been sent back from the dead to do.

The only problem was she had no idea what that was.

Her steps slowed at the corner, but not because she was uncertain or lost. She was terrified.

Life had transformed Agnes, formerly an aging grandmother of five. No, correct that. *Death* had transformed Agnes. And she couldn't forget how easily death could happen again.

Which was why she'd come up to North Carolina in response to what was surely a begrudgingly issued invitation to an engagement party. No doubt the whole family thought their boorish, complaining, self-centered old Yiayia would want no part of celebrating the pending nuptials of her not-so-beloved daughter-in-law, Katie Santorini, to a man named Daniel Kilcannon.

And who could blame them? They didn't know what happened to Agnes last year, because she'd never told a soul, not even the doctors. And for the forty years Katie had been married to Agnes's son, there'd been very little love lost between mother and daughter-in-law. Even at Nico's funeral, Agnes had been cold to the woman whose only real fault was not being Greek.

Oh, Agnes Mastros Santorini. No wonder you weren't allowed in...up there.

But then, she'd changed. Or was *trying* to change.

She passed a store window and caught her reflection, where that change was most evident. Gone were the gray, unstyled locks, dyed to something called warm espresso and cut to match a picture from a magazine. A few thousand dollars' worth of Botox and filler had smoothed out her face, eliminating the deepest creases that almost eight decades of scowling had etched. Complete denial of everything delicious, daily two-mile walks with one of her dogs—the fat one could go only a few blocks—and regular visits to the Jacaranda Lakes Fitness Center had whittled down her formerly matronly figure. Today, she wore a size-ten sheath and kitten heels.

But her brush with death had transformed so much more than Agnes's face and body. During seemingly endless moments, she had floated toward the light and felt inexplicable peace, and then she got there, to the brightest center of joyous brightness…only to go careening back to a stretcher in the middle of an Olive Garden. That had altered something deep inside her, and it wasn't just that she'd never eat in a second-rate chain restaurant again.

Agnes wanted to be better. No, no. She *had* to be better. Otherwise, next time, she might not get a second chance, and she'd get sent…somewhere else. But "better" was a challenge for an old battle-ax like her.

All her life, negativity had come naturally because she bitched the way most people breathed. Constantly and without much thought. And her deeply ingrained cultural bias that anything Greek was better than the rest of the world reared its ugly head on more than one occasion. Like every single day.

Changing her body, face, and hair had been a breeze. Changing on the inside? Much more difficult. Oh sure, she could fake it with friends for an hour or two of playing cards, but something told her the change had to be with her family. To really work, her change had to be directed at people she'd hurt the most.

So, after weeks of ignoring that invitation on her kitchen counter, she'd packed her bags, locked her condo, gathered up Pyggie and Gala, and climbed into her Buick Regal for the long drive to North Carolina with one goal: to be *New Yiayia* to her family.

And speaking of family…she sucked in a noisy breath at the sight of her granddaughter, not one block away.

Holy sh…

Oh. Dang. She squeezed her eyes shut and erased the curse word, replacing it with the closest thing she knew to a prayer. *Please God, don't let me screw this up.*

Then Agnes pinned her gaze and all her hopes on the young woman on the other side of the street, headed straight for Santorini's Deli.

Cassie walked next to a little old lady with white hair and the same kind of button-down sweater and slacks that Agnes used to wear. She even had the rubber-soled shoes and a frumpy handbag hanging on her arm.

The famous Gramma Finnie, Agnes surmised.

All of what Agnes knew about this new extended family had come from Cassie, who was the only grandchild who called frequently to fill her in on what had happened in the Santorini family over the last few months.

If Cassie wondered why Agnes hadn't busted a gut when she found out that Nick, her oldest grandson and Cassie's brother, wasn't a *Santorini* at all, but a love child conceived in a dorm room back in the seventies…well, the girl was too smart and classy to ask. Or maybe Cassie thought, *Yiayia lost her marbles*—which was closer to the truth.

Cassie had detailed the whole story of how the man who was Nick's biological father, Daniel Kilcannon, had fallen in love with Katie, proposed to her, and they'd set a wedding date for this fall.

The *old* Yiayia—the one Katie had no doubt reluctantly invited to her engagement party—would have blown a gasket over the news that her precious grandson wasn't her grandson at all. The old Yiayia would have rolled her eyes and delivered a hate-filled diatribe about how she'd never liked Katie all that much and reminded them all that Nico Santorini was a very great Greek man who deserved better than this sad legacy. The old Yiayia would dip into her deep well of mean to remind her own daughter-in-law that she *liked* her but didn't *love* her because she wasn't Greek.

Shame, regret, and a wayward brick nearly buckled her at the knees.

"I'm sorry," she whispered with a glance to the sky, regaining her balance.

So what would the *new* Yiayia do?

She'd wish the happy couple well and raise a glass to a long life together. Would that be enough? Was that her "purpose" in this second chance at life? To be nicer? Maybe. But there might be more, and she had to figure out what it was before...before her heart stopped again, which could happen in the next five minutes based on the way it was slamming against her chest right that moment.

Taking a deep breath, she watched the two women cross at the corner, heading toward the restaurant. No surprise, Cassie didn't even notice Agnes. She was deep in conversation with the little white-haired granny, laughing as they reached the front door of Santorini's Deli at the very moment Agnes did.

They all stopped, and for a second, Agnes pressed her hand over her chest and closed her eyes, vowing to *be nice*.

"Oh, sorry, 'tis closed today," the older woman said in a rich brogue, likely mistaking Agnes's turmoil for disappointment. "But surely you can come back tomorrow and enjoy some delicious Greek food."

"That's redundant," Agnes said, looking at Cassie. "All Greek food is delicious."

"Oh my God." Cassie croaked the words, her dark eyes widening like the black olives she loved to steal from the restaurant back bar when she was a little girl. "*Yiayia?*" Her voice rose in utter shock. "Is that you?"

Never the most affectionate person on earth, Agnes forced herself to lift her arms to reach out to her granddaughter for a stiff hug. "I made it. No doubt the earth will stop revolving now."

Cassie let out something between a shriek and a laugh, stepping forward to fold Agnes in a warm embrace whether she wanted one or not.

"Look at you, Yiayia!" Cassie eased back to stare at Agnes, who was used to the reaction. It happened every time she ran into someone who hadn't seen her in a while. "I would never have recognized you until I heard your voice. Oh my *gawd*," she cooed, putting her hand on Agnes's cheek and blinking. "You look ten, no, twenty years younger!"

Agnes smiled into those familiar Santorini eyes. "And you are as beautiful as ever, *koukla*."

Cassie gave her another quick hug at the use of her childhood Greek nickname. "Mom is going to freak," she said. "She never dreamed you'd come."

Never *feared* she'd come, more like. "I wanted to

surprise her," Agnes said, glancing at the other, older woman. "And meet this new family of ours."

Cassie pressed her knuckles to her mouth, too overwhelmed, it seemed, to make introductions. "Who are you and what did you do with my Yiayia?"

"I left her at the gym, the beauty salon, and…" She tapped her cheek. "A sweet little business called Palm Place Plastic Surgery where they give out Juvéderm like it's candy." She added a casual shrug. "'Do not go gentle into the good night.' Isn't that what they say?"

Little grandma lifted one knowing and very white brow. "They also say, 'The older the fiddle, the sweeter the tune.'"

Agnes flicked off the comment. "Even a Stradivarius gets refurbished once in a while. You must be the Irish leprechaun that Cassie has told me about."

"Lepre—"

"Gramma Finnie, this is my grandmother, Agnes Santorini." Cassie slipped between them as if she expected blows to be exchanged. "And Yiayia, this is Gramma Finnie, who will be…" She hesitated for one awkward beat.

"Katie's new mother-in-law," Finnie finished for her with a gleam in crystal-blue eyes that Agnes couldn't quite interpret. "I suppose that gives us quite the common bond, lass."

Agnes let out a sharp laugh. "Lass? Now you're just mocking me."

"Not a bit," the woman said. "I'm shamrock green with envy at your fine self. Hard to believe we're of the same generation."

Well, Grammie, there's Betty White, and then there's Jane Fonda. I choose Jane.

8

Agnes bit her lip to keep from spilling out the bitter brew she used to serve to everyone. "Well, you've been wonderful to my family, Finnie," she said instead. "Cassie has told me so much about the Kilcannons and the Mahoneys, and I'm thrilled our dear Katie has found love again."

Cassie inched back a bit, making a face. "Wow. Somebody's on her best behavior."

Oh yes. Somebody was.

Before Agnes could answer, Finnie leaned in closer, her sweet smile at odds with the inner strength shining through from behind her bifocals. "I already love Katie like she's my own daughter," she said softly. "The whole family, in fact, has wormed their way into this old Irish heart."

For a moment, the two of them just stared at each other, something intangible hanging in the balance. They could be friends, enemies, competitors, or conspirators. Whatever, Agnes sensed they were polar opposites.

But she had no doubt this little old Irishwoman wouldn't be turned away from the pearly gates, and it would behoove Agnes to get on her good side. She might need a reference someday.

"How blessed they are to have you," Agnes said, the very words like sandpaper in her mouth despite the sweet voice she tried to use.

The tone must have worked, because Gramma Finnie angled her head and let out a little whimper of joy. "And blessed to have you here today, lass. And I mean that term of endearment as a true compliment on your beauty, inside and out."

9

Wait. Did she say *inside* and out? Agnes couldn't hear it over the sound of angels singing.

"Whoa," Cassie muttered, giving the side-eye to Agnes. "This family is certainly growing... complicated."

But Gramma Finnie slid her hand around Agnes's arm and snuggled her closer. "The more we grow, the stronger we get," she said, nodding to the park on the other side of the street. "Just like that big old tree in that town square, always spreadin' with new branches. Come meet my clan. They're going to love this lovely and sweet new grandmother they just found."

Lovely. Sweet. New.

Agnes pressed her hand over Finnie's knotted knuckles. "From your lips to God's ears, my friend."

And she'd never meant anything more.

Oh, the good Lord sure worked in mysterious ways. Finnie settled into her chair at the main table of the engagement party, oblivious to the crowd, her attention on the new addition to the ever-growing Kilcannon-Mahoney-Santorini branches that made up her beloved family tree.

First, He'd sent the lovely Katie to change Daniel's life from dark to light. Then He'd tied both families together with a child Katie and Daniel had unwittingly conceived forty-three years ago. And now, He'd brought forth a person who might have been a thorn in Katie's side during her forty years of marriage to Agnes's son, but now obviously wanted nothing but a fresh start with a new family.

Why, yes, the woman seemed a wee bit uncomfortable in her own skin, most likely because that skin had been pulled, pricked, polished, and puffed. She simply needed a friend to help her navigate these new waters, and Finnie would certainly—

"I still can't believe she's here." Cassie slipped into the chair next to Finnie, setting down her champagne glass so hard the fizzy stuff splashed a bit.

"Oh, Cassie darlin'." Finnie took the young woman's hand. "'Tis a surprise, but a happy one."

Cassie gave her head a negative shake. "You could have knocked me over with a feather when she opened her mouth."

"Must admit, lass, she's not what I expected based on the bits and pieces I've picked up from you and your mother."

Cassie's eyes tapered to dark slits directed at her grandmother across the crowded room. "I don't know what she's up to, Gramma Finnie. I'm not going to lie, something is weird."

"Weird? She seems perfectly lovely."

"Right? *Wrong.*" She picked up her champagne glass and took a deep drink. "She always has a motive. And it's usually to make my mother's life worse. Or somehow intervene in ours to make things happen the way *she* wants them to happen. Just her being here scares me, but this…this…" She waved her hand up and down in the direction of Agnes. "This extreme makeover? Something isn't right."

"Child." She squeezed Cassie's hand. "People change. Especially as they get old. She's lookin' at eighty, right? Oh, it's a mighty dauntin' number. Makes you want to do crazy things." Finnie leaned closer. "Maybe learnin' that her grandson wasn't her grandson at all, but *mine*, put somethin' sweet on her heart."

Cassie gave her a skeptical side-eye. "Nothing sweet has ever been within a mile of her heart. You don't know her, Gramma."

"You said she was gracious when she found out that Daniel is Nick's biological father."

"Exactly. Who uses 'gracious' and 'Yiayia' in the same sentence? No one."

Finnie sighed and slid a look to the table where Agnes was now deep in conversation with Cassie's brothers, twins Alex and John. Agnes was pointing to the food and nodding enthusiastically, so that would make Alex the chef happy, and she seemed to have a very cordial relationship with John.

"I think you should be grateful she's here, lass."

"I think she should go home and not try to ruin my mother's happiness, Gram."

Finnie tsked. "Unkind words can turn your mouth rotten."

"Then hers must be growing mold."

"Why don't you give her a chance? Remember, she buried a son and a husband in her life. I can tell you from my firsthand experience, you're never quite the same after pain like that."

Cassie looked at her, her shoulders dipping with a tiny bit of resignation. "You're so good, Gramma Finnie. I love how you give everyone the benefit of the doubt."

"Not everyone, but family. Family is the bedrock, the only thing that matters. You best remember that, lass."

"My grandmother doesn't think like you," Cassie said on a sigh. "If she did, our family would have been a lot happier."

"Well, when your mother marries my son, I'll be your step-grandmother," Finnie said, patting Cassie's hand. "And as such, my first order of business will be to ask you to love the one God gave ye."

"I *do* love her. I just don't trust her."

Finnie added a little pressure on Cassie's hand and jutted her chin in the other direction. "Oh, look, Braden's standing all alone."

Cassie rolled her eyes. "Subtle, Grammiecakes. Real subtle."

Finnie laughed, amused as always by this refreshing lass. "Well, if you won't talk to him, I will." She started to push up, but Cassie circled her wrist, holding her in place.

"Why don't you talk to Yiayia instead? People always confide in you, Gramma Finnie. See if you can suss out her ulterior motive for the unexpected arrival."

"What if she doesn't have one?"

Cassie notched one of her perfectly arched dark brows. "Twenty bucks says you're wrong about that."

"Twenty bucks says she's here to love and appreciate her family."

"You are one for the books, lady." Cassie leaned over and planted a kiss on Finnie's cheek. "The world would be a better place if more people were as optimistic as you."

"Phooey on your optimism. I want my twenty bucks." Finnie pushed up and headed off to prove a point.

On the way, she lifted two champagne flutes from the bar. She'd have preferred a shot of Jameson's, but maybe that was too Irish for a fine Greek goddess like Agnes Santorini. Still, a wee lubrication of the tongue wasn't a bad idea.

Finnie arrived just as the matching lads were rising to their full stature, both of them wearing pleased but puzzled expressions on their handsome bearded faces.

"I have to check on the food," Alex said, his dark gaze still on his grandmother. "But I have to say, Yiayia, you look amazing."

"And you seem so…happy," John added, adjusting his glasses as if he could somehow get a better look at Agnes and make sure it was really her. "And I'm sorry I haven't visited you down in Florida for so long."

"Nonsense, Yianni." The Greek version of her grandson's name rolled off her tongue, making Finnie suspect she'd called him that since he was a babe. "I'm the one who should have come back to North Carolina more often. And I will now, I promise." She gave a quick laugh. "Who knows? I may never leave."

As soon as they stepped away, Finnie moved in, placing the glasses on the table and getting comfy in the seat across from Agnes.

"You know what the Irish say about grandchildren?" Finnie asked.

"They're better than potatoes?" Agnes bit her lip as soon as that came out. "Oh God. I don't mean that as an insult."

"None taken," Finnie assured her, inching Agnes's glass of champagne closer in invitation. "They say, 'Children are the rainbow in life, but grandchildren are the pot of gold.'"

She sighed and smiled. "That might very well be true, Finnie. I only have five, but they are all golden to me." She wrinkled her nose, which might have been the only thing on that face that *could* wrinkle. "I guess I only have four now."

"Don't ever say that." Finnie leaned in and held the other woman's gaze. "Nick might be *my* son's biological child, but he was raised into a fine lad by *your* son." She waited a beat before adding, "And Katie."

For a millisecond, her dark eyes widened, but almost immediately, she managed a smile that wiped away whatever her initial reaction would have been. "I hear Nick didn't take the news well at first."

Finnie gave a shrug, but well remembered that fateful Saint Paddy's Day when the handsome doctor confronted his biological father. "'Tis the past," she said. "After a few weeks, Nick made his peace with it all. Of course, he's in Africa now, and I understand he's in love."

"I've heard that, too."

"Although…"

Agnes raised both brows with open interest. "Yes?"

Finnie waved it off. "Needless gossip."

"Is there any other kind?" She put her hand over Finnie's. "It's not gossip if it involves our grandchild. And in this case, he is *both* of ours."

For a long moment, Finnie didn't say anything, then she smiled. "'Tis a strange and wonderful twist of fate, isn't it? Us having the same grandchild and the same daughter-in-law."

"It does give us a unique bond." Agnes didn't

sound like that bothered her, though. "Otherwise, we might never be…friends."

But could they be? "You're different than what I expected," Finnie said softly.

The observation made Agnes's expression shift into something that could be described only as satisfaction. "Really? You think so? Has anyone else said that to you about me?"

"Just my own observation, dear." When the other woman's face fell a little, Finnie remembered her mission. "You've done a kind thing for Katie by showin' up," she added. "I do believe you've shocked your family."

"That's the idea."

"Is it?" Finnie pressed, suddenly worrying if Cassie had been correct. "So you're here to…shock them?"

"In a manner of speaking, yes."

Oh no. "You think you'll be spendin' some time with Katie, then?"

"I don't know. Does she spend any time with anyone other than Daniel?" There was enough wryness in her tone to make Finnie certain she'd noticed the couple was virtually inseparable. Did she want to change that, or was it just an honest observation?

"They're together a lot, and I would know, considering I share the house with Daniel and Katie's all but moved in. Redecoratin' everything, too."

Agnes nodded. "She's very good at that."

"She's making it her home now," Finnie told her. "'Tis beautiful, but…different."

Agnes eyed her closely, clearly intrigued by the tone in Finnie's voice. Well, every good friendship did begin with honesty, and Finnie hadn't confided her concerns to anyone yet. "I'm getting used to it," Finnie added with a smile she hoped didn't look sad, because her new role as the second lady of the house didn't make her sad, just restless. Which was both a blessing and a curse for a woman her age.

"I can't wait to see Waterford," Agnes said. "Cassie told me that it's not just a homestead, but a large canine rescue and training center."

"Aye, 'tis the largest in the state. And I built the original home with my husband when we came here in the 1950s."

"I didn't know that."

Finnie took a breath to start the story, then stopped herself. This woman hadn't quite earned the history—long or short version. And everyone knew Finnie told only people she liked the long version.

"Could I bring my dogs there?" Agnes asked.

"I wasn't aware you had dogs with you."

"I never go anywhere without Pygmalion and Galatea, my doxies. They're named after the famous Greek lovers. Of course they made the drive up from Florida with me."

"Well, yes, you should bring them to Waterford," Finnie said. "How long will you be in town?"

"I don't know…" She looked around for a moment, scanning the faces in the room. "I'd like to stay for a while," she mused. "I've missed my family."

Bingo. Finnie was right, and Cassie was wrong.

Agnes leveled her gaze at someone across the room. "Who is that tall and handsome young man who seems to never be more than five feet from Cassie?"

"Braden Mahoney, my daughter Colleen's

youngest son," Finnie said without looking. "I had such high hopes for those two."

"Excuse me?"

"I thought for sure they'd be the next, what with the way they are both so anxious to leave Wednesday night dinners and go dancin' with the others and always teasin' each other, but…" She sighed and looked across the room where Daniel and Katie gazed into each other's eyes, laughing about some secret joke. "My son seems to have forgotten his matchmaking magic now that cupid's arrow has struck him."

"His matchmaking magic?" Her full attention on Finnie, Agnes put her elbows on the table and rested her chin on her hands. "What are you talking about?"

"Just look around and you'll see. In the past two years, my son orchestrated six different romances. It sealed his nickname as the Dogfather, a man who knows how to pull strings and make things happen."

"The Dogfather?" She chuckled at that. "What was his trick?"

"Special dogs. Perfect timing. Common sense and a wee bit of nudging, 'tis all. Liam and Andi happened thanks to a fateful trip to the hardware store and Liam learning she needed a guard dog. And there's Darcy and the landlord who didn't want pets that her father just happened to find for her. Aidan and Beck were forced to share custody of Ruff. My darling Molly? The pregnant one, she—"

"Wait. Wait." Agnes held up her hand. "I met more than one pregnant woman, and there's a newborn in the bunch, too."

"Exactly." Finnie crossed her arms and sat back. "All results of matches helped along by the master, my son. But now we have all the Mahoneys—they're my daughter Colleen's kids—and, of course, Daniel's future stepchildren, who happen to be your grandchildren."

"That's a lot of strings for the Dogfather to pull."

"The Dogfather is too in love to pay attention to anyone but our sweet Katie," Finnie noted. "But we need more happy endings around here, and I can't get him to settle down and get the job done."

Agnes turned her attention from the crowd to Finnie. "If he can do it, so can we."

Finnie drew back, not expecting this response.

"How hard can it be to find them partners and prod them along?" Agnes asked, her voice rising with a bit of excitement. "What's keeping Cassie and Braden apart? I mean, other than the fact that he's obviously not Greek."

"An ex-girlfriend who hasn't seemed to completely disappear." Finnie shook her head. "And some notions that firefighters don't make ideal partners."

Agnes waved that off as if it was balderdash. Which it was. "And Cassie?"

Finnie gave a slow smile. "She teases him, and I've caught her starin' a few times across the dinner table at the family gatherings. Caught him starin', too. The seed is planted, but it might need a little waterin', if ye catch my drift."

"You know what else I catch?" Agnes suddenly clapped her hands once, as if turning on a lightbulb in her head. "A purpose!"

"Pardon?"

"A good one, too. And I've been searching for one of those for eight long months."

She had? "What happened eight months ago?"

The other woman didn't answer, but bit her lower lip and stared at Finnie. "I have an idea, but I warn you, it's big. So, so big."

Finnie laughed and came closer, magnetically drawn to this fascinating stranger. "Tell."

Agnes reached over the table, around the untouched glasses, and put her hands on Finnie's arms. "When the spirit moves me, I listen."

"And you're...being moved?"

"Absolutely. From there to here."

Finnie stared, a little breathless.

"You feel the need to leave Waterford Farm," Agnes said.

Finnie gasped. "I said no such thing."

"You didn't have to. I can read between the lines, and I think you're struggling because Katie is the mistress at Waterford now."

"I love Katie," she denied hotly. "I simply adore her. And I came back to Waterford Farm after Daniel's wife, Annie, passed and—"

"And now he's getting married again."

Finnie eyed her suspiciously. "What are ye gettin' at, lass?"

"Let's get a place in town. You and me. And the dogs, of course. We'll find something nice and make it our own. And then we can set our two minds together and help our grandchildren—*all* of them— find true love."

Finnie's jaw might have hit the table. "Move in with a perfect stranger?"

"Why not? Why not try a new chapter in your life? Take it from someone who's turned a page, there's nothing better than a fresh start. Even at your age."

Finnie gave her a look. "*Our* age."

"Oh, oh, of course. Sorry. But think about it, Finn." She was still holding Finnie's wrists, a look of hope so powerful in her eyes it sent a chill up Finnie's back. A chill of...*possibilities*.

For a moment, she was transported in time, taken back to a cold winter day in Ireland more than seventy years ago. To another person who sometimes called her "Finn." She'd done something impulsive then, and the result had been a long and happy marriage to Seamus Kilcannon. She could see his smile and feel that same indescribable pull that had a hold of her heart right now.

When Finnie finally looked away, her gaze landed on Daniel, who was moving to the middle of the room to make a toast. To his bride. To his new life. To his doubled-in-size family.

It was time for Finnie, who'd stepped in when her son needed her, to step out and let him live without his old mother breathing down his neck. "I've been prayin'," she confessed on a whisper, "that I might know where to go so as to not be in the way."

"Praying, have you?" Agnes squeezed a little harder. "Then *someone* must have sent me as the answer to your prayers."

"But I don't know you at all." But maybe that good Lord who worked in mysterious ways was sending Finnie in to do a job with this other grandmother. Or maybe Seamus was looking down and encouraging his Finola to take a chance. He'd done that so many times in their long marriage.

"We could rent and test the waters," Agnes countered. "And we'll take a trial run at this match-making project. Start with Cassie and Braden and see how we do?"

"'Tis perfect, since she's your granddaughter, and Braden's my grandson."

Agnes gestured to where Daniel and Katie stood, their arms intertwined, their gazes locked. "Since the Dogfather seems to have taken a permanent vacation from matchmaking."

In the middle of the room, Daniel slowly let go of Katie to tap his glass and quiet the room, but that did nothing to slow Finnie's thoughts.

Sweet Saint Patrick, was she going to do this?

This wasn't what she'd come to this table to accomplish! But in all honesty, Finnie had been putting dents in the floorboards walking them at night, wearing her rosary to nubs. She didn't want to live alone at her age, yet couldn't bear to impose on Colleen, who was busy running a store in town. And the grandchildren? They were all starting new married lives and families, and she was nearing the end of hers.

Daniel began his speech, drawing every eye to the tall, silver-haired patriarch whom they all loved and admired. He spoke of change and children, of the past and future, of love and loss and second chances.

Everyone needed a second chance in life, he told them.

Oh, Danny Boy, you're so right.

She turned to Agnes, who was staring at Finnie like she'd hung the moon. She wasn't a bad person, despite what Cassie said. She wanted to live near family and shower them with love—and help them find it. A purpose, indeed. And a fun one. Finnie needed that in her life, and Agnes needed family.

"So join me in raising your glass…" Daniel's voice echoed through the restaurant as Finnie and Agnes followed the order, lifting their champagne glasses. "And drink to love!" he finished.

Finnie held her glass to Agnes's, took a breath, and whispered, "To my new roommate."

Agnes gasped and threw her head back with a laugh, finally looking truly comfortable in that sleek skin of hers. "To Finnie and Agnes. The Dogmothers."

"The Dogmothers?" Finnie hooted and clinked her crystal glass against Agnes's. "Well, that surely has a nice ring to it."

And while the whole room chattered and cheered, Finnie told Agnes about how she came to live in Bitter Bark. The long version.

Chapter One

One Month Later

"One, two, sweep, *extend*. One, two, sweep, *extend*." Cassie Santorini called out the dance steps to the familiar pluck of the mandolin strings, knowing full well that trying to teach a bunch of silly, slightly inebriated, incredibly distracted Irishmen and women how to perform the sirtaki was a waste of time.

Whoa, they were bad at Greek dancing.

But she wasn't complaining. Not at all. Truth was, it wasn't exactly a hardship to have Braden Mahoney's muscular arm draped over her shoulders. And she didn't completely hate that his hips and thighs occasionally brushed hers when he did the wrong step. Which was frequently.

She actually liked the bolt of pleasure that ricocheted through her whenever they touched or had eye contact or teased each other mercilessly. But a few sizzling seconds was all this flirtation could be, and Cassie would do well to remember that every time their

24

contact felt more than casual or "cousinly," and their shared laughs did fluttery, buzzy things to her body.

Obviously, her hormones had no way of knowing she was planning The Great Escape now that Mom was settled and her brothers had opened the new restaurant in Bitter Bark. Her lady parts didn't care that with their families so connected, she'd have to see him two or three times a week, which would only make things complicated. And her heart—which had no business sliding into this debate—couldn't possibly realize that she and Braden were genuine friends, and anything else would just ruin the fun.

But her head knew *all* that, which made her step away from Braden as the music ended and something more modern started up. It had been happening this way on Wednesday nights for a few months now. The younger, childless members of the Kilcannon, Mahoney, and Santorini families always left the midweek dinner at Waterford Farm and headed to Bushrod's for a nightcap and dancing. Because the local bar wasn't crowded on a Wednesday, her brother John usually convinced the DJ to play "Zorba's Dance" so Cassie, John, and Alex Santorini could teach their Irish friends how to *really* dance.

And somehow the smokeshow of a firefighter always ended up next to her.

On the way back to the huge table they'd filled, Braden high-fived his brother Connor.

"Please don't celebrate like you actually danced," Cassie quipped as she snagged her glass of water from the table and lifted her heavy hair to get air on her damp neck. "At this point, you couldn't make it through the first hour of a Greek wedding."

25

"Speaking of weddings." Braden leaned down close to her ear, the low timbre of his voice and his warm breath wrapping around her and sending heat through her whole body. "Our family has three coming up in the next few months. You'll need to keep teaching me until I get it right."

Our family. He loved to do this, loved to tell her they were going to be cousins. Was it a ploy to keep their playful flirtation from tumbling into dangerous territory, or did he actually believe that?

"We are not *family*, Braden Mahoney. How many times do I have to explain that to you?"

"When my uncle marries your mother? We'll be cousins." He leaned back to take a swig of beer, eyeing her with that constant tease that flickered in his too-blue eyes.

She let her gaze coast over the hollows of his cheeks, all shadowed with whiskers that grew dark when he had a few days off between firefighter shifts. She finally reached his mouth, which just made her envy the bottle of Miller Lite and imagine her own lips could trade places with the amber glass.

"Cousins. Pffft." She flicked her hand, letting her fingertips casually graze his broad chest. "You don't become cousins because two people you're related to get married."

"But your brother is Daniel's biological son."

"Which makes us nothing, Einstein." She rolled her eyes. "Honestly, for a genius with a degree in fireology—"

"Fire *science*," he corrected.

"—you can be pretty dense. Yes, my brother's biological father is your uncle. Yes, your Kilcannon cousins are now my stepsiblings. But that doesn't make *us* cousins, first, second, third, or once removed, so quit trying to horn in on my cool Greek heritage. Be Irish. Eat potatoes."

He grinned, the bottle back at his mouth, his lips stretched into a smile that reached right up and made his eyes glint like blue gas flames. "Shame, isn't it? If only we weren't cousins."

"If only you weren't an idiot," she countered, wishing he'd stop flirting with her and also wishing she'd stop enjoying it so much.

She turned to the rest of their group to notice that Ella Mahoney and Darcy Kilcannon were gathering their bags, while Darcy's fiancé, Josh Ranier, stood and pushed in his chair. Braden's brothers, Declan and Connor, were laying down cash and on the way out, too.

Too bad. She was having fun and didn't want Wednesday night at Bushrod's to be over.

Maybe John and Alex would stay. She glanced at her brothers, but the Santorini twins were knocking back the dregs of their drinks and about to call it a night because the breakfast rush started early at Santorini's.

At least Braden wasn't moving. She sneaked a peek only to find him staring at the door. The smile he'd worn had faded into a dead expression, his eyes cool and narrow, his strong jaw set in a way that told her he was clenching his teeth.

She followed his gaze, already suspecting what—or who—she'd see. Yep. There she was. The *ex* who just happened to pop up with increasing frequency. He wasn't moving because Simone London had walked in.

"Oooh," Cassie cooed. "I see London, I see France, I see Braden…in a trance."

That made him smile a little, even though she could tell he didn't want to. "Shut it."

"Truth hurts, big guy."

He finally tore his riveted gaze from the new arrival, who hadn't even noticed him yet, proving she was both blind and clueless, and shot Cassie a dirty look. "You don't know what you're talking about."

"I know enough. Your sister told me you used to date her. Your uncle Daniel told my mother you took the breakup hard. And you get a little red and uncomfortable if her name is casually mentioned at a family dinner."

"I did date her. No breakup is pleasant. And if I look uncomfortable, I'm probably trying not to belch at the table." He ran his hand through short-cropped brown hair. "I have no feelings for her."

"If by 'no feelings,' you mean longing, lust, and lingering hope, I believe you."

"You're—"

"G' night, Cassie." Darcy Kilcannon, Braden's *actual* cousin, interrupted his pathetic self-defense as she came around the table to give Cassie a hug, her long blond hair tumbling out of her ponytail, loosened by the dance. "I'll see you Saturday, right?"

"Saturday?"

"Moving day for the grands," Darcy reminded her.

Oh yes, *that*. "I still can't believe my grandmother is moving *to* Bitter Bark and will be living with Gramma Finnie." Cassie shook her head at this impossible turn of events.

"I know!" Darcy's blue eyes glinted with that

infectious Kilcannon optimism. "I just hope they don't have too many problems with that old Victorian they're renting."

"Don't worry, my grandmother can scowl even an inanimate object into doing her bidding. Plus, your fiancé is a contractor."

"I haven't seen Gramma Finnie this happy in a long time. It's like she has a whole new reason for living. Isn't it wonderful?"

"That remains to be seen," Cassie said, not wanting to throw cold water on all that positivity, but none of them knew the real Yiayia. Yet.

What they knew was this...this *stand-in*. At least Cassie had her mother and two brothers to discuss the new weirdness that was Yiayia. None of them understood the changes in the woman, and they were all certain it was just a matter of time before the veneer fell off to reveal her sharp tongue and cold heart.

"Are you helping with the move, Braden?" Darcy asked.

"I'm picking up a half shift tomorrow at the fire station, but if there's still work to do when I'm done, we'll swing by."

We. Cassie caught the word and wondered if he meant his dog, Jelly Bean, who was frequently with him, or the woman he was tracking with his gaze.

"Lunch on Friday, Cass?" Ella Mahoney, Braden's younger sister, scooted up next to them, running a hand through her super-short hair to spike it in a way few women could wear. But the pixie look only accented her big brown eyes and movie-star bone structure. "We need to nail down some of the details for the Paws for a Cause fundraiser. I really want Bone Appetit to shine on our day and organizing this shindig is not in my wheelhouse."

"Count on it," Cassie promised, so grateful to have the event-planning work to beef up her résumé. Without it, she'd never get the kind of job in the kind of place that she wanted, but there was no reason to share that with Ella or any of the family yet.

When she was ready and able to make that career move, she'd break the news that she was leaving. Until then, she wouldn't give anyone a chance to try to talk her out of it, because she'd waited long enough to start living her life.

"You leaving now, Braden?" Ella asked her brother.

"Nah." He shook his near empty bottle. "I'll stay for another round."

Ella choked softly. "Yeah, I just saw your 'next round' cruise over to the bar."

"Mind your own biz, Smella."

She just smiled at the nickname her brothers must have hung on her as a child and gave another hug to Cassie. "Stay with him, Cass," she whispered. "He was in a funk after they split up, and I don't think she's done with him yet. Keep an eye on him."

"I will." Both eyes, probably. Since they almost always glued to Braden when he was in a room.

With a few more goodbyes, that group headed out, but Braden made no move to leave, although to his credit he'd stopped watching Simone. Cassie hadn't, though, noticing the woman and her two friends were looking for seats at the bar. Simone's blond head turned in Braden's direction frequently, so she had noticed him. Not that you could miss a six-foot-two firefighter with shoulders that could make a woman whimper.

"So how bad a breakup was it?" Cassie asked, curious now. "I mean on a scale of no-big-deal to wanted-to-rip-your-heart-out-just-to-stop-the-pain?"

He almost smiled. "'Bout a three."

Really? "Then why the eye-stalking?"

"I'm not eye-stalking."

No, but Simone was. Cassie took a step to the left, blocking the view from the bar. "So what happened? Who dumped who?"

"It was mutual."

"You think you're both over it?"

"Yep. Don't listen to my sister," he added. "Smella's imagining things."

"Why on earth do you call that beautiful girl Smella?"

He grinned. "Inside Mahoney joke. We're not cousins, remember? So don't try to horn in on my cool Irish heritage. Read Homer. Be Greek."

She took a sip of water, eyeing him and knowing him well enough to have no doubt he actually *did* read Homer. "So you want her back?"

He shot her a look, but didn't answer.

"You want her to notice you're still on the planet, or do you just want her to go away?"

His gaze flicked toward the bar. "She knows I'm on the planet, and it's a small town, so she can't go away. Actually, she did go away, right into the arms of an *actuary*." The word rolled off his tongue as if it tasted like fried tar.

"Whatever that is."

31

"Safe," he said. "That is safe."

"So she chose safe over…" How could she describe Braden? She thought about the opposite of safe, and he wasn't that, either. He was solid. Grounded. Focused. Well-read and crazy-smart. Loved his family and did heroic work. Also fry-your-eyes hot. "Over *you*?"

He looked down at her, the glint in his eyes saying he'd picked up the compliment buried in her subtext. "Contrary to rumors you may hear, it really *was* mutual," he finally said.

"So mutual that your entire being changed when she walked in the door?"

One more time, he stared at her, silent.

She crossed her arms and let out a sigh. "You know, when I want something—anything, really—I go for it. I take action. I make my needs known. I seize the day, every opportunity, and let nothing and no one stand in my way."

"Do you?"

"Haven't you noticed?"

He lifted a brow. "You? Yeah, I've noticed."

"So what would Cassie do?" she asked. "When life doesn't go exactly as planned or sucks a little bit too much, Cassie Santorini doesn't sit around moaning about it or staring. She takes action."

"Does she?" Amused, he took a sip of beer. "And she talks about herself in third person."

"Sometimes…she does." She glanced past his shoulder, zeroing in on the attractive blonde who'd finally found a stool facing the dance floor. Two guys had already moved in.

Was *that* what was bothering him?

"What would Cassie Santorini do in this case, if the tables were turned?" Braden asked.

"You mean if someone chose an actuary over me and made me mope around for a few months?"

"I am not moping, and I wasn't…" His voice trailed off, his argument lost in the first few notes of a Sam Smith ballad that filled the bar. "Come on, Cass." He suddenly closed his hand over her wrist and tugged her toward the dance floor. "This way."

"Oooh. Confrontation. My specialty."

"We're not confronting anyone," he said as he slid his arm around her, leading her forward.

"Just talk, then? Buy her a drink? Demand answers? I can be your representative from the female species. We speak the same language."

"Cassie, shut up." He reached the dance floor and stopped, turning her to wrap his hands around her waist. "We're going to dance."

Right in front of the ex, it would seem. "The old make-her-jealous trick. I should have thought of that."

He pulled her closer, the sudden full-body contact shocking her with how warm and solid and big he was. Greek dances weren't like this. Greek dances weren't…sexy.

But he was. And so was the look in his eyes and that shadow of a playful, daring smile. "You *sure* we're not cousins?"

"Einstein. You're killing me." In more ways than one.

"Then do me a favor," he said, his voice a little rough as he leaned closer and put his lips against her ear. "Act like you like me for once."

For once? Acting like she *didn't* like him was the real challenge.

Sam Smith crooned a high note as Cassie slid her hands up Braden's shoulders, taking it slow like this charade called for, but it was a nice excuse to appreciate each cut and dip and bulgy bicep she'd been eyeing in the months since they'd met.

"Little closer, cuz." He splayed his big hands over her back, adding just enough pressure that there wasn't a molecule of air between them.

"So she buys it?"

"Yeah." The word was gruff, low, and almost lost to the music.

As he turned her a half step, Cassie peeked at the bar and locked gazes with one very interested Simone London.

"Oh, she's buying," Cassie assured him.

"Really?" He pressed his lips to her hair, the contact zinging through her.

"Very realistic," she whispered. So was the knot of need forming low in her belly. Too realistic.

He looked down at her, doing his part by slaying her with a slow, bedroom-quality smile. "Think she believes we're a thing?" he asked, swaying with far more grace than he ever showed when attempting the sirtaki.

"Maybe." They turned, and she got another look, noticing that Simone's eyes had tapered to an intense stare, and she'd stopped talking to her friends. "On a scale of doesn't-give-a-crap to ready-to-flip-her-stiletto-at-me? I'd say she's a definite six."

He threaded his fingers into her hair, nearly making her collapse at the knees. "Gotta raise the stakes." Their hips brushed, pressed, and electrified them both for one long moment.

Oh. Something was about to *raise*, and it wasn't just the stakes.

"Brace yourself, cuz," he whispered the words as his mouth came down on hers, searing her lips. She sucked in a surprised breath, but then they both stopped moving completely as he angled his head to deepen the kiss.

Heat crawled up her chest and down her back and all the way out to the fingertips that clung to him. His mouth moved against hers, sweet and insistent, with the beat of the music and her pounding heart. Large, strong hands covered her back to cradle her closer, making her feel safe and terrified and a little like she was floating on air.

Whoa. This definitely felt...*real*. Or was it?

She peeked out from under one partially closed lid to see Simone staring hard at them.

"I think it's working," she murmured into his mouth. *Something* was working. Like all her nerve endings and a few she hadn't even known she had.

He added some pressure and slid his hands a little lower, resting them in the curve of her lower back, his long fingers grazing the pockets of her jeans.

"I think we better try...harder." He kissed her again, this time letting their tongues touch and tangle. Their hearts hammered against each other, and somehow, every single person in the bar seemed to disappear except for Braden.

Suddenly, the music scratched to a stop, then shifted gears into a fast beat, leaving them frozen and shell-shocked and speechless.

Cassie managed to inch back, swallowing against a desert-dry mouth and her pounding pulse. As she caught her breath, she saw Braden look right at the bar.

Slowly, like she was moving through molasses, Cassie followed his gaze, which landed on one empty barstool.

"Sorry, Romeo," Cassie said. "Not exactly what you wanted."

He turned, locking eyes with her. That smolder was still evident, the blue irises dark and direct as he stared at her. "Oh, it was exactly what I wanted."

The kiss or the disappearing ex?

He let go of her and swiped his lower lip with his knuckle, holding her gaze one beat too long. "I better walk you home before the Doublemint Twins come after me with a rolling pin and a spreadsheet."

She wanted to laugh at the perfect description of her brothers, but she needed all her focus to walk with curled toes, weak knees, and a low-grade boil of need in her blood. Braden, on the other hand, seemed unfazed by what just happened on the dance floor.

In fact, he was perfectly normal as he took her to her apartment and gave a very cousin-like and playful salute when he said goodbye.

It wasn't until she was inside, alone and behind a locked door, that Cassie finally let out a groan of complete frustration and despair. She could *not* crush on Braden. Except she was. Hard.

Well, the crush would die a natural death. When she got into her car, kissed small-town America goodbye, and got a high-rise and a big job.

Hey, a girl could dream.

She headed off to bed, where she probably wasn't going to dream of apartments and a new career. No. Her dreams would be built like a towering inferno and kissed like sin on a stick.

Chapter Two

There could be only one reason Uncle Daniel would ask Braden to come over to Waterford Farm on a Friday morning.

He knows about that kiss.

As Braden's truck rolled down the long drive, he peered into the late afternoon sunshine pouring over the expanse of lawns and dog pens that made up the canine rescue and training center his uncle ran with all his cousins.

Surely Braden wasn't going to get taken to task for a quick peck on the dance floor?

Okay, not exactly a *peck*. That kiss with Cassie was incendiary, unforgettable, and sent him straight to a twenty-minute cold shower when he got home. Which was exactly what he'd known it would be and why he'd had to use that lame Simone excuse to experience it.

He couldn't have cared less about making his ex jealous. If anything, she needed to know that her semiregular "accidental" appearances in his life were getting annoying. Why did she bother?

She wanted something he could never give her, and

he hoped she found it with the actuary. But Cassie...with that smart mouth and sweet laugh and a body like she was a real-life Greek goddess? Oh, Cassie Santorini pushed every button he had, and Wednesday night...he just got sick of *not* kissing her.

But he couldn't let that happen again. If they got that close too often, he'd be right back in the same boat he'd been in with Simone, only way worse because...well, because *Cassie*. From the minute he'd met Cassie a few months ago, he had a weakness for her that constantly tested him.

And at Bushrod's the other night, he damn near failed that test. As sweet and sexy as that defeat had been, it wouldn't happen again. Because Cassie could never be casual, and Braden could and would do only casual for as long as he was a firefighter, which would be for as long as he could stand, run, and carry the line.

Would he have to explain that to his uncle? God, he hoped not.

But as he parked the truck behind the bright yellow Waterford Jeep, another thought slowed his hand as he shut off the engine. This was the *Dogfather*. Steer him away from Cassie? Hah. He might have exactly the opposite in mind. Another *marriage* in the family.

Oh, no, Uncle Daniel. Take the matchmaking games to the other Mahoney kids. The only permanent partner Braden wanted had four legs, gray fur, and a tongue that hung out when he was happy. Jelly Bean was Braden's partner in life and, if everything went according to plan, his partner in work.

Because Braden's plan was to expand his role at the fire station to handler of a trained Accelerant Detection Canine, or arson dog. He'd finally found the perfect one-year-old Weimaraner online and had driven five hours to a shelter in Atlanta to pick up Jelly Bean. He'd had the dog by his side for more than a year now.

During that time, Jelly Bean had been through every level of obedience training, and this past month, he started the final phase: accelerant scent detection. Once he nailed that, they could get certified by the ATF and start working all over the tricounty area. Getting that certification was all that mattered to Braden, and his uncle knew it, and knew why.

Because, for Braden, it was one thing to fight a fire, which he could do along with the best of them. But that wasn't enough. It would never be enough.

Since he was thirteen years old and the fire chief knocked on their door at three in the morning and told them Dad wouldn't ever be coming home from his shift, Braden swore he wouldn't just fight fires, he'd use the brains he'd been given to stop them. And the way to stop something was to figure out how it happened in the first place. That's where Jelly Bean came in.

He pushed open the truck door and climbed out, scanning the pens where a number of dogs were in the middle of distraction training. Of course, Jelly Bean wouldn't be there, unless he was showing the rookies how it was done.

He spotted his uncle almost immediately, leaning against the fence, deep in conversation with Braden's cousin Liam, the oldest of the six Kilcannon kids. Well, guess it was seven now that Nick Santorini—and his entire Greek family, including one sizzling little sister—appeared on the scene.

Daniel and Liam turned as he approached, waving him over and sharing one more bit of conversation before Braden was in earshot. They looked serious for a moment, then Uncle Daniel broke into a wide smile and gave Braden a bear hug and a slap on the back.

"There he is," he said, his blue eyes twinkling more than they had for years. Of course, Nick's arrival in the family came with Nick's mother...who was now a permanent fixture in his uncle's life. And honestly, it couldn't have happened to a nicer or more deserving guy.

"Hey, Uncle Daniel." Braden greeted him easily and nodded to Liam, who wasn't much of a hugger. He wasn't much of a smiler, either, but his dark eyes looked particularly serious today. "S'up, Liam?"

"Oh, you know. Dogs."

Braden chuckled at the simple, no-nonsense answer he'd expect from his older cousin. Sure, marriage and fatherhood had loosened up the former Marine who ran the law enforcement K-9 division of Waterford, but it would never make him talkative.

That, among many other reasons, made Liam one of his favorite cousins, though Braden was closer in age and interests to Aidan, and the two of them with their rhyming names had always been tight. But where K-9s were concerned, Liam knew his stuff, and he'd been instrumental in guiding Braden—and Jelly Bean—toward success.

"Tough day in training?" Braden asked, expecting another shrug and single-syllable answer in response.

"Actually, it's been a very difficult day. That's why we wanted to talk to you." It wasn't the length of Liam's reply that surprised him, it was the tone.

"Is Jelly Bean okay?" he asked, looking from one man to the other for a clue.

"He's fine," Uncle Daniel assured him. "But let's go get him and have a talk."

He did not like the sound of that. "Sure."

He followed the other two men into the kennels, a large, bright building that reflected the care and quality that the entire Kilcannon family had put into Waterford Farm when they built the facility. Braden and his brothers and sister had helped a lot in the early days, but now Waterford ran like a Swiss watch, with a constant stream of trainees and rescues and a growing array of programs, like service dog training and Liam's highly regarded K-9 program.

"He tried valiantly today," Liam said as they rounded the corner of the kennel where the K-9s were housed during training sessions.

Tried? Jelly Bean never "tried" anything. He mastered. His intelligence and willingness to please had been evident from the first. But Braden stayed quiet, waiting for more of an explanation.

Liam's section of the kennel reflected his personality—clean and streamlined, organized and purposeful. The only "art" was an illustration of the Marine bulldog mascot with the words *USMC Teufel Hunden*, meaning Devil Dog, like the tattoo on Liam's shoulder. In the kennels, most of his trainees, almost all German shepherds and Belgian Malinois, stood at attention at the sight of him.

Behind the last gate, Jelly Bean did the same, although his green eyes flashed when Braden came into view. He tilted his head in silent greeting, and his tongue curled out of his lips as it always did when he was trying to be good but really just wanted to slather Braden with kisses. But affection might be a sign of weakness, and Jelly Bean rarely showed that.

"Hey, JB," Braden muttered, coming close to the kennel and waiting for Liam to unlatch it.

When he did, Jelly Bean glanced at Liam first, waiting for a signal to go forward. Being the super dog he was, Jelly Bean knew that at Waterford Liam was the leader of the pack. Liam nodded and snapped his fingers, as Braden had learned to do in handler training sessions, and immediately Jelly Bean came closer for a nuzzle.

Braden ran his hands over Jelly Bean's soft, sleek, mouse-gray coat. Taking one floppy ear in his hand, Braden flipped it between his fingers, and instantly Jelly Bean dropped to a soldier-like at ease, head up, tongue out.

"You're a good dog." Braden leaned over to deliver the assurance right to his face, then he straightened and looked from his cousin to his uncle. "Isn't he?"

"He is a very good dog." Uncle Daniel put his hand on Braden's shoulder, the two of them eye to eye at a matching six two. "And I know you've worked tirelessly to get him ready for the final stage of training with the ATF. I know that being a handler for an arson dog and using your keen intelligence—and his—to not only fight but also figure out fires means the world to you, and that dream should never die until you realize it."

His stomach churned at the speech. "What's the 'but,' Uncle Daniel?"

"I don't believe Jelly Bean is going to qualify for that training."

43

Braden drew back at the gut-punch of disbelief. "What?"

"I've seen this before," Liam said. "He's a rescue, so we don't know what he was exposed to in the first year of his life, but someone might have tried to train him in scent detection and done it wrong."

"How?" Braden asked.

"If a dog's been trained and rewarded for more than one scent, there's room for error." Liam reached down to give Jelly Bean a stroke on the head, as if he knew his news might hurt the dog's feelings. "And now, he sometimes seems to identify multiple scents, barking at various tests we have in the field. He's successfully identified marijuana, explosives, some people, *and* accelerants."

"And that can't be trained out of him?"

"Possibly," Liam said. "He certainly has the intelligence for that kind of retraining, but..." Liam looked at his father as if he needed backup, and Daniel stepped forward.

"It might not be a training or intelligence issue," his uncle said. "If it wasn't poor training in his past, then there's a possible defect in his olfactory system. That means he might not have the ability to discern one scent from another, which, obviously, an expert scent-detection dog would need."

Disappointment squeezed as Braden tried to process this news, but couldn't. "He smells treats from a mile away," he said. "He can smell when I've been around another dog and sniffs like hell when you take him out in the world."

Uncle Daniel nodded in understanding. "He can smell, Braden, no question about that. But he may not be able to differentiate specific smells. Which could be a problem you might be able to fix with very extensive and specific training, or it could be a physical problem that will never change. You just don't know until you try."

"Okay, then we'll try," Braden said. "I'll do whatever it takes to fix it. What's involved with the training? When can we start it?"

Liam shook his head. "It's a complex and long-term undertaking and not one we're equipped to do here at Waterford either in terms of staff or space or even know-how," he said. "I know of two places in the state that specialize in accelerant training specifically for arson investigation and might be able to work with a special case like Jelly Bean."

Special case? The words sliced him. It was like they were talking about another dog, not this superstar. "And if I don't do that, he can't qualify for the ATF certification?" Braden asked.

His uncle let out a slow breath. "We have to sign an affidavit that confirms our professional opinion that he is ready for the final certification, because they won't even take him in for testing without that. I can't sign that for Jelly Bean."

Braden closed his eyes at that, rooting around for any other option. "Is there any chance you're wrong, Uncle Daniel? That it's not a training or a systemic problem? Is there a third option?"

"There is the slightest chance that he has a temporary condition, similar to a cold or virus in a human. In my professional opinion as a vet, that's not the case with Jelly Bean, but I have been known to be wrong."

Rarely.

Braden felt his shoulders drop as it all settled on him. To start over with another dog would be a huge setback for him personally, since he'd trained so hard to be Jelly Bean's handler. Not to mention that he loved the dog with every cell in his body. Enough that...

"What's the special training cost?"

Liam swallowed. "Ten thousand at a minimum."

Braden swore softly. Of course, that was why Accelerant Detection Canine units were rare and nearly unheard of at a fire department the size of Bitter Bark's. But Waterford had done all this training gratis with the firm belief they'd be handing Braden, and the fire department, a dog ready for certification.

Next to him, Jelly Bean sat down again and tipped his head back to stare at Braden, patiently waiting for his next command.

But he couldn't command the dog to distinguish smells.

All he could do was let out a heartfelt sigh, which made Uncle Daniel place a firm but always loving hand on Braden's shoulder. "We can work with you to find another dog. It might take a while, but—"

Braden shook his head, silencing his uncle. "Don't. He understands."

He loved his uncle for nodding and not even questioning that. "You think about what you want to do. Jelly Bean's been through every stage of training. He could easily become a different kind of working dog."

"I could teach him almost anything but scent detection," Liam said. "The dog's a freaking genius

46

who understands more words than my seven-year-old son. That's why I was so stymied when he made so many mistakes in the training. He wants to get it right. You show him a reward once, maybe twice, and he'll work like hell for it, but…"

Braden held up his hand, almost not able to take the truth. "What if I kept working with him?" he asked. "I've watched enough of the process here to know how. If I could teach that scent discernment on my own, would you sign that affidavit? Or if I could prove to you it was a cold and not something chronic?"

"I'd need absolute black-and-white proof that he could distinguish smells, and not just once or twice in testing," his uncle said. "I'd need to see it happen without fail, repeatedly. Then he'd need to come back here and run through all these advanced tests again."

"If you make some headway with him, I'll test him again," Liam said quickly. "And you can test him with other scents as long as they're food or food-related. Or, of course, an accelerant, which will be his rewarded nonfood scent if he becomes an ADC."

Not *if*, Braden thought. *When.*

"And if you succeed and he tests out," Uncle Daniel added, "you can bypass the expensive training. But, Braden, if it's a physiological problem, no amount of training will make him a scent-detection dog."

His gut twisted. "What would you do?" he asked his uncle.

The older man took a moment to consider his response, as he always did when facing a big decision. "In all honesty, I'd seriously think about a different dog, but," he added quickly, no doubt reading Braden's expression, "the other option is advanced, specialized training. However, you're essentially gambling ten grand, and that's a high price for failure."

He glanced down at Jelly Bean, whose keen green eyes looked as if the one word he didn't understand was *failure*.

"I don't have that amount lying around," he admitted.

"Is there any way the fire department could pay for some of the training?" Liam asked. "God knows it would be a major coup for them to have an arson dog, and you two could farm out to every other fire department in a fifty-mile radius. Maybe Holly Hills and Chestnut Creek could all pitch in?"

No small-town fire department had that kind of cash on hand, and the red tape to get other departments involved would be daunting. "I gotta think about it," he said, shaking off his disappointment to split a look between the other men. "I really appreciate all you've done for him."

"I wish I had better news, son." Uncle Daniel's piercing blue eyes narrowed. "I can keep an eye out for another dog."

That he would hate.

But Braden nodded and signaled to Jelly Bean to follow him out, not even wanting to look at the other dogs in the pen or talk to any of his Kilcannon cousins who might be around. He just wanted to get home and figure out a way to scare up ten grand. Or prove to his uncle that Jelly Bean's olfactory system was in top working order and this whole glitch was *temporary*.

But right at that moment, that seemed impossible.

Chapter Three

A fast getaway was not meant to be, Braden realized as he spotted an oversize U-Haul van that had pulled into the driveway, blocking his truck. Of course, tomorrow Gramma Finnie was moving out. He might not be able to help with the move, but he was here now, so he should offer to do what he could to get her stuff loaded.

Crossing the driveway with Jelly Bean, he spotted his cousins Aidan and Shane heading into the kitchen, both carrying large moving pads that they must have brought from the back of the U-Haul.

The two men disappeared through the kitchen door, and Braden followed, not bothering to knock since Waterford was as much his home as the house he and his two brothers and sister had grown up in together just north of town.

"Oh, hello, lad." Gramma Finnie was at the counter, putting some utensils in a box, talking to the woman he recognized as the Santorinis' grandmother and Gramma's new roommate. The other woman, who looked quite a bit younger than Gramma Finnie, was tucked into the long bench at the kitchen table, each of her arms wrapped around pointy-nosed dachshunds who seemed totally at ease sitting at the table.

"Ladies." He gave the women a smile. "I can offer some muscle for the move if you don't mind me letting Jelly Bean in."

"Of course." Gramma abandoned her box and came right to him to give him a hug. "Your sweet arson investigator pup is always welcome here, lad."

The two dogs at the table instantly jumped down, barked, and headed over to sniff the new arrival. "Well, he's not an arson investigator yet. Maybe…" He blew out a breath, unwilling to finish and distracted by a cream-colored dachshund circling his legs and another, nearly black with a light beige snout, who waddled over with a little less enthusiasm but a mighty wide gut.

"Who are these cute little guys?"

"Well, you remember Yiayia," Gramma said, lifting her brows. "This is *Cassie's* grandmother Agnes."

He smiled at the description since she was also Alex and John's grandmother and Katie's mother-in-law. "Of course. Hello, Mrs. Santorini."

"It's Yiayia to you and anyone else in a five-mile radius," the other woman said. "Unless you're over seventy and single. Then it's Agnes."

He grinned at her, instantly seeing where Cassie got her spunk. "Is that Greek for 'grandma'?" he asked.

"It is. Also Greek for anything and everything wonderful. And that's my Pyggie currently making himself at home on your boot, and Gala is the one sniffing your dog's butt like it's fresh baklava from the oven."

He cracked up. "He's a little wide, but is it fair to call him Piggy?"

"It's short for Pygmalion, and Gala is short for—"

"Galatea," he finished. "One of my favorite stories in mythology. I love how Aphrodite brought Galatea to life for her creator."

The woman's eyes widened. "Well, *you're* not just another pretty face."

He laughed as Gramma Finnie put an arm around his waist and patted his chest with grandmotherly pride. "Braden graduated first in his class in high school and got a scholarship to college. When he was fourteen, he read a hundred books in the Bitter Bark Library and won the Reader of the Year prize."

The other woman looked suitably impressed. "Oh my, I like a thirst for knowledge."

The only thing he'd been thirsty for that summer was an escape from reality, but he just gave a humble smile.

"He's also a heroic firefighter who is always the one to go into a burning building with the hose in hand," Gramma bragged.

"I like a good hoser," Yiayia said, letting her gaze cover him like she was the hose and he was the fire.

"And he has been studying to be a handler for an accelerant-detection dog," Gramma Finnie finished. "Can you tell I'm proud of this grandson of mine?"

"Get a cookie for being so smart." Yiayia rose and pointed to a tray full of sweets. "*My* grandson Alex made kourabiedes. Can you cook, too?"

"Not like Alex." He pointed in the general direction of Gramma Finnie's third-floor suite of rooms.

"Thought I'd go help those guys move whatever you need first. That way, I'll earn it."

"But a cookie is good for the heart, lad." Gramma slid the tray closer. "And I understand yours is broken."

He gave her a questioning look, wondering if it was time to start letting his family know that he wasn't *that* broken up about Simone. Nah, then they'd all want to know what was really bothering him, and they'd never understand that.

"Daniel told me about…" She pointed at Jelly Bean, then tapped her finger to her nose. "'Tis a darn shame 'bout his smellin' issues."

Oh, of course. News traveled at lightning speed around here. "Yeah, it is. But I'm not ready to give up. I just need to come up with ten thousand dollars to gamble on him." He added a rueful laugh. "Maybe I need that cookie, after all."

"Ten grand?" Yiayia chimed in. "That's a lot of cabbage."

"More than I want to scare up." He reached down to give Jelly Bean's head a scratch. "But this guy is so close to certification. I don't want to give up yet."

Yiayia came closer, hands on her hips and brown eyes pinned on him. "What about that Paws for a Cause thing that everyone is talking about? Aren't there all kinds of people doing crazy contests and events with dogs to raise money for the entire month of June?"

"The fire department has already been roped into something called Date with a Dog, and there's a firefighter competition," he told them. "I think the whole department would punch me in the throat if I asked them to do anything else to raise money."

"Date with a Dog?" Yiayia snorted. "Is this something I want to enter my Pyggie and Gala in?"

"It's a glorified bachelor auction for some black-tie event at a local winery. You bid on a firefighter and his dog as your date." He looked skyward, and Jelly Bean swatted his paw on the ground as if he, too, thought being auctioned like a piece of meat and then having to wear a tuxedo as your punishment was the stupidest thing he'd ever heard. "And anything we raise is going straight toward the new pumper truck."

Both women moved a little closer, Yiayia openly studying him. "You ought to fetch a few drachmas."

He managed a smile, not sure if she was serious or kidding. Yep, Cassie in fifty years.

"But, lad, you could do something separate on your own to raise money for yer cause." Gramma placed a cookie on a napkin and pressed it into his hand. "What would stop you?"

He looked down at the cookie. "I don't have any idea how to do that."

"Hmmm." Gramma crossed her arms and nodded. "Cassie does."

"Oh yes, she does," Yiayia chimed in. "She's not just a catering expert, you know. She's always talked about managing special events, like parties and luncheons."

"And *weddings*," Gramma added, sharing a bright-eyed look with the other woman. "Cassie will help you."

"Cassie?" He took a bite of the cookie and hoped that any color that rose to his face looked like a result of how good it was.

"Don't know if you don't ask," Gramma said, heading toward the refrigerator as if he'd asked for the milk that he knew was forthcoming. Because... Gramma.

Yiayia bent over and picked up the smaller of the two doxies, curling the dog into her arms and stroking her head as she stared at Braden with unabashed interest. "Cassie's doing your sister's event, you know. And I think she would like more opportunity to showcase her talents."

"Her...talents." Which happened to include kissing like she was a one-woman five-alarm fire. He took another bite of the cookie.

"Oh, she is quite a wonderful girl," Yiayia practically sang. "So she has so many wonderful... connections."

"Wonderful everything," Gramma added with a slightly yellowed but totally sweet smile.

"Cassie could be your..." Yiayia frowned. "What do you call it?"

Distraction? Fantasy? Cause for concern?

"Go-between," Gramma supplied.

"Go between what?" His sheets? He covered the thought with a gulp of the milk she gave him.

"So you don't have to deal directly with all the things." Gramma squeezed his arm with her gnarled but always tender fingers.

"I guess I could ask Cassie," Braden said, finishing the milk as the women shared a quick look, apparently satisfied they'd meddled or fed him enough.

Just then, his cousins came into the kitchen, carrying a dresser between them.

"Dude." Shane lifted one wry brow at the empty

glass of milk in his hand. "Nice of you to come in for your after-school snack while we bust our backsides."

Jelly Bean barked in doggy defense.

"We had very important business to discuss with him," Gramma said, her own defense as fast and heartfelt as Jelly Bean's.

"Don't worry," Aidan said. "There's a recliner up there that has your name on it."

Braden laughed and started to walk his glass to the sink. "Great."

"I'll take that." Gramma Finnie relieved him of the empty glass and smiled up at him. "Cassie will be here tomorrow to help with the move, lad."

"I'm picking up a half-day shift and studying for a final in electrical system forensics, which I thought would help as an ADC handler." But without a canine to handle, why bother?

"Don't give up," Gramma said, as if she could read his thoughts. She always was pretty good at that.

"Come to our new house in the afternoon." Yiayia was suddenly on his other side. "That's when Cassie is going to be there."

"It's on Dogwood Lane, if you can believe that twist of fine fate." Gramma jotted something on a notepad and tore off the paper. "Here's the address."

He looked from one to the other, suddenly feeling like he was in the middle of a grandma sandwich. "I'll...try."

"Greeks don't *try*," Yiayia said.

"I'm not Greek."

"I'm overlooking that." She gave him a nudge. "Now get that recliner and..." She leaned in. "Talk to Cassie, okay?"

"I'll think about her…er, it." *Think about her some more* was what he meant.

Yiayia raised a fancy drawn-on eyebrow.

"Don't tell me. Greeks don't think," he guessed.

"The country that gave us Socrates, Plato, and Aristotle? All we do is think." She leaned closer. "And then we *act*."

Who knew the need-for-action gene was hereditary?

Gramma eased the other woman away. "Come and visit us tomorrow at our new place, lad. The more family around, the better."

Yes, *family*. Which, in some stretch of the imagination, was what Cassie was to him.

But that didn't stop him from thinking about the idea as he headed toward the stairs to haul the recliner.

"Oh, Finnie," he heard Cassie's grandmother whisper as he left. "A cause and a dog. Could it be better?"

Wow, what a sweet old lady to care so much about Jelly Bean. And was she right? Could Cassie help him raise ten grand to help Jelly Bean? Maybe.

Was it worth the low-grade torture of being around her all the time? Possibly.

Would it end up with another one of those blistering kisses? God, he hoped so.

Chapter Four

Standing on a step stool in the basement pantry, Cassie listened to the banter of the two most unlikely roommates as they set up housekeeping. With each exchange that floated down the stairs, the question pressed on Cassie's heart.

What is Yiayia up to?

After more discussions with Mom, the only answer was *no good.* Cassie's mother was low-key terrified that her former mother-in-law was here to screw things up. And it wouldn't be the first time Agnes Santorini meddled and muddled and manipulated her family into doing what she wanted.

The question was—what did she want? And why was she acting so *nice*? For a month now, she'd kept up this Sally Sunshine act. *Why?*

Cassie burned to know the answer and was determined to get it today. Before Yiayia did any of the damage that Cassie and Katie and all the Santorinis knew she was capable of.

"Sweet Saint Patrick, you have a lot of wooden spoons, Agnes," Gramma Finnie mused. "Who needs more than one?"

"A Greek cook, Finnie. How else do I stir the orzo?"

"And, oh my, you're going to use this entire cabinet for spices?" Gramma Finnie's voice rose with dismay.

"And a shelf in the downstairs pantry." Yiayia let out a soft sigh. "I mean, if that's okay with you."

"Of course it's okay, but spicy food makes my stomach scream unholy words at me."

Cassie smiled, then froze at the sound of Yiayia's footsteps, moving pretty quickly considering how steep those stairs were.

"Then cook your own damn..." Yiayia stopped at the pantry door and cleared her throat, staring up at Cassie on the step stool. "Oh, I forgot you were in here."

"And almost acted like yourself again."

As she always did now, Yiayia waved off the comment as if she hadn't even heard it. "I have more olives for you."

"Because these five thousand won't be enough."

"I'm sure we'll work out the cooking," Gramma called down to her.

"We will!" Yiayia replied, still holding Cassie's gaze. And then she added, "It'll be fun!"

Cassie put the olive jar on the shelf with just a little too much force. "Who *are* you?" she asked in a hushed whisper.

"Don't put the kalamatas too high, Cassandra. Gramma Finnie won't be able to reach them."

"But you *always* keep the kalamatas high, Yiayia, so no one can steal them. Including your new roommate."

"Well...maybe I want to share my kalamatas."

Cassie dropped down a step. "And maybe Santa Claus wants to wear lavender and come at Easter."

Yiayia blinked. "That would confuse the poor children."

"Exactly. Like this one." Cassie tapped her own forehead. "Totally confused." She put her foot on the floor, face-to-face with a woman she knew almost as well as she knew her own mother. "When are you going to tell me?"

"About the olives? I would just put them on a lower shelf myself since you're doing such a lovely job, and I appreciate the help so much." She added a stiff, fake, but very wide smile.

Cassie leaned in, studying one eye, then the other, doctor-like in her examination. "Did you make a deal with the devil?"

In the harsh fluorescent light of the pantry, it was easy to see Yiayia's fine Greek skin go a little…green.

"Am I right?" Cassie urged. "Some kind of bet with someone? Or you *lost* a bet." She snapped her fingers and pointed. "You lost a bet and have to be nice for a month."

"Cassandra."

But Cassie shook her head, knowing her grandmother didn't gamble. "It's a man. That Ted guy. You're trying to get him back from Iowa by showing him how much you really like your family."

"Cassandra Katherine."

She gasped. "Yiayia, you don't have a terminal disease, do you?"

Yiayia let out a sigh and dropped her shoulders just enough to make Cassie reach out and squeeze. "You do?" Blood drained from her head as the possibility that she might lose Yiayia hit like an unexpected blow. Yes, the woman drove her crazy, but she loved her just the same.

"Gala's scratching at the door!" Gramma Finnie called.

Yiayia looked relieved, backing up. "I'll take her out. *Dear.*"

Cassie grabbed her elbow and squeezed. "Oh no you won't. *Dear.* You will tell me the truth, Agnes Santorini, right this very minute."

"Uh, actually, Finnie, could you take her?" Yiayia called. "*Pretty please?*"

"Already leashed!" Gramma's rubber-soled footsteps and the slamming of the screen door that needed an extra push to close meant they were alone in the house. Cassie moved in a little closer.

"*Pretty please*, Yiayia? Really? Since when do you say that?"

"Since—"

"Are you dying?" Cassie demanded, the idea, now planted, even more terrifying.

"No. Maybe. Someday. We all are, so can we just forget about this conversation?" She turned, accidentally knocking over one of the spices, which tumbled to the floor and spilled everywhere, making the small space suddenly smell like Nico Santorini's famous lemon chicken.

"Oh, the rigani!" Yiayia started to bend over to clean it up, but Cassie stopped her with two hands, forcing her to stand.

"I am not kidding," Cassie ground out the words. "If something is wrong, you have to tell me."

For a long moment, Yiayia didn't say a word. Then she blinked again, and this time, tears threatened. Actual tears.

"Are you crying? I've never seen you cry. Not even at my father's funeral did I see you cry."

"Well, I did, I just hid it. Someone had to be strong. Your mother was a useless dishrag."

"A useless dishrag." Cassie leaned back, crossing her arms, weirdly satisfied. "There you are, Yiayia. Welcome back."

"No, no!" She wiped the words away with a sweep of her hand. "Your mother was understandably distraught and grieving, so I tried to hold everything together for the family. The family I love. With everything I have." Her face crumpled. "Why don't you believe me?"

"I believe you love your family, but I also know *how* you love us."

She closed her eyes as if Cassie had slapped her. "Isn't it possible that I've just seen the light?" She added a mirthless smile. "Literally."

"What are you talking about?"

She glanced over her shoulder as if Gramma Finnie could walk into the pantry any minute, or maybe she was buying some time. Cassie gave it to her, waiting for a legit answer, because after all this time of watching Yiayia behave as if an alien had taken over her body, she finally felt close to an explanation.

But then Yiayia gave her head a quick shake, as if second-guessing anything she might have said. "People change, Cassandra. People change."

"Not you. You don't change. I don't believe it."

"Because you don't want to," she shot back. "You

want to believe the worst of me, and when I act out of character? It makes you uncomfortable."

That actually wasn't too far off the mark, and *that* made her uncomfortable. "Well, it's weird."

"Maybe it is, but you'll just have to trust me."

She never had trusted her grandmother before, though. Why would she start now? "So what brought on this massive change?"

Huffing out a breath, Yiayia shrugged in a way that looked somehow practiced and staged. "Age, I suppose. Facing my mortality. Father Time and Mother Nature. And I'd appreciate it if you'd stop getting in the way of that and help me."

Getting in the way? "How can I help you?"

"Quit asking me if I'm going to die or meet the devil or *whatever*." Her voice was just sharp enough to sound familiar again. "And help me achieve my purpose."

She had a purpose? "Which is?"

"You'll see."

Frustration zinged. "Why are you being so cagey, Yiayia? If this purpose of yours is honorable and not calculating, then you should be able to tell me. Because if it's to hurt my mother or end her happiness—"

"No! I won't do that." To her credit, she sounded vehement. And honest.

"Then what is it? You have to tell me."

She swallowed. Hard. "If I tell you, it won't happen."

The screen door banged upstairs. "Oh my heavens above, Agnes!" Gramma Finnie's excited brogue floated down the steps. "Where are you? You won't believe who just pulled up in the driveway."

Yiayia didn't answer, still holding Cassie's gaze.

"It's Braden!" Gramma called in a hushed whisper, barely audible over the dogs barking at the new arrival. "Where's Cassie? She didn't leave yet, did she? It's our big chance to get them alone together."

For a long, long minute, neither Cassie nor Yiayia said a word, but both raised knowing eyebrows during the stare down. Yiayia's shot up in an expression of hope. Cassie's look had to reflect what she was thinking: *You have got to be kidding me.*

"Agnes Santorini," Cassie hissed. "*That's* your purpose?"

Yiayia smirked and almost looked like her former calculating self again.

"Not possible," Cassie said. "You would never be happy if I went anywhere near a guy who isn't Greek."

"Like I said, people change."

"Not *that* much. Yiayia, I can still taste the vasilopita in my mouth on New Year's Eve. I got the coin in my piece, remember? And while everyone was cheering, you leaned down and whispered, 'You'll marry a Greek man, *koukla.*' Then you said, 'You won't make the mistake your father made. You won't water down the line. You won't bring shame upon the name. You and your brothers will marry Greek because you are Greek, no matter about your mother.'"

Yiayia stared at her. "You couldn't have been three years old."

"Five. And you repeated it often enough that I've spent a good deal of time trying to make that happen, but I've never met a Greek man who measures up to my father."

She made a smug snort. "Nico set the bar high."

"But now you want me with…" She pointed up, in the general direction of the driveway.

Yiayia's eyes shuttered, and she let out a guilty sigh. "That's my purpose, Cassandra."

A man who wasn't Greek? Cassie snorted. "And I think I see a flock of pigs soaring overhead." She leaned in even closer. "Really, Yiayia? You can say anything, but I know you would never push me into the arms of someone who doesn't meet your one and only qualification: Greek."

"I am telling you the truth…*koukla*."

Cassie huffed at that. Manipulation with pet names, of course. It was a Yiayia signature move. "You know, I should call your bluff. I should play your game. I should waltz up there and throw my arms around him and pronounce him *all mine*. And your hair would light on fire."

"You're wrong, Cassandra."

"Am I? I've seen you with my mother my whole life. I've seen the way you look at her because of what she *isn't*."

"I swear to God and all that's holy and on the body of my dead husband: I've changed." Yiayia delivered the oath at Cassie with the most sincere expression she'd ever seen on the older woman's face.

"Agnes, where are you?" Finnie called from the kitchen.

"Coming!" Yiayia notched her head toward the floor. "Will you clean up the rigani for me before Pyggie comes down here and Hoovers it up like it's his afternoon snack?" She tapped Cassie's cheek. "And maybe…put a little lipstick on? And do something with…this?" She flipped some of Cassie's hair. "You look a bit wretchy."

"Wretchy?" She choked softly. "Now that sounds like the Yiayia I know and love and kind of miss."

Her grandmother's eyes closed as if the comment hit its mark. "Don't miss her, Cassandra. She's gone and not coming back." With that, she turned and left the pantry.

Cassie just stood stone-still, stunned, and more confused than ever. Yiayia's purpose was to set her up with Braden? No, that simply didn't ring true.

What if Yiayia really was sick? It would be like her to hide an illness—maybe something serious. Maybe that was what brought her back to her family. Or maybe she did have some insidious, secret motive.

Cassie bent over and brushed the spice into her hand, only because Pyggie *would* lick it and probably get sick. She looked around for a trash bag and, not seeing one, mindlessly stuffed the flakes into the pocket of her cutoffs, still buzzing.

But not with anger. Not with frustration or the need to know. No, this hum in her head was quite familiar. This was the need to take action. To control the outcome. To bend the will of the universe to meet her immediate desires.

Maybe, in that way, she was just like Yiayia.

Cassie had to do something to get her grandmother to come clean about her game. Whether she was up to no good or very sick, it didn't matter. Cassie had to come up with a way to wrest the truth out of her. But what?

She had no idea, but she wasn't sticking around here to have Yiayia smash her against Braden and hope for the best. She'd smashed against Braden enough, and all it did was make her want to…smash some more.

Pausing at the pantry door to listen for any voices, she stepped out to make a quick getaway, slamming right into the big, broad, muscular chest of the man she was hoping to avoid.

Chapter Five

"Oh!" They bounced off each other and let out the exclamations in perfect unison, making Braden laugh. But Cassie didn't seem to find bumping into him the least bit funny. "Sorry," he added, mostly because she looked so serious. "I was supposed to put this in the pantry." He handed her a jar her grandmother had stuffed into his hands when he walked in. "She said it was urgent that I get this into the pantry."

Cassie's rolled her eyes as if she understood that urgency and didn't like it. "I'll take it." When she put her hand over the jar, their fingers brushed, and she blinked as if she felt the same electrical shock he did.

"Okay. Thanks. Bye now." She turned and climbed a step stool, placing the jar on a shelf that had about ten identical ones.

"I see she's got olives covered in case of the zombie apocalypse."

"Mmm. Well, I gotta get out of here."

He just laughed a little. "So, that's how it's going to be? Awkward?"

"It's not going to be anything, Braden." She climbed down and stepped closer, but only in an effort to get out of the walk-in closet. "I'm going home now. I think they want you to move a sofa or something upstairs."

"Gramma Finnie already offered your help for that."

"I'm sure she did." She managed to slide by, barely brushing him, but the contact held a zing anyway.

He stood still for a minute, moving out of the doorway to watch her climb the open-riser stairs that didn't exactly look like they met building codes, but the cutoff shorts? Those definitely broke a few laws.

"Hey, Gramma! Yiayia!" she called when she reached the top of the stairs. "I'm headed out now that—"

Jelly Bean's bark echoed just as he lunged right at Cassie, knocking her off-balance. She shrieked as Braden launched forward, taking the steps three at a time in time to catch Cassie before she tumbled backward.

She landed hard against his chest, but years of training had his feet planted and arms sturdy, except the years of training didn't include Jelly Bean forcing himself at her again.

"Hey! JB! Down!"

He backed off, but kept barking at Cassie like…like he'd made a find.

"You okay?" he asked, easing her away from him.

"Yeah, whoa." She straightened, grabbing the railing for support. "What the heck, doggo?"

"Jelly Bean!" His voice was stern enough to silence the dog, but Jelly Bean didn't take his sharp gaze off Cassie's midsection. "Stay!" Braden pointed at him, holding his finger in place as he guided Cassie up the last step into the kitchen.

The dog followed the command, but his eyes were bright with alarm, along with the rumbling growl consistent with his training for hitting a target.

"Hey, chill, honey." Cassie caught her breath and held out one hand, inching away from the dog. "Just trying to slip out unnoticed here."

Unnoticed? Why?

Jelly Bean snarled as if he had the same question. Braden stared at her as the only explanation occurred to him. Cassie? Really?

"What's all the ruckus?" Gramma Finnie came in with the little dachshund under her arm, and Yiayia was right behind her, hauling the fat one. "Doesn't Jelly Bean love you, Cassie?"

She gave a dry laugh. "Apparently not." She tipped her head, matching JB's questioning look. "I thought we were good, big guy."

Jelly Bean got up and took one step closer, staring at her hips and growling low, then letting out one sharp, clear bark. Exactly the way a dog trained to detect a scent would behave. Except... *Cassie?*

Braden eyed her, his own gaze dropping to her shorts, lingering there for a second, and not only because her thighs were exposed and pretty much perfect.

"Well, never mind about that," Gramma Finnie said, clapping her hands like a schoolteacher about to send them out for recess. "Agnes and I are going to go upstairs and plan out the furniture for our rooms, and while we do, you two can sit and chat."

Yiayia pulled out a kitchen chair. "Right here."

Cassie looked from one slightly crazy old lady to another. "I have to go, Yiayia."

"No, you have to talk to Braden." Gramma Finnie pulled out the other chair and patted Cassie on the shoulder. "He needs your help, lass." She came around the table and gave Yiayia a gentle nudge out of the room. "Let's go upstairs, Agnes."

Cassie shook her head, refusing the offer. "Sorry. Not a good time. Shoot me a text, Braden, and let me know what's up." She wasted no time grabbing her purse from the counter and darting to the door. "Bye, all!"

There was no way he wasn't laying down the law about this. This was his grandmother's home, and she needed to respect that. "Cassie, wait," he said. "I do need to talk to you."

"On my way to the car!" she called as she slipped out a squeaky screen door that flapped a little, not hitting the latch.

He gave Jelly Bean a signal to stay and followed her outside, finding her rushing through the side yard toward the street. "You can try to run away, but that isn't going to change what I know," he said as he caught up with her.

"What you…" She stopped midstep and looked up at him, frowning. "Trust me, if you knew what those two sweet old grandmas are up to, you'd want me to run. I'm doing us both a favor."

"I know what you're hiding."

"What *I'm* hiding?" She glanced over his shoulder to the house behind him and then gave a wry laugh.

"What's funny?" he asked.

"Yiayia and Gramma are in that window watching us like two old ladies who just tuned in to *Days of Our Lives*."

He didn't look because he suspected it was a deflection, and she didn't want to be busted. "It's not cool, Cassie."

"No kidding."

"Bringing pot to my grandmother's house is not cool."

For a moment, she stared at him. "Excuse me? Did you say *pot*?"

"My dog is trained. He smelled it. My guess is it's right there in that pocket." He pointed to her hip and tried like hell to keep his eyes off those tight thighs. Failed, but he tried.

"Pot. In my pocket." A little of the color drained from her cheeks, as it would from a person caught red-handed.

"Unless you have a bomb in your pocket, or a container of kerosene. He can identify those, too." *Sometimes.*

"Hate to break it to you, Einstein." She slipped her hand in her pocket and pulled out something that brought the liner with it, then placed her hand under his nose. "Take a whiff."

"It smells like...pizza." He had to be honest. It hardly reeked of any marijuana he'd ever smelled. But—

"Because it's Greek *oregano*." She croaked a laugh. "Maybe Jelly Bean's the one I should call Einstein."

He stared at her hand, slowly reaching for it and bringing it to his face to sniff again. "Oh man."

"You sound disappointed."

71

"I am."

She snorted. "You wanted me to have pot in my pocket?" Shaking her head, she glanced up at the window, giving a wave. "Move along, ladies. There's nothing to see here." She headed to the front of the house, leaving Braden to stand there feeling like the world's biggest idiot.

"Cassie." He hustled to catch up with her in the driveway. "I'm disappointed because oregano is what they use in drug-detection training as a decoy."

"It's also what Greeks use in every single recipe."

He huffed out a breath and reached for her arm. "I'm sorry, Cassie."

"It's fine." Once again, she looked over his shoulder. "And they're at the front door now."

He glanced in that direction. "Why are they watching us?"

"If I told you, you'd cry."

"Try me."

"No. Go inside and teach your dog how to smell." She headed to the sidewalk where a little red Ford Escape was parked. "I'm going home to do a line or two of Splenda."

He huffed out a breath. "He can smell oregano. Maybe he was trained as a drug-sniffing dog when he was little."

"Oh? Well, remind me to avoid his line at the airport."

"Cassie, stop joking. This is huge. Maybe his olfactory issue comes and goes. Maybe he *can* pass the accelerant test, too."

She stopped to fish her keys out of a handbag. "What are you talking about?"

He studied her for a long time, thinking of the positives and negatives. Was this a smart thing to ask? He didn't know. He just knew what he needed. "I need your help."

"Sure. What do you need?"

"About ten thousand dollars."

She hooted. "Hey, I like you, but not that much."

"Please help me come up with some kind of fundraising idea, then make it happen during Paws for a Cause. I can't do it without your help, and I have to raise the money so Jelly Bean can go to a special training course and be the Accelerant Detection Canine he was born to be."

She squished up her face, confused but maybe a little intrigued. "Maybe if he wasn't named after Easter candy?"

"He came with that name." He stepped closer to make his plea. "I believe in that dog, Cassie. I've pinned all my hopes on him for a year, and I want him to succeed so much. I want to give him every chance. You're an event coordinator. You're already doing this for other people. I'm not asking for the moon, just some help on an idea and maybe the nuts and bolts to make it happen. I don't expect to raise a million dollars, but any help I can get could be the answer to what Jelly Bean needs. I could give up on him, I could get another dog, but I don't want to."

He took a breath, damn near winded after the speech, and noticed that her attention was split between him and the house behind him.

"They're still in the window watching us."

"Cassie, please."

She coughed a laugh. "Does she think I was born

yesterday? That I don't know this whole thing is a cover for what she really wants? Except I have no idea what that is, and I need to know. I *have* to know."

He frowned and looked over his shoulder for a second, seeing the two old ladies in the front window, but still completely confused by what she was saying. "I don't know about them, but I really need your help."

"Okay."

Did he hear that right? "Okay? Did you say okay?"

"Of course I said okay. Did you think I wouldn't help you after that impassioned plea? But, Braden, you have to help me, too."

"Anything."

She raised an eyebrow. "Be careful. You don't know what I'm going to ask or why I'm going to ask it."

"I'm telling you, Jelly Bean's training means everything to me. I've wanted the department to have this dog for so many years." His whole life, really. "So name your price, Cassie. You need me to tell the world you're doing this to help your business? Ask around if other people want your help? Or...or..." What else could he give her? What did she want? "I won't tease you about being cousins. I'll learn to dance that stupid Greek dance. I'll—"

"Hey. It's not stupid."

Damn. Shut up, Mahoney. "The point is, whatever you want, I'll do it, I promise."

Her smile widened, but her attention was still on that window behind him. Then she lifted her hand slowly, as if reaching for him. "Take my hand."

He did, closing her slender fingers in his much bigger hand. "And?"

74

"Now pull me closer. Not too fast. Kind of slow, like it's the first time and you're a little unsure."

He tugged her hand, bringing her close enough that she had to look up at him, which she did, with the strangest, most enchanted look on her face.

"Now what?" he asked.

"A kiss. Quick. Light. Easy. Nothing like the other night. We don't want Gramma Finnie to have a heart attack."

"You want me to kiss you. On the lips. In front of our grandmothers." Nothing about this made sense.

"*Kiss* me."

He didn't have to be told twice. Lowering his head, he used his free hand to tilt her chin toward him and lightly brushed his lips over hers, which were as sweet and soft as he remembered. And he'd done a lot of remembering the past few days.

"Like that?" he asked, inching back.

She leaned to the right and peered at the window. "Son of a...they're *clapping*. Yiayia is clapping."

"Why?"

"That's what I'd like to know. And I'm going to find out." She took a slow, deep breath, slid her hands over his shoulders, and locked them behind his neck. "Braden Mahoney, will you be my boyfriend?"

"What?"

"Just for a little bit, just for pretend. Just until that woman comes clean and tells me what the heck she's doing."

"I couldn't be more confused," he admitted.

She smiled up at him like he'd just told her she was the most beautiful woman on earth. And, hell, right then, in his arms, with affection in her eyes, and her hair tumbling around her face? She was.

"I'll help you raise your money, and you'll help me dig out the truth. She won't be able stand it if I'm *really* with you and—"

"Neither will I," he muttered. He couldn't fake liking Cassie. He could barely fake *not* liking her. He wasn't a fake.

"Oh, no worries. I'm not here for long. We'll have a clean, amicable breakup the minute my grandmother returns to normal. And in the meantime, we'll get Jelly Bean the money he needs. Deal, cuz?"

Oh hell. He was probably going to regret this. No, he already regretted it, but he couldn't help himself. "Yeah, but then we really can't be cousins."

She gave him a sly smile. "*Kissing* cousins."

Now that part, he was going to like.

Chapter Six

He got it.

But then, did Cassie expect anything less from the man she called Einstein? She explained enough for him to flirt playfully while they moved the sofa, and then he seemed eager to finish up and head off to talk—alone. Well, with Jelly Bean, who still eyed her with distrust, avoided contact, and occasionally growled like she was clearly getting away with criminal behavior.

Gramma Finnie practically pushed them out the door, and Yiayia was right there encouraging them to spend lots of time planning the fundraiser together.

But now, as they sat down with iced coffees at one of Bitter Bark Brew's outdoor tables, Cassie braced for a barrage of questions about her unorthodox plan. Why she thought it would work, or what she expected her grandmother to do, maybe why she suspected she was sick, as she'd mentioned to him.

"Are you really leaving Bitter Bark?"

Oh, she didn't see that coming. Or the slight note of disappointment in his voice, but wasn't that how she expected everyone to react when she finally shared her plans?

When she didn't answer, he added, "You said, 'I'm not here for long.' Is that what you meant? You're leaving Bitter Bark?"

"I'd like to, but, Braden, please. I haven't told my mother or my brothers that I'm planning to move away."

"Why not?"

"Because they'll try to change my mind. My mother wasn't thrilled years ago when I announced my plans to take a job in Boston. Nobody was happy with that idea except me."

"So what happened?"

She looked down at her coffee. "My dad got cancer, and everything changed. Everything. I had to step in and help my brothers run the business, for one thing. But I couldn't dream of leaving while he was sick. Then, after he died, my mom needed me more than ever."

"I can tell you two are close."

"She's my best friend," Cassie told him. "And she went through hell taking care of my dad. But now?" She lifted a shoulder and smiled. "She has a new best friend, and I am finally going to spread my wings and live in a city."

He curled a lip, making it clear what he thought of city life. "Where are you going?"

"Wherever I can get a job in event planning, with the only criteria that the population has to be over…" She gave a casual glance that encompassed the whole small town that surrounded them. "This."

"What's wrong with this?"

"Nothing, but haven't you ever wanted to leave?"

"I've left enough. I traveled and went to school, but…" He shrugged. "My family's here, and my job. I love the weather and the Blue Ridge Mountains, and I love…" He looked down at Jelly Bean, who'd finally given up monitoring Cassie's every word and now snoozed under the table. "My soon-to-be-trained dog who's going to be the best arson investigator in western North Carolina."

She smiled at that. "I can certainly appreciate the unique beauty of this place," she said. "I grew up a little over an hour away from here. But I need to experience more. I want the vibrancy and hum of the city."

"That's called traffic."

"The challenge of being in a job with people who are the best of the best."

"Coworkers with big, fat egos? No, thanks."

She brushed off the negativity. "I want to live in a high-rise that looks out over the city lights and wonder about all the stories and all the people."

"You want to live in a box with a thousand other people sharing the same walls and laundry room?" He shook his head. "Cassie, if you want to be high above it all, get a house on a mountain, breathe clean air, and start your own business. Then you know you'll be the best of the best."

"Look, it's just something I've always wanted. I'd like to experience big-city life and a big-city job." But having him throw cold water on her dreams was not cutting it right now. "But frankly, I need to pump up my résumé so I can get that dream job in a big city. So let's talk about your fundraiser and forget about my future, please."

He studied her for a minute, thinking and making her wonder if he wasn't quite ready for the change of subject. But then he asked, "How do we make ten thousand dollars?"

Finally. "Big number, but not impossible if we can come up with the right event and promote it and get people interested. If we cook up something creative enough to really bring the crowds, we can do it." She opened her bag and grabbed one of three notebooks. "Let's get to work."

He looked down at the cover where she'd written Paws for a Cause in black Sharpie.

"Look, I feel a little dumb asking this, but what exactly is this whole Paws for a Cause thing?" He pushed his coffee to the side to lean on the table and get closer. "I know it goes on for the entire month of June, and it's kind of a spinoff of the Puppy Parade we've had in the past, but how did it get to be a month long, and how exactly do people make money?"

"*People* don't make money," she explained. "Organizations and good causes do. But it's really not a dumb question at all, since it's new. Bitter Bark had a Puppy Parade when the town was in its Better Bark phase."

He nodded. "Shane's wife, Chloe, came to town to increase tourism and had that wild idea to rename Bitter Bark *Better Bark* for a year and turn the town into the most dog-friendly destination in America."

"It worked."

"In a big way," he agreed. "The name's back to Bitter Bark, but as you can see…" He gestured toward the other tables, several with dogs sleeping or sitting on their owner's lap.

"Well, the Puppy Parade was a huge hit with tourists, who spent a ton of money at the booths," she told him. "So the tourism committee decided to move the whole thing to a summer month and spread the wealth to every Bitter Bark organization, person, or nonprofit that wants to raise money for an approved cause. There's an event or contest or party happening almost every single day, and each one is designed to bring in cash."

"But not just for dogs?"

"Oh, no. Anybody can hold a fundraiser as long as the event includes dogs and the money goes to a worthy, altruistic cause."

He nodded. "Equipping the fire department with an Accelerant Detection Canine and his handler is a very good cause. So, we won't have any problem getting on the schedule, right?"

She flipped the notebook open to the calendar page, skimming the mostly-full dates. "We're a little late. June is right around the corner, and I don't think there are a lot of slots available, but I've made some friends in the mayor's office. I think I can pull a few strings if we come up with a great idea. There are already a ton of really imaginative events planned."

"Such as?"

She ran her finger over the squares that marked June and read the event names. "There's a dog race, of course, the Five K-9, sponsored by the sheriff's department. The hospital is doing America's Got *Tail*ent, which is…"

"A doggy talent show?" he guessed on a laugh.

"Yep, and they are charging big money for a spot in the show and admission." She angled her notebook so he could see the calendar.

"What's Artsy Animals? Don't tell me dogs paint."

"No, but that's not a bad idea. It's a craft show put on by the local Rotary, but all the items for sale are animal-related." She pointed to June first. "Of course there's the big kickoff event, Date with a Dog, with all the hot single firefighters and their dogs. Winners go to Yappy Hour, a black-tie cocktail party at Overlook Glen Vineyards the following night."

He looked skyward. "I can't imagine any of us will be pulling in big money."

She gave his hand a playful tap. "I'll bid for you, Einstein."

"You will?"

"If Yiayia's in the audience, sure, I'll part with a Benjamin or two, especially since Jelly Bean comes as part of the package…" She reached down to pet his head, but he jerked away and gave a low snarl. "If he'll let me."

"I'll tell him to let you." He inched a little closer and let his gaze drop over her face, landing on her mouth. "It's the only way I could get what I wanted."

Which was help with an event, right? Or…his words from the other night at Bushrod's came back to her. *It was exactly what I wanted.*

She swallowed hard. "Wait a second. You do realize I mean a *fake* relationship, right? Like, it doesn't include all the side dishes that come with the full meal."

His lips curled in a half smile. "So it's an à la carte romance? Buffet-style? Pick what you want and leave the rest?"

She met him halfway across the tiny table, close enough to whisper her answer and put her hands over his to make her point. "There will be no more smoking-hot dance floor kisses."

His brow flickered with a little humor. "It was smoking hot."

Just the way he said it made her insides fire up again. "Exactly. Just let my grandmother think I'm falling for a non-Greek guy so I can get the truth out of her in a moment of weakness, when she's chomping at the bit to talk me out of this relationship. Until then, we'll just spend a lot of time together raising money and helping Jelly Bean, letting her think we're dating." She slid her hand out from under his, picking up a pen that was clipped to the side of the notebook. "Maybe we should write down those rules."

"So, no sex."

"Did you *think* a fake relationship included sex? Is that why you said yes?"

He didn't answer for a long time, studying her with a look that said he most certainly did—or at least wanted to. "I said yes because you said yes to helping me. Now, I'm just trying to make sure I know the rules."

She looked down at his large hands, still resting on the table, taking in his blunt-cut nails and tanned fingers, with nicks and scars and the lightest dusting of hair on his knuckles.

As she stared, a slow burn started deep in her belly, winding its way up to her back and down her tummy and settling right…where she wanted those hands. Her mouth went bone-dry, her blood ran burning hot, and for a moment, everything in her wanted to change the rules of the game before they were even set.

Would sex be so bad?

No, it would be earth-shattering and amazing and delicious and worth every possible pain and regret because—

"Cassie?"

She looked up, falling into blue, blue eyes with navy flecks and dark lashes and just enough hope and heat that she almost said yes.

But then she'd never leave Bitter Bark. Because Braden Mahoney could be a fake boyfriend, but he could never be a one-night stand.

"No sex," she confirmed, easing her hands out from under his. "That would be stupid, Einstein."

Wouldn't it?

Well, well, well. At least all that chemistry wasn't a product of his imagination.

Braden studied Cassie's profile as she flipped to a clean page in her little notebook and wrote *Braden's Event* at the top. None of the details of her features were new to him, but that didn't make it any less fun to memorize them.

He was already familiar with her fine bones and the smooth, olive-toned complexion she must have inherited from her Greek father. He'd already imagined running his hands through the nearly black hair she had pulled into a thick, sloppy ponytail and tracing the defined lines of her jaw, the soft curve of her throat with his fingertips. Or lips. He was no stranger to the depths of her ebony eyes or the way her long lashes cast a shadow over her cheekbones.

Fact was, he'd been into Cassie since the day he met her. And now that he knew she was moving away? Cassandra Santorini just became his ideal woman. Except for the *no sex* and *fake dating* part.

"Maybe we could think of a way to piggyback off Ella's event," she said, scribbling the word *Ideas* on the first line.

"Yeah." Except...damn. He had no clue what that event was. "What exactly is she doing again?"

"Dude, your own sister? Do you not talk to her?"

"I haven't done much but study and work for months," he admitted. "So humor me. What is Ella's fundraiser? She can't be raising cash for Bone Appetit, because her dog treat business isn't a nonprofit."

"No, but her charity is. Kibbles for Kindness donates treats to shelters," she said.

"Oh, I remember." Ella and his mom had told him about this. "A dog baking contest?"

She laughed, turning the page to another that was covered in multicolored ink. "No dogs will be baked, but treats will be, and the best-tasting one—according to the canine judges—gets grooming for life at Darcy's shop. Entrants to the Pawsbury Bake-Off are paying a lot of money because Ella also got some big muckety-mucks from the Family First Pet Foods company interested in her event."

"I did hear about that," he said. "Aren't they cosponsoring the whole event or something?"

"They're underwriting Paws for a Cause for PR purposes, but they're also looking for a new line of organic treats, possibly homemade by a customer who lives in Bitter Bark, since we are the dog-friendliest town in America."

"What a cool idea."

She smiled. "Thank you. I'm proud of it."

"Your idea? Impressive." Like everything else about her. "Got any more just like it for me or are all the good ideas taken?"

"Have faith in me, Einstein." She poked him with a pen. "I always have more. But there are some good ones on the schedule, like the costume contest and parade, the funniest-video contest, and, of course, the Waterford Dog Show, with all proceeds going to Uncle Daniel's friend Marie, who is starting a cross-country rescue transport business with her niece. But we can think of something, I'm sure. We just have to brainstorm. So, quick." She snapped her fingers, and Jelly Bean sat up. "Not you, Wonder Dog. You." She pointed the pen at Braden like it was her sword in battle. "What comes to mind when you think of a dog?"

He looked down at Jelly Bean, who looked from one to the other, then returned to his nap. "Unconditional love?"

She smiled. "Maybe something a little more basic that we can turn into a contest. Sleeping? Eating? Sniffing?"

He gave a sad smile. "Don't mock my dog's disabilities."

"I'm sorry." She put her hand on Braden's arm in sympathy, drawing his eyes to her long, lean fingers and pale pink nails. "If we put him on a hunt for oregano, he'd bring home the…"

"Basil," he joked, enjoying her easy laugh in response. "Don't put him on a scavenger…" He didn't finish the sentence, but blinked at her, and for three long seconds they held each other's gazes as their minds clicked.

"A scavenger hunt!" She drummed excitedly with the pen.

"There isn't one on the calendar yet?"

"Not yet. Every team could have to have a dog," she said, starting to write. "Who sniffs out the clues. We can call it…"

"Lost and Hound," he suggested, making her eyes flash and her smile nearly blind him.

"Einstein, you *are* a genius!"

He grinned at the praise and returned her high five. "But how does that raise money?"

"Entry fees, for one thing." She started scribbling like crazy. "And people can sponsor teams. There are professional scavenger hunters who'll pay up to a thousand dollars to win a big prize, which we can have donated."

"A thousand dollars? Then we'd only need ten teams. That's easy."

"Not totally easy." She jotted more on the page. "Let's see, we have to set it up, organize it, find a donor for the prize, and promote it, of course. But first we have to get it approved by the committee, which I can do." She scratched her pen furiously.

"Do you write everything down?"

"If you don't commit it to paper, you won't commit it to action." She looked up from the page. "My father taught me that. Said that's how businesses are run and worlds are changed and nothing gets misunderstood or forgotten. I have at least half a dozen notebooks going at any given time. This project will be one big to-do list, which…" She bit her lip. "Kinda makes me happy."

"Good, because a list like that makes me sick." At her horrified look, he added, "You know what my shifts are like."

"Twenty-four on and forty-eight off, right?"

"With the occasional ten hours a day for four consecutive days," he added. He shook his head and glanced down at the dog. "And I really, really wanted to work on training with Jelly Bean on my off-hours. Ideally, I could bypass this whole ten-thousand-dollar training program if I could prove to Uncle Daniel that Jelly Bean's scent issues are temporary."

"Explain to me what he told you was wrong again," she said, putting her pen down and shifting her focus directly to him. "I didn't get the whole gist of why he won't sign the affidavit."

As he told her about the conversation and detailed his options, Braden absently reached down to pet Jelly Bean, answering Cassie's questions and appreciating how interested she was, even taking notes.

As they talked and discussed his options, she also clicked on her phone a few times, googling for information on olfactory problems in dogs and then searching for the closest arson investigation canine training centers.

"You love to find answers, don't you?" he mused as she read to him about one not too far away, in-state. "You're such a problem solver."

She laughed. "I told you I'm a woman of action."

"You're like Jelly Bean on a hunt for that one elusive thing."

"Nice to know I remind you of your dog," she said while writing something else.

He reached forward and put his hand over hers. "Cassie, that is the highest-possible compliment."

Her return smile was a little shaky, but real. Almost immediately, she looked back at the phone, tapping it. "Look at this, Braden. This one training site lists all their tests so you can get your dog ready for that certification."

"I think I've seen that."

"I'll send you the link."

"Thanks, Cassie." He reached for her hand again, constantly drawn to that spark that he got every time they touched. "I could never do this without you."

She eased her hand away again, as if the contact was too intense for her. "And I get my non-Greek boyfriend, which will make my Yiayia crazypants until she tells me the truth."

"So, she finds out tomorrow? At Waterford Farm's Sunday dinner? Because I'll be there."

She bit her lip. "I guess we could, you know, drop a few bread crumbs in front of Yiayia."

"And your brothers. And mother. And my siblings and cousins and mother and uncle." He grinned at her. "That's more like a loaf of bread, not crumbs, Cass."

"Yeah." Her eyes narrowed as she thought about that. "Not sure I can lie to my mother. I might have to let her in on our secret. But, *oof.*" She made a face. "Then she'll tell Daniel, and he'll tell one of his kids, and then it'll slip out, and Yiayia will know exactly what I'm doing and why. But..." She dropped her head back. "I *cannot* lie to my mother."

"So don't lie."

She gave him a confused look. "I just told you what would happen if I tell her the truth."

One more time, he took her hand, curling his fingers into hers tight enough that she couldn't slip away. "It's not a lie if we really are dating."

But she gave a good yank free. "*Excuse* me?"

"You heard me. Why fake it? Be my girlfriend, Cassie Santorini."

The flush that crawled up her cheeks was as satisfying as it was terrifying. He braced for her to smack the table with a resounding *Are you out of your mind, Einstein?*

But she just stared at him.

"That way, you wouldn't be lying and…"

"You'd get sex," she finished.

He shut his eyes with a snort. "Honestly, that's not what I was thinking."

"Then what were you thinking?"

"Look, you're out of here in, what, a few months? The minute you get a job in Boston or New York or DC?"

She nodded, silent.

"And, Cassie, I'm going to be straight with you. I don't believe in…permanent things."

"You don't?"

"Not when someone has a job like mine," he admitted. "I don't think it's right or fair to be in a serious, long-term relationship. My work's too dangerous, and I refuse to give someone a guarantee of a future. That—at my age of thirty-three?—usually sends women packing after a few dates."

She considered that, studying him before asking, "So, what exactly are you proposing?"

"That we don't fake a thing. We just give it an expiration date."

"I don't know," she said. "Anything 'real' almost always comes with connections and plans and trust and intimacy that will lead to…side dishes and detoured dreams. And I won't let you do that, Braden. I won't."

He heard the vehemence in her voice, and that just made him more certain this was a good idea. "Then we both agree it's temporary. Nothing will be detoured, I promise. Go ahead…" He pressed her hand to the notebook. "Write that down and make it so."

But she didn't, still studying him. "And side dishes?"

"They can be on or off the table, Cass. You're the one setting it."

She shot up a dubious brow. "Do you seriously think we could date for real, spend any amount of time alone with each other, and not…" She swallowed. "Repeat that kiss?"

No. Not for a minute. "We could try."

"Then what difference does it make if it's real, fake, or temporary if there's no sex?"

"Because I'm not a fan of lying, either," he said. "So be my temporary girlfriend, and let's just have a little fun before you blow out of Bitter Bark."

"Fun?"

"Could be." So much fun.

Her lips curled up just enough to give him hope. "I'll let you know tomorrow at Sunday dinner."

"I can't wait."

Chapter Seven

Cassie knew what her answer would be long before she arrived at Waterford Farm the next day. Simple, straightforward, uncomplicated...no.

There was absolutely no way she'd let herself consider Braden's suggestion. Make this *real*? Was he nuts? *Real* would be dangerous. *Real* would be risky. *Real* would mean he'd tug on her heart and slip off her clothes and slide into her life and make her give up her dreams.

You fall for a firefighter, and you fry.

Holding that thought, she climbed out of her car, taking inventory of who'd already arrived at the weekly *festuche* they called Sunday dinner at Waterford Farm. Oh yeah, pretty much everyone was here from all three contingents.

It wasn't that she didn't enjoy the event—the Kilcannons could toss back Bloody Marys like pros, and there was always something fun planned, like ATV rides or meeting a whole new set of puppers that had arrived for training or rescue. Cassie had easily found like-minded friends with Darcy Kilcannon and

Ella Mahoney, the sister-close cousins who were her age, and she always managed to steal her mother away from Daniel long enough to catch up on life.

The food had left a lot to be desired in the early days, when Daniel and Gramma Finnie were in charge of cooking, but now that the Santorinis were included, the menu had improved—and gotten more Greek—every week. Her brother Alex frequently cooked and always brought sides and desserts from Santorini's, which closed after brunch on Sundays.

In addition to the oodles of Kilcannons and their spouses and significant others, there were the cousins. Colleen Mahoney, Daniel's sister, though quiet, had a sweet, calming influence and, like Gramma, knew all the secret stories that the old house had to tell. Her three sons were scarce due to fire station shifts, but when Braden was there, the whole day had a slightly more magical feel.

Which was why she could not, would not, let this little idea of hers snowball into something real, even if he wanted to label it "temporary." And she'd tell him they needed to bag the whole plan today. There had to be another way to coax the truth out of Yiayia.

"Hello, baby girl."

The minute she saw her mother step out of the kitchen door onto the wraparound porch, Cassie felt good about her decision. She couldn't lie to Katie Santorini if her life depended on it. But what if Yiayia's life depended on it?

"I was starting to wonder if you weren't coming."

"Hey, Mommy." She slipped into her little girl name mostly for giggles, but also because it bonded them. "Did the Irish folk start drinking without me?"

She pointed to the side of the house, where the porch spread to a large deck, the noise telling her they were all out there talking and toasting.

Her mother laughed, a sound that Cassie was still getting used to hearing on such a regular basis. The years nursing Dad had been hard on her, and laughter had been rare. And just when Mom started to emerge from a fog of recovery and grief, there was the shock of that DNA test that revealed her oldest son was not Nico Santorini's, but the son of a young vet student she'd dated briefly in college.

And while he and Mom tried to figure out how to break the news to Nick, who was currently in Africa with Doctors Without Borders, Cassie had to lie to him when he'd asked repeatedly about the results of the tests. Just those few moments on the phone had gutted her because Cassie didn't have a lying bone in her body.

So the sooner she told Braden the deal was off, the better. She'd still help him with the scavenger hunt, which was all he wanted in the first place. Well, not maybe *all* he wanted, but it would have to be enough.

"You look great, Mom," Cassie said as her mother crossed the porch, her dark hair swinging around her chin and her sweet brown eyes dancing. "Like you were born to live in this gorgeous place." Cassie gestured to the rambling yellow farmhouse and the hundred acres of rolling hills around it.

"That's because I'm so happy and in love." As Mom gave her a hug, she squeezed extra hard and put her lips close to Cassie's ear. "But newsflash. Impostor Yiayia is here in full force. She baked, Cassie."

"That's not unusual."

"And brought handmade presents for babies, born and yet to arrive. And…" She leaned back to finish. "She handed me a bag of fresh lemons because she remembered I love lemonade in the summer."

"Oh dear."

"I know," Katie said. "It's so *thoughtful*."

"Downright scary," Cassie agreed, making a face. "Anything else?"

"Oh, I saved the best for last. She's talking nonstop about you and Braden. How you're going to do a fundraiser together. And surely you'll bid on him at the bachelor auction. The next thing you know, she'll have you two dating."

Cassie stared at her. "That would be…"

"Crazy, I know. As if she'd approve of anyone for you who isn't Greek." Of course her mother understood that about Yiayia. "What do you think she's up to?"

"No good," Cassie said. "I confronted her, but she wouldn't come clean."

"Do you think she's—"

"Hey, Cassie." Daniel came around the corner, wearing the same expression of happiness and contentment that his bride-to-be had, giving Cassie a hug, but immediately draping his arm around Mom's shoulders. "Great news about the fundraiser with Braden."

"Yeah, it is."

"Although, I don't want you to get his hopes up too high."

"How's that?" she asked, wondering if she'd already done that. "I really think a scavenger hunt with dogs could raise the money he needs."

"I have no doubt of that," Daniel said. "But I believe there's a strong possibility that something's wrong with Jelly Bean's olfactory system, and training won't fix it. I'm afraid our boy is in a little bit of denial."

"Well, Jelly Bean almost threw me down for having oregano in my pocket," she said with a sad smile. "So he can smell."

"But that proves he can't discern. Training might fix it, but I'm not sure. I'd hate to see Braden be disappointed." Daniel added a look she couldn't quite interpret. "You know he's had a lot of that lately."

Ah, yes, Simone. Except he didn't seem very destroyed over that breakup, at least not to Cassie.

"Cassandra!" The next arrival to the porch party managed to suck all the oxygen and fill all the space, even though her body was quite a bit smaller than it used to be.

"Hi, Yiayia," she said, glancing at the glass of water with lemon that she held. What was up with that? *Real* Yiayia would never miss a chance to day-drink. "I heard you're showering the fam with presents." She added just enough of a look so that the woman would know Cassie, for one, wasn't fooled.

"And I have a little something for you." She started to gesture for Cassie to come into the house, then stopped. "Oh, how rude of me. I didn't mean to cut in on this conversation."

As if she weren't the Queen of Ill-Timed Interruptions. "No, it's fine, Yiayia, I'm just—"

"Braden's here," Yiayia said, waggling her eyebrows like a lunatic, which made Daniel laugh.

"And I thought I was pushy," he joked.

"Oh, your days are over," Yiayia said to him. "There's a new matchmaker in town."

That made Daniel chuckle. "Well, have at it, Yiayia," he said, giving Mom a squeeze. "We keep forgetting about that while we're planning our own wedding."

"But, Yiayia," Mom's eyes narrowed in skepticism, "haven't I heard you say a thousand times that our Cassie is going to fall in love with a man exactly like her father?"

"Strong, smart, loving, funny, and capable?" Yiayia shot back. "Check, check, and check again."

"And *Greek*?" Cassie added.

Yiayia shrugged. "Some things are more important than nationality."

On what planet? Cassie's jaw darn near hit the porch.

But she contained her reaction and let it fuel her, giving her grandmother a fake smile and mentally drawing her sword. Oh yeah. A bluff needed to be called. And hard.

She glanced at her mother. Yes, lying to her was impossible, but she had to fool Yiayia, which meant she had to fool everyone. Which meant…she couldn't lie.

This had to be *real*.

"Hey."

They all turned at the sound of Braden coming around the corner. She tried not to react at the sight of him, not to notice how his eyes were the same color as the blue chambray button-down he wore, or how strong his forearms looked in the rolled-up sleeves. And just forget those shoulders.

Those shoulders alone could make a girl say yes to all kinds of trouble.

"Hey, Braden." Her voice came out thick through a dry, tight throat, and she could have kicked herself for not keeping it light and calling him by the proper nickname.

"We were just talking about you," Yiayia said in that singsong voice she must think made her sound nicer. "Cassie's so excited about helping you with the fundraiser."

He looked at her, a question in his eyes. "Is she?"

"She is," Cassie said softly.

"Oh, when she talks about herself in third person?" Braden's smile grew. "She means business."

"Yes, she does." Taking a deep breath, Cassie stepped closer to Braden and very deliberately slid her arm around his waist, looking up at him. "How's my gorgeous boyfriend?"

His eyes flickered for a millisecond, then lit like a Christmas tree. "Depends. How's my gorgeous girlfriend?"

"She's…yours."

Cassie turned back to the others, expecting shell-shocked reactions. But Daniel's expression was bemused, and her mother appeared strangely satisfied. But Yiayia? She looked positively rapturous.

Oh no. Was this whole thing going to backfire and blow up in Cassie's face?

"You're just in time to take Jelly Bean for a walk." Braden secured his arm around Cassie just in case she suddenly threw her head back and yelled, *Just kidding!*

"A walk sounds great. Is there time before dinner, Daniel?"

"There's time!" Yiayia answered for him, coming closer to them to wave them off the porch. "Alex is making lamb kleftiko, and it's taking forever. Go, you two. Walk. Take your time."

"Jelly Bean's in the pen with all the other dogs. Come on." Braden finally released his hold, but snagged Cassie's hand as she dropped her purse on a wicker chair and gave a quick wave to the audience of three.

"Sorry if I blindsided you," Cassie said under her breath as they walked down the stairs and crossed the drive and lawn toward the penned-in area where all family dogs played on good-weather Sundays.

"Not a bit. I thought your timing was perfect, and your delivery?" He gave her hand a squeeze and leaned close to her ear. "Hell, for a minute there, I believed you."

She looked up at him, silent.

"Don't tell me," he whispered. "Is that a yes?"

"A temporary, qualified, provisional, highly controlled, full-of-restrictions yes."

He couldn't help laughing.

"It's not funny," she said.

"No, but you are. Relax, Cass." He put his arm around her again and tucked her into his side, loving the warmth of her against him. "Controlling a fire is my specialty."

"I just couldn't lie, so…" She let out a little grunt of regret.

"Don't worry," he assured her. "Now we don't have to lie. We can just hang out together until you head off into the sunset. No strings, no broken promises, no disappointments. Come on, let's tell Jelly Bean."

They reached the edge of the main training pen, which was full of an array of family dogs, including three pitties, a tan border collie, one crazy boxer, an old setter and the golden who never left his side, and several more.

Cassie leaned on a wooden slat of the wire fencing, staring at Jelly Bean, who made his way dutifully through the sea of cousin dogs toward Braden, but slowed to a stop when he spotted who was next to him.

"Uh oh," Cassie joked. "You brought the neighborhood oregano pusher, and he doesn't like it."

Braden signaled the dog to come closer. "Too bad. I like it." He opened the gate and bent over to greet Jelly Bean, who accepted the affection, but didn't stop staring down Cassie.

After Braden told the dog they were going for a walk, Jelly Bean did a little circle of joy, which made Cassie laugh.

"You do know he speaks English?" he asked.

"Oh, he does?" She gave a skeptical chuckle.

"Go ahead, doubt. You'll find out the truth soon enough." They headed off toward the path that led to the lake where Braden had spent about a thousand hours of his youth fishing with his cousins and brothers.

He and Cassie followed, quiet at first, the only sounds the distant barking from the pen, the occasional hoot of laughter from the house, and some birds calling back and forth.

Then he felt her gaze on him. "Can I ask you a personal question, Braden?"

"Of course."

"If you wanted a girlfriend so much, why did you break up with Simone?"

Did he want a girlfriend "so much"? Or did he just want Cassie and this was the perfect chance to have her for a short time, which was all he could offer.

He thought about that, not answering while they rounded a cluster of trees to reach the lake, surrounded by a wide expanse of spring-green grass broken by swaths of purple patches and massive oak trees.

"She really wanted something I wasn't able to give her," he finally said.

"But everyone said you were upset about it."

"I was unhappy about the inevitability of the breakup, which has happened to me more than once."

"Why?"

He led her to a smooth rock he knew well, where she could sit and not get grass stains on her white jeans. "Because I have some deep-seated beliefs about how I should live my life."

She settled on the stone, stretching out her legs, giving him a glimpse of turquoise-painted toes in white sandals. "That's what you meant yesterday when you said someone in your job doesn't get permanent?"

"Precisely."

"Lots of firefighters are in permanent relationships," she said. "It sounds to me like an excuse that suits a commitment-phobe."

He laughed and reached down, plucking one of the flowers that grew next to the stone. "What are these called?" he asked, handing it to her.

"I think that's a common violet. Also known as a weed."

"It's pretty for a weed. They're all over this area in the summer. I used to bring them home to my mom after I was fishing here with my cousins and brothers."

"Mmm. Way to change the subject and talk about flowers."

"I wasn't. I was about to explain why I don't do permanent relationships."

"By telling me about flowers for your mom?"

"By telling you *why* I brought my mom flowers."

She looked up at him, reacting to his serious tone. "Because you love her?"

"Because I knew she'd spent the day crying."

Drawing back, she looked down at the flower in her fingers as a frown tugged. "Because of your dad?"

"When I was thirteen, he died fighting a fire."

"I heard that." She let out a sad sigh. "I'm sorry for you. For your whole family."

He nodded, because even to this very day, the pain of how his father died burned at a hole that never seemed to leave his heart. Braden had been sound asleep when Joe Mahoney had left for that twenty-four-hour shift and had never said goodbye. Twenty years later, that still stung.

She put a hand on his forearm, adding some gentle pressure. "And I've been around here long enough to know he was a great husband and father."

"Yep."

"Not that it's anything the same, but I know how it feels to lose a father. Of course, we knew it was happening and I was an adult, not a kid, but..." Her voice trailed off, letting her touch do the sympathizing.

He stared out at the water, thinking of that kid, turning fourteen right after Dad died. He could smell the pot roast his mom would be making when Aunt Annie dropped them off at home after he'd spent a summer day at Waterford Farm. Braden would present those flowers the very minute he walked into the house that his mother worked so hard to keep normal when things were anything but that summer.

"She'd take the flowers and make a big fuss," he said. "She'd always put them in a little jar that she used for making jelly. And she'd say, 'It's okay, Braden. I knew what I was getting into when I married a fireman.'"

He heard Cassie's soft moan. "I can't imagine how that affected your family."

"All of us handled it differently. I escaped into books. Declan grew up in a big fat hurry and became the father, at least in his eyes. Connor went off the deep end and rebelled like a classic sixteen-year-old. And Ella ran away."

"She ran away from home?"

"Repeatedly, but she always came back. When she was old enough, she started traveling a lot, always taking off somewhere, lots of times with Darcy. But us boys? We all had to be firefighters. We all had to follow in his footsteps, because that's what he wanted."

"It's a lot safer now, isn't it? Don't you have better equipment and more technology?"

Safer was a relative term. "I still have to go through fire, Cassie. I still have to suit up and get in the truck and go on every call, without knowing for sure that I'll come back. Now I don't live in fear, and a lot of the time, I don't even think about it. The crew is amazing, and we know what we're doing. The real danger is rare, but real, and I never forget that."

She nodded, too smart to argue that fact. "I remember a few years ago when this whole area had terrible forest fires."

"I fought a lot of them, and yes, they're mighty. They're big. They're deadly." He turned to her, taking her hands. "I don't particularly like living alone or not having a plan for a future with someone and for kids of my own. And like I told you, most women want that. You don't."

"Oh, I do, someday. I just want the experience of living a different way for a while."

"That makes you perfect."

"Really? And here I thought it was my quick wit."

"You mean that thing you haul out when someone tries to get close to you? That wit?"

She narrowed her eyes. "That should be off-limits, too."

"What? Wit?"

"Getting close. Analyzing each other. Getting… connected."

He studied her for a long time, feeling himself drawing closer, aching to kiss her and seal this deal.

"One more inch, Einstein, and all bets are off."

He lifted her chin with his fingertip. "What are we betting on?"

"That we can actually spend time alone, be six

inches apart, and keep our hands off each other. Pretty sure we'll lose that bet."

He didn't move. "I could do it. Not sure I want to, but I could."

"Mmm." She flicked her tongue over the very spot on her lip he wanted to taste. "Side dishes cost too much."

"How much?"

She narrowed her eyes. "They cost intimacy and heartache and regret and probably a whole change of plan."

He tipped his head, a little surprised by the fierceness in her response. "They don't have to, but I promise that's not my end goal here."

"Oh, really? You merely want to have a girlfriend stamped with an expiration date and no sex?"

Of course he didn't, but he wanted Cassie around more than he wanted to get laid. "Look, I wouldn't sleep with you on the first date if I'd just met you on the street and asked you out. It's not my style, and you're too special for that. I would, however, kiss you."

"Then we'd never stop."

"I have self-control, Cassie."

"Go you. I, on the other hand, might not have a shred of it."

He laughed and leaned back. "Okay. Your rules. Your temporary, qualified, provisional, highly controlled, full-of-restrictions rules. I'm in as far as you'll let me and give you my word that I'll do nothing but blow a kiss in your general direction when you're ready to leave."

Before she could answer, Jelly Bean barked from across the field, his paws at the water's edge. With a quick whistle, Braden called him back, both of them watching the dog trot toward them.

"Your uncle is really worried his scent problems are not temporary or trainable," she said softly. "I hope he's wrong."

"He's wrong," Braden said, believing the words as he said them.

"Then let's prove it." She pushed up and brushed off. "Let's raise money so he can be trained and prove everyone wrong."

He smiled as he stood next to her. "My woman of action," he said, sliding both arms around her.

She stiffened. "I'm not your woman."

"For a little while, you are." The very first tendril of wishing it were more than that threaded its way up his chest, but he managed to cut it down and ignore it, as he planned to do *for a little while.*

She eased out of his arms to offer the flower he'd given her. "Want to take this to your mom?" she asked.

"Yeah." Bending over, he snagged a few more. "She'd like that."

"Oh man," Cassie muttered as she started walking away.

"What? Oh man, what?" No doubt she'd sling back with *You're so mushy, Einstein.*

But when she turned to him, she wasn't smiling. The breeze blew her black hair over her face and almost hid her eyes, but he could see the fierceness there when she pointed at him.

"Do not make me like you, Braden Mahoney. *Do not.*"

He just laughed and brushed her nose with the little flowers. "We both know it's too late for that, Cass."

Chapter Eight

Sunday afternoon with their families had unfolded with barely a sideways glance, sly smile, or any needling from the sharpest in the clans. Not only did no one seem very surprised by this "relationship," Yiayia seemed downright giddy. And, like most Sundays, Braden and Cassie sat next to each other at the table and were partners in the Mario Kart tournament.

In some ways, it was like any other Sunday, except Cassie managed to gracefully fend off a private chat with her mom. She wasn't ready to be hit with a barrage of questions about Braden. It was all too new. Still not *real* no matter how she defined that. But Mom settled for an extra hug at the end of the evening, whispering, "You look happy, honey," when they said goodbye.

But the questions would start now, Cassie knew, as she walked down the steps of the town hall with her approved proposal for Lost and Hound under her arm and a confirmed date for the event on June twenty-ninth as part of Paws for a Cause. From here, she had a meeting scheduled with Ella to go over the Pawsbury

Bake-Off details, and then they had a conference call with their contact at Family First Pet Foods.

She crossed the square and turned the corner on Ambrose Avenue, pausing to let a lady and a massive Saint Bernard out of the door of Bone Appetit before stepping inside the little shop.

Sure enough, Colleen was behind the counter, checking out a customer with three lively little white puppers all getting tangled in their leashes. The store wasn't big, but Ella and Colleen had made it one of the most warm and welcoming places in Bitter Bark. They modeled it after an old-fashioned candy store by using bright, cheery pastels and printed wallpaper, and two long glass counters full of gourmet treats. There were more packaged goods for sale in a retail area and a large penned-in play area for four-legged shoppers and guests.

An open doorway led right into Friends With Dogs, where the clipping, snipping, and "beauty" took place. The dual businesses were perfect for Darcy and Ella, who Cassie knew had been inseparable their whole lives.

"Hi, Cassie," Colleen called after she gave freebie treats to the three little dogs, finished with the customer, and then came around the corner. "Ella's on the phone in the office, but she told me to send you back when you got here."

As always, Colleen's long hair, nearly to her waist, was pulled off her face with a simple gold clip. She never wore a spec of makeup and didn't seem too concerned about the fact that her hair was more gray than brown. But instead of seeing a plain, middle-aged woman, Cassie suddenly imagined Colleen twenty years ago, with four kids and a husband who didn't come home from work one day.

The idea softened Cassie's heart, making her reach for Colleen and add a hug in greeting that really wasn't necessary but felt right.

"Yes, we need hugs today," Colleen said, returning a light embrace. "Ella's doing her conference call with Family First."

"What?" Cassie checked her watch with a soft intake of breath. "It wasn't supposed to start for half an hour."

"New guy, new rules," Colleen said.

"What are you talking about?"

"She got an email an hour ago that the company contact had changed, and he moved up the call time."

"Oh, did I miss a call or email about that?"

Colleen shook her head as if that hadn't even been considered. "You were at the town hall getting Braden's event approved. That's just as important, and we know it."

"I would have rescheduled that to help Ella. I know the corporate calls can stress her out. Who's the new guy?"

"Apparently, he's the just-named head of public relations for Family First Pet Foods, and he's all over this whole event," Colleen said. "Not just our Bake-Off, but all of Paws for a Cause."

"Well, they are underwriting most of it." She started walking toward the back office, and Colleen stayed with her.

"And I think he thinks that means he can call the shots."

"Call, yes? Change at this late in the game? I hope not." Cassie added a reassuring pat to Colleen's shoulder. "And the Pawsbury Bake-Off is going to be amazing."

"Oh yeah. He's changing that name. Too close to Pillsbury."

Cassie gave her a look. "Seriously? We have flyers and ads created already."

She shrugged and gave her a nudge to the door. "Go and listen. She's got the call on speaker."

"On it." Cassie tapped the door to the back office, wincing at the sight of Ella pacing and stabbing her fingers through her spiky-short hair, the desk covered with papers, her cell phone on speaker in the middle of it all. From it, a man's voice boomed.

"Hey," Cassie whispered, making Ella whip around to give her a horrified look and mouth, "Oh my God, help me!"

"These entrants have to be serious bakers with legitimate products, Ms. Mahoney," Boomy Voice continued. "We're not going to splash this all over the trades and media only to have a second-rate winner."

"Oh, Mr. Demakos. My event planner, Cassie, is here, and I know she can help answer all of your questions."

"Like exactly how many entrants have signed the waiver to give us their recipe when this is over?" he demanded.

Uh, none. Cassie took a deep breath and slipped into the guest chair, because the small sofa was covered with boxes of inventory. Staring at Ella, she racked her brain for something to say.

"Demakos?" she asked. "Are you Greek?"

For a moment, there was nothing but silence, then, "Uh, yes, I am. Second generation, as a matter of fact."

"So am I! Well, third gen. Cassandra Santorini is the name."

She heard a chuckle. "Named after an aunt or grandmother?"

"Aunt and, well, mythology."

"I'm Jason, after my grandfather, two uncles, and, of course, the Argonaut."

Cassie laughed. "That sounds about right. So your Easter eggs are red, you're never hungry, and your papu slips you five-dollar bills after church?"

"You've obviously been to my family's house in Chicago," he said, still cracking up. "Opa!"

"So you're at the Family First headquarters in Chicago, Mr. Demakos?"

"Call me Jace, Cassie. Yep, right in the heart of the Windy City, which, as you probably know, has the third-largest Greek population in the country."

"I didn't know that. Fascinating. And, oh my gosh, I didn't mean to hijack this conversation."

Ella made praying-hands and whispered, "Please. Hijack away."

With a thumbs-up to her friend, Cassie pulled out the right notebook from her stack and flipped it open. "Can you send us the waivers for us to have the entrants sign...Jace?" She added a smile, but directed it to Ella, who practically fell into her desk chair with relief.

"Of course. I'll have my assistant send them right out."

"And..." Ella leaned closer to the phone, looking a little tentative. "We need to talk about the name," she said. "Mr. Demakos isn't a fan of Pawsbury Bake-Off."

"I totally get that," Cassie said, giving a quick wave to Ella so she didn't panic, mentally planning how to fix the flyers. "Wouldn't want to confuse people about who's underwriting the event."

"Exactly. I was wondering if we could do something that plays off our name. Like First in the Family or—"

"How about Family Fur Bake-Off?" Cassie suggested. "It sounds like Family First, but not exactly."

"I love it!" Jace exclaimed. "That's brilliant."

Ella threw her hands out in surrender. "Take it away, Cass," she whispered, too soft for the man on the phone to hear.

Cassie nodded, on a roll now. "Have you guys discussed having the five finalists do video interviews for your website yet?"

"Is there such a thing as a video crew in that little town of yours?" There was just enough condescension in his voice to make Ella roll her eyes.

"There will be a crew on-site at the event," Cassie promised. "The Paws for a Cause planning committee already has three different video professionals lined up for the whole month to do interviews and make B-roll that they'll send out with daily press releases."

"Oh." His whole tone changed immediately. "So it does sound like the whole event is being professionally managed."

Ella made a face at the phone. "I hate him," she said silently.

Cassie bit back a laugh. "Of course it is, Jace. Your company is underwriting an amazing, professional event that's going to raise thousands of dollars for wonderful causes and elevate the visibility of Family

First with its most important audience—dog owners. Have you had a chance to talk to the committee chair in the mayor's office who's managing the entire month?"

"Actually, I started this job last week." He sounded just sheepish enough to be forgiven. "And this is the first call related to this event I've had. I'm talking to…uh…William Maddox this afternoon."

"I just left Bill's office," Cassie said with a wink to Ella. "He's Mayor Wilkins's right-hand man and I can assure you, he has everything under control."

"Okay, I haven't even talked to Mayor Wilkins yet. I hope he's a good guy."

"*She's* a wonderful person," Cassie countered, trying not to laugh at Ella throwing her hands up in disgust. "To be perfectly fair, Jace, Ella's focus is not only her business, but the awesome Kibbles for Kindness program that she started single-handedly when she opened Bone Appetit. I'm the person who's worried about the details, but Ella is the one with a heart of gold."

Ella blew a silent kiss, making Cassie grin.

"So are you coordinating all the events, Cassie?" Jace asked, not terribly interested in Ella's heart.

"Only two officially. This one and a dog-related scavenger hunt. Of course, I'll help back up my brothers with the food booths, since they own a Greek deli in town, Santorini's."

"That's where your family is from? Of course, that's your last name. We're from Mykonos."

"Practically neighbors," she joked.

"Well, I can't wait to meet you, Cassie. It'll be nice to know there's good spanakopita in that little

113

Podunk. I admit I was dreading having to spend so much of June there."

Ella stuck out her tongue at the phone, and Cassie covered her mouth to silence a laugh. "I think you'll be pleasantly surprised, Jace. Bitter Bark is the most dog-friendly town in America, and our tourists have pets. Plenty of them. That makes us your most important little Podunk."

He chuckled. "You're right. I came over from a pharmaceutical company, and sometimes I forget that the consumer for our product has four legs."

"Well, the people with the dollars to spend have two," Cassie reminded him. "And they are in Bitter Bark in droves next month. So, congrats on the new job. How do you like it?"

"I like being vice president of public relations," he admitted. "I'm not a fan of learning curves, though."

"Oh, I get that," Cassie crooned, pretty sure she had this guy's number. "We should get a feature article done about your new position in the *Bitter Bark Banner*. I know it's not exactly *The New York Times*, but the people who visit this town read the *Banner* religiously, and we actually have a whole section called Gone to the Dogs that appeals to pet owners. I'll definitely talk to the Paws for a Cause planning committee about getting you an interview."

"That would be fantastic." He sounded more than pleased with that idea. "You know your stuff, Cassie."

She looked down at the notes she'd taken. "Just trying to help. If you send those waivers over, we'll get them signed. Was there anything else?"

"Nope. It sounds like you have all the bases covered."

Ella curled her lip.

"We're working on it," Cassie assured him.

"Then I look forward to meeting you," he replied. "And you, uh, Ms. Mahoney. Your cause sounds... wonderful."

She made a face, then fake-smiled. "Thank you, Jace. Can I call you Jace, even though I'm not Greek but sitting in the same room as one?"

He laughed, a thousand times more relaxed now, and they signed off. As the call ended, Ella stretched out her arms. "This is me loving you for smoothing out that pompous jerk with promises of interviews and spanakopita."

Cassie laughed. "I know my way around a Greek man," she said. "And you looked overwhelmed."

"I'm not gonna lie, this event-planning stuff? Not my thing. I run a store and love dogs and didn't know where to begin to answer his questions, Cass. No wonder Braden got you to help him. Did you get the scavenger hunt approved?"

"I sure did. And he'll love the date, too. It's toward the end of the month, so we have plenty of time to plan."

"We." She raised her brows. "And the family grows even more complicated."

And here we go. "We're not technically family."

"Oh, I know. And no one is technically shocked. You know that, don't you?"

She stared across the desk, processing that. "That we're...dating?"

"Cass, everyone's kind of surprised you didn't go official sooner. You two have been attached at the hip since you moved here."

115

"No." She shook her head. "No hips have been attached. I swear that hips have not even come close to attaching."

Ella laughed and stood up. "But they will be."

"No, no, they won't."

Ella shot her a look as she came around the desk. "Girl. You're dating him. Your hips better get attached, and soon. We need some little Mahoneys to balance out all those baby Kilcannons."

"Little Mahoneys?"

Ella shot out the door. "Mom! Cassie saved my backside. She can marry your son now!"

Cassie just sat there with her mouth wide open, listening to the two of them giggle. And she almost joined them, because the idea was so preposterous, it was funny. Except, when they hit the expiration date...would all these people who weren't surprised be disappointed?

Chapter Nine

B raden's truck rumbled into Pine Woods Grove, the residential neighborhood he called home, at six thirty on Monday night, and all the stress of a long shift disappeared at the sight of Cassie's red compact SUV parked in his driveway.

For some reason, he'd wondered if she'd really come over, thinking that maybe the evening they'd planned together to grab a bite at home and then work on the scavenger hunt would feel too intimate.

Fact was, Braden had rarely been alone with Cassie. Other than an hour at a coffee shop and a few minutes on Sunday out by the lake, someone in the family was almost always around them.

Now, they had a whole evening together, completely alone.

As he'd suggested, she'd used his pass code to open the garage door, promising to handle dinner so they could go to town and scope out some scavenger hunt stops before it got dark.

He put his hand on Jelly Bean's back, where his dog was curled up on the passenger seat next to him.

"Lesson one, my friend. Never underestimate Cassandra Santorini."

Jelly Bean rose from his resting position immediately, peering out the windshield, letting out a quick bark at the sight of an unfamiliar car, then a few more, followed by his guttural growl that somehow had managed to translate into Cassie's name.

"Can it, JB," Braden warned. "We got ourselves a brand-new girlfriend."

Chastised, he dropped his head, but Braden whistled with a second wind after a long day. He climbed out, grabbed his duffel bag, and let Jelly Bean out. As he walked toward the bungalow he'd been renting for two years, the front door opened and Cassie stood with one hand on her hip and a wooden spoon in the other.

"Hi, honey, you're home."

He wanted to laugh or at least fling back a one-liner, but...for a moment, he was simply off-balance. Was this what it would be like to come home to Cassie? Because he didn't hate the idea. At all. In fact, he kind of wanted to stand in the doorway and beam at her like a loon.

After a second, he got control. "You cooking?"

She opened the door to let them in. "Or possibly rap your knuckles like my Yiayia did with her wooden spoons."

As he stepped inside, he had to fight the urge to lean over and kiss her hello. It seemed so natural and right, but he held back. "No knuckle rapping. I was very good today," he said. "And so was JB." He looked down for the dog, but didn't see him. Turning, he found him on the patio, refusing to come in. "What the heck?"

"Pretty sure he hates me," Cassie said.

"Then he needs more than scent-detection training." He signaled for Jelly Bean to come, which he did, but then he made an actual effort to walk around Cassie and not look at her. "Jelly Bean," Braden chided. "What's up with you?"

The dog headed to the kitchen in search of dinner, leaving Braden to stare at him in disbelief.

"No worries," Cassie said, tapping his chest with the spoon. "Do you always finish a ten-hour day in a clean shirt and smelling like manly soap?"

"I showered at the station." He tossed the bag on a table near the front door and took a deep sniff of something wonderful. "Speaking of smells. Whoa."

"Don't be impressed." She gestured for him to follow her to the kitchen. "I'm just heating up some souvlaki and dolmades I got from the restaurant."

"Sounds exotic."

"Because you're Irish and ketchup on meat loaf is a culinary adventure." She moved with grace and familiarity in the kitchen, which was surprising because she'd been to his house for a party only once, and a few months ago she and Ella had brought him soup when he'd had the flu. "Souvlaki is skewered meat and vegetables. Dolmades are—"

"Stuffed grape leaves. I get them every time I go to Santorini's."

"No octopus?"

He grinned, heading to the pantry cabinet to get some dinner for Jelly Bean, since the dog was already making circles around his empty bowls. "We'll work up to octopus."

She leaned against the tiny island and pointed to a glass of white wine. "Do you mind that I raided that little shelf over there?"

"Of course not. It's left over from the last time I had people here. Is it any good? I prefer beer."

"It's fine, and I did bring over a six-pack of Miller Lite for my host. It's in the fridge."

He tapped his hand over his heart in gratitude. "Why do I feel like this good fortune can't possibly last?"

"Because...expiration date, remember?"

Ah, yes. Of course. "Well, speaking of dates, can I take you on one this weekend?"

"That was fast." She lifted her glass, eyeing him over the rim.

"We gotta have a little time in the public eye, or nobody will believe us."

She stared at him for a moment, then took a big gulp of wine.

"Why does that bother you so much?" he asked as he turned to fill the dog food bowl.

"I've done such a good job of avoiding it for so long, that's all."

Letting that sink in, he fed JB and opened the fridge to help himself to a Miller Lite, then asked the only obvious question. "Why?"

"I already told you, I'm planning to leave."

"And that's kept you from dating *anyone*?"

She went to the stove, stirring something in the pan. "I'm thirty, and dating isn't going to be super casual. Dating someone and having no future is like shopping with no money. You can't really get satisfaction."

"So that's satisfaction to you? The whole enchilada? Like, marriage, babies, and white picket fences?"

She stared at the food, the wooden spoon still. "I'm Greek," she finally said. "We place a high value on that. And honestly, I've only seriously considered Greek men, and they seemed to all fall short."

He held the beer bottle midway to his mouth, thinking about that. "So, you actually agree with your grandmother? You think you have to marry a Greek guy? Why? Your dad didn't marry a Greek woman."

"I know, but I think it's…right. It's comfortable to me. I've grown up around Greek men, they understand my culture, they respect the family, they…" She turned to him, her brows lifting when she saw his jaw hanging open. "What?"

"That's so…limiting. And closed-minded. And old school. What if you fell in love with a guy who wasn't Greek?"

She shrugged. "Not saying it couldn't happen, just that's not what I think I want. And what I want is to move out of small-town America. For that, I need to have an amazing résumé. So, will you get me some plates so we can eat and get started working on the scavenger hunt plan and concentrate on what's important here?"

He didn't move for those plates, still staring at her, taking it all in, processing it, understanding why, which was always the question that plagued him.

"Why are you looking at me like I have two heads?" she asked. "You're the one who won't settle down because of some imaginary fear of never coming home."

He opened his mouth to argue, but shut it. She was absolutely right. "So, what about Saturday night? Chief Winkler's turning fifty, and his wife is having a surprise party for him. Will you be my date, or am I not Greek enough?"

"You'll never be Greek enough, but sure, I'll go to a party with you." She slipped by him, opened a cabinet, and grabbed the plates she'd asked for.

He put down the beer to get napkins and forks, the first half of her sentence stinging.

You'll never be Greek enough.

He tamped down all the feelings that threatened and shifted to safer, more solid ground.

"I hardly went out at all on calls today, which gave me hours to research scent-detection training. I actually downloaded a textbook and read about half of it."

"Of course you did, Einstein."

There. Safer ground. He had to remember to stay here. "So, before we go out, I just want to run a quick test with JB, and then we can try him out when we head to town."

"Sounds good."

He easily kept the conversation on scents and scavenger hunts the whole time they ate dinner together.

"You're adorable." Cassie crossed her arms and leaned against the porch post in Braden's backyard and watched him work.

"Why do I think you're mocking me?"

"Oh, because you just spread out an array of junk

that includes..." She picked up a metal jar. "Kerosene, Q-tips cut in half, Tupperware you ruined with holes, disposable gloves, and tweezers. Where did you get all this stuff?"

"At the station. I collected it all day and made my very own scent-detection kit." He took the disposable gloves and slid them on. "Can you take Jelly Bean inside, away from the scents, while I load the vessels with the appropriate Q-tips?"

"Wouldn't it be better to leave this up to the experts that you're raising ten grand to access?"

"Wouldn't it be better if I can prove to my uncle that Jelly Bean's issue was that temporary thing he said was a remote possibility and I don't need to spend ten grand at all?"

"Can't argue that." With one more glance at him holding the Q-tips in his glove-covered fingers like he was a surgeon heading into the OR, she reached down to slip her hand into Jelly Bean's collar, but the dog backed away, turned, and evaded her.

"Aw, come on, Mr. Bean. We need to let Dr. Strangeglove finish his science experiment."

Jelly Bean barked once, his eyes nothing but defiance.

"I really do think Jelly Bean has issues with me."

Braden snorted a laugh. "Nah, he's just letting you know this is his house and he calls the shots."

"I don't know." Cassie held her hand out to the dog, who averted his eyes. "Haven't you noticed that since we, uh, became a thing, Jelly Bean wants no part of me?"

"He still thinks you're responsible for Bitter Bark's tragic oregano problem."

But she didn't laugh, too frustrated with the dog. "I think he knows I mocked his Easter candy name. Can I lure him with a treat?" she asked. "Or would that ruin your experiment?"

"Sure. He can't resist peanut butter. Try a spoonful of that from the pantry."

She went inside and followed that order, heading back out with a spoon slathered in Skippy, holding it in the air to coax the dog closer.

Instantly, he came. "Well, he can smell that."

"He can smell," Braden said. "The problem is discernment."

"Follow me, pup." She walked back to the house, and he trotted along and into the kitchen, where she closed the door. She instantly rewarded him with the peanut butter. The whole time he licked the spoon, he kept his gaze on her.

"Are we friends now?"

He turned around and stared at the hallway.

"I'm going to take that as a no."

"Hey, Cass. Bring him out now?"

Jelly Bean shot toward his master's voice, and Cassie followed, disheartened but not ready to give up on getting the dog to like her.

Outside, Braden held out one of the destroyed Tupperware containers, and Jelly Bean went right to it, sniffing. Instantly, Braden slipped him a treat from his pocket. He walked a little farther, repeated the whole thing, and again, until they'd gone around the whole backyard, Jelly Bean getting a treat each time.

"All right. Now we have to go far away, to an open area, like the square in town. I'd like to go ahead in my truck so I can hide the kerosene-covered Q-tips, if you don't mind driving him separately."

"If he'll get in my car," she said.

"I'll just tell him. He speaks—"

"English. I know," she finished on a laugh. "So while we're there, can we walk through the first scavenger hunt station, and figure out what we're going to ask hunters to do? Like take a picture with their dog in front of that statue of that guy who founded Bitter Bark?"

"Thaddeus Ambrose Bushrod? That guy?"

She blinked in surprise. "Is that why the bar is called Bushrod's? And Ambrose Avenue? I didn't know that."

He put his arm around her. "See? So much to love about Bitter Bark, Cass."

"But no high-rises or busy intersections."

"Exactly."

She rolled her eyes. "Meet me in front of Big Bad Thad in ten minutes."

Jelly Bean wasn't thrilled with the transportation arrangements and, in fact, stayed in the hatchback of Cassie's little SUV, nose pressed against the window like a prisoner dreaming of a better life.

Fifteen minutes later, Cassie had Jelly Bean on a leash, and they walked together across the south side of Bushrod Square, headed straight to the statue in the center that was surrounded by stately oaks that always had white lights flickering at night, no matter the season.

But the lights weren't on yet, since daylight was hanging on to this late May evening. The square was crowded with kids at the playground, dogs on the path, and lots of residents and tourists taking strolls.

"See, we can be pals," she said to Jelly Bean, keeping him close with a short leash. "This isn't so bad."

He replied by stopping to pee on the grass.

"That's okay, you do you, Mr. Bean. We'll get there." As she got closer to the center of the square, she caught sight of Braden standing near the statue, and of course her heart did a little tumble and flip. Oh yeah, the man had something. Something that made her want to be very careful.

When Jelly Bean spotted him, he barked, but didn't tug her forward.

"Good boy," she said, rounding a large shrub that formed a five-foot wall around Big Thad, suddenly seeing that Braden wasn't alone, but stood talking to...Simone London.

Really?

The minute Jelly Bean spotted her, he jerked forward, letting out a series of barks.

"Whoa!"

He yanked the leash to pull her with him, his barking rising to a frantic crescendo.

"Hey, JB, slow down, baby."

He didn't, but his noise made Simone turn and let out an equally deafening squeal as she threw out her arms to the dog. "Jelly Belly!" she called.

Cassie gave up, let go of the leash, and Jelly Bean broke into a full run until he reached Simone, jumping up to thoroughly slather the woman with kisses. Cassie caught her breath, watched the exchange, and gave in to the ugly green monster that crawled into her chest.

Who's jealous of a kiss now, Cass?

Simone was nearly rolling on the ground with the dog when Cassie reached them.

"Sorry." She looked up, a pair of sky-blue eyes pinned on Cassie. "I just love this dog to death." She had one of those sweet Southern accents that Cassie somehow never picked up, despite a lifetime in North Carolina.

"He's a great one," Cassie agreed.

"Ooh, he is!" Simone rubbed her hands on either side of his head, getting a face-lick in response.

Braden was next to Cassie in a flash. "Simone, have you met Cassie Santorini?"

"Yeah, she's your cousin, right?"

"No, we're not cousins," he said with a quick chuckle. "Just..."

Cassie waited a beat, but he never really did answer, saved by Jelly Bean's happy bark as he circled Simone, licked her hand, and pawed at her for attention.

"He's certainly happy to see you," Cassie said. "And nice to meet you, Simone."

Simone gave her a quick smile in response, then shifted her attention back to Jelly Bean. "Well, we were good pals during those long days and *endless* nights when Braden had to work, weren't we, Belly boy?" There was just enough of an edge in her voice for Cassie to imagine how those conversations unfolded when Braden got off work. "Anyway, I guess I better be going. Good to see you, Braden, and thanks for your kind words. But honestly, this is for the best. Frank and I just weren't ever going to be...well, you know. Rebounds never work."

Frank. The actuary. They broke up? Wait, he was a *rebound*?

Cassie looked from one to the other, trying to read the communication between them, all the while tamping down one more uprising from that same green monster.

But Braden didn't look like he suddenly wanted to fall down on his knees and win Simone back. His whole body seemed on alert, protective, and tense. In fact, the only one with puppy dog eyes was Jelly Bean, who gazed up at Simone like she was sprinkled with bacon bits.

"So anyway, I'll see you around, Braden. Oh, and Cassie, I finally got into your restaurant the other day. Really great food. What a nice addition to Bitter Bark."

"Thanks." Cassie smiled. "I'll tell my brothers, since they're the ones actually running it."

"The twins with the beards?" She laughed. "Yeah, they're also nice additions to Bitter Bark."

The comment was just enough to make Braden stand ever so slightly taller, a subtle move that most people wouldn't have noticed, but told Cassie everything she needed to know. Now that green monster had a hold on him.

"Yes, that's Alex and John, my brothers," she said.

"Well, I'll be sure to stop in again. And good to see you, Braden. Take care." With a quick smile and a few too many kisses on Jelly Bean's head, Simone headed across the square. For a moment, Cassie just stood there, not sure what to say.

"Awkward," Braden mumbled.

"Not for everyone," Cassie joked, pointing to Jelly Bean, who lay panting on the grass, staring in the direction that Simone had gone.

"Plus, the scent vessel is a foot away from him in that bush. And he has no idea."

"Well, he obviously can discern the scent of a woman he really likes."

Braden took a step closer. "So can I." For a long moment, he looked into her eyes, long enough to make some butterflies soar. "But can I say that I like that you're jealous?"

"Of Jelly Bean, not you."

He grinned. "It's a start."

"Except we're not supposed to start anything, Einstein. Remember? Temporary? Qualified? Full of restrictions and highly controlled?"

"Oh yeah." He reached down and tapped her chin. "I keep forgetting."

"Don't worry. I wrote it down."

"I'm sure you did."

Chapter Ten

Cassie slid the ticket across the pass-through and ducked under the stainless-steel warmer to get Alex's attention away from the grill. "Four more spanakopita, big guy. What'd you put in it today, crack?"

He laughed and made a stern expression she immediately recognized. "It's the dill, *agapi mou*. Never go light with dill and..."

She pointed at him with the same frown and gave her own imitation of their father's voice. "Use an extra layer of phyllo to soak the oil." They both smiled at the memory, the image of Dad as clear as if he stood in the Santorini's kitchen with them.

Alex's smile turned to a sad sigh, though those had become far less frequent since they'd come to Bitter Bark and opened a new Santorini's. Maybe it was better for him to not be in the literal shoes of his father, as he had been at the Chestnut Creek deli.

"Rush almost over?" he asked, setting a platter of moussaka on the pass for table four.

"Just a few stragglers and..." She cocked her head

at the sound of the front door opening. "And the usual latecomers."

"Go get 'em, Cass."

She rolled her eyes, beyond sick of being a waitress in a Greek deli, a job she'd done off and on most of her life. Flipping the parsley and lemon garnish onto the platter, she reached to scoop up the plate, but her brother extended his hand into the pass-through to cover hers.

"John and I are interviewing, I swear." Alex pinned her in place with his dark gaze. "You'll be able to be a full-time event planner soon. I know that's what you want."

She gave him a quick smile, affection for her brother welling up, even though she suspected those interviews were going slow because they were so used to her being there for them. "I know, Alex," she said. "And that is what I want to do."

Except...not in a small town like this.

"Just a few more weeks, I promise. We're really getting this place off the ground. Bitter Bark was a great move for us." He dipped his head to get a better look at her. "And not so bad for you, right? I mean, with you and Braden finally making it official."

Finally? Official? Oh boy. She considered a bunch of responses, but discarded them all. The last two evenings, she and Braden had met after he was off work, done a sniff test or two with Jelly Bean, then taken a drive through town to scope out another station for the scavenger hunt. Being with him didn't feel fake or wrong or anything but...good and, yeah, official.

Holding hands was surprisingly natural. Easy hugs were, well, easy and frequent, as were casual touches and playful conversations. The only reason they resisted a kiss good night was because they both knew that once they started, they'd never stop.

She took the plate, the very scent of it reminding her that if she didn't make her move out of here, somehow she'd end up being the head waitress of Santorini's with a side business of catering and planning two-bit events and…coming home to Braden every night.

Only one part of that didn't completely suck.

"What?" Alex asked. "Don't try to pretend you guys haven't been into each other since you met."

She stared at him, then closed her eyes. "Just keep interviewing, Alex. I can't build my event business if I'm serving your moussaka all day long."

She took off for the dining room, where she instantly saw who had walked in. Gramma Finnie and Yiayia were setting up at a two-top by the window, taking their usual seats across from each other, leaning forward to gossip and giggle like the teenagers from Bitter Bark High.

And of course, Gala and Pyggie were tucked under the table, waiting for phyllo dough crumbs.

"Hey, Gramma. Yiayia," Cassie called as she sailed by to deliver her order. "The usual?"

They looked at each other and shared a conspiratorial smile, then Yiayia waved Cassie closer. "We need to talk to you."

What? Big change? No feta on Yiayia's salad? Hold the tzatziki on Gramma's gyro? "Just a sec."

She gave the waiting customers their plates and a smile, refilled a water, placed a check on the next table, and finally made her way back to the front

132

window, confident that she had two minutes to pull a chair from the next table and join the women. Gala licked her leg, and Pyggie nestled closer.

"What up, sweet grandmothers?" As she used the half-sarcastic—the Yiayia half—nickname, she stole a glance at her grandmother, catching a quick flicker of smug satisfaction disintegrate to a frown.

"Santorini's employees don't sit," she said under her breath, sounding very much like the woman who'd run a family restaurant for forty years.

"Nonsense, Agnes!" Gramma Finnie patted Cassie's hand with one that was wrinkled, spotted, and so very tender. "Rest your tired feet, lass. Not a person in Bitter Bark is judging you for that."

Oh, *one* person was. Cassie gave a tight smile to Yiayia, whose whole expression instantly changed into something...soft.

"Which is what I love about this little town," Yiayia said quickly, managing to get back into the caricature of herself she'd been dragging around for weeks now. "Go ahead, Finn," Yiayia insisted. "Ask her."

Finn? Who called Gramma Finnie *Finn*?

"Ask me what?" Cassie urged when Gramma didn't reply right away. Maybe she couldn't speak because someone just called her *Finn*.

"We had an idea," she finally said, shifting in her chair and adjusting her glasses with slow movements.

"We're ready to move on," Yiayia added, clearly impatient with Gramma's buildup.

"Move on?" Cassie's eyes widened. "Are you going back to Florida?"

"Of course not!" Yiayia exclaimed. "Finnie and I are having the time of our lives, especially now that you and Braden are settled down."

She nearly choked. "Settled down?"

"Well, in a manner of speaking, lass." Gramma leaned closer. "My darling Pru said she saw the two of you walking outside the library last evening." She lifted her brows. "And not just walking, if you know what I mean."

She knew exactly what she meant. Braden had had to drop a book off, and while they walked, they'd held hands. Maybe they stopped and wrapped their arms around each other. They did everything *but* kiss, because the fire was constantly burning between them.

"What's a fourteen-year-old doing slinking around town at nine o'clock at night, might I ask?" Cassie's hackles raised at the infringement of privacy. Couldn't a person return a library book without "family" lurking around every corner?

No, not in Bitter Bark when your family was Kilcannons, Mahoneys, and Santorinis.

"Pru volunteers at the library helping the little ones read to some of the dogs of Waterford," Yiayia said, rising to the teenager's defense. "It's open in the evenings until September, you know."

"I do know, and by the way, nobody's *settled*." She had to get that much straight.

The two women shared another look, this one a little bit horrified.

Gramma put her hand over Cassie's. "I thought you two were an item now."

"An item is something on a menu, Gramma, and we're just..." She gave a sideways glance to her grandmother, who was, she had to remember, the root cause of all of this. "*Dating.* Which is a far cry from *settled.*"

"But you're off the market," Yiayia said.

Cassie let out an exasperated sigh. "What are you two getting at, anyway?"

"We have an idea for the Date with a Dog bachelor auction," Gramma said, pulling out her big bag to dig for something. "But we need a third opinion."

Cassie took a quick look around the restaurant. The spanakopita for the two older couples in the back booth had to be ready, since it was served room temp. And table six needed a check.

"Here's our list," Gramma Finnie said, pulling out a piece of paper. "Yiayia loves to write everything down, did you know that?"

"It's a curse of the genes," Cassie said, putting her hand on whatever the list could be, not even sure she wanted to know. "What is this, exactly?"

"A matchmaking list," Yiayia said cheerily.

"You're seriously matchmaking?" she asked, directing the question to Gramma Finnie because the woman couldn't tell a lie. Yiayia, on the other hand, lived one.

"Someone has to do it, lass. The Dogfather has fallen in love and forgotten his role in this family."

She snorted a soft laugh. "His role is to be father and uncle and, soon, a husband. Anyway, I know he and my mom have joked about continuing his streak, but these things need to happen organically. Don't try and push them." Then she turned to her grandmother, the question burning. "Are you honestly telling me you don't care that I'm seeing a guy who isn't Greek?"

She saw the struggle in Yiayia's dark eyes, but it disappeared quickly. "I'm honestly telling you that."

Cassie would have sworn the old battle-ax was telling the truth. For a long moment, they held each other's gaze, nothing but a challenge in Yiayia's eyes, daring Cassie to believe her.

Why?

"Here's a list of women in town we think would bid on either Connor or Declan," Gramma Finnie said. "They'll both be up for sale."

"For auction." She grunted. "It's not a meat market."

"Oh, but it is," Yiayia said. "We had a bachelor auction at Jacaranda Lakes once, without the dogs or firefighters. Just the widowers and divorced guys, and let me tell you, it got heated. Ted went for three hundred and fifty dollars." She grinned. "But he paid for my dinner."

Gramma tapped the paper. "Do you know any of these women?"

She looked down at five names, three she didn't recognize, one she happened to know was gay, and... "Simone London?"

"She's single now," Gramma Finnie said. "I saw her at Waterford Farm yesterday."

Cassie blinked, feeling her blood drain a little and praying they didn't notice. "What was she doing there?" She tried so hard to keep her voice level. And failed.

"Donchya worry, lass. She knows Braden's taken. I made sure of that."

"Gramma!"

She drew back. "Isn't he?"

"Well, yes, but..." She didn't dare look at Yiayia. "It's complicated."

"Love is never easy," Gramma Finnie said.

Love? This was one step from pretend, not love. "But why was she there?"

"Lookin' to rescue, she told us. In fact, she asked Garrett to find her a Weimaraner, if you can believe that."

"Oh, I can believe it." A dog exactly like *Jelly Belly*? Ugh, that nickname. She wanted to wipe it from her brain but couldn't.

"But Garrett explained to her that getting a rescue isn't like going to the store to pick your favorite color and size." Gramma took a sip of water. "So we talked a bit on the patio, and I've always thought she was a nice girl."

"Did you know her well when they dated?" Cassie asked, unable to stop herself from finding out more about this girl who'd dated Braden.

"He never brought her to Sunday dinner, if that's what you're askin'. But she came to Waterford a few times with Braden and Jelly Bean. Nice girl. Not from around here, but she went to Vestal Valley College," Gramma Finnie said, referring to the small university that was part of Bitter Bark. "She lived for a while in California, but then came back to work in the college's admissions office. That's what she does now."

"I see." Not that her resume interested Cassie. She tried to swallow, surprised at how tight her throat was on the subject of Simone. Which was crazy because Cassie and Braden were simply hanging out together, enjoying the zing of a little chemistry, both knowing this was temporary.

But sometimes he looked at her, and she wondered if he really believed that. If his *I can't get serious because of my job* excuse was just that—an excuse.

"Do you know why they broke up?" Cassie asked Gramma. "I mean, the real reason."

"He's not telling you the real reason?" Yiayia inched closer. "I don't like deception."

Cassie almost tripped over all the layers of irony in those four words. She kept her gaze on Gramma. "Did he ever tell you or anyone in the family what broke them up?"

"He didn't," she said simply. "But she told me yesterday."

"And?"

Gramma just stared at her. "You really don't know, lass?"

"All I know is that it was mutual," Cassie said. "That she wanted more than he did."

"Well, he wanted…somethin'," Gramma said pointedly. "The last time they were together as a couple was at the end of January."

Cassie tilted her head, frowning. "January?" And then she realized exactly the significance of that. That was when Cassie and Braden met, four months ago. And something slipped inside her chest. Braden said Simone left him, but that it was mutual. Had Cassie's arrival affected all that?

"But nothing happened between us," she said softly. "I mean, nothing really has yet, so…"

Yiayia patted her arm. "You needed a little help from the Dogmothers."

"The *Dogmothers*?"

Finnie giggled. "Oh, Agnes. Every time you say that I must laugh."

Cassie dropped her head in her hands, not knowing whether to laugh, cry, or run. "Please tell me I imagined this whole conversation."

"We're matchmakers," Yiayia said. "Like Daniel, only female and twice as effective."

"The…" Dogmothers? She couldn't even say it. "No. Don't try to make that a thing. Please, it's not a thing."

Yiayia got her best smug look. "Too late. Isn't it, Finn?"

"I think it is, Agnes."

Cassie looked down at the list again, staring at Simone's name, which right now seemed like a much bigger problem than these two lunatic grandmothers. Cassie didn't want to have any role in their breakup, even unwittingly. Not when she knew that, eventually, she'd be leaving.

A familiar buzz started in her head, making Cassie's limbs ache a little for…action. On a sigh, she pushed up, hearing the soft bell of an order up in the kitchen.

"Leave Simone off this list," she said, sliding the paper back to Gramma Finnie. "And I'd check to see if any of the others haven't already dated Connor, since he seems to get around. And Declan? He's a confirmed bachelor."

"No such thing," Yiayia said as she grabbed Cassie's wrist before she could get away. "And help us with Alex and John?"

"Is no one safe from you two?"

"No one," Gramma Finnie said, pushing up. "It's

our mission. And now my mission is to use the ladies' room."

"Again?" Yiayia demanded. "You went ten minutes ago. For heaven's sake, Finn, suit up with a Depends when we're going out."

Gramma Finnie blinked at her, hurt deepening the blue of her eyes. That icy tone probably sounded strange to Gramma, but it sounded very much like Cassie's childhood.

"Not that you need them." Yiayia instantly corrected her course with a saccharine tone and smile. "Please, dear. Take your time in the ladies' room. We're in no rush here."

Gramma relaxed at that, patting Cassie's shoulder as she stepped away. "Remember, lass, the Irish say, 'What the heart knows today, the head will understand tomorrow.' That's what makes love so excitin', and that's why you're askin' all the questions about Braden."

With that, she walked away, her rubber soles mewing on the linoleum, her words echoing in Cassie's heart.

"What my head doesn't understand," Cassie said to her grandmother, "is why you are pretending to be someone you're not."

Yiayia's whole face fell. "I'm not pretending."

Cassie gave her a dubious eyebrow.

"Please, Cassie. Every time you fight me or question me, it takes me three steps away from my goal."

"Which is?"

When Yiayia opened her eyes, a tear threatened. A real tear. "I think the word people use is redemption."

Cassie had no earthly idea how to respond to that, so she picked up a napkin from the table and handed it to her and headed back to work.

Fake Yiayia was one thing. But this woman? Cassie was lost.

Chapter Eleven

When the lights went out and the dining room turned pitch-black, Braden slid his arms around Cassie's waist and pulled her back into his chest. Lowering his head to whisper over the sounds of the tipsy jokes and nervous laughter of about twenty of his friends and co-workers, Braden nestled his nose in Cassie's hair.

"Did I tell you how gorgeous you look tonight?"

She looked up, tilting her face toward his. "I think you did." She added a smile. "Four times before we got here."

"Too much?"

"Nah, but shhhh. It's surprise time."

"They're coming up the walk!" someone said in a loud whisper. "Everybody shut up!"

More laughter, more comments, and more of that insanely sweet smell of Cassie's hair made Braden tighten his grip around her, loving the feel of her back and body against him.

Since he'd picked her up for Chief Winkler's surprise birthday party, Braden had had a hard time keeping his hands off her. Hell, that'd been the case for a while now. Tonight, he was sick of fighting it.

So he pressed his nose on her hair again, making her chuckle. Or maybe shiver. He couldn't tell, but he wanted to know.

"Now! Quiet!" That was Cal, a young probie who'd started a few months ago. The new kid took some immediate grief from a few of the veteran firefighters in the group.

But the guests finally went silent in the darkened dining room which, like the back patio of Owen and Liz Winkler's house, was currently festooned with balloons and banners.

He heard Owen's voice, as loud and distinct as the fire chief himself, first, after the door opened, then he heard Liz and footsteps as they crossed the living room floor.

In a moment, the lights went on, "Surprise!" rocked the room, and the chief's eyes bulged bright white against his dark skin.

"What the…" He blinked, scowled, and looked like he was about to throw out an order that they'd all be docked pay for giving him a heart attack, but he just shook his head, fighting a laugh. Then he turned to the petite woman smiling up at him with a look of utter victory. "How did you do this, boo?" he asked. "What? Why?"

"Because I love you." She slid her arms around him and took a fierce kiss from the man who stood at least six four and still packed almost as much muscle as he did when he was a linebacker for UNC thirty years earlier. But his comments were lost on Braden, who was watching the couple cling to each other, the crowd cheering as Liz reached up and playfully rubbed Owen's big ol' bald head. They looked so…complete.

The chief had been fighting fires since he got out of college. Why hadn't he worried about the dangers of his job? He'd spent decades risking his life, but that hadn't stopped him from falling in love with a beautiful, wonderful woman and having three kids.

Looking around the room as if he was just taking in the moment of joy among the men and women who worked to keep Bitter Bark safe, Braden realized that all the firefighters, EMTs, and volunteers who had come to the party were either married or in a relationship. Even Cal, the kid who'd told them all to be quiet, was living with someone and made a lot of noise about popping the question after his probationary period was over.

All…except for him. And his brothers, of course.

Those two were closer to the front of the room, high-fiving and bro-hugging Owen. Declan was alone, as always, but the woman Connor had brought tonight—Maya? Malia?—would not be present at the next gathering because, well, Connor.

He didn't get a chance to mull that over as he and Cassie moved closer to greet their hosts.

"Big Bray." Owen reached out and pulled Braden into a big bad bear hug, patting his back so hard he might have left a bruise. "Is my wife something or what?" He leaned back and put a beefy arm around Liz again, who was dwarfed by the man's sheer size.

"She is something," Braden agreed, giving Liz a hug and a kiss on the cheek. "This is Cassie Santorini, by the way. Liz and Owen Winkler."

"Oh, hello," Liz said. "Santorini, like the new restaurant?"

"Guilty," she said. "My brothers actually own it, but I'm helping them by working there."

"That food is amazing!" Liz exclaimed. "I had no idea how much Bitter Bark needed a Greek deli until that place opened."

"Thanks. I'll tell my brother Alex, the chef." Cassie turned to Owen and extended her hand. "Happy birthday, Owen."

"Thanks." He bypassed the handshake to give her his usual hug. "Really glad you're here." When he leaned back, he frowned. "But you're way too pretty for this egghead. Always imagined him with a librarian."

She laughed as Owen winked and turned to the next person, but Liz got closer to Cassie, leaning in to whisper something in her ear that Braden didn't catch over the party noise.

Cassie just looked up at him and held up one finger. "Be back in a sec. Liz wants me to meet someone." She slipped away with the hostess and headed for the patio, replaced almost immediately by his brother Declan, who was holding a beer Braden would bet good money was his first and still full.

"You and Cassie look like you're having fun," he said, glancing in the direction she'd gone. "So it's *official* official?"

"*Official* official?" Braden made a face. "You been hanging around Pru, Dec?" he joked, referring to their cousin Molly's teenage daughter.

"You know what I mean. Cassie's your girlfriend."

"Newsflash. We came out at the last Sunday dinner. Weren't you there?"

"I was." He eyed Braden with intense brown eyes that came squarely from the Mahoney side of the family. "She's not going anywhere, you know."

Braden frowned, thinking of all the different ways that could be taken. First of all, she was, sometime. But no one knew that yet. Or did he mean she and Braden were a long-term thing, at least longer than he'd been with Simone? Or was he prognosticating the future and sharing that in his older-brother way?

"Not sure what that means," he admitted. "But she's here now."

Declan lifted the beer bottle, but, no surprise, didn't sip. Nothing made their captain lose an ounce of control. "What I mean is that Cassie is part of our life."

"We're not actually cousins," he said.

"But she's always going to be at Sunday dinners, birthdays, weddings, and every single event that brings family members together. So if this thing goes south..." Still holding the beer, he moved one finger from Braden toward Cassie's general direction. "You don't have anywhere to run or hide."

"I'm not worried." He took a real sip of his beer and glanced toward the patio, missing her already.

"Then you don't think you two will ever split up?" Declan's question held enough skepticism for Braden to know what *he* thought. And since this was not Connor, who would deserve an actual smart-ass reply, Braden didn't say a word, but seriously considered the question.

"Because when you do, it could get awkward," Declan said.

"When, not if?" he asked with a laugh. "Such confidence."

Declan didn't smile. "I know you pretty well, bro. They never last."

"Whoa." He held up his beer. "You *do* know I'm not Connor?"

That made him laugh. "No, he's in a whole 'nother league."

As if summoned by the two of them joking about him, Connor came closer, his date nowhere in sight. "What's so funny?"

"You," they answered in perfect unison, then toasted with their beer bottles.

Connor rolled his eyes, long used to the two of them ganging up on him. It had always been that way, even when they were little. Declan and Braden vs. Connor and Ella. And after Dad died, it was the four of them vs. the world.

"At least I'm not dating my cousin."

"Shut the hell up," Braden said.

"At least he's not dating the fortieth woman in this calendar year," Declan added.

Connor grinned and ran a hand through his thick, chestnut-colored hair. "And it's only May."

They laughed, and Owen came back to their group. While they talked, Braden observed his two brothers and wondered, not for the first time, how the three of them all managed to stay single. Declan was nearly forty, and Connor was thirty-six.

It wasn't the first time he wondered if their father's death affected them in the same way it had him, wrecking permanence in every relationship. And what about little Smella? Truth was, they didn't really talk about it, not individually or as a family. Joe Mahoney was revered, mentioned frequently, and never forgotten, but the impact of his loss on each of their lives has stayed firmly locked up and undiscussed for twenty years.

"Hey." Cassie came up to him with that beautiful smile that wiped away every other thought.

"Hey." Couldn't help it, he put his arm around her. "Where'd Liz take you?"

"To meet her sister because they're planning a family reunion and needed some advice."

"Oh? A new client?"

She shrugged. "I gave them some ideas, but…" She shook her head. "I can set them up with catering from Santorini's, but they really do want full-blown event planning, from creative invitations to organizing the room blocks and activities."

"Isn't that kind of what you want to do?"

"Not exactly. I mean, I could, but the reunion's in six months and…"

She'd be long gone by then. "You'd rather do that job for a big company in a high-rise."

She winked at him. "Top floor, baby."

His heart betrayed him and dropped like it had been tossed from that floor. "Aim for the penthouse," he joked, pulling her closer to join the conversation with the others, which she did, easily.

But all the while, he kept hearing his older brother's warning.

She's not going anywhere.

Oh man, Dec. That's where you're wrong. And the sooner Braden stopping thinking about changing that fact, the better off he'd be. But he thought about it.

Thought about her staying, about *temporary* becoming *permanent*, and all those side dishes they could enjoy.

He thought about all that way more than he should.

There were a few stragglers still at the Winklers' party when Cassie and Braden said good night, heading into the night to walk the few blocks to Braden's house, where he'd left his car after picking up Cassie.

It seemed natural to walk hand in hand down the sidewalk, through the quiet streets of the residential neighborhood, especially after they'd been so publicly together all evening. Plus, it felt good to have his big hand around hers, making her feel warm and safe.

"So, how'd I do on my first major girlfriend outing?"

He laughed softly. "Owen said you're out of my league. Ray Merritt figured you lost a family bet. Luella Holmes told me to wipe the shit-eating grin off my face. And Declan warned me that if things go south, there will always be awkward Sunday dinners. So, overall an A."

She slowed her step, looking up at him. "Wow, you talked to a lot of people for a man who was basically attached to me all night."

"Not all night, and yeah, I got some input." He leaned over and kissed her on the top of the head for the twentieth time, ready to take his mouth lower and longer against hers. "All in all, they liked you and seemed to think we make a nice couple."

"My dad would say, 'Couple of what?'"

He chuckled. "He sounds like he was a good guy."

"The best," she said. "A tad temperamental, like Alex, but a great father and husband." She felt a familiar prick of pain. "I miss him."

"I get that," he said, squeezing her hand in sympathy.

She looked up at him. "So Declan thinks we're going south, huh?"

"He didn't say that. He said 'if,' not 'when,' and sure, he knows the complicated extended-family situation."

"And your history."

This time, he slowed down, just in front of the house, actually bringing them to a complete stop. "Not sure what that means. My history?"

"Of ending relationships because they get too serious," she said.

"Wait. Did Declan corner you at some point that I missed?"

"No, I was thinking of Simone."

"That makes one of us," he quipped.

But she didn't laugh. "Unless that's not really why Simone broke up with you. If she broke up with you at all."

He turned to her, a question in his eyes. "That sounds like you're accusing me of lying, Cassie. Why would you do that?"

"I'm not, but I'm just…wondering. She called Frank the Actuary a rebound, remember?"

"Not really. I barely remember when we saw her." He sounded, and looked, completely confused.

"And she was at Waterford looking for a Weimaraner to adopt," she told him.

He considered that for a minute, then gave his head a shake. "That's weird. She did really like Jelly Bean, and maybe seeing him unearthed this deep need in her to own a Weimie. Good for her."

"You don't think she's trying to win you back?"

"Because she's adopting the same dog I have?" He laughed. "No, especially because—let me be perfectly clear here—she split up with me. I knew it was coming, I knew her reasons were valid, and I was relieved because I knew the ending was inevitable."

But was it? "That doesn't mean she might not want you back. And you might want her."

"Cassie." He put his hands on her shoulders. "I can't believe you're jealous. I mean, I'm all kinds of flattered, but—"

"I'm *not* jealous." At least, she didn't think she was. "I'm worried that…that you should be with her, not me."

"Why?"

"Because she's in Bitter Bark, and she's a nice girl, and she wants the kind of life you can offer, and…I don't."

He let out an exasperated sigh. "You're in Bitter Bark now, you're the nicest, if occasionally snarkiest, woman I know, and I'm not offering anybody anything." He was quiet for a moment, the only sound Jelly Bean barking on the other side of his front door. "Except for you to stay for a while, since if we get right in that car and I drive you home, JB will be wrecked."

"Of course." She went inside with him, where Jelly Bean tried his best not to show how totally happy he was that Braden was home and, of course, treated Cassie like a pariah.

When they took him to the backyard, Braden didn't turn on any lights but let the dog wander around the fenced-in area, standing at the edge of the patio stones to keep an eye on him. Cassie dropped onto an outdoor sofa, letting her eyes adjust to the dim moonlight.

"What makes you think I should be with Simone?" he asked in a tone that made her guess he'd been staring at the yard and dog but thinking about their conversation.

She took in the grill, outdoor TV, and seating area, all of it screaming *stability*. "I think you're a guy who's more ready to settle down than you realize."

"Then we would have moved in together, which is what she was pushing for. And even if you are right, and I want that kind of...of living situation, it wouldn't have worked with her long-term."

"Why not?"

He thought about it for a moment, sliding his hands in the pockets of his khakis with a sigh. "Because I need magic. I need sparks. I need...something that wasn't there. I mean, she's great on paper, you know? Very pretty, smart, said and did all the right things, but sometimes I thought she just wanted to close the deal so much, she'd say anything."

"Whoa. Brutal."

"I don't mean to be, but I'm trying to be one hundred percent real with you."

"Are you sure you gave her a fair chance?"

He dropped down next to her, close enough that their thighs touched, and that sent the usual heat through her body. Some things never changed with Braden. They just got more intense.

"You don't have to give magic and sparks a fair chance, Cass. They happen instantly."

She could feel his gaze on her and knew that if she turned her face ever so slightly, they'd be lined up for...magic and sparks. "Instantly?"

"The moment you meet."

"Really."

He took her chin in his fingertips and turned her to face him. "I remember you walking up the driveway of Waterford with your mother. I remember the first thing we talked about was a little lesson on Greek names."

"And you were the first non-Greek person I've ever met who knew Cassandra was a princess and a prophet and not a goddess."

"And I've been called Einstein ever since."

She held his gaze, inches away, slipping back to the chilly winter day and her first thoughts about him. "Shoulders," she whispered.

He lifted his brows in question.

"My first thoughts were not actually about your impressive brain. It was..." She put a hand on his shoulder and pressed. "Your impressive brawn."

His lips curled up in a smile. "And I took a dive into your eyes and didn't come up for air all day."

She had to ask. Had to. "Had you and Simone broken up yet?"

"Yes, for a few weeks, all but for the returning of things left at each other's place, which actually happened the day after I met you."

She flinched a little at the mental image of that exchange. "Because you met me?"

"No, it just happened that way."

"Do you think you two might have reconciled if you hadn't been eye-swimming the day before?"

He laughed softly. "No, we wouldn't have. She'd already met Frank the Actuary."

He drew her face a little closer. "So you can't take credit, Princess and Prophet Cassandra."

"Credit…or blame."

"Semantics." He held her gaze a few seconds longer, making each breath harder to take, as she knew they couldn't wait a minute more. "Like…is this going to be our first kiss or not?"

"We kissed once at Bushrod's."

"But you weren't my girlfriend."

"Temporary girl—"

He closed the space and silenced her with his mouth over hers, sliding his palm against her cheek to hold her there.

Closing her eyes, Cassie gave in to exactly what her whole being wanted. Sinking into the kiss, she parted her lips and invited his tongue to touch hers, letting out a soft moan as electricity zapped through her.

"See?" he murmured. "Magic and sparks. Or is it sparks and magic?"

"Semantics." Slipping her hands around his neck, she let him pull her all the way against his chest, a little shocked at how quickly his heart was beating. He broke the kiss, but kept his lips against her jaw and throat, pressing kisses to her skin, searing everything he touched.

She was vaguely aware of Jelly Bean's paws on the patio, bracing herself for a bark of disapproval. But none came, then she heard him go back into the house.

154

"Now we're finally alone," Braden whispered into her ear, making her laugh softly as his hand grazed over her collarbone and pressed on her heart. But that laugh dissolved into a whimper of pleasure when his fingers brushed over the skin exposed by the V-neck of her top.

All her nerve endings danced with a need that moved her even closer and let him pull her down onto the sofa so they were horizontal with her whole body on top of his. Under her, everything was muscle and man, drawing her in to touch and inhale and lose herself against him.

"We sure as hell better not be cousins," he joked as he stroked her back and slipped his hand under the shirt.

"Mmm." She bowed her back, because there was no way she could resist the pure pleasure of being against his body. "We're not."

"Cassie." His whole hand gripped her ribs and waist, holding her in a firm grip, dragging his palm around to touch—

A hand slammed on her back, making her jump and turn and come face-to-face with Jelly Bean. So, not a hand. A *paw*.

"Hey, JB. Not cool, man." Braden's voice was thick with frustration.

Jelly Bean didn't bark, because he held something in his mouth, but it was too dark to see exactly what it was. A dish towel? Clothes? He smashed his snout into Cassie's arm, making her push up.

"What is it?" She reached for Jelly Bean's mouth, but Braden swore softly and beat her to it, snagging whatever it was from the dog's teeth and balling it in his hand. "Braden." She tried to open his fingers. "What did he bring out here?"

"His opinion." Very slowly, he opened his hand, and Cassie reached for it, then instantly drew back when she realized it was a lacy thong.

"Oh my. I guess she didn't get all of her stuff out of here."

"Or Jelly Bean kept a stash."

She couldn't even laugh at that. "He *is* the world's smartest dog," she said, pushing all the way up and straightening her top.

"Cassie, you're not going to let—"

"Yes I am." She gave Jelly Bean's head a quick rub before he could escape her touch. "Thanks for the wake-up call, Mr. Bean. I almost forgot that temporary, highly controlled, qualified, and…whatever it was…didn't include making out on the sofa. I need to go home."

"Or you could bend the rules and stay all night," Braden said, making no effort to sit up all the way or even move off that sofa. His eyes were dark with arousal, and his lips were…warm, sweet, and inviting.

What was she doing leaving this man?

Taking action…and the action she needed to take was to protect both of them. "I need to go home, Braden."

That's all it took for him to get up. He walked toward the door, pitched the thong in a trash can next to the barbecue, and gestured for Cassie to go first.

"I'll deal with you later," he said sternly to Jelly Bean. "Just know you've had your last drop of peanut butter for a month."

Chapter Twelve

I t was rare that his schedule gave him two Sundays in a row at Waterford, but Braden had no complaints as he pulled up to the big yellow farmhouse for the weekly afternoon tradition.

He spotted Cassie's Escape almost immediately, which put a smile on his face and tweaked his slightly guilty conscience. He'd left Jelly Bean at home today, which was unusual. Not that the dog was being punished, though Braden did give him a stern talking-to that morning while he searched his house and all of JB's favorite hidey-holes for any more remnants of Simone.

He just wanted Cassie to be comfortable, and Jelly Bean always seemed to express his dislike or distrust of her.

Yes, Simone and Jelly Bean had a tight bond, but this was ridiculous.

As he came up to the side porch of the house, the first two people he spotted were Cassie and her mother sitting on a glider together, drinking lemonade, deep in conversation.

"There are two beautiful women," he teased as he came up the stairs.

Cassie smiled at him, her casual Sunday face and ponytail every bit as gorgeous as last night when she'd worn makeup and her hair all tumbled around her pretty face.

"Oh, Braden, hello." Katie rose to greet him, reaching out for a hug that seemed even warmer than usual. "Where's your better half?"

He looked at Cassie over Katie's shoulder, pointing at her. "Right there," he mouthed, making Cassie laugh softly. "Jelly Bean's in the doghouse, so to speak."

As soon as he said it, he saw Cassie's eyes flash in surprise and realized he now had to explain why. And telling her mom that JB interrupted their make-out session with his ex's underwear wasn't going to cut it.

"He's still not discerning smells?" Katie asked.

"Not a one," he said, unable to keep the disappointment out of his voice.

"He smells the things he likes," Cassie said dryly. "I'm going to tell Daniel you're here. He wanted to talk to you the minute you arrived."

"I'll get him," Katie offered quickly. "You sit in the sun with Cassie."

"No arguments from me." Braden went right over and sat close to her. "Happy Sunday, gorgeous."

She narrowed her eyes to near-black slits. "You're not seriously punishing that dog because he not only sees *London* and France, he stole her underpants?"

He laughed, reaching for her to bring her closer and kiss her lightly. "Why are you so funny and hot and irresistible?"

"'Cause I'm half Greek. Seriously, why isn't Jelly Bean here?"

"He just isn't. Does it matter?"

She drew back and gave him a look he couldn't begin to interpret. "Well, brace yourself, okay? I think Daniel has a plan, and you might not like it. Or maybe you will, I don't know."

What was that supposed to mean? "A plan? Do you like it?"

She shrugged. "I'm not in this equation."

"Hey, Braden." Daniel's voice came from the other side of the screen door, pulling them apart.

"Hi, Uncle Daniel." Braden got up to greet his uncle, his curiosity piqued.

"It's a treat to get you two Sundays in a row," Uncle Daniel said. "How did Declan and Connor both have duty and you got off?"

"The whole schedule is juggled because of next weekend."

"Which is?"

"That Date with a Dog auction on Friday night," Braden explained. "Then there's a black-tie event the next night, which means more people not on duty. Trust me, I'm working every day this coming week and a few nights."

"Oh, that's right. The Paws for a Cause kickoff. And Cassie's been telling us about the scavenger hunt you two have been working on."

"This is the week to really go after entries," Cassie chimed in, getting up to join the conversation. "Unless we don't have to do any of that at all."

Now Braden was really confused. "Why wouldn't we?"

"Come with me, Braden." Daniel gestured toward the yard, and Braden started to follow, then turned to Cassie with an expectant look.

"You go," she said. "Come back and tell me what you think."

Completely perplexed, he walked across the lawns, waiting for some clue from his uncle and getting none. There were a few dogs in the pen, but on Sunday, no training was going on, and so few of the family had shown up yet that Waterford felt a little deserted.

"How's Rusty doing?" Braden asked, not seeing Daniel's beloved setter, or his constant companion, Goldie. Rusty had suffered a mild heart attack back in March, following surgery to remove a benign tumor and, at almost fourteen, was definitely slowing down.

"He's hanging in there." Daniel gave a tight smile that didn't hide the bit of sadness in his eyes. "It's helped he's found love again in his old age."

"Just like his master," Braden joked.

"God willing, Katie and I have a lot more years ahead, but Rusty?" He blew out a breath as they reached the kennels. "All I can tell you is that I know what it's like to love a dog, and I know you love Jelly Bean."

Of course he did. So where was this going?

"But loving a dog might not be enough for what you need as an arson-dog handler, assuming you're serious about that."

He choked in disbelief. "Since I've taken hours of extended education and training courses to be his handler, yeah, I'm serious. Hell, a dozen more credits, and I can get certification as an arson investigator myself."

"Is that what you want to do?" he asked as he opened the door.

"No, I want to be a firefighter like my father, and my brothers. But I can also be the handler at a fire scene with a wonderfully trained and talented dog."

"Yes, precisely what I want to show you."

Braden stifled a sigh. "Show me?"

"A wonderfully trained and talented dog." Daniel led them down the main hall, past snoozing dogs, beyond Liam's K-9 section, to a set of kennels in the back, usually reserved for newcomers. They stopped at the first gate, face-to-face with a stunning black Labrador with eyes as blue and intense as Daniel's. "Meet Jasmine, our newest arrival."

His chest tightened as he finally figured it all out. "Jasmine," he repeated.

"She goes by Jazz, has been a therapy dog for three years, living with a woman at an assisted living facility outside of Charlotte, but her owner's passed away."

"What's she doing here?"

"A friend of mine is the owner's son, and he can't take her, and the facility won't keep her, so he called me. Garrett went out to pick her up a few days ago, and whoa. She's amazing, Braden." Uncle Daniel unlatched the gate and stepped inside. Immediately, the dog walked up to him and poked his nose toward his hand, asking to be petted. "Very play-motivated, loves her toys, cooperative, athletic, independent, but highly owner-aware."

All characteristics that made for a great scent-detection dog. "Don't tell me. Her olfactory system is A-plus-plus."

Uncle Daniel laughed. "You know we can't test for that, but she hasn't been scent trained at all. So there's no *un*training to do, which will make it so much easier for you to work with her."

"Easier than, say, Jelly Bean." He couldn't keep the unhappiness out of his voice, and the look he got from his uncle said it came through loud and clear.

"Like I said, I know what it feels like to love a dog. But with a job as critical and potentially life-saving as a canine arson investigator, a working dog can't be selected on emotion and connection. The dog has to have special qualities." He added a meaningful look. "Not everyone is cut out to be a firefighter, as you know. Doesn't mean a person can't want it, but you know there are certain physical and mental characteristics required. It's no different for a working dog."

He let out a noisy exhale, but didn't reply.

"You want this dog to do his or her job flawlessly. Now, no dog is flawless," Uncle Daniel added quickly. "They lose interest, they get tired, they might not be on that day."

"Jelly Bean never loses interest, is tireless, and is always on." He managed a dry laugh.

"If I sound defensive, it's because I am."

"I get it," he said. "And I respect your opinion. But come and meet Jazz. She really checks off every box for what you need."

Couldn't he be the judge of that? Braden made no effort to step into the kennel, swallowing hard against all the objections he had. But one *had* to be said.

"I can't manage two dogs, Uncle Daniel. I'm gone for twenty-four hours several days a week, and I have to bring my dog to work. I can't bring two there, it's against policy. Jelly Bean…" Damn. He couldn't even think about that.

"Someone was in here this week looking to adopt a Weimaraner."

Braden grunted and closed his eyes. Of course. "My ex?"

Daniel tipped his head. "I was going to tell you, but I wanted to get your reaction before including that bit of information. Does it matter?"

"Yeah," he said. "It matters because I'm not giving up on Jelly Bean. I don't care if the greatest ADC that ever lived is standing right here in front of me. I'm sure this dog is astounding, and she should have her job, whatever it is. Give Jazz to another handler and get her trained. I'm committed to Jelly Bean." He held up a hand, hating to be anything but respectful to this man. "Sorry, but it's important to me."

"There's nothing to be sorry about, Braden. If anything, I apologize for blindsiding you. Are you sure there isn't any way to keep Jelly Bean *and* work with a different arson dog?"

"Maybe. Possibly. I don't know, because I'm not mentally there yet." Of course, Uncle Daniel was right. If JB couldn't be retrained and his scent-discernment issues fixed, he would never be an ADC. He wouldn't check all the boxes, like Jazz did.

After a second, he stepped into the kennel and knelt down in front of the dog.

"You're a beauty," he said, scratching her head. "A showstopper." He looked up at his uncle. "But I love the one I have."

Next to him, his uncle shifted from one foot to the

other as if he didn't like what he had to say. "But if you can't get Jelly Bean certified, Braden, you are going to have to either give up your dream or get another dog."

"I don't want another dog," he said simply.

"I know, but the right ADC doing the job could mean life or death. If he stops one arsonist in his lifetime, he's a success."

Braden stood slowly, holding his uncle's gaze. "I know about life-or-death decisions, Uncle Daniel. And I know you're telling me to make this one with my head and not my heart. But I'm not ready to give up yet."

"I'm not suggesting you give up, just looking for another option." Uncle Daniel gave Jazz a treat and another head scratch, then walked out with Braden, latching the kennel. "I do know a little about making decisions with the heart and not the head."

Braden gave him a quick smile. "That's what makes you the Dogfather, right?"

His uncle's features relaxed. "I think my reign is over, based on the way my mother and her new best pal talk. But I am taking credit for this string of weddings we have coming up." He added a sly and totally unsubtle look. "Three, is it?"

Braden just smiled. "At the moment."

"Hey, an old uncle can hope." He added a playful elbow jab. "You know if you and Cassie work out, you'd get a promotion from nephew to step-son-in-law." He laughed. "At least, I think that's a promotion."

But right then, Braden didn't find anything amusing. "Don't get your hopes up, Uncle Daniel."

The other man looked genuinely disappointed. "You mean it's not serious?"

"It's…" *Temporary. Qualified. Provisional. And even my dog knows that.* "New," Braden said. "Very, very new."

"Can I offer unsolicited advice?" he asked as they stepped outside into blinding afternoon sunshine.

"I guess as my uncle and Cassie's stepfather-to-be, you have every right."

"Only if you want it."

Braden nodded, slowing his step to look at a man he admired with every bone in his body. "Yes, sir, I do."

"Very simple advice," he said. "When you know you have the right one, don't let go."

Braden hoped his smile belied the thud of worry in his chest. "You mean a dog or a woman, Uncle Daniel?"

"Both."

"Considering what Daniel's proposing, I guess it's a good thing Braden left Jelly Bean at home." Mom settled back down on the glider after the men headed to the kennels, picking up her lemonade for a sip. "But why do you think he did that?"

"Because that dog hates me," Cassie said dryly. "Loves his ex, though. Hates me."

"Ooh, Cass. Jealousy is not a good look for you."

She snorted. "I'm not jealous, Mom. Worried that I'm the wrong girlfriend for him, but not jealous."

"Why would you be the wrong girlfriend for him?

165

At the risk of sounding like a pushy mother, I think you two are perfect together. Daniel's always thought that, to be honest. Long before you two got together."

"He can't take credit for this," Cassie told him. "This little…" What should she call it? Romance? Relationship? "*Thing*…is all Yiayia's doing."

"That's what she claims," Mom said.

"Well, she did push for me to help Braden raise money, and then with all the time together…" She shrugged. "But it wasn't out of the kindness of her heart."

"Wait. Her heart has kindness?" Mom joked, then held up her hand. "I didn't say that. She has changed."

"Oh, come on. You know as well as I do she's up to no good."

"Well, it can't be all bad if she got you two together."

"Mmm." Cassie covered with a sip of lemonade. It wasn't like she was lying to her mother, because she and Braden were together, at least at the moment. But it was temporary, and she really didn't want to get into that level of detail with Mom. Not yet, anyway. No reason to break her heart in advance.

"What do you think he'll do?" her mother asked, gesturing toward the kennels.

"If I had to place a bet?" Cassie thought about Daniel's plan to offer a new, better-equipped dog for the ADC training. "He'll keep fighting for Jelly Bean, but at some point, digging your heels in for something destined for failure seems kind of dumb, and if there's one thing that man is not, it's dumb."

Cassie leaned back on the sofa and closed her eyes, enjoying the summer breeze.

"Honey, while we're here alone, I need to talk to you about something."

At the serious note in her mother's voice, Cassie leaned up to see if her expression matched. It did. "Is everything okay?"

"Yes, of course. Couldn't be better. What I need to talk about is the wedding."

"Oh, good. What do you need?"

"A wedding *planner*." She lifted her brows. "You know anyone good with event management?"

Cassie stared at her. They were getting married in late October. Four more months? After all these years of waiting?

"What do you need a planner for?" she asked quickly. "You said you want to keep it to under sixty people, Santorini's will cater, and you're getting married here."

She shifted in her seat. "We agreed we're not going to get married at Waterford Farm."

Cassie drew back, eyes popping in surprise. "Since when?"

"Since…" Her mother let out an uncomfortable sigh. "I want a real wedding, honey. You know I didn't have one when Dad and I got married because I was 'in the family way.'" She rolled her eyes. "My mother refused to book the country club, and Yiayia didn't think my non-Greek pregnant self would have been welcome at Saint Catherine's."

Cassie shook her head. "Imagine if anyone had known that baby you were carrying wasn't even half Greek?"

"Everyone's life would have been so different," Mom mused. "And Daniel and Annie married here, for the same rushed reason. So we both agree we want a real wedding. I don't mean a long white gown and veil, obviously. But we don't want the reception in our house, and I feel like we should find somewhere grand and glorious. And I don't want it catered by the family restaurant. I want my son to be in the wedding party, not cooking for it. I want waiters with trays and a jazz band and a big cake and..." She cringed as if she'd just heard herself talking. "Would you die of embarrassment if we had that kind of wedding?"

"Not at *all*." But she didn't want to stay here for an additional four months to plan it. "I understand wanting that. It's just that..." She looked out to the yard, past her mother, trying to think of a gentle way to get out of the responsibility of planning it. "I thought I was going to be the maid of honor, not wedding planner."

"Of course you're the maid of honor!" Mom patted her arm. "You don't think you could do both? Isn't most of the planning work done by the time the day rolls around?"

"I could, but..." She swallowed. Maybe it was time to tell her mother what her plans were. Why wasn't she? "It's just that—"

"Oh my gosh, Cassie. I didn't think this through." She put her hands on her face. "How selfish of me."

"Think what through?"

"Planning a big, fancy wedding when you haven't... you aren't...you are..."

"An old maid?" Cassie gave a hearty laugh. "Please, Mom."

"But you're the right age for a big splashy wedding, and I should be out shopping for that MOB gown you told me years ago I'm not allowed to wear to it." She leaned closer. "You know, with one of those matching jackets that covers everything."

"In lavender with sequins."

Mom took her hand, holding her gaze, both of them smiling at the old joke, a feeling of affection welling up in Cassie's chest.

"I'm so happy for you, Mom," she said as the laughter faded. "You worked so hard taking care of Dad when he was sick, and Daniel is truly a great guy who adores you."

She bit her lip and nodded. "I love the hell out of him, I'm not going to lie. He makes me feel so alive and secure and grounded, all at the same time."

Cassie blinked at her, the description settling on her heart. *Alive and secure and grounded.* What a beautiful testament to love. "Well, then you should have the wedding of your dreams, Mom."

"Will you help me plan it?"

She could do that, couldn't she? Even if she ended up moving? Maybe she'd just stay through the holidays and move in the new year?

Oh God. How many times had she said those very words, year after year after year?

"No." Mom shook her head. "Never mind. You're right, you shouldn't plan it."

"Yes, I should."

"No, I can see you don't want that responsibility, and you're absolutely right. I want you by my side as my maid of honor, not running around checking on the appetizers. I'll hire a planner, if I need one. Or maybe I'll find a venue that offers planning services. But this isn't your worry, honey. You have a life to live." She leaned in to whisper, "And a brand-new boyfriend to think about."

Cassie glanced at the kennels. "It appears that way," she said.

"He sure seems smitten," her mother said, pressing her hand on Cassie's leg. "Are you?"

"He's…" Hot, funny, sexy, adorable, and perfect. "Going to be your stepnephew. That's kind of weird, don't you think?"

"There is no such thing as a stepnephew, and is that what's keeping you from falling hard for him? Because, before you try to deflect that with a quick one-liner, I'm going to remind you that this is me, and I know pretty much your every thought."

"Not every," she said dryly. "Some thoughts I have about Braden, I'm relatively sure you don't want to know."

Mom laughed softly, but didn't disagree. "Well, he's not related to you. But as for the family thing? Just think how easy the wedding plans will be—people can sit on both sides of the—"

"Mother!" She laughed, but held her hand up to stop this line of conversation.

"Sorry. But we're curious."

"We. You and Daniel?"

"That's who we are now. A couple."

"A couple of what?" Cassie joked, making Mom give that bittersweet smile she saved for a nice Dad memory. "Do you think Dad would like him?"

"Yes," she answered without a nanosecond of hesitation. "So, is it serious?"

"It's…fun," she replied, the closest thing to the truth she could come up with. If she admitted this relationship suffered from planned obsolescence, Mom would pester and needle until Cassie told her she wanted to leave Bitter Bark.

Just then, she was saved by Daniel and Braden leaving the kennels. "Oh, here they come."

"I wonder how Braden took the suggestion."

She squinted at him, studying his serious body language as Daniel talked, then suddenly Braden laughed. "He said no," Cassie decided. "Otherwise, he wouldn't find anything funny."

"Oh well," Mom said on a sigh as some cars and trucks pulled into the driveway. "And here comes Yiayia. Let's see if she's still drinking her Nice Kool-Aid."

But Cassie's attention was on Braden, where she knew it would stay all day.

Chapter Thirteen

Jelly Bean trotted through the crowds in Bushrod Square like he was the reason they'd all come to the Date with a Dog bachelor auction. The dog was proud, fierce, confident, and…unaware he'd failed every scent-detection test Braden had attempted that week. Braden blamed himself for a crazy schedule that had him at the fire station on duty far more than at home, so how could he work with the dog?

The week hadn't just been rough on JB. Braden hadn't seen much of Cassie at all, and that left a weird emptiness he didn't understand. Fortunately, that was about to end in five minutes.

"Where you going?" Connor asked as Braden started to veer away toward the bleachers that had been set up and would stay for the whole month of events.

"I'm meeting Cassie first, then I'll go backstage. Declan's over there already."

"Of course he is." Connor laughed. "Because it's fifteen minutes early."

"And he's doing the opening with the chief," Braden reminded him. "I'll be there in a few minutes."

"You better not bail," Connor warned.

"Why would I bail? I already know who's bidding on me. You, on the other hand, could get ignored by God knows how many former flings you have running around this town."

Connor laughed. "It's not me they'll want, it's Jazz." He gave the leash a tug, but it was obvious the tether wasn't necessary. A dog like Jazz would walk next to her owner into a fire…and when it was over, back in to find the cause.

Uncle Daniel had given Connor his choice of any of the dogs in residence at Waterford, and it was no surprise he'd picked the best and brightest. And their cousin Darcy had groomed her to gleaming perfection, complete with a hot pink bandanna.

As Braden moved away, Connor shot him a look.

"Or are you just tryin' to hide, bro?" Connor asked.

"From what?"

"*Who.*" He notched his head to the right. "Incoming. Two o'clock."

Jelly Bean saw Simone at the same time, jerking forward with a loud bark. A quick tug and command got him to stop, but there was nothing Braden could do to slow down the woman coming right at him.

She tipped her head to the side and gave a wave, blond hair flying and a short skirt fluttering around her legs as she picked up her pace.

"Jelly Belly!" she called, arms outstretched, but Braden held firm to the leash.

Connor shot him a quick look. "Speaking of former flings."

"She wasn't a fling," he said.

"Then it looks like you might have two bidders

today." Connor grinned as he nodded hello to Simone, then headed for the stage as she reached Braden and Jelly Bean.

"Hey, baby." It sure sounded like her greeting was directed at him, but Simone crouched down to love on the dog. "I bet you make the fire department oodles of money today." She looked up and winked. "And Jelly Bean should do okay, too."

He gave a quick laugh. "Well, it's for a good cause."

"Mind if I join in the fun?"

He frowned, not sure what she meant.

"If I bid," she clarified. "I don't want you to be upset if I...*win*."

She'd bid on him? "Simone, I'm seeing someone."

"Your cousin?"

"She's not my—"

"This is for charity, Braden. I want to see the department get that pumper truck."

Jelly Bean answered for him, jumping a little for more of her attention and basking when he got it. Why didn't he ever treat Cassie that way?

Speaking of Cassie, he tugged the leash gently. "I gotta go," he said. "I'm late to see my girlfriend."

"Braden." She straightened and looked him right in the eyes. "I need to talk to you. Every time I see you, you're busy. I need to tell you something very important."

"What?"

She shook her head. "Not here, not now. But soon."

"Sure. But I have to go."

She folded over to give Jelly Bean another hug, then stepped closer to give one to Braden. "Good luck today," she whispered in his ear. "May the best woman win."

"Simone—"

She gave him an unwanted kiss on the lips, another flippy wave, and trotted away with her skirt ding-donging. What the hell?

He stood staring for a few seconds, trying like hell to figure out what she was up to, long enough for Jelly Bean to let out his low, slow, distrustful growl. Even before he turned, he knew who he would come face-to-face with.

Cassie. And she looked stunned.

"Hey, Braden." Declan came hustling up on the other side. "They just announced the order, and you're second. Get your ass over there. Sorry, Cassie, but this man's gotta make some cash."

She finally smiled and nodded. "I completely understand."

She didn't, but he'd explain after this was over. Assuming she won the auction.

He was gone before Cassie could say a word, any word—like *It doesn't matter*, or *I know she doesn't mean anything to you*, or *Why the heck does that dog love her and hate me?*

All those retorts got swallowed up in a moment of disbelief and hurt.

Nursing the latter, she headed back to where she'd been sitting on some temporary bleachers with a small group that included Ella, Darcy, Gramma Finnie, Yiayia, Aunt Colleen, and her mother, none of whom would be bidding, but were all there for moral support.

And she could use some of that right now because…was she doing the right thing? Should she be "with" Braden when another woman was so very much in the picture?

As she came up behind the bleachers, she spotted Ella talking to a tall man she didn't recognize, looking up at him with an expression that hung somewhere between terror and uncertainty. But her whole face changed when she saw Cassie, and she broke into a smile of pure relief.

"Oh, there's Cassie!" Ella exclaimed.

The man turned and pinned her with a dark gaze that was somehow familiar and haunting and, whoa, handsome. Tall, dark, and dimpled, with thick black hair, a jawline that could cut diamonds, and a long, lanky frame that was somehow powerful but without the brawn she'd been getting used to the past few weeks.

"Me?" she asked, coming forward.

"Cassie, this is Jace Demakos, vice president of public relations for Family First."

Holy…*whoa.* "Jason the Argonaut," she joked.

He beamed at her, blinding her, of course, with a set of gleaming pearly whites. "Cassandra the goddess, I'm guessing."

Oh, strike one, dimples. Read that mythology again. "Welcome to Bitter Bark." She held out her hand, and he took it, giving it a warm shake.

"It's as quaint as I expected. And you're…" He gave her a nearly imperceptible once-over. "Definitely Greek."

"Only half, but my grandmother is here if you're looking for one hundred percent."

"I'm looking for..." He glanced around. "I was supposed to meet Bill Maddox, but I was late, and he texted me to watch the bachelor auction." He added a snort. "As if that would be something I'd like to do."

"Well, it's not the usual bachelor auction," she told him. "There are dogs involved, and dogs are..."

"Our target market." He pointed to her. "You are correct, Cassie. So, take me to your dog and bachelor auction, but don't expect me to bid."

"You're off the hook," she said. "I, on the other hand..." *Was supposed to be bidding on my boyfriend, who just kissed his ex in the middle of the square.*

"You will have to step in and tell this big-city guy everything I need to know about this town and its dogs."

A big-city guy. A *Greek* big-city guy. Oh boy. "I'll be happy to."

"At least half my family and some of Cassie's are in these bleachers," Ella said, pointing to the stands. "You're more than welcome to sit with us."

"Thank you, ladies, I'd love that."

"Well, just be warned," Cassie said. "It's bleachers full of women. This is a bachelor auction, you know."

He laughed easily. "Bleachers full of women? Doesn't sound too awful."

As they made their way up the steps, every one of the women at the top levels stared. Every woman on every level, to be honest. And the single ones were probably wondering why this particular eye candy wasn't up for bid.

But it was her grandmother's expression that

caught Cassie's eye as they climbed. A look of shock, joy, disbelief, and a lifetime of hope, all stamped on one filler-pumped, Botox-injected Greek grandmother's face.

"And who is this?" she asked, practically climbing out of her seat as Cassie reached her.

Jace extended his hand and somehow managed to nod just enough for it to look like he might be bowing. "Yassou, Yiayia. Ti kaneís?"

His inflection was as perfect as his accent, and for a moment Cassie thought her grandmother might actually faint.

Oh, Yiayia. Your game is *over*.

Chapter Fourteen

Backstage at a bachelor auction was the last place Braden wanted to be when he was aching to clear up that misunderstanding with Cassie. She had to know that that kiss was one-sided and unwelcome.

"Can you switch that schedule around?" Braden asked Liz Winkler, whom Chief Owen had roped into managing the firefighters backstage.

"I'll pretend I didn't hear that." She looked way up at him, since she couldn't be five two in heels, silencing him with an expression that probably had her kids running to their rooms to make their beds and do their chores.

"But, Liz, I have a personal emergency."

"And we need a pumper truck." She patted him on the arm as if he were one of those kids. "Braden, you're going to get the highest bids. We need you to kick things off with those big ol' shoulders, stud."

He didn't laugh. "I have to talk to my girlfriend."

Tapping a clipboard, she shook her head. "Tell her to bid, because money talks, my friend. You're on in two minutes, right after Cal." She snapped her fingers and pointed to the younger firefighter, who wore bunker pants with his navy station T-shirt, holding a little brown dog with pointy ears on a leash. "Don't forget to take off your shirt, probie."

Cal blinked once, then gave a hoot, pulling at the T-shirt. "Yes, ma'am."

"Not now, numskull." She gave him a playful smack with the clipboard. "While you're standing out there with your dog. You're our number one piece of meat, Cal. Make it count."

The kid grinned at Braden. "Sucks to be number two, Mahoney."

Liz was having none of it, slamming him one more time with the clipboard. "When my husband and the captain are done talking, you're on. Don't come back in here with less than five hundred dollars for that fine ass, son."

As Cal scooted away, Braden went in for another shot. "Liz, listen. My brother Connor is on the schedule second to last. I'll switch with him."

"Oh no you don't," she said, her dark eyes flashing. "He's another hottie, and we don't want the bids to fall flat at the end." She added a grin. "But you don't have to take your shirt off, Braden. Cal doesn't have your brains or smile, but lawd, that boy has abs for days."

"You hear that, bro?" Connor put his hand on Braden's shoulder. "The probie's got you beat in the abs department."

"Now you." Liz jabbed Connor with the edge of the clipboard. "You take off your shirt and pray there's a woman out there you haven't pissed off yet."

Connor's jaw dropped, and a few others around them cracked up, but Braden just grunted with frustration. If Cassie thought...and Simone bid... *damn it.*

On the other side of a large curtain, Chief Winkler was introducing Fred Flintstone, a border collie who'd lived at the firehouse for years. Since the chief wasn't being auctioned, Declan, the second-highest-ranking Bitter Bark firefighter, would be the member of the team escorting Fred. At the rousing applause for the dog and Declan, who was well known and loved in this town, Braden knew he'd lost this battle.

Hopefully, Cassie would give him the benefit of the doubt. When this was over, he'd explain it to her.

"Let's get the bidding started," Chief Winkler called out on his microphone. "Our first bachelor is what we call a probie. That's because he's on probation and finishing his training. Ladies, get out your wallets for a date with Cal Norton and his Yorkie named Toto." That got a big cheer, and Cal marched out with the toy-sized terrier.

Declan came over to join Braden and watch from behind the curtain. "Is he seriously going to strip off his shirt?" Declan asked.

"Mrs. Chief's orders," Braden told him.

"Then it's brilliant," Declan joked as the chief started calling out bids.

"Ladies, we will open the bidding at twenty-five dollars. Do I hear twenty-five?"

"Twenty-five!" a woman's voice replied.

"Thirty-five!" another called.

"Remember, you get Probie Cal...and Toto, too!" Chief's high-pitched imitation of a *Wizard of Oz* character earned a cheer from the crowd, but Braden took a step closer to see past Cal to the packed bleachers. It took exactly two seconds for him to see the two rows at the top of the middle section, where in a sea of familiar female faces, only one mattered.

He found Cassie almost immediately, getting a jolt of relief to see her laughing with his sister, Ella, and...who the hell was that? A guy in the middle of the Kilcannon-Mahoney-Santorini all-female cheering section?

He'd never seen the man before, but he was sitting next to Cassie, leaning back to talk to Yiayia behind him, who had not one but two hands on his shoulders as she yakked in his ear.

Cassie turned to them, joined in whatever was so freaking hilarious, not one of them paying any attention to poor Cal as he stripped off his shirt and got bids over a hundred bucks.

"You gotta beat whatever he gets," Connor said, coming up on Braden's other side.

"Yeah, you do," Declan agreed. "Mahoney pride at stake."

Braden ignored them, squinting into the sun at the bleachers. "Who is that guy up there?" he asked. "Second row from the top, with Ella and Cassie."

Connor inched closer and looked. "I don't know, but maybe he'll bid on you."

Braden shot him a look. "What's he doing with them?"

"Do I hear two twenty? Two twenty-five?" Owen drowned them out as the inexpensive sound system crackled with his booming voice. "Going once. Going twice. Sold for two hundred! Congratulations to the young lady in the red dress. You are going to the Paws for a Cause Yappy Hour at Overlook Glen

Vineyards with Cal and Toto tomorrow night!"

Declan gave Braden a nudge. "You can beat two hundred with your eyes closed."

"Cassie said she'd go up to five, so we're good."

"Do you have to pay her back?" Connor cracked.

"Ladies, put your hands together for our next bachelor!" Some stupid music that sounded like the theme song of an old TV show started playing as his brothers gave Braden a push onstage.

He signaled for Jelly Bean, who marched out first as if he was born to be auctioned off to the highest bidder, easily able to follow orders with no leash.

"He's handsome, buff, smart, and furry...oh, but that's Jelly Bean." Over applause and laughter, Owen continued his schtick. "His owner is one of three brothers who serve the good people of Bitter Bark. Ladies, let your dollars fly for our own Braden Mahoney."

Braden gave a wave, feeling beyond stupid, but the women were clapping and hollering, and he had to laugh. He kept Jelly Bean right next to him, and together they walked down the stage, and he winked at a woman in the second row.

"One hundred dollars!" she called out, getting a huge response from the crowd.

"That's what we like," Owen said. "Do I hear one twenty-five?"

"One fifty!"

Braden turned toward where the voice had come from, knowing it couldn't have been Cassie. Recognizing the voice, he spotted Simone in the first row of the far-right bleacher stand, two of her friends on either side, clapping.

"Nice work, Big Bray," Owen teased, using the nickname he'd hung on Braden back when he was a probie. "Do I hear two hundred?"

For a moment, no one bid, and then he saw movement at the top of the stands. "Two hundred!"

He grinned up at Cassie, who smiled back. It was a good smile, a real smile, a trusting smile, but then she turned to that guy next to her, and the smile became a hearty laugh as she tipped her head back at whatever he'd said.

"Three hundred!" Simone called out, making the whole crowd hoot.

He walked the other way, toward Cassie's section, knowing she'd come through.

"Take off your shirt and start a fire!" A group of women in the front clapped and hollered.

He teased them with a little pull of his T-shirt, getting the expected reaction, which made him laugh.

"Three fifty!" Cassie called.

"Four hundred!" This from one of the women in the front. "Five if you take it off, baby!"

"Work it, Braden." He could hear Liz's command from behind the curtain.

He reached down to Jelly Bean and flicked the navy bandanna he wore, pulling the loose knot and dragging it off very slowly, making everyone laugh and cheer. He twirled it in the air, and another woman in the front group yelled, "Five hundred!" and he tossed it to her.

Amidst the chaos, he shot a quick look to Cassie, who was leaning forward, taking it all in. Ella leaned over and whispered in her ear, and Cassie nodded.

"Six hundred," she called out.

That's my girl. He winked and gave her a thumbs-up, hoping this particular hell was about to come to an end. He held his breath, turned, and his gaze landed on Simone, who stood now with her hands on her hips.

"Seven hundred!" Simone called.

What?

The women in the front chatted with each other, and one shook her head as they all sat back down. So it was going to be between Simone and Cassie?

"Seven fifty." Cassie called her bid with a little less enthusiasm, and who could blame her? Five was their agreed-on top, and he'd figured that would take any other bidder out of the running.

Of course, he hadn't counted on Simone, who held up one finger like she was at Sotheby's bidding on a Rembrandt. "Nine hundred dollars," she said.

Good God. The crowd went wild as Owen repeated the bid, and Braden could even hear the cheering backstage. The noise was intense, making Jelly Bean look from side to side and pant a little as they walked.

"Hang in there, buddy," Braden said with a brush of his fingers on the dog's head. "This has to end soon."

He just hoped it didn't end *badly*.

He could see Cassie's whole body leaning forward, no doubt seized by her need to take action and change the course of events. "Nine twenty-five," she called.

He blew her a kiss, but Simone instantly stepped forward. "Nine fifty."

Jelly Bean spun and barked, searching the gasping, cheering crowd for the familiar voice.

"Holy Moses!" Owen sounded more stunned than overjoyed. "That's...that's a record. Do I hear one thousand?"

Almost the whole crowd turned to look up in the direction of the second bidder, finding Cassie staring straight at him. Braden gave an infinitesimal nod to her, as if to say, *It's okay, we'll cover it together.*

Jeez, he really *did* have to repay her for the bidding.

"Nine seventy-five!" Cassie called, and the whole group around her hooted, many of them on their feet. And the guy, whoever he was, leaned back, looked at her, and said something that made her reward him with a billion-watt Cassie Santorini smile.

"One thousand dollars." Simone stepped right up to the stage. "For the firefighter and Jelly Belly!"

JB barked again, spotting her now, batting his paw in excitement.

"One thousand dollars?" The chief sounded like he was about to implode.

"You heard me." Simone leaned a little closer and gave a quiet whistle that probably no one else in the whole crowd heard, but it was enough. Jelly Bean launched toward her, adding to the wild chaos of screaming and hollering.

Jelly Bean reached the edge of the stage where Simone stood with her arms outstretched, and he leaped to give her a lick on the face. The crowd went insane, but Braden looked up at Cassie, wishing he could do anything at all to change this.

Along with the rest of the audience, she watched the woman and the dog with a cool half smile. Leaning back, she crossed her arms and shook her head a tiny bit in response to something Ella asked her.

"Can we top one thousand dollars?" Owen bellowed.

Nothing.

"Going once. Going twice. Sold to the woman who loves that dog."

Simone giggled loudly, and Braden had to fight not to give her a dirty look when he went to get Jelly Bean.

"See you tomorrow, Braden," she said sweetly.

He gave a silent nod, then walked backstage with Jelly Bean and ignored the high fives and fist bumps of his team.

"Watch him," he said to Declan, guiding the dog close to his brother. "I have something to do."

With that, he set off to find Cassie.

"Cassie! Why didn't you outbid her?" Ella demanded, shock in her eyes as the chief dropped the final gavel. "My brother doesn't want to go to Yappy Hour with Simone."

"What, and break Jelly Bean's heart?" Cassie managed a casual shrug.

"Wise move on your part," Jace said from her other side. "That woman wasn't about to be outbid."

"But Braden's her—"

Cassie held up her hand, not because she didn't want Jace to know Braden was her boyfriend. He'd surely figured that out by now. But Jace's arrival had taken this from a fun afternoon to something more professional. He was the underwriter for Paws for a Cause, and she was the planner for more than one event.

"This is a huge coup for the fire department," she

said brightly. "A thousand is going to go a long way for that new pumper truck."

Jace leaned a little closer. "I have to go to that event at the winery tomorrow, as well," he said. "I even had to pack a tux. I'd love if you'd go with me and introduce me to the people I need to know, Cassie. Otherwise, I'm pretty sure I'll end up tagging along with Bill Maddox."

"And his wife," Cassie added, turning the offer over in her brain. It couldn't hurt to socialize with the representative of the underwriting corporation, and it would easily turn the event into "work" for her.

"Spare me that?" he asked, adding a devastating smile.

Yiayia leaned right between them from the row behind. "That's not a bad idea, Cassie."

Cassie slid her a side-eye with enough *I told you so* to silently make her point. Matchmaking her with Braden as Yiayia's purpose in Bitter Bark would soon be forgotten, as all other men would pale in comparison to a Greek.

But suddenly, Gramma Finnie was on the other side, inching in to offer her opinion. "I'm sure Braden would be happier if you were there," she said.

Jace laughed softly, clearly no stranger to the meddlesome grandmother. "I know I would be," he said.

She gave a quick glance to Ella on the other side, looking for an assist. Cassie didn't mind escorting the new guy, but it couldn't be a date. "Ella, why don't you come, too?"

If looks could kill, Cassie would be six feet under. Ella still wasn't over the phone call, it seemed, and had done her level best to avoid even cursory conversation with Jace. "I'm actually already tagging along with your brothers Alex and John. They wanted to check out the wines to see if they could include them on the Santorini's menu. I figured you were going with Braden, so…"

"Why don't we all go together?" Cassie suggested, giving her another pleading look. "A group would be fun."

Ella just stared at her. "Fun."

"Ella," she whispered as Jace got involved in a lively conversation with Yiayia behind her. "I don't want him to think it's a date. Please?"

Ella sighed and rolled her eyes. "Only for you."

"Perfect," Cassie said, giving her friend's leg a squeeze, then turning back to Jace. "We'll go with Ella and my brothers."

He inched forward to look past Cassie at Ella. "Great. Thanks." He said it as if he knew exactly how *not* great that was for Ella.

"I haven't lived here that long," Cassie said quickly to cover the awkward exchange. "But Ella knows everybody."

"Sounds good," he said, pulling out his phone. "Let me get your number so I can text you about getting to the winery."

As she was giving it to him, she glanced up to see just how smug and satisfied Yiayia looked. But she and Gramma were exchanging looks that didn't seem very smug at all. Gramma looked a little horrified, and Yiayia looked panicked.

Okay. Enough of this. "Aren't you supposed to meet Bill Maddox here?" Cassie asked Jace.

"If you can tell me where to find…" He tapped the screen. "A guy named Thaddeus Ambrose Bushrod?" He cracked up. "Bushrod? You can't make this small-town stuff up."

Next to her, Ella could barely contain a disgusted sigh. "He's this *small town's* founder, and you're sitting in Bushrod Square."

"Oh, I…" He started to smile, but then just lifted a brow. "Looks like I need to dial back my big-city snark."

Whoa, trouble left and right up here. Cassie stood and gestured for him to do the same. "Well, dialing back snark isn't usually my strong suit, but I'll show you where the statue is. Come on. Be right back, you guys."

Jace said goodbye to everyone—including an actual kiss on the cheek for his "new Yiayia"—then they headed down the bleacher steps. As Cassie reached the bottom, she couldn't resist a glance over her shoulder, past him, to see if she could catch Yiayia practically drooling.

Except she wasn't drooling. She and Gramma Finnie had their heads close in deep conversation and—

"Oh!" She walked right into someone coming up. "I'm sor…" *Braden.*

"You're looking the wrong way, Cass."

"Hey, sorry. Nice work up there." She gave a sly smile. "Where's Jelly Bean? Still licking the auction winner?"

He closed his eyes, looking unhappy with the auction outcome. With everything at the moment. Including the man right behind Cassie.

"Oh, Braden. This is Jace Demakos from Family First Pet Foods. You know, the Paws for a Cause underwriter?"

The fire chief's voice over the loudspeaker drowned out the introduction, so they stepped around to the side of the bleachers, away from the crowd.

Jace shook Braden's hand then. "Congrats on all that cash," he said. "Got pretty fierce for a while."

Braden searched his face for a moment, maybe sizing him up, maybe just wanting to get the conversation off the auction. "Well, it's a good cause, but..." He shot a wry look to Cassie. "Guess our five-hundred-max plan didn't work."

"Who could have guessed that fabulously well-behaved dog of yours would throw the auction?" she joked.

But Braden shook his head, clearly not able to laugh about it yet.

"Well, I better get to my meeting," Jace said. "You stay here, Cassie. I can find it."

She pointed to the center of the square. "Head toward those trees, and you'll see a statue. But if you want, I can walk you over there and introduce you to Bill Maddox."

He gave his head a quick shake. "Bill can find me. I told him to look for a tall Greek guy," he said on a laugh. "Thanks for making me feel comfortable, and I'll see you tomorrow night for, uh, Yappy Hour? I'll text you."

"Okay, great." She extended her hand, suddenly seeing this exchange through Braden's eyes and knowing he might not realize this was business. "Bye, Jace."

They shook, and he took off, leaving Cassie and Braden alone in the shade with the echoes of another auction behind them.

"You're going to the black-tie thing with him?" Braden asked, obviously working valiantly—and failing—to keep any emotion out of his voice.

"With a big group," she assured him. "He doesn't know anyone else involved with the event—"

"Except Bill Maddox."

She blew out a rueful laugh. "So, you're going to come over here and get jealous after your ex just paid a thousand dollars to make me look like an idiot *and* snag you as her date?"

"You know I didn't want that to happen, Cassie."

She lifted a brow.

"And I know you saw her get all kissy with me before it started."

"I did."

He reached for her hands. "And you know she's been just this side of a stalker lately."

She searched his face for a long time before responding. "I trust you," she said simply, and his big shoulders dropped with relief.

"And I trust you." He glanced in the general direction that Jace had gone. "Is he really Greek?"

"Oh yes. And he knew all the right things to say to my grandmother."

He looked skyward. "And he's taking you out tomorrow."

"No, he's coming with my brothers and your sister, and it didn't even cost a thousand dollars."

"Exactly. I'd have lost my job if I said no to that, but you have no excuse." She heard the tease in his voice, but there was an edge, too. An edge she wanted to resent, but didn't. Damn it, she kind of liked that he cared so much.

"Is this our first fight?" she asked.

He almost smiled—finally. "Yeah."

"It is?"

"And you know what that means."

She bit her lip. "Makeup...kiss?"

He reached for her and stepped them both under the bleachers, which were rocking with cheering, hollering women. "Kiss for now," he said gruffly, sending an unholy thrill right through her. Then his mouth came down on hers as he pulled her whole body against him and opened his lips and melted her right into the grass of Bushrod Square.

She clung to him, digging her fingers into his shoulders, holding him close so the delicious, slow, hot kiss didn't end too soon.

"We should fight more often," he murmured into her lips, stealing a little more contact before reluctantly breaking away.

"Mmm. Big fight."

He smoked her with a look so sexy, she would have swayed if he hadn't been holding her. "In fact, let's have one tomorrow at that event," he said. "Then come home with me and we'll make up."

She could barely breathe at the sexy invitation. "I thought we...weren't..."

"What? Getting jealous of other people? Wanting more than a kiss? Feeling things for each other?"

Oh Lord. "Are you?"

"All of the above." He stopped her response with another long kiss, adding pressure with his big hands running up and down her back. "I have to work a twelve-hour shift starting at seven on Sunday morning," he whispered. "So it can't be a late night. Come over after the winery thing, and...we can compare dates."

Heat coiled through her, making her ache with need and impatience. "He's not a date, but you can't say the same about Simone. She's crazy about you."

"Don't know, don't care." He inched back. "But what about this woman? Isn't she crazy for me?"

This woman isn't going to stick around here long enough to ruin every dream by falling head over heels in love with this big, gorgeous hunk of human perfection.

"She's crazy, all right."

"And speaking of herself in third person. That means...she's going to take action."

She let her gaze fall over his face and shoulders and body and back to his face, settling on his mouth. "She might..." she said on a whisper, "consider helping you take off the bow tie...with her teeth."

He laughed, hugging her closer. "Her teeth, huh? I..." His voice faded as he cocked his head, listening to the crowd and the auctioneer.

"Going once! Going twice! Sold to the woman in the second row! You just bought Connor Mahoney and Jazz for a record-setting eleven hundred dollars!"

"He beat me." He grunted and closed his eyes. "Why do women love that guy?"

Cassie reached up and kissed him. "Don't know, don't care. But *you* have one date for the party...and a different one for the after party."

"Do I?"

She nodded slowly, so tired of fighting the attraction. "I'll be there."

He held her gaze with one that was so real and sincere and hot that Cassie almost whimpered. "I can't wait."

Chapter Fifteen

"This place looks different." As Braden parked his truck in a crowded lot, he peered into the early evening light that poured over the entrance of Overlook Glen Vineyards. The rambling fieldstone farmhouse sat about ten miles west of Bitter Bark, perched high on a hill with a commanding view of the Blue Ridge Mountains.

The last time he'd been here was on a call with the fire department because the owner, an older man, had smelled gas and was afraid there could be a leak. The winery had been run-down and nearly abandoned, the rolling hills of the vineyard nearly barren then. But tonight, the landscaping was sharp, the stonework looked like it had been repaired, and rows of rich green grape vines were visible all around.

"I've never even been here before." Simone shifted in her seat, adjusting the skintight white dress that kept creeping up her legs.

"I'd heard it was going to go out of business," he said. "But I think there's a new owner." He shot a glance to the woman in the passenger seat, catching her wiping her palms on her thighs. "You nervous, Simone?"

She gave him a quick smile. "Should I be?"

"To go to a cocktail party? No."

"To go to a cocktail party with my ex-boyfriend? Yes."

He considered how to answer that and stuck with the approach he'd taken since he and Jelly Bean had pulled up to her apartment complex to pick her up for the black-tie event. He played it straight, unflirtatious, uninviting, and cool. Every time Simone flipped a little flirt his way, he refused to volley back.

This was a fundraising arrangement, not a date.

"Well, your best pal is right there in the back." He pointed his thumb to Jelly Bean, who sat on his haunches, looking out the window, unconcerned that he wore a bow tie that Simone had insisted on wrapping around his neck.

Oh, and speaking of bow ties…Braden took a cursory scan around the lot, skimming over the groups and couples headed to the main entrance of the winery. The men all looked alike in penguin suits, the women, like Simone, decked out in a lot of sparkle and bling. The dogs, sure enough, wore either bow ties or glittery collars.

Would Cassie get all dolled up for her "business" meeting with…*Adonis*?

"What's the matter?" Simone asked, putting a hand on his arm.

"Nothing," he lied.

"You look like your stomach hurts or something."

"I'm fine." But trying to act like this "date" wasn't the most wrong thing he'd done in ages was kind of making him feel sick. He had to be cordial to a woman he'd long ago stopped thinking about, because she'd *bought* him, all the time knowing that the woman he wanted at his side was with another man.

She squeezed his arm. "You're mad at me."

"Nope. I'm happy the fire department got all that money." He flipped off his seat belt, and she did the same, reaching down to the floor to slide her shoes back on. He noticed that the heels were about the height of an extension ladder, and the entrance to the winery was a decent walk from here.

"You sure you can make it across the parking lot in those things?"

She laughed. "I always wore high heels on our dates, Braden. How could you forget?"

"Because we broke up," he said dryly, unable to hide the undercurrent of frustration that punched at him. He felt like a damn prisoner tonight, one who had to be polite and nice and fake that he was having fun.

"So that means you forget how I dress?"

"It means I…" *Don't think about you, ever.* "Don't want you to trip in a crack or a pothole."

"You're so sweet. Did you hear how sweet he is, Jelly Bells?" She threw the question to the passenger in the back. "Braden is a caring, kind man."

"Simone." He turned to her, knowing he had to set some ground rules before they walked in and she did something that would easily get misinterpreted. "I really appreciate what you did for the fire department, but—"

"Chief Winkler said I set the bar, and that's why so many of the bids reached four figures." She actually sounded like she thought outbidding Cassie had been her civic duty.

"And like I said, that's great, but like I also said, I'm seeing someone. You know that, right?"

"I've heard, and, of course, I saw you eating her face off at Bushrod's." She dropped her chin, but looked up at him through lashes so thick, he'd bet good money they were fake. "I know you were trying to make me jealous, and God, Braden, it worked."

"I wasn't trying to make you jealous, and you're too smart to play this game."

"I'm not smart," she said on an achingly sad sigh. "Or I would never have broken up with you."

His gut tightened. He'd known that was where this was going. From the moment she'd said she had something to tell him in the square yesterday, he'd known it was this.

"Well, you did," he said. "And that was for the best, so—"

"No. It wasn't." She reached out to him again, curling her fingers over the sleeve of his dress shirt. "I'm not even sure why we broke up, but I know it was a mistake."

"You wanted to move in together, and I didn't."

"Because you have this bizarre reluctance about getting married and having kids."

Getting married? Didn't take long to get there. "Even if I didn't feel that way, I wouldn't have wanted to move in together."

She flinched as if he'd hurt her.

"I'm sorry," he added. "But I've moved on, Simone. I'm happy right now. I thought you were, too."

"But what about when you have the same thing happen with her?" she said. "When you tell her that

199

you have this…this hang-up that you should be alone, and she gets restless, like women our age do, and decides to move on?"

"I already—"

"Then I'll be waiting," she said, leaning so close he thought she was going to kiss him. "I will be waiting for you, Braden Mahoney. And I won't care that you won't commit to me or move in with me or even marry me."

He stared at her, not even sure how to respond.

"I'll be the very girl you want. We can have great sex, good times, nice dates, and I swear I won't complain when you work twenty-four-hour shifts." She dug her nails into his arm, desperation transforming her features into something far less attractive.

"I'm not interested in a relationship like that," he said simply.

But she shook her head as if his words didn't matter. "You know how I feel about you, Braden. Nothing's changed. Even when I was with Frank, I missed you every single minute." Tears welled and threatened her sparkly makeup, but she didn't seem to care. "I wanted to wait until we had a drink and maybe had some fun before I told you this, but, Braden, I want to get back together. I really do."

Jelly Bean barked, hard, right between their faces, as if he thought he had to be the one to stop this insanity. Braden used the excuse to pull away, putting his hands up as if that could halt her.

"See? Jelly Belly understands," she cooed.

But JB didn't understand anything. He barked again, staring out of the car, then a low, menacing growl rumbled from his chest.

Braden turned to follow the dog's gaze, his own gaze landing right on the woman he wanted to be sitting with in this truck. Cassie was about fifteen feet away, shimmering in a shiny pink dress that wasn't sprayed on, but fit in a way that made a man want to do nothing but take it off.

Ella, Alex, and John were behind her, but Cassie was walking side by side with her Greek god, who looked down at Cassie with an expression that said he knew he was the luckiest guy at this shindig tonight. And then he laughed so hard, Braden could hear it inside the truck.

"See? Jelly Bean knows," Simone said softly. "He never barks or growls unless he doesn't like someone."

The damn shame of it was that was true.

"He's not dating her, I am." He gave a stern look to Simone. "And you and I are here as friends because you paid for the night. Please, Simone, don't say another thing you're going to regret."

"I don't regret anything except breaking up with you." She reached for her bag and the door handle, not waiting for him to get out and open the door for her. "And you have nothing to worry about, Braden. I can fake that we're just friends who mean nothing to each other. I won't do anything to sabotage your relationship. I care about you too much for that."

Relieved, he nodded. "Thanks."

As he climbed out of the truck and reached for his jacket, he took one more look at the lady in pink, just in time to see the man next to her put a casual hand on her back and lead her to the front door.

He should never have let himself fall so hard for Cassie Santorini, but it was too late to change that now. He just had to get through this cocktail party and know for sure that Cassie would be in his arms tonight, and no one else's. He hoped.

"Welcome to Overlook Glen." A tall, slender blonde greeted Cassie and Jace as they entered, extending her hand and adding a warm smile. "I'm Grace Donovan, the new owner and oenologist."

"Hello, Grace. Cassie Santorini, and this is Jace Demakos, who's with Family First Pet Foods, the main underwriter of the Paws for a Cause event."

"Oh, hello." She turned her attention to Jace, her blue eyes widening with the appreciative look Cassie had already noticed he got from pretty much every female around. Except Ella, who treated him about the same way Jelly Bean treated Cassie.

But, yeah, Jace was a ten and a half and didn't seem to even realize it. "Wonderful to have you here," Grace gushed. "I hope you'll take the tour of our newly renovated winery, taste some of our product, and have a wonderful night."

Cassie glanced around, taking in the oversize reception area and what looked like a banquet hall beyond it, all of it spilling to a large terrace already populated with partiers.

"An oenologist?" Alex asked, coming up behind Cassie to shake Grace's hand and hold her gaze for a moment. "Then you're not the winemaker?"

"I've hired someone as a vintner," she said. "But my interest is the science of winemaking."

Alex gave a soft snort. "There's more passion than science in winemaking, like food."

She slowly withdrew her hand and tilted her head, looking up at him. "I couldn't disagree more, Mr. Santorini. Without science, there would be no wine."

Alex inched back as if the very idea hit him hard. Or maybe Grace Donovan did.

While the others greeted her and exchanged pleasantries, Cassie took in the scope and beauty of the place. Huge, high windows flooded the whole area with the golden glow of the sunset, and the stonework on the walls gave it the feel of an old castle.

"Do you hold a lot of events here?" she asked Grace as the rest of her party moved on. Well, all but Jace. He seemed glued to her side.

"We're starting to ramp up this summer," Grace said. "We just haven't quite established ourselves yet, but we hope to."

"Would you do a wedding?" she asked.

"Oh!" The woman looked from one to another, her smile growing. "Are congratulations in order for you two?"

"No, no," Cassie said quickly. "I'm actually thinking of my mother's wedding coming up in October. She's looking for a venue just like this."

Her whole face brightened. "How awesome. Just call me and set up a tour and appointment. We'll be harvesting then, and the fall colors will be spectacular."

"I will," Cassie said. "Don't let anyone steal the second Saturday in October if you still have it open."

"I think I do."

"Fantastic." Cassie reached out for another handshake. "I'll call you, Grace. Thanks."

As they walked on, Jace leaned down a little bit to talk over the noise. "I see you never turn off your inner event planner," he said.

She laughed and looked up at him. "It does run hot sometimes, but my mother recently asked me if I could help her find the right place for her wedding."

"So, your mom is getting married? You cool with that?"

"Absolutely. She's marrying Ella's uncle, as a matter of fact."

He frowned, slowing his step until he stopped. "Wait a second. Ella will be your cousin?"

"Not really, just extended, unrelated family."

"Whew, that's good to understand." He glanced over her shoulder and fought the tiniest smile.

"Why?" She frowned at him. "Do you say that because you don't like Ella for some reason?"

"Ella doesn't like me for some reason," he said. "But I was a little confused because you were bidding pretty hard for a date with her brother, the firefighter. So he's also like extended family?"

He sounded just a little too interested in her relationship with Braden, and she had to nip that in the bud, pronto. "Jace, I've been seeing him."

"Oh, is it serious?"

"It's…" *Temporary.* She opted for the same thing she'd told anyone who poked around this relationship. "Fairly new."

He searched her face as if considering that, then gave his head the slightest nod in the other direction. "And it explains why he was staring at me like my mother when I steal the last koulourakia."

She wanted to laugh at the all-too-true analogy, but

couldn't resist turning, and sucking in a soft breath of surprise.

For the love of God and all that was holy, Braden Mahoney in a tuxedo ought to be illegal. And he wasn't staring at Jace now. In fact, he was talking to the winery owner, introducing his date, who looked like she'd stepped off a magazine cover and seemed to always have one hand on that shoulder that Cassie liked so much.

And of course, Jelly Bean was glued to Simone with his tongue hanging out.

Cassie turned back to Jace. "Never steal the last koulourakia, *agapi mou*." She grinned up at him. "That's me channeling my inner father, who made those cookies all the time."

"Really? My mother's recipe is the best."

"You'll have to debate that with Alex."

They chatted easily as they walked out to the terrace and looked for the others, but Alex had already gone to inspect the buffet, John was talking to a Santorini customer Cassie recognized, and Ella had flat-out disappeared.

"Let's get drinks and sit over there," Jace suggested. "There's nothing I love more than talking about growing up Greek."

And have Braden walk by her cozy little tête-à-tête? "First, let's go talk to Mayor Wilkins. Have you met her yet?"

He smiled. "You're right, Cassie. We're here to network, not relive our childhood. I admire that work ethic."

She led him to Blanche Wilkins, who was just finishing up a conversation, and introduced Jace without bothering to explain his connection, because by the look on the older woman's face, she knew exactly who he was.

In fact, she clapped her hands with picture-perfect Southern charm. "Well, if you aren't the guest of honor here, I don't know who is. Thank you, Mr. Demakos, for underwriting such an important event for our wonderful town. How do you like Bitter Bark so far?"

"It's…"

Cassie shot him a sneaky *don't snark* warning look, which she knew he got.

"Quite possibly the cutest town I've ever visited."

Mayor Wilkins lifted her wineglass in appreciation. "And how long will you be staying, Mr. Demakos? Maybe there's time to do something special for you. I don't know what, but we have to make a big deal out of your company's generosity."

Cassie stepped closer. "How about a Family First Day, Mayor?" she suggested. "Bitter Bark is all about families, and their pets. We could celebrate the brand and have it be the 'official dog food of Bitter Bark.'"

"I love that idea!" Mayor Wilkins exclaimed.

Jace inched back a little, giving Cassie a look of surprise and approval. "Did you just dream that up now?"

"Kind of, yeah." She gave a nervous laugh. "Unless you hate it, then I absolutely stole it from Purina."

He cracked up. "It's genius, Cassie. And yes, Mayor, I'll be here almost the entire month, though I do have to fly back to Chicago for a few meetings."

"Oh, then you'll have to come and tour our town hall and historic sites. Thaddeus Bushrod's home, too."

"Ah, the founder." He winked at Cassie at the very moment that Braden and Simone walked by on their way to the bar.

Of course he'd cruise by at the worst possible time. But when her gaze shifted and locked on Braden's, hot adrenaline shot through her. Simone pretended like she didn't see Cassie, and the mayor was chattering to Jace, so for those few heartbeats of time, it was just the two of them, and the rest of the world sort of faded away.

Why weren't they together tonight?

His expression mirrored her thoughts, but then Simone took his arm and pulled him toward a friend, and the moment was lost.

"You're in good hands with Cassie," Mayor Wilkins was saying as Cassie dropped back to earth and the stupid, mundane work talk she didn't want to be having. "Every idea she has is gold. We'd kill to have her on our tourism committee." The mayor gave her a playful nudge. "But every time I ask, she's got something else going on."

Because she didn't want to get embroiled in Bitter Bark. She wanted to leave. But...out of the corner of her eye, she saw Braden look past his date's shoulder at Cassie.

She had to fight the urge not to look back and let him know—let everyone know—how she felt about him.

Talk about getting *embroiled*.

"I'm happy to consult as needed," Cassie said smoothly. "And, oh, Jace, you need to meet Lisa Stillman. She's the features editor of the *Bitter Bark Banner*. She's right over by the buffet."

They said goodbye to the mayor and headed toward the food.

"I underestimated you," Jace said under his breath as they walked. "You're a powerhouse in this position."

She smiled up at him. "I told you tonight was work."

"From one workaholic to another, I appreciate that."

She took him straight to Lisa Stillman, made the introductions, and in ten minutes, an interview was lined up. They drank a glass of wine, had a bite of quiche, and Cassie started looking for her next networking opportunity...preferably as far away as possible from Braden, who seemed to be just ten feet from her at every turn.

"Oh, great." Cassie pointed to a man on the other side of the terrace. "You need to meet—"

"Stop." Jace put his hand over her finger and guided her hand down. "You need to come with me to that table under that tree. I want to talk to you."

She stared at him, her whole body tightening. Oh God. He liked her. It was obvious from the way he smiled and how attentive he was, from the way he praised her skills and made little comments about her being Greek.

She could no longer beat around the bush. "Jace, I hope I made it clear that I'm not on the market. You do know that, don't you?"

"Which market?"

She frowned, not understanding the question.

"Come with me, Cassie." He put a light hand on her back just long enough to send her in the direction of the empty table. Not sexual, not flirtatious, not even overly friendly. But still...

They sat down, far from any other people, and he turned his chair to face hers.

"The job market," he said simply.

"Excuse me?"

"You asked which market I meant. My question is, are you on the job market?"

This time, the adrenaline rush was for a completely different reason. "I might be," she said, purposely vague. "I guess it depends on the job."

"I need someone to head special events at Family First. Right now, I'm using an outside agency, and I'd prefer in-house. Special events fall under the PR division, which is mine, and I have a good budget for the position. I'm looking for—"

"In Chicago?" The question came out as a croak of disbelief.

He leaned back. "Is that a deal breaker? Yes. The offer would be good, but I'd want you to relocate."

Holy moly. "Chicago," she muttered. "That's a... big city." It totally qualified as *dreamy*.

"Does that scare you, Cassie?"

She almost choked. "It's perfect."

His face lit up. "Really? You want to leave Bitter Bark? I couldn't tell, since you seem pretty well settled here, so—"

"No, no, not settled. I'm living in an apartment with my brothers because they opened a new restaurant and needed help."

He glanced out at the terrace, and she didn't have to guess who he was looking for. "And the guy you were ready to spend nine hundred and seventy-five bucks for tonight? I don't mean to pry into your personal life, but I had this idea before we even got here, and now that I see you in action? I'm going to be crushed if you don't take the job."

He didn't like her...he wanted to hire her. For a great job in a huge city.

"Is he...enough to keep you here?" he prodded.

Well, if that wasn't the million-dollar question.

"Most of my family is here in Bitter Bark now," she said slowly, deliberately steering the conversation away from Braden. "But I..." She closed her eyes. "I'd like to think about it, obviously."

"Obviously. I have to go back to Chicago this week, and when I'm there, I'll have HR put together an offer package. You can think about it as long as you need to. Well, not too long. I need you for a Family First event in Millennium Park."

"What's that?"

"A massive headache that we're sponsoring. I've got the local agency working on it, but I need someone smart with boots on the ground that weekend." He leaned closer. "Your boots, Cassie Santorini. On the Fourth of July."

She gulped. "So, you'd want me to start in July?"

"I know you've committed to this." He gestured toward the terrace, but obviously meant the whole Paws for a Cause. "Unless you could leave sooner? I know you said you have some scavenger hunt thing, but maybe someone else could handle that, and you could get set up in Chicago by midmonth."

Midmonth? Some scavenger hunt thing. Braden.

"I couldn't do that," she answered without a second's hesitation. "I couldn't let down my..."

"Your client, of course," he finished for her. "That's okay. You can start July first. It'll be baptism by fire, but something tells me you're not worried about getting burned."

Just worried about burning…the firefighter. Which was precisely why she hadn't wanted to give in to this attraction in the first place.

"Let me get you some wine," he said. "You look like you need it."

She just nodded, still not quite wrapping her head around the last ten minutes. The second he was gone, she heard her phone buzz from inside her evening bag. She slipped it out and stared at the text from Braden.

Nine o'clock? My place? This nightmare should be over by then. He added a little picture of a bow tie, which normally would have been cute and funny and sexy, but…

July? In Chicago? *Forever?*

File that under *be careful what you wish for.*

Letting out a breath, she lifted her gaze to meet Braden's across the crowded terrace. The sun was setting behind him, backlighting him in a glow that made him look…

Her mother's voice echoed in her head.

He makes me feel so alive and secure and grounded, all at the same time.

How did this happen? She'd been so determined not to fall, but one secret half smile and a scorching look, and Cassie's heart was fluttering and floating and betraying her.

If she went to his house tonight, if she climbed into his bed and made love to that man…she could kiss Chicago goodbye. She'd never want to leave him. Once they had that intimacy, once she looked into those blue eyes while their bodies joined, once he held her all night long…so long, big city.

From the corner of her eye, she saw Jace coming back with two glasses of wine, sidestepping a crazy little Pomeranian in a pink lace bandanna who barked like she could be the poster dog for Yappy Hour.

Cassie had to make a decision about tonight…fast.

She tapped the phone screen with a simple reply.

Second glass of wine. Better not drive tonight.

And even from this far away, she saw those broad shoulders fall in disappointment. And, no surprise, he didn't text back with an offer to pick her up.

Of course not. Braden Mahoney had been hurt enough, and the closer she got to him, the more it was going to hurt when she left.

If she left.

No, no, no. *When* she left.

"To new beginnings." Jace held out his glass and waited for her to toast with him.

And unexpected endings. "Cheers," she whispered.

Chapter Sixteen

Everything about the last twenty-four hours sucked wind. No, actually, everything about the last thirty-six hours had blown. From the moment Simone begged for a second chance, to right this minute, Braden itched with discontent and frustration. And since he'd just done a hard twenty-four-hour shift on top of a sleepless night of wanting a woman who he knew wasn't going to show, he was bleary-eyed exhausted.

The fact that Cassie hadn't come over for their post-party date had grated on him for the whole shift, when he'd run on autopilot in between shots of adrenaline during two brush fires and four medic calls—including one for an old man who'd had a tractor accident and was still in critical condition—and about six hours of filling out forms.

So when Braden pulled up to his house and saw Cassie's red Ford in the driveway at seven thirty Monday morning and Jelly Bean sat up and started growling, Braden's reprimand was a little sharper than it should have been.

When JB shot him a startled look, he put his hand on the dog's head in apology. "Just quit growling at her, boy. I realize you're rooting for the wrong team, but that car there? Seeing that is pretty much the first time I've been anything but miserable since Saturday, so drop your disapproval."

One bark was all he got in response.

"Now let's figure out what the hell she's doing here."

Another single bark.

"Sex? Doubtful. Breakup? Possible. Maybe she brought food and coffee, and that would be just fine, too." Braden dragged himself out of the truck, glancing down at his dirty clothes that covered his sweaty body. He'd have showered at the station if he'd known she was coming.

Cassie opened the front door before he even got there, looking all kinds of beautiful and fresh in jean shorts and a white tank top that clung to a body that he'd wanted to cling to since the day he met her.

"Morning," she said with a tenuous smile.

"You're late," he said dryly. "By about thirty hours."

She tipped her head to the side in an unspoken apology, which made her thick dark hair fall over one of her shoulders, and all he could think about was how that silky hair would feel in his hand.

"I brought bougatsa."

"Bougwhatsa?"

"Greek pastry."

He let out a sigh and closed his eyes. "Yes. Let me shower first."

"Take some coffee with you?"

Laughing softly, he slid his hand under her hair and cupped her jaw. "You have to be perfect, don't you?"

"Far from it. I just want you to forgive me for breaking our date."

He let his gaze slide over her without trying to hide it. He was too wiped out to play games. "You had me at pastry, and you know it. Unless, of course, you spent the night with...Hercules."

She gave his arm a push. "Give me a break, Braden. You know me better than that."

He nodded in acknowledgment, still holding her face and gaze. "I know you well enough to guess I'm taking that shower alone."

For one millisecond, her eyes glinted, dark and interested. Then she eased out of his touch. "I'll take Jelly Bean out back and give him some food."

He snorted. "Like I said, perfect."

"No, perfect would be taking the shower with you."

"Yeah, you're right." With one more longing look, he headed toward his bedroom, standing in the doorway for a moment, listening to her steps and voice as she talked to Jelly Bean and opened the back door to let him hit the grass.

The shower would have been...amazing. But she was here, and that was really all that mattered.

Holding that thought, he didn't even bother to close the bedroom door, and in two minutes he was stripped and standing under scalding water. It permeated his body and melted his skin as he put his head back, closed his eyes, and let the water sluice over his face. He couldn't really think right then, or figure out why she was here, but he didn't care.

Water, soap, heat, steam, and Cassie in the next room was enough. As he opened the shower curtain, he saw Jelly Bean in the doorway, staring at him as if to say something wasn't right.

"Put a towel on," Cassie called from the bedroom. "Because I'm in here."

"And he's not growling."

"I bribed him with bougatsa."

He grabbed a towel, swiped it over his hair, and wrapped it around his waist, securing the corner as he walked into the bedroom.

Cassie was on his bed with a plate of food and a cup of coffee and the sweetest look he'd ever seen. "Do you allow eating on your bed?"

"If the waitress stays."

"You look like you might fall into your pastry at the table."

"Rough shift," he said, heading to the dresser to grab a pair of thin sweats and taking them back to the bathroom. After he pulled them on over his wet body, he went back out to join her.

She sat cross-legged on the bed with a plate that was filled with a flaky pastry dusted with powdered sugar and oozing cheese and smelling like heaven itself.

"That looks ridiculously delicious." He smiled at her. "Food looks good, too."

She patted the space next to her. "I bear Greek food and good will, *agapi mou*."

"Been to church enough to know *agapi* is love. *Mou* has to be…" He lifted his brows. "My love? You *do* want me to forgive you."

"It's like sweetheart or darling, but yes, your translation is technically correct. You shouldn't have to forgive me," she added. "I didn't do anything wrong."

Settled on the bed next to her, he picked up a piece of pastry and accepted the napkin she offered as a makeshift plate. "Well, thank you for this. Are you having some?"

She nodded and took a piece, not tasting it until he did. Then she laughed when he closed his eyes and moaned.

"Are you kidding me?" he mumbled around a mouthful as powdered sugar snowed from his lips. "This is…" He moaned again. "Holy hell. Bougatsa means 'best thing I ever tasted.'"

"Greeks have it all over the Irish when it comes to food."

He nodded in enthusiastic agreement, taking another bite. "Okay…no talking. I'm eating."

She chuckled softly, tasting hers with far less gusto, eventually pulling her legs up to wrap her arms around her knees and rest her head to watch him eat.

"My father would cry if he saw you eat like this," she said.

"Why?" He brushed his hands over the plate and went for the next piece.

"People loving food was like his reason for living. Alex is the same way, but my dad? I never saw a man happier than when someone tasted something he made for the first time. 'Is it good?' he'd ask over and over again. Like he didn't know his food was perfection."

"Mmmm. Perfection." He finished the last bite, and finally, for the first time in hours and hours, his stomach felt something other than black and empty and unhappy. He gulped a little of the coffee she'd made him, which was easy since it wasn't burning hot and she'd put plenty of milk and sugar in it.

"How do you know how I take my coffee?"

"You drink it on Sundays a lot, before we eat. Don't you think I notice things like that?"

He eyed her. "What else did you notice?"

"Besides your shoulders?"

He lifted one, enjoying the way she looked at it like he'd looked at her pastry.

"How smart you are," she said, resting her cheek on her knees. "You know something about everything."

"I don't know about you."

She lifted a brow. "Open book. Just ask."

In one way, he had so many questions for her. He wanted to know everything, from her first memory to...what happened the other night. When he didn't ask any questions, she moved the empty pastry plate to the nightstand, then slid down on her side, propping herself on her elbow.

Looking at her lying next to him on his bed, he did the only thing he could possibly do right then...slide down next to her, prop his own elbow, and lay face-to-face and body-to-body.

About a foot separated them, and in that space was hope and anticipation and an explosion of pheromones and chemistry.

"Waiting for your question," she said softly.

There really was only one thing that mattered right then. "What happened Saturday night?"

She stared at him for a long time, blinking once, staring some more, silent.

"Oh, I see," he said. "You want me to guess?"

"You won't."

He sat up a little. "Let me try. A, you got scared because I looked so good in a tuxedo. B, you got jealous of that nitwit Simone pawing me. C, you showed up and Jelly Bean threatened to attack while I was asleep. D, you got drunk on expensive wine and passed out alone. E…" He was fresh out of ideas except the one that ate away at him. "E, you met someone who has something you want more than you want me."

When her eyes shuttered, he just let his head drop off his hand and hit the pillow with a grunt.

"Yes, it is E," she whispered, the words stabbing at his chest. "Also A and B, because, damn, Einstein, you did rock the tux, and good God, I could claw Simone's eyes out. Oh, and I could get past your dog with a jar of Skippy, and I have never passed out drunk in my life."

He didn't hear anything past *It is E*.

Then…this guy meant something to her. How? Why? "Well, he's Greek," he said, answering his own mental questions. "And he's, you know, tall, and I guess that's what you'd call good-looking, what with the manly jaw and all. And he's Greek. Oh, and he lives in a big city with, guess what, a bunch of Greek people?" He gave a mirthless laugh. "Have I missed anything besides the fact that he knows what *agapi mou* means and can probably make bougwhatsa with his eyes closed? And he's Greek."

"Are you finished?" she asked.

He turned his head to look at her, but that hurt, too, because damn it all, the girl was beautiful. "Am I?" he asked. "You seem to hold all the power."

She sighed. "I don't want to hold all the power."

He shifted his whole body so he could easily reach his hand out and stroke the fine lines of her jaw. "You do," he said softly. "Because I'm stupidly and completely into you. I think about you for about twenty-three of twenty-four hours. And when I get that one hour of sleep, I dream about you. I want to be with you. I want to sleep with you. I want to eat with you. I want to—"

"Shhh."

"And she shuts me up."

"Because it hurts, Braden." The words came out ragged, with her eyes just damp enough to slice right through him.

"Why?" He stroked her shoulder and eased her closer. "Why does it hurt to know how I feel about you?"

She shook her head, silent.

"What? Because it's temporary? I know that, but temporary doesn't make me feel any less or want you any—"

"He offered me a job in Chicago running special events for Family First."

"He...did?" His hand stopped moving on her as this news hit. Hard. This was much worse than if she liked the guy. He could win that battle. He could weather that storm. But...her dream job in a big city? "Wow."

"That's what I said." This time, she touched his face, lightly stroking one finger along the whiskers that had grown during his long shift. "Especially when he said he needs me on July first, no later."

July...*first*? "You're only here for another month?"

"I didn't say I took the job."

"Of course you're going to take it." He started to sit up as the reality exploded in him, but she grabbed his arm and kept him beside her.

"Braden."

"It's exactly what you want. Exactly. You don't even need my stupid scavenger hunt to build up your résumé. This guy spends one day with you, and he knows when he's struck gold. He sees...what I see."

"He sees a good employee," she said.

"Well, I see..." He rolled a little closer. "Heart and humor and...home."

"Oh." She curled into him, the two of them coming together in the most natural way, her body fitting into his. "Why do you say that?"

"I don't know," he admitted, cuddling her closer and putting his hand on her head so it rested on his shoulder. "Home is more than a place, obviously. It's a state of mind. It's comforting and easy and what you want at the end of a shift." He squeezed his eyes tighter with every word. This was like walking into an uncontrolled blaze without equipment or backup. "And yours is going to be in Chicago."

She splayed her palm on his bare chest, and pressed just enough that he was sure her handprint would be burned on his skin forever. "I thought you didn't want someone at the end of the shift. You said it scared you and kept you from getting serious with anyone. I thought you wanted...temporary."

He'd thought he wanted that, too. But right now? With her body against his after a long, brutal day, he wanted...

When he didn't answer, she lifted her face to look up at him.

"Right?" she asked. "Temporary."

He stared at her, lost in her eyes, thinking about something he couldn't quite put into words. "Right."

"Then this is good," she whispered, her words fluttering warm breath on his skin.

"Good?" In whose universe was this good?

"If I go, it makes our breakup so natural and…"

If.

He clung to two letters like they were a lifeline, but he already knew this line would break. "Cassie. You've already decided." And he'd just have to accept it, which he would, once he wasn't beat up and worn down.

"That's why I didn't come over after the party."

He turned his head to look at her, guiding her face up again so he could see into her eyes. "I don't follow."

"If I had come, my decision would have been made for me." She gave a soft laugh. "Ten more minutes on this bed next to my favorite shoulder in the world, and it might happen after all."

"What might happen?"

"Three guesses, Einstein."

He searched her eyes, so dark he could practically see his own face reflected back. "How would that affect your decision?"

She gave him her *you really are a moron* look. "Braden, if I…if we…" She shook her head with a laugh. "You know what will happen."

"Um…pleasure? Satisfaction? Extreme physical release? Mind-blowing gratification? Einstein's out of euphemisms, but if you want, I can get more detailed." He pulled her whole body closer and stroked her side and hip with his hand, his body tightening. "Or I could show you."

She sucked in a shaky breath, melting a little into him. "I won't leave."

"And the problem with that is...?"

"That I won't leave," she repeated.

"I'm off for three days." He dragged his hand over her waist and hip. "All we need is food, water, and—"

"Ever."

He stilled his hand, silent.

"I won't leave Bitter Bark. I won't leave you. I won't live my dreams or take that job or see beyond the horizon of the Blue Ridge Mountains."

None of that sounded...bad. Except those were the things she wanted, and he was acting like a selfish, love-sick jerk. "That would be bad." He tried to sound like he meant it, but knew from the look on her face that she knew he didn't.

"You're different, Braden," she said softly. "You're not like any other guy I've ever met. The few I've been intimate with never made me think beyond a couple of months. But you're *different*."

Different enough to put an actual ache in her voice.

"So are you," he said, bringing his hand back up to hold her face. "You make me want to take chances, Cass. You make me want to break my personal rules. You make me want to think about things I've never—"

"Stop." She put her fingers on his lips. "I get it. We both like each other a lot."

He nodded, holding her gaze.

"And I'm telling you, if I sleep with you, if I let you into that place in my heart and body, I'm not going to want to leave you."

Then don't leave me.

He swallowed the words and snuggled her closer, closing his eyes to inhale the scent of her. "So now what?"

She let out a long, low, miserable exhale. "Why don't you get some sleep?"

"I don't want you to…" *Leave.*

"I won't," she promised, proving that she could mind-read, or he was crappy at hiding his thoughts. "Take a nap. I have work to do and lists to make. I'll be here when you wake up."

But not…*in July.*

He squeezed his eyes shut, his lids burning like they always did after a long shift. He kept them closed, but didn't let go of her, holding her against his body, memorizing the curves of her hips and breasts, the garden scent of her hair, and the sound of her steady, soft breath.

Temporary.

Totally crappy word, but he'd take what he could get. And if that was falling asleep with Cassie in his arms, then he'd take it. *Temporary* beat *nothing.*

And nothing beat *this.*

Chapter Seventeen

Holy cow, this was big. This was...*big.*

Cassie dashed into the house and through the kitchen and tiny hall to Braden's bedroom, where she stopped at the door. There, she danced from one foot to the other, tapped her hands in a silent clap of barely contained exuberance, and checked the time. He'd been asleep for three hours. Was that enough? Wouldn't he want to know this?

"Braden," she whispered as she tiptoed into the room she'd dimmed by closing the blinds when he'd crashed.

He was flat on his stomach, arms outstretched to either side, one cheek pressed into the pillow, lids sealed. The comforter she'd covered him with had moved all the way down, exposing the muscles— many big, beautiful muscles—in his back as it rose and fell with each steady breath.

"Braden!" She ditched the whisper, but tried not to scare him and make him jump and growl like her brothers did when she woke them. "Wake up."

Nothing, not a flutter.

She sat on the bed and gingerly put one hand on his

back, grazing the skin with her fingertips. God, he was hard and smooth and nice to touch. Also, dead asleep.

"Aren't you a firefighter?" She leaned a little closer to his ear. "Don't you sleep lightly?"

He took in a huge breath and flipped his head with a grunt, then slipped back into slumber.

She braved her way closer, getting her mouth to his ear. "Braden, I have something very exciting to tell you."

"Mmm." The response was half moan, half growl and came from somewhere deep in his chest. He lifted his hand and crooked his arm around her neck, pulling her down with another groan.

She went, sliding next to him. "I have big news." She sang the announcement. "You want this."

"What I want is..." He pulled her into him and kissed her, rolling onto his side to get more of her. "This."

Heat wended through her as their bodies lined up, and she could feel every muscle in his body. "Oooh." She couldn't resist rocking against his hips. "Someone's having a nice dream."

"Not a dream, Cass," he murmured into the kiss, sliding his hands over her. "Don't leave me, baby."

Now...or ever?

She pushed the question away and gave in to a few seconds of sweet pleasure as he explored her body, and she felt every cell liquefy and surrender.

Without opening his eyes, he started to guide her under him, sliding over her to press all of him against her, sending fire right through her body and erasing everything she might have been thinking when she came in here.

His hands caressed, his hips rocked, and her legs just seemed to relax under his.

One peek at his face, and she realized it was entirely possible he was still asleep. Which was not what she wanted.

"Jelly Bean could tell the difference between pepper and vinegar."

He stopped moving.

"I tried it three different times. I set up a whole testing field in the back and used things he wouldn't want to eat but that have distinct smells."

He stopped breathing.

"And three times he was able to tell the difference, because I rewarded him for vinegar but not for cayenne pepper and…"

Finally, his head lifted, and he looked down at her with warm, sexy, but very much alert eyes. "Did you record it?"

"Every minute."

He pushed farther away, making her momentarily doubt the wisdom of her timing, but the look on his face was worth the sacrifice of a seriously nice make-out session.

"You did that?"

"Come on." She gave him a gentle nudge and got a look that hovered between reluctance and fascination. "I'll show you." She added some pressure, and he gave up the fight, letting her roll off the bed and following her out the door to the kitchen. "There's my field test."

"Those pots?"

All along the grass, she'd placed terra-cotta pots upside down. "I found them in your garage," she said. "I hope you don't mind."

He looked down at her, fully and completely awake now. "Mind? I think I just fell a little harder for you, if that's possible."

She laughed lightly, but only to cover up what the words did to her on the inside.

"Come on. Let Jelly Bean show you, and we'll go for round four."

Outside, JB lay sprawled on the grass, soaking up the sun after all that work. He barely lifted his head when Braden came out, and he certainly didn't growl at Cassie. Not after all those peanut butter rewards.

"You need to go inside, bud."

He rolled on his back and looked up at her.

"In the house," Braden said, snapping his fingers and pointing.

"Don't look," she called after him, then smiled up at Braden. "He knows what that means."

"English is his superpower." Braden took a few steps closer to the pots.

"So is playing hide-and-seek." She gestured toward the picnic table under an awning where she'd set up all her materials, including a notebook with *Jelly Bean Training* written at the top of the page.

There, she sprinkled red pepper on a plate, then soaked two paper towels in vinegar and handed one to him. "Go pick two random pots and hide each of these under a different one. I'll go get Sniffy."

Braden hesitated only long enough to shoot her a smile. "My woman of action."

"And your dog of wonder. Go." She flicked her hand toward the pot. "Before he outsmarts us both."

She backed into the kitchen to see which pots he used, then found Jelly Bean waiting patiently by his food. First, she scooped some peanut butter onto a spoon, gave him a lick, then waved the vinegar towel in front of him, then gave him more peanut butter.

"You ready?" she called to Braden.

"Yep."

"Brace yourself." She pulled her phone out of her pocket to record the moment and followed Jelly Bean, who trotted out to the grass. "Find the vinegar, Jelly Bean," she called.

He walked by the pots, slowing at the one with cayenne pepper, which she'd let him taste only once, then continuing to the second from the last, lifting a paw, and slapping it on the pot victoriously.

"Yay, Jelly Bean!" Cassie called, hustling closer to crouch down and reward him with the spoon of peanut butter.

"Cassie!" Braden choked her name in disbelief.

"I told you." She beamed up at him. "This dog knows the difference between vinegar and pepper. If he can't work in the fire department, we could always give him a job at Santorini's."

"It *was* temporary," he said, reaching down to bring her up for a hug. "His inability to discern smells must have just been a cold or something. It was temporary."

"See? Some temporary things can be good."

He seemed at a loss for words, just scanning her face with his deep-blue eyes as if trying to guess where to best plant a kiss. The mouth won, and the next thing Cassie knew, she was folded in strong arms, smothered with sweet lips, and high on life and her doggy training victory.

"We have to tell my uncle," he said, breaking the

kiss as if the thought had just hit him. "We might not have to take the ten-thousand-dollar training course. Maybe he'll pass the program at Waterford, and Uncle Daniel will sign the affidavit."

She inched out of his arms. "Let me text my mom and find out if he's at Waterford. We'll go now."

"Now?"

"Of course. Let's take Jelly Bean and my recorded proof, and you can make the case."

As she started to text, he took her hand and lowered the phone.

"You don't want to go now?" she asked. "What if Jelly Bean loses his scent sense again?"

"No, that's not..." He shook his head. "I just don't even believe you."

"You want to see all three recordings showing that he did it every single time?"

"I don't even believe you...exist." His voice softened, and she finally understood what he was saying.

"Oh..." She smiled. "Here I am, sticking my nose into your dog issues and trying to fix them. That's what I do."

He let out a sigh and hugged her closer. "Thank you," he said softly. "For everything."

"Even the tease on the bed?"

"We're not done there, but...this boy..." He threw a proud grin at Jelly Bean. "Text your mom. I can't wait to see if my uncle will retest him."

Not ten minutes later, they were on their way to Waterford Farm in his truck.

"What's the name of that movie?" Braden asked as they pulled out. "*While You Were Sleeping*?"

She laughed. "While you were sleeping, I read one of those scent-detection sites and started taking notes. Then I couldn't help it. I had to try and set up a test field, especially once I found vinegar in your cleaning supplies, since that's what they recommend testing with. You know, I started with some peanut butter just to totally butter him up, pun intended. Then he seemed so responsive, I tried food in one closed fist and soap in the other. Then I just buzzed."

He gave her a side-eye. "You buzzed?"

"That's how I feel when I just have to get something done. I can't be stopped."

"You're a powerhouse, Cass. No wonder this guy wants to hire you."

Oh, Jace. Family First. Leaving Bitter Bark. "All that work with Jelly Bean made me forget," she said.

"Not me," he admitted. "Although getting a job offer is a little better than what I was worried you were doing with him."

"Yeah, no need to be jealous."

Curling his lip, he turned into the massive entrance of Waterford Farm. "How could I not be? Big Greek dude was all over you in your shiny pink dress."

"Oh, you noticed my dress?"

"Waited all night to take it off you."

She closed her eyes at the reminder of how difficult it had been to stay home and in her own bed that night. "How did it go with Simone, by the way? I forgot to ask."

"I forgot to care." He grunted. "She wants me back."

"What?" She shot forward. "Way to bury the lead."

"There's no lead," he said. "I'm not interested."

"What did she say?"

"Just that she…" His voice faded away. He was obviously uncomfortable with the subject. "Doesn't matter, Cass." He turned into the long drive, the yellow house and sprawling canine center coming into view. "I'm not on the market."

But if Cassie moved to Chicago, he would be.

"Well, it pains me to admit it, but you guys made a really nice couple," she said.

He grinned at her. "Couple of what?"

Her heart stuttered for a moment. Right then, with his sweet smile and good heart and silly pun…he was more like her father than any Greek man she'd ever met. She managed a laugh, but nothing about that thought was funny. It was scary and intriguing and gave her doubts about…everything.

"There are a lot of dogs in the pen," Braden said, jutting his chin in that direction. "That's more than a typical training day."

She followed his gaze, but it landed on a big old black Buick that would never look like it belonged here. "Yiayia's here," she said. "What is she doing at Waterford on a Monday morning?"

"I don't know, but my mom's here, too." He gestured to a compact car. "And by the looks of that obstacle course, dogs are getting ready for a show. Isn't that this coming weekend?"

"Oh, yes, the Waterford Farm Dog Show is Friday, and the Family Fur Bake-Off for Ella's fundraiser is Saturday." But her attention was on that Buick. "I'm going inside to say hi to my grandmother for a sec while you find Daniel. Can I meet you over there? Here, take my phone. I'll unlock it so you can show him the video."

"Okay."

She tapped the screen, then handed him her phone. When she turned to open the door, he put his hand on her arm and drew her back. "Hey. Wait one second, please."

She looked at him. "Yeah?"

"Kiss for luck?"

"Is that what the Irish do?"

He drew her closer, slid his hand under her hair, and angled her face, studying her for a long moment. "It's what this guy, who is crazy about you, is about to do. You good with that?"

"I'm…getting good with it." Which made things messy. She covered with a joke. "Never sure how Jelly Bean will respond, though."

"Let's find out." He eased her closer and kissed her, just so very gentle at first, as if he wasn't sure what might happen next. When it was quiet in the back seat, he added pressure, deepened the kiss, and Cassie leaned into him to go along for the ride.

He tasted like toothpaste and sunshine and the sexiest man she'd ever kissed. Heat crawled up her skin, making her cling to his impossibly perfect shoulder and slide her hands up into his hair.

With a soft moan, she shifted her head to the other side, let their tongues play and time stand still. At that moment, there was just this warm, inviting kiss in a truck on a dog farm with a guy who made her feel so good. The rest of the world—big cities and their big decisions—was a million miles away. And she didn't want to be anywhere else on earth. For now, at least.

They separated, neither one of them rushing to

open their eyes. And the truck was dead silent but for their soft sighs.

"Well, what do you know?" she whispered.

"Jelly Bean passed another test."

"Way to go, Junior Einstein." She glanced in the back to find the dog watching them, but quiet. "Now, go sniff like you've never sniffed before."

Chapter Eighteen

"It looks like Westminster over here," Braden said as he greeted his cousin Shane, who'd just stepped out of the training pen to grab a water.

"Hey, Braden." Shane gave him a sweaty high five and reached down to greet Jelly Bean. "Please tell me he's entering this dog show. You know he'd win."

"He's not a show dog."

Shane snorted and thumbed in the direction of the pen. "Are any of them? You know how my dad is about 'show dogs.' You do realize that the main event is Wiggliest Butt or Best Kisser, right? But none of them follows commands like this genius."

But this genius was going to be a scent-detection dog.

Braden eyed the "obstacle course," which he could see now was pretty downgraded from a real dog show. A kiddie pool, a few ramps, and his cousin Darcy was in the middle of it, waving a hula-hoop at Braden. "Hey, Bray!"

He waved back and turned to Shane. "I actually brought Jelly Bean in for a little test today. Is your dad around?"

"He's down in the K-9 pen with Liam doing bite work." He crouched down in Jelly Bean's face. "How's the old sniffer, JB?"

"I think it's working again," Braden said. "That's why I'm here."

"Really? That'd be awesome." His attention was pulled away to the pen. "Hey. Hey! Ruff! Do not eat the swimming pool! None of that!" He gulped the rest of the water, tossed the empty in a bin, and held his hand up. "You really should enter Jelly Bean. He'd show them all what's what."

He took off, and Braden watched for a second, trying to imagine his dog jumping into a kiddie pool, running around two cones, then diving through a hula-hoop. He could do it, of course, with about two rounds of practice. But Jelly Bean was an arson investigator, not some trained circus act.

"Come on, boy," he said, guiding him into the kennels. "Let's go where the grown-up working dogs are."

Braden made his way around the back of the kennels and down a slope to where another large pen was in use. Here, two German shepherds were deep into training with Liam and two men, no doubt some of the many law enforcement personnel from all over the East Coast who trained here. They all wore padded bite suits and helmets, the dogs and men panting in the heat.

His uncle was leaning against the fence, talking to Braden's mom. Not far away, Uncle Daniel's Irish setter, Rusty, snoozed under a nearby tree, and the red golden, Goldie, paced back and forth in front of her sleeping charge.

"Hey, Uncle Daniel. Mom."

They turned, and both flashed surprised smiles.

"Oh, hi, honey." His mom came closer with her arms outstretched. "This is a nice surprise. We were just talking about you."

"What are you doing over here?" he asked after giving her a hug.

"Gramma Finnie and Yiayia are using the kitchen for a project and needed some input from me, so I stopped by to chat with my brother."

Uncle Daniel greeted him with the usual hug, and Jelly Bean barged into the mix to get closer to the veterinarian every animal in the state loved. Of course, that got Goldie and Rusty to shake off and come over, too.

After the hellos, Braden got right to the point. "I think Jelly Bean is discerning scents again."

"He is?" Uncle Daniel's eyes popped in surprise.

"I have it recorded here on Cassie's phone."

"You smellin' right again, boyo?" Daniel got down in JB's face, giving him a good rub and a close inspection. "That's great news."

"So maybe it was just a cold or temporary thing," Mom said.

Daniel looked up, squinting his blue eyes against the sun. "Are you sure he was able to discern and not just smell?"

"Here's the proof." Braden pulled Cassie's phone out of his pocket and tapped the screen, going to the photos app to find the videos she'd shown him before they left the house. "Take a look."

He did, watching the first three videos, then nodding enthusiastically. "This is very promising,

Braden. Come on, let's check him into a kennel. Can I keep him a few days?"

A few days? "It'll take that long?"

"To do it right and make sure the change is lasting. Plus, we're swamped with the fundraising dog show." Daniel gestured for him to follow, and they all headed back to the kennels at an easy pace, and on the way, Braden told them both everything that had happened that morning and how Cassie had successfully tested him.

"Speaking of fundraising, how's the scavenger hunt going?" his mother asked.

"Well, we don't have nearly ten thousand dollars' worth of entries yet, but Cassie says it's early. Plus…" He gave a hopeful look to his uncle. "You sign that affidavit, and we can donate whatever we earn to something else. Maybe that new rescue transport business you said Marie's niece wants to start."

"Are you trying to bribe me?" Daniel asked with a laugh.

"I know better."

Back in the kennels, Jelly Bean barked a few times, circling and sniffing the place where he'd spent so much time.

"He's happy to be back here," Braden noted.

"That's good. We're up to our eyeballs, so I'm going to have to put him in a kennel with another dog, if that's okay. It'll only be for…" He stopped and frowned as if an idea occurred. "Unless you'd do me a huge return favor."

"Of course," he replied. "Anything you need."

"Would you take this little lady home for a few days?" As soon as he paused at the corner, Braden knew which "little lady" he meant.

"Jasmine?" he guessed.

Daniel put a hand on Braden's back and led him the few steps to where the gorgeous black Lab stood staring out at them with her haunting blue eyes.

"I'm pretty sure she was the one who got the big auction bid, not Connor."

Braden gave a soft laugh. "Safe bet."

"And she has the nose of a bloodhound. In fact, we've had a few offers to adopt her out, and I just can't do it."

Braden frowned in question. "Why not?"

"Jazz isn't a family dog," Daniel said. "Well, she could be, but this girl is not happy unless she's on some kind of project or mission. She could be a service dog, but her scenting skill set is so exquisite, I—"

"I get the point," Braden assured him, trying not to let any irritation into his voice. "I still think you should hook her up with the ATF or one of the big training sites looking for candidates for ADC training."

Daniel sighed, not answering, because he didn't have to.

"You're saving her in case I change my mind," Braden guessed.

"I'm only asking you to board her for the week," Daniel said.

"In hopes that I fall madly in love with her and start her ADC training next week?" Braden smiled and threw his mother a sideways glance. "He's *still* the Dogfather, pulling strings to get his way."

Daniel shook his head. "Braden, you know how I feel. I want you to have your dream of being an arson dog handler, with the right partner. And, anyway, don't you and Cassie need a dog for the scavenger hunt setup? Jazz will be perfect for that."

"I have a feeling Jazz will be perfect, period." Braden gave a wry smile.

"Thanks. I'm going to head back to bite training. Liam and I will start Jelly Bean later this afternoon, and we'll keep you posted." He flipped a leash off the wall and opened Jasmine's kennel. "Remember to give her a job, if you can. She needs a mission."

"I will," he promised, clipping the leash on as his mother came closer.

"I'll walk back to the house with you, Braden," she said.

As they passed the training pen, Shane did a double take. "In with one and out with another?"

"Looks that way." Braden glanced down at the dog who seemed so unfamiliar next to him. Different color, different gait, different soul.

"You're handling this well," his mother said, walking on his other side.

"I'm really optimistic about Jelly Bean," he told her. "And taking in a dog when Waterford is this crowded is the least I can do after all Uncle Daniel and Liam have done for Jelly Bean."

"That's good," she said, inspecting him with that all-knowing Mom look. "You look like you had a long shift."

"Brutal," he said. "I slept a few hours this morning, though."

She nodded and put her hand on his shoulder. "Are you doing okay, honey?"

"I am," he assured her. "Better now that Jelly Bean can smell."

"And...Cassie?"

He threw her a sideways smile. "Cassie can smell, too."

She laughed. "You know what I mean. I don't like to meddle, but...the whole family's pretty excited about this union."

"Then they should get unexcited, Mom. It's temporary with a capital T."

That slowed her step. "Why? How do you know that?"

Cassie's job offer wasn't his news to share, so he just shrugged. "We've agreed on that."

"That's sort of...odd."

That was one way of putting it. "Neither one of us is looking for anything serious."

"But you seem so happy."

The words stabbed. "Yeah, I know. I am," he admitted. "But...you know me. My relationships never last."

"No, they never last with Connor. With you..." She stopped walking and studied him. "You get scared and sabotage the relationship."

Did he? Was that his MO? "Scared of what?"

"History," she said softly, then squeezed his arm. "While that makes sense, it's not a smart way to live." For a long time, she looked at him, taking a moment to choose her words, just like her brother frequently did. "Honey, at the risk of spouting off something my mother would embroider on a pillow, you do know that there's truth in the saying 'it's better to have loved and lost than never to have loved at all,' don't you?"

He blew out a slow breath. "Not for the person left behind, Mom."

"Oh, I beg to differ." She narrowed her eyes and straightened her frame, the inner strength that was so much like Gramma Finnie's shooting out of every pore. But she stayed silent for a long time. Talking about things like this was damn near impossible for Colleen Mahoney.

But Braden really needed help from his mother right now. "Can you elaborate?" he asked.

Her eyes shuttered a bit with a slow sigh as she obviously dug for whatever strength she needed to open up. "Braden," she said softly. "I wouldn't give up a thing in my life, not one year with your father and not one minute of the time we had, even if it meant saving myself from the grief of losing him."

He understood that, he really did, and every day he inched closer to letting go of that old hang-up. But his fears weren't the only thing between them. "The choice might not be mine to make, Mom. Don't tell anyone yet, but Cassie might be leaving Bitter Bark for good. She has a job offer in Chicago."

Her eyes flashed in surprise. "I had no idea."

"She hasn't even told her family yet, but I'm going to have to live with whatever she decides."

Her brow furrowed, then her head tilted. "They have fires in Chicago, you know."

Leave Bitter Bark? "How would you feel if I did that?"

She reached a hand up and patted his cheek like he was six, and her hand still comforted him. "I just want you to be happy."

Would moving away from his family, friends, home, and job make him happy? Even if Cassie were right next to him? "It would depend…"

"On how real this relationship is," his mother finished. "Oh, I see Katie pulling in." She gestured toward the driveway.

"Please, not a word about Cassie's decision. She doesn't have the offer yet."

She zipped her lips and locked a pretend key. "Promise."

When she headed off, he stood for a long moment in the sunshine with his new dog. His *temporary* new dog. That *could* become permanent, if he just said the word. But that would mean giving up—

The phone in his pocket buzzed. Out of habit, he pulled it out, only to realize when he looked at it that it wasn't his phone. He'd left that in the truck when he took Cassie's. A text message flashed on the screen from Jace Demakos.

Taking off for the Windy City in 10 min. Be back in BB by Friday—offer in hand. Hope to make it easy for you.

He curled his lip at the screen. "Hope to make it impossible for you, Zorba."

But even as he said it, he knew he might fail. Just like Jelly Bean might fail his scent test.

As he lingered, Jazz looked up at him with a question in her blue eyes.

"I don't know, girl," he murmured. "Maybe the solution to my problems is something I never imagined. Kind of like you."

She stared back, her expression blank.

Of course, because only one dog really understood English.

🐾

Cassie paused at the screen door, her step slowed by the sound of Yiayia's guffaw floating out from the kitchen.

Had she ever in her entire life heard her grandmother laugh from the belly like that? Was it possible she *had* changed?

Yes. She had changed. But Cassie still didn't know why or how long it would last. Real change would be permanent. Real change would be for a good reason. Real change would be—

"But, Agnes, did you see that kiss? I tell you, lass, that wasn't the kiss of friends in that truck."

Oh, so now Yiayia had Gramma Finnie spying on her?

"Oh, no. They were definitely kissing like lovers. Do you think—"

Cassie's jaw dropped, and Gramma tsked noisily. "As long as they're happy, right? Isn't that what we agreed, Agnes? You're only as happy as your least happy grandchild, I say." She laughed. "Well, someone I loved very much used to say that. But it's true."

Not for Yiayia. Cassie inched closer, waiting for Yiayia's retort. *Who cares if they're happy as long as I am?*

"And with the right person," Yiayia said.

Ah. Of course. The arrival of Jace Demakos changed everything. Deep inside, Yiayia, no matter her motivation, would never go against the possibility of another Greek in the family. At least that hadn't changed.

"Who could be better?" Gramma Finnie countered.

And Yiayia was dead silent, the only sound from the kitchen a spoon scraping against a bowl.

For some reason, Cassie breathed a sigh of relief. Not that she wanted Old Yiayia back, but at least all was right with the universe if this new version of her grandmother turned out to be a fake.

Still, a relationship with Braden hadn't brought out the real Yiayia like Cassie had thought it would. Got Cassie all confused, hot and bothered, and tempting fate with ten-minute kisses, but Yiayia remained steadfastly...*nice*.

"I think they are wonderful together," her grandmother finally answered, the words ground out in that high singsong that Cassie had learned to recognize over the past weeks as Fake Yiayia.

"And we have lots of weddings coming up," Gramma Finnie cooed. "If this month of working on the scavenger hunt together does what we hope, then she'll catch one of those bouquets for sure. Maybe all of them!"

No surprise, Yiayia was quiet. Then suddenly, she gasped, "Oh, Finn, stop! You can't roll the dough that way! It looks like a worm, not a cookie. Here, here, let me do it."

Cassie bit her lip against a smile. Score one for Old Yiayia.

"It's for a dog, Agnes," Gramma Finnie shot back with laughter, not shame, in her voice. "And my goodness, sometimes I see where Cassie gets her cutting wit and that need to control everything so it's done the way she wants it."

Cassie blinked. *Yiayia slips into her old self, and that reminds Gramma Finnie of me?*

Yiayia forced a laugh. "I apologize," she said, sounding freakishly sincere. "You get right back here

245

and roll, dear. Sometimes I just fall into old habits. And if Cassie is like me? Well, someday she'll grow out of it. Hopefully, before it's too late."

What the heck did that mean?

She wasn't sure, but she had to find out. She had to do something to make her grandmother come clean, even if that made Cassie...control everything so it's done her way. Was she really like Yiayia?

She tamped down that thought for later examination. Now, she knew exactly what would show Yiayia's true colors and force her to be honest.

Clearing her throat, she reached for the door and called, "Do I hear grandmothers baking? This sounds like fun."

"Oh, Cassie!"

"There's our sweet lass! We were just talking about you."

Both of them came at her instantly, one on each side—a blue-eyed sparkle of joy and a dark-eyed look of distrust, which softened when Yiayia smiled. On their heels came one fat doxie and one wiggly one, all demanding a greeting.

"We are bakin', lass," Gramma assured her with a kiss.

"Why here and not at home?"

"Oh, that oven is a piece of ancient cra...broken," Yiayia said. "And we have a large group of taste testers. If we relied on Pyggie and Gala, Pyggie would gain five more pounds."

Cassie drew back, a little confused. "What exactly are you baking?"

"We're entering the Family Fur Bake-Off with our own recipe called Dogmother Delights," Yiayia said.

"Dogmother Delights?"

"Finn's working on a tag line for us," Yiayia added. "Because she didn't like 'When bland Irish meets tasty Greek.'"

Both of them threw back their heads and howled like a couple of college girls with an inside joke. And as much as Cassie wanted to join in, all she could do was marvel at this unexpected friendship.

"Oh, I got one," Finnie said, poking Yiayia's arm. "How about 'You're only as happy as your least happy dog!'"

Yiayia clapped and held her hand up for a high five. "Good one, Finn!"

Cassie looked from one to the other, still stunned.

"And maybe," Gramma Finnie added in a whisper, like the walls had ears, "since Agnes hit it off so well with that nice Greek man from Family First? Maybe we'll win the grand prize and be rich and famous!"

"Oh, yes, you liked Jace, didn't you, Yiayia?" Cassie asked.

Her grandmother gave a tight smile, like she had to work to contain it. "He was nice. How was the event on Saturday evening? We were surprised not to see you here for Sunday dinner, Cassandra."

Because she'd holed up in her apartment and tried to figure out what to do with Jace's job offer, and knew she couldn't have kept it to herself if she'd spent the day here. "Oh, I was tired."

"So it was a big night out?" Yiayia prodded.

Cassie sighed and took her hand. "Gramma Finnie, can I steal Yiayia for a minute? I have to talk to her about something." This was the person to tell, she decided. Plus, once she knew about Jace's offer, she might come clean about why she'd changed.

"Of course, lass. I'll be right here rollin' up my worms." Gramma Finnie waved her hand to send them both out. "And comin' up with clever tag lines."

Yiayia giggled again and then followed Cassie to the wide side porch to sit on two rattan chairs.

"Yiayia, I have to tell you—"

"No." Yiayia held her hand up, the single syllable as sharp as any she'd ever spoken.

"You don't even know what I'm going to say."

"You're going to stick your little face in mine and demand to know what's going on, what's wrong with me, and how you can change it."

Cassie blinked, stunned by the accusation, Gramma Finnie's words echoing in her ears. "Do I really try to change everything?"

"You like the world to bend to your will, Cassie," she said, adding a wry smile.

"Just like you."

"Just like I *used* to." She smiled and patted Cassie's hand. "Now what did you want from me?" She leaned closer to whisper, "I need to hurry back in because between you, me, and the lamppost? That woman cannot bake or cook to save her life. How do you get to be near ninety and not know how to make a puff pastry?"

Cassie searched her face. "Almost. That's *almost* you."

She sighed and looked annoyed—maybe more with herself than Cassie. "Please let me change, Cassie. Don't constantly stand in my way."

There was no answer to that because...she was

absolutely right. Cassie was standing in her way. And that was wrong.

"Now, what do you need, Cassie?"

She'd brought her out here to tell her about Jace's job offer and see how fast she dropped her push for Braden. But now? She wasn't so sure what she wanted from her grandmother. Maybe… "Advice."

Yiayia drew back. "That's a first."

"I don't want to talk to my mother, so please keep what I'm about to tell you a secret."

She gasped. "You're pregnant!"

"Stop!" Cassie flicked her hand lightly against Yiayia's arm.

"A great-grandmother can hope, you know."

"You'd really be happy if I was that serious with Braden? Even…after meeting Jace?"

Her dark eyes flashed. "Jace isn't for you."

She felt her jaw slip. "You don't think…because he's Greek…you don't want us…"

"Oh heavens, *koukla*. We've got him lined up for Ella."

Ella? She almost couldn't respond. "She gags at the sight of him, Yiayia. She can't stand him. She doesn't even want to talk to him."

"Finnie says that's called 'frenemies,' and it makes for a great love story."

Cassie dropped her face in her hands, not knowing whether to laugh or cry.

"Well, she knows these things because she's a blogger. Also, young Prudence is just a fountain of knowledge and words like that. I enjoy that girl. We're thinking of making her an honorary Dogmother."

"Jace lives in Chicago, Yiayia. Surely Gramma Finnie doesn't want Ella to move there? Her business is here, one she shares with her mother. Her family is here. Her brothers would be wrecked if their little Smella moved..." Her voice faded as she realized what she was saying.

"We'll figure out a way to lure him here," she said, utterly confident.

"And if they continue to dislike each other?"

"Dislike?" She gave a soft hoot. "You didn't see how many times they sneaked peeks at one another during that bachelor auction, then. Of course you didn't. You were too wrapped up in that man right there." Yiayia pointed to Braden, who was leaving the kennels with a large black dog on a leash, talking to his mother. "Oh, and speaking of our fine lad."

"Lad? Hello, you're *Greek,* Agnes Mastros Santorini. Did you forget that, too?"

She just laughed. "That's just more of Finnie rubbing off on me." Her eyes danced with something that could only be called joy. "And you know, that gives me so much hope."

"Hope?" Cassie choked on the word. "As if that word is in your vocabulary."

Her whole face fell as if Cassie had slapped her.

"I'm sorry, Yiayia," she said, reaching for her, shame warming her face. "That was awful of me to say."

"No, no." She gave Cassie's hand a squeeze. "We can have sharp tongues, you and me. I might have even been the one who taught you that, but, of course, yours is usually tempered with humor. And you know..." She stroked Cassie's hand in a way that was much more Finnie than Agnes. "There's nothing wrong with cutting wit as long as you don't slice someone you love."

Slowly, with disbelief and confusion, Cassie inched back. "That sounds like something Gramma Finnie would say."

"Nah." The other woman gave a smug smile. "That was straight-up Agnes Mastros Santorini." She looked up at the sky as if trying to deliver that news to someone far above them. "What do you think?"

"I think..." Cassie sighed. "I was wrong. You've changed. And I'm...impressed."

Yiayia beamed, her dark eyes welling up. "Thank you, Cassandra." After a second, she patted Cassie's hand. "Now what is this advice you're seeking?"

"Never mind," Cassie said, pushing up, not wanting to force Yiayia to make some kind of decision between Jace and Braden. Her true colors had come out and, honestly? They were not ugly at all. Just the opposite. "It's not important."

Chapter Nineteen

"And…she finds it." Braden shook his head, a mix of amazement and frustration in his voice as he and Cassie followed Jazz to the farthest, darkest, most out of the way back corner of the basement of Bitter Bark Books. There, he stood silently in front of the shelf where Cassie had hidden the scented towel on this, the fourth stop they'd devised for the scavenger hunt that afternoon.

And every time, Jazz had sniffed out the clue with ease.

"You don't sound happy about that," she mused as she backed up and looked at the books, trying to figure out what the challenge should be for the hunters who got to this spot.

"She's a pro, is all." He gave the dog a quick rub on the head, nothing like the affection he showered on Jelly Bean.

Turning to the books, Cassie pulled out a gold-embossed copy of *The Canterbury Tales*. "I bet you've read this."

He glanced at the title. "Not a huge Chaucer fan."

She smiled and looked for inspiration from the

next book, but her real attention was on Braden and his poorly masked jealousy. "And not a huge Jasmine fan, either."

"She's a great dog," he insisted. "I mean, she could smell her way out of a black hole."

"And you hate that."

He gave a guilty laugh. "Jelly Bean couldn't do this once, Cassie. How many times in the last two weeks have we tried a test scavenger hunt—"

She spun around. "He did it this morning," she insisted. "Give him a chance."

"Yeah, I know." He gave Jazz another pet, a little more enthusiastic this time. "It's not your fault you're smart and talented, Jazzer. And even know to stand at attention when you reach a target, like a good scent-detection dog."

"There's more to this scavenger hunt than the dog, though," Cassie said, scanning the rows of books. "We're in classic literature, so I need to give them a riddle, have them take a picture of the book that solves the riddle, then leave a clue for the next destination." She grazed the spines and snagged one. "*A Tale of Two Cities*?"

"Great book," he said enthusiastically. "A masterpiece."

She turned, as amazed by him as he was by Jasmine. "Did you read it in college?"

"I read it on Easter Sunday when I was nine years old," he said without hesitation.

"You read this? When you were nine? Einstein!"

He laughed. "Not that edition," he admitted. "My dad put a kids' version of it in my Easter basket."

"Which would have caused mutiny in my house on Easter. You were a strange child."

"He always gave me books," he said, his gaze a little distant as he slipped into the memory. "Like your dad taught you to put things in writing? My dad was all about reading. Thought it made a well-rounded man."

"He was probably right."

Braden reached for the book spine. "I remember that year because I was sick with a fever, and everyone was going over to Waterford Farm for a big Easter celebration. My dad stayed home with me, and we read it together. It turned out to be the best Easter, even though I was sick."

"Banished from Easter dinner? The very idea brings this Greek to tears." She took a step closer, eyeing him. "But I love that image of you and your father reading Charles Dickens."

"'It was the best of times, it was the worst of times,'" he quoted, sliding into a sad smile. "And that was the best. I remember him closing the book that day and handing it to me, telling me to keep it on the condition that one day I would read it to my own son or daughter. He made me promise."

She looked up at him, a strange pressure on her chest she recognized as the longing she'd felt for her father since he died. "And you promised?"

"Oh yeah. I have it on a bookshelf at home."

She let that sink in, and felt her heart slip a little at the thought of him carting a children's book around for almost twenty-five years to keep a promise to his father. "So what would he think of your decision to not ever get married and have kids to read to?"

"I..." He gave a dry laugh. "I wouldn't have made that decision if he were still around," he reminded her. "But I can tell you this. When he died, books were the only thing that kept me from curling up on my bed and crying nonstop. I read a hundred that summer, as Gramma Finnie likes to brag. The Bitter Bark librarians felt so sorry for me they let me take out ten a week. And a lot of times, when I had nothing to read, I read that kids' version of *A Tale of Two Cities* again and again."

She tried to imagine that boy, barely a teenager, burying himself in books because his father was gone.

"That's all I did that summer. Read and...grieve."

She slid her arms around him, washed with affection and charmed by this big, bright, incredibly sweet man. "You're so much more than great shoulders, Braden Mahoney."

He smiled, the sadness disappearing from his eyes. "We have a lot more stops to create on this scavenger hunt and only have Genius Dog for a few days. Better stay focused."

"I am focused," she whispered, pressing into him. "On you."

"Yeah?" His brow flickered with interest. "I should bring you to the classic stacks more often, then." He turned her around to face the books, keeping their bodies in total head-to-toe contact, sliding her hand across the row to another book. "Here. Go with *War and Peace* for the scavenger hunt."

"Why?"

"It's the ultimate classic."

"I won't tell Yiayia you didn't say *Odyssey*."

"Overrated and overwritten."

She laughed. "Okay, then help me figure out a riddle that will lead people to *War and Peace*, but not too easily. Tell me something about it."

He thought for a minute, planting a kiss on her shoulder, then straightening. "Well, the main themes are spirituality and love, and family, of course, since it's kind of a warm, loving family and one that's cold and calculating. So it's about navigating a place in the world and society..." His words trailed off as she turned in his arms to look up at him. "What?" he asked at her bemused expression.

"You know, sometimes I forget that this..." She tapped his temple. "Is almost as sexy as this." And placed her hand on his shoulder. "And maybe we could just go with who wrote it, what year, and where the author is from."

He snuggled her closer. "Leo." Then lowered his face to brush her lips. "Tolstoy." Added some pressure. "Eighteen..." Slipped his tongue over hers. "Sixty-five." And wrapped his other arm around her and pulled her all the way into him. "Russia."

She dissolved into the warm, slow kiss, wrapping both arms around his neck to return all the affection. She breathed him in, dizzy for a moment as every sense overloaded with Braden.

"What else do you want to know?" He feathered some kisses on her jaw and ran his hands up and down the length of her back.

"Everything."

Taking a step, he eased her against the bookshelf, kissing her again and sliding his hand under her T-shirt, making her suck in a breath at the heat of his palm on her skin. "Like a full book report?"

She managed a laugh, but lost it to the next kiss, this one a little more frantic as heat and need ribboned through her. He leaned against her, the wood of the shelves jabbing her back and the whole of his body searing her front.

"Cassie." His hand coasted up her stomach, his thumb grazing under her bra. "We should go home. Now."

"Mmm. So far away."

He broke the kiss, glancing left to right around the deserted, dusty bookshelves. Disinterested in their kissing, Jazz had assumed an off-duty snooze a few feet away where sun came through a window about six feet off the ground.

"It *is* a fantasy of mine," he admitted with a smile. "Sex in the stacks."

"Nerd." She got up on her tiptoes and kissed his mouth, tracing it with her fingers, then kissing it again. "But damn, Einstein. Who knew that could be so…hot?"

"I did." He slid his hand over her breast, his smoky gaze as intimate as his touch. "But do we really want our first time to be in the basement of Bitter Bark Books?"

Right about then, she didn't care. "How 'bout foreplay?"

"We could play." He slipped one hand behind her, unhooked her bra, and lowered his head while he lifted her T-shirt.

All the blood in her body rushed to the place where his mouth came down, making her helpless and tense and suddenly desperate for release. And just as suddenly, his head shot up as if someone had punched him in the back. And Jazz barked once in the direction of the stairs.

"Someone's on the way down here." His voice was gruff as he reluctantly let go of her. "Let's head home."

"Yes. Home." Barely able to string words together, she reached behind her to reclip her bra, and he helped, sliding a look at Jasmine when he did.

"Of course she's also the perfect guard dog," he muttered.

She smoothed her T-shirt back into place and poked him in the chest with one finger. "Jelly Bean is awesome and probably right this minute acing a scent-discernment test."

Hooking his arm around her shoulders, he walked her to the steps, nodding to two older women who'd just reached the basement. At the top of the stairs, he stopped suddenly when his phone made a melodic ding she'd never heard before.

"Hang on." Pulling it out, he glanced at the screen for a split second, then murmured something she didn't get.

"What's wrong?"

"I have to get to the station. There's a warehouse fire out of control in Simon's Mill Run. They're calling in backup from multiple counties and asking anyone off duty to come in. Our engine's leaving in less than five minutes."

"Oh God, okay. Take your truck. I can walk home. I'll keep Jasmine."

He nodded, his whole face and body transformed as he mentally prepared to go. "Good. Thanks. I'll…" He was already moving away, but stopped and took a breath. "Wait for me at my house. I'll be home. I'll… be home."

She held his gaze and nodded. "I know you will, Braden. And I'll be waiting."

He closed his eyes as though grabbing hold of the words, then shot off, leaving Cassie in the middle of Bitter Bark Books with a dog.

Jasmine looked up at her with a question in eyes as blue as the ones she'd just gazed into. "Well, what do you know? Life with a firefighter. Want to keep working or…" She stepped outside and looked down the street, taking in the awnings, flower boxes, and warm brick buildings of Bitter Bark. In the distance, a siren screamed, tightening her gut just as her gaze landed on a dog bone hanging as a sign.

"Let's go get a treat at Bone Appetit," she said, tugging her leash in that direction.

Jazz seemed good with that plan, prancing down the street without even a sideways look at other dogs and people. As Cassie reached the entrance, she peeked in and saw Aunt Colleen behind the counter and Ella and Darcy playing with some puppies in the pen.

"Family and friends," she whispered to her canine companion, a little surprised by how much the sight of them gave her a sense of hope and relief. "That's something I wouldn't have in Chicago. Along with the possibility of sex in the stacks."

"Cassie!" Ella spotted her and rushed to the door, pulling it open. "Oh, and Jasmine! Come in here, you two." She practically pulled Cassie in and hugged her with a little bit more ferocity than normal. "Did Braden leave?"

"Just now. An engine is leaving the station in—"

"Three minutes," Aunt Colleen finished for her, holding up her phone. "Dec's on that one, too. Connor was on duty, so he's there already." Her features looked a little drawn, but there was still a warm light in her eyes. "I'm glad you came here."

She came around the counter to greet her and give Jasmine a treat.

"Where else would she go?" Ella asked, drawing her deeper into the store. "When there's a bad fire, we always stick together."

Cassie immediately felt some tension release from her muscles as she looked past Ella to the other women in the store. Darcy leaned in the doorway between the two businesses, and her sister Molly, in vet scrubs that showed off a decent-size baby bump, leaned on a stool near the pen where some dogs were playing with her daughter, Pru, who sat in the pen with them.

One scan of their expressions and Cassie had the sense that anytime there was a fire like this and the Mahoney men were involved, most of the rest of the family quietly gathered around Colleen.

"You can all help me finish the ideas for the scavenger hunt," Cassie said brightly, guiding Jasmine to the pen to join the other dogs.

"I love scavenger hunts!" Pru called, opening the gate to let in the new arrival.

Aunt Colleen came back to Cassie, holding a glass of lemonade. "We start with this, and if the night gets long, there's some Jameson's in the back."

She laughed and took the glass. "Of course there is, because you're Irish."

"We're family," Colleen said. "And you're part of that now."

Cassie lifted the glass in a toast. "I guess with my mom and your brother getting married…"

Aunt Colleen just smiled, and Cassie saw the hope in her eyes. Would they ever forgive her for leaving? And worse, would she forgive herself?

This wasn't Braden's first trip to Simon's Mill Run, a town about a third of the size of Bitter Bark. With nothing but an understaffed volunteer department, it wasn't unusual for Bitter Bark, Holly Hills, or Chestnut Creek stations to respond to a call out there.

But it was unusual for all three stations to show up, and that, Braden realized as the engine screamed toward a massive blaze in a warehouse section that abutted a recently gentrified section of the town, was because this was no simple job.

Two warehouses were scorched and engulfed in flames, with a sizable crew working. Next to those buildings, a small row of two- and three-story brick residences, not five feet apart, were clearly threatened by proximity to the blaze, but didn't appear to have caught fire. Yet.

Sheriff's deputies had cordoned off the buildings, and a small crowd of residents had gathered. From the radio calls in the front of the truck, Braden learned that all the structures had been cleared, including the homes.

Mike, the engineer driving this rig, zoomed along a row of pumpers and engines, taking them to the end.

"Bet we're going to check the residences for fire," Ray Merritt, the firefighter next to Braden in the back of the truck, said. "That blaze could jump easy."

Cal, the young probie, dipped his head down to get a look at the situation. "Holy shit," he muttered, squinting into the flames being hosed by a dozen firefighters on the ground. "There must be six lines stretched."

"And four men on the roof," Ray noted.

Braden looked up the row of ladders to see the group with axes, attempting entry by breaking through the roof.

"Ten bucks says your brother's up there," Ray added, giving an elbow to Braden, who barely smiled and knew better than to take that bet. Connor was the first up the ladder on any job.

That would account for both brothers, Braden thought, knowing that on every job where the three Mahoney men got separated, he didn't fully relax until both Connor and Declan had checked in. Right this moment, Declan was up front in this truck, next to the chief who, like the rest of this engine's crew, had been off duty when the call came in.

That meant Declan didn't have the usual authority he would as captain, outranked by the chief. It also meant Declan would go in, which was good. There was no one he trusted in a fire more than one of his brothers.

From the front of the truck, Chief Winkler turned around to command their attention, a phone still at his ear.

"Indoor attack," he informed them. "Command is sending us to the residence closest to the burn.

Homeowner reported second-floor smoke, no fire, but it could have been coming in through a window. We need to find it."

Everyone copied.

"Mike and I will stay with the engine and run the line, communicating with Command. Ray and Cal are on backup. Declan and Braden will carry the attack line. Braden, you got the tip. Take the TIC and a drywall hook 'cause you're going to pull walls and ceiling if windows are closed, but for God's sake, remember this is somebody's home. Don't destroy what you don't have to."

Once again, they copied, and as the engine stopped, they unloaded, grabbed equipment, and moved on instinct and muscle memory. And fast. Hustling toward the building, Braden got his mask in place, then the helmet, ear flaps down. He buckled up his gloves and didn't touch the respirator, saving air for the moment he entered the house.

Cradling the fat nozzle with his left hand, his right poised over the bail that could release up to a hundred and fifty gallons in a minute if he had to, he shot a look at Declan.

Right then, Declan could have been Joe Mahoney's twin brother, not his son. His eyes narrowed in determination behind the face shield. And he knew exactly what Dec was about to say.

"Godspeed, kid." He said it every time Braden headed into a job.

Holding the thought, Braden nodded, and they took off into a house that was probably built in the forties, but had been extensively remodeled. It was home to a family with at least one baby, he surmised as he passed a playpen in the living room. Right this minute, it could easily have a fire hidden in the walls or attic, especially if that remodeling job wasn't entirely to code.

They disregarded the first floor after Declan did a cursory check, heading up the stairs. Declan led, the drywall hook like a javelin in one hand, his thermal-imaging camera in the other, aimed at walls as he looked for hot spots behind them.

They stopped at a small, square hallway, with open doors that led to two bedrooms and a tiny bathroom. Declan stepped into one, checking with the camera and looking for the attic door.

"Attic access is in here." Braden pointed the tip of the hose toward a ceiling panel, his voice and breath echoing in his helmet and shield.

They both headed for it, the line growing too tight for Braden to rush. "More line!" he called down to Cal and Ray. "Found the attic access!"

Instantly, his line freed, and he got into position next to Dec, who used the hook to slide the attic door open.

A second later, gray smoke billowed down.

He heard Declan swear and swing around, looking for a way up. A dresser about three feet away would do the trick. Braden, knowing he couldn't drop the nozzle for any reason in heaven or hell, yelled into his comm for a man.

Cal was in the room in seconds, and he and Declan dragged the dresser across the floor so Braden could climb up and hose the source of the smoke. As soon as he did, flames rushed at him. He jumped off the dresser, but kept the spray pointed into the attic as Dec and Cal hustled around, pulling ceiling down to give Braden more access to the fire.

Braden called for more line and focused every ounce of concentration and energy on managing the nozzle and fire. With practiced precision, he made steady slow circles at the flames, getting wet on red, the way he was trained.

As Dec busted the ceiling piece by piece, Braden stayed right with him, hosing the crap out of the flames that had already eaten away at the rafters and roof and some incredibly old and probably illegal I beams holding it all up.

If one of them burned through, everything would fall—on them. He had to get this fire out before that happened. But the blaze was alive, crawling, crackling, and rolling orange and hot toward the other bedroom.

Braden aimed and shot, the only sound his own respirator as he systematically battled the flames. He worked with Dec like they were in a choreographed dance, tearing and hosing, ripping and wetting, pulling and soaking in silent, furious concentration to stay one step ahead of the blaze.

In the hall, the fire brought a huge section of ceiling down, revealing another massive rafter engulfed in flames.

"It's gonna fall," Braden called out to Declan when he saw that I beam burning through.

"Put it out!" Declan ordered.

"I am." He ground out the words so hard he felt his teeth grind. His boots braced, his legs locked, his arms tensed, and his whole body prepared for the fight.

"Go get the second line," Dec ordered Cal. "We need another stretch up here."

Cal shot back downstairs, but the moment he disappeared, the ceiling over the stairs dropped. Cal made it out, but with a noisy crack, the fat, fiery I beam fell from one end, swinging down in a shower of orange embers to smack Dec in the side and knock him over.

He swore hard as he fell, then the beam broke and pinned him to the ground.

Instantly, Braden dropped to his knees, holding the nozzle up on the flames. "Backup!" he called, fighting the line with one hand and trying to get the burning beam off Dec with the other. But the stairs were blocked, and he knew backup wasn't coming for at least a minute. Maybe two.

"Declan is down! We need men up here."

Above him, the blaze roared, cracking and popping as it found fresh oxygen in the hall.

"Put it out!" Dec managed to say, pushing at the beam himself.

Braden ignored the order, making a split-second decision to shut off the spray and use both hands to save his brother as flames licked over him and the beam weight damn near crushed him. He took one second to look up, in time to see a second beam on fire, certain to fall on both of them.

"I got this," he assured his brother, placing his hands on the beam to push. "Can you get up if I free you?"

"Can you free me?"

Braden shot him a look and used what felt like superhuman strength, shoving the burning beam just high enough for Dec to roll out. Instantly, he hopped to his feet and grabbed the nozzle himself, spraying like hell. Cal and Ray made it up with the second line, which Braden took, flipping it on and taking it in the other direction where the fire had traveled.

Damn near blind from smoke and the adrenaline rush of freeing Dec, he attacked the flames with every ounce of strength, training, and power he had. As the fire died and lost the fight, Braden finally let himself relax and put out the hot spots.

As they backed out, he noticed Declan wincing in pain.

"You okay?" Braden asked his brother on the way down.

"I think I cracked a rib," he admitted.

"Oh man," Braden said. "Go see the medic."

"I will." He turned as they got to the bottom of the steps. "Thanks, bro," Declan muttered. "Dad would have been proud."

Braden just nodded and got his brother out the door.

Outside, there was more work, more orders, more backup positions to hold. It was hours until the all-clear was called. By then, Declan was wrapped up, his ribs bruised and possibly broken, so Chief sent Braden to Command on behalf of their engine.

Braden hung back, listening to the chatter of the other firefighters in the aftermath of a massive battle, the relief damn near palpable.

"Second one in five weeks," he heard one of the volunteers say.

"This one was worse, though."

Braden stepped forward and greeted the two men with a nod. "Second fire here in Simon's Mill Run?" he asked. "I didn't hear about the first one."

"Dumpster," one guy said. "We handled it with locals. Didn't have an investigation on that, but we will on this."

The other man snorted. "Better do it fast, before the next one. Someone hates the landlord."

Braden just stared at him, heat and anger coiling through him.

"Bitter Bark Engine 75!"

At the call from Command, Braden stepped over to the center of the controlled chaos to sign some papers. There, the chief from Holly Hills FD was on the phone. "Then call Charlotte or Asheville or Boone, damn it. We need all possible resources on this investigation," the man demanded. "Don't give me budget shit. We need to stop this."

Yes, they did. But could one lone investigator figure out the source? Without someone—some four-legged one—with eight hundred times the receptors in his snout?

Only if those receptors worked.

He signed his name, let out a sigh, and suddenly ached like hell to be home.

Chapter Twenty

When the word came in that everyone was safe and on their way home, Cassie, with Jazz faithfully by her side, left Bone Appetit and the gathering of women that had somehow managed to soothe a soul she hadn't even known needed soothing.

She walked to her apartment, got a change of clothes and a toothbrush, stopped by Santorini's and got some dinner, then drove to Braden's house without one tiny shred of doubt of where she'd spend the night.

Sometime in the last few hours, she'd stopped thinking about Chicago, a job, and the threat that falling for Braden represented to that lifelong dream. Tonight, she had to be with him, no matter what the future held.

She fed Jazz, who never snarled or gave her the stink eye, not once. After that, she took a shower, towel-dried her hair, and pulled on a pair of pj shorts. Snagging a navy Bitter Bark Fire Department T-shirt from a pile of folded laundry in a basket next to Braden's bed, she climbed onto his bed to reread

Braden's last text—*Home in 20 min, you better be there*—sip a glass of wine, and work on her to-do list for the upcoming week.

When she heard his truck door, that list fell to the floor, and Jasmine jumped up to greet him. Cassie sat up, took a deep breath of anticipation, and stayed right where she was.

"Oh, it's you." Braden's voice carried in from the front. "How's it going, Superdog?"

Jazz barked a few times.

"Sure, I'll follow you. There better be something good in there." He stepped into the doorway of the dimly lit room, and Cassie sucked in a soft breath.

"Oh," she whispered, letting her gaze slide over him.

"Oh is right. You're clean and fresh and a sight for red eyes."

"You're…not." His face was filthy, streaked, and his hair stuck out in four different directions. He had on what was probably a white T-shirt once, but looked gray and stuck to his skin. The blue firefighter uniform pants weren't much better.

"I decided to shower here," he said. "Hoping for company."

She smiled. "Here I am."

"Company in the shower."

"I just took one," she said, fluttering her still wet hair.

"Then…" He dropped a duffel bag on the floor and took a few steps closer to the bed. "Take another one."

The command sent heat through her. "I'll watch you."

"Watch?" His lip hitched up on one side in a half

smile. "My woman of action? If I know you, you'll lather the soap and dispense the shampoo."

"I'll bring you dinner in bed."

He shrugged a shoulder. "I'm not hungry." Then he narrowed his eyes and let his gaze take a long, slow trip over her body, lingering on her bare legs, then returning to her face. "For dinner."

She sank a little deeper into the bed, like need and desire were pressing her down.

Without another word, he tugged at the neck of his T-shirt and yanked it over his head, flipping it on the floor next to the clean laundry. She tried not to moan at the sight of his pecs and abs, the muscles glistening from sweat and bunched with tension—and a few bruises she hadn't seen last time he'd had his shirt off.

He propped on the only chair in the room, bending over to take off his boots and socks, then stood, flipped the button of his pants, unzipped, and stared at her, and for the first time she saw something hurt and hollow in his blue eyes.

"How bad was it?" she asked.

He blew out a sigh of deep frustration. "It was arson, Cass."

"Really?"

He notched his head in the direction of the bathroom. "See you in there." It wasn't a question.

She bunched the comforter in her fists as the familiar hum buzzed through her. She had to do something, to help him, to heal him. She slid her legs across the bed, fueled by her need to fix whatever was wrong.

She knew exactly how to take the sadness out of his eyes. Yes, there might be a price. A regret. A difficult decision yet to be made. But right that minute, the only thing she cared about was Braden.

On a slow breath, she walked toward the bathroom door, which was ajar with some steam rolling out. She inched the door all the way open, able to see the silhouette of his body behind a semi sheer white shower curtain.

He stood with his face up, letting water pour over him.

"I heard a beam fell on your brother," she said.

"Yeah, but he's okay." After a second, he added, "How'd you hear that?"

"I was at Mahoney Central, also known as Bone Appetit."

She saw his body go still in the act of pouring shampoo from a bottle. "Really." It wasn't a question, but the single word held plenty of surprise. "Why'd you go there?"

She thought about it, not entirely sure of the answer. "It seemed natural to be with…family."

"They're not your family, cuz. Otherwise, you wouldn't be allowed in here."

Laughing softly, she leaned against the small vanity, her gaze locked on the shower curtain. Even in shadow form, he was sexy. His backside round, his thighs thick, his…whoa.

Those shoulders just dropped to second place.

Her hands shook a little as she flicked at the bottom of the T-shirt she wore, inching it up. "I brought Jasmine, too."

"Yeah." He huffed out a breath and turned to let water sluice down his back. "Jasmine."

"Don't hate her, Braden. She's a good dog."

"I don't hate her." He sounded resigned. "Far from it."

"So you're not mad she's here and Jelly Bean isn't?"

"I'm mad you're out there and not in here."

She smiled and ducked out of the T-shirt, letting it drop silently on the floor. She stood in nothing but pj shorts, taking deep, deliberate breaths to steady her heart. But that didn't work. Nothing steady on her. Everything was vibrating with the need to take…

Oh, who was she kidding? The need was for Braden. Not action. Just him. *Now.*

She slithered her shorts down her legs, holding the counter since she was light-headed and off-kilter. Then she took a step toward the shower, pausing for a moment at the curtain, closing her eyes as if she'd have to be mentally prepared for what she'd see. And what she'd do. And all the many things she was about to feel and risk and enjoy.

Then she opened the curtain wide enough to step in.

He faced the other way, giving her a plain view of his entire back engulfed in puffs of steam.

"You like the water hot," she whispered, watching every muscle tense as he heard her behind him.

His shoulders rose and fell with the same sigh she'd just let out, the same undercurrent of anticipation.

She closed the space between them, slid her hands around his waist, and stepped into the heat of scalding water and rock-hard man. "Hey, Einstein."

"Hey, cuz."

She spread her fingers on his soaking-wet chest, pressing against the muscles to feel the wild beat of his heart. "I want to make you feel better."

"This is a good start." He turned in her arms, his eyes that gas-flame blue of intensity that always took her breath away. "Is that why you're in here? To help me?"

She shook her head very slowly, bowing her back to press her chest against his and dropping her head so water splashed her face and ran down her neck. "I'm here because there is nowhere on this earth I'd rather be."

His hands opened, and he coasted them up her back, around and over her breasts, then into her hair for a long, wet, intentional kiss. She rose on her toes to get more, grabbing hold of the slick granite of his body, leaning in so he could hold her upright since her weak knees might not do it.

"Nowhere I'd rather have you," he murmured into her mouth. "You and me. It's good, Cassie. It's right."

She couldn't argue with that. Instead, she let her hands and mouth explore every inch of skin and muscle, taking the soap from his hand to wash him while he kissed her and touched her and pulled her under the spray to melt them both together.

He knew why she'd come to him. He knew exactly why. And he didn't care.

If her will to heal his heart with sex was all he ever got of Cassie Santorini, Braden would take it and relish every blissful, mind-blowing moment of making love to her.

Which wasn't going to be a quickie in the shower. Not the first time. Not if it might be the *only* time.

"Let's get out," Braden whispered, reaching back to flip the water off.

Cassie inched away, black hair flattened to her head, water streaming off her long lashes and over her face. "We're just getting started."

"Do you know how often EMTs are called for shower-sex accidents?" He opened the curtain, and steam billowed out. "It would be hilarious if half of them didn't end up in the ER. Bed's safer."

She scanned his face, blinking water. "Nothing's safe about this, Braden."

No kidding. Like how easy it would be to say things he knew he'd regret, to make promises she'd never let him keep. Totally unsafe to make *love* and not mention...*love*.

"I have what we need to make it safe, I promise." He stepped out and reached for her. "I put them in the nightstand drawer the day you agreed to be my girlfriend. My real girlfriend who I am right now taking to bed."

"Well, that'll be...*real*."

"Yep." He turned and grabbed a towel from the rack, wrapping her in it and helping her out of the tub. "And it could take all night and most of tomorrow morning, so...yes?"

"I'm naked, soaked, and begging, Einstein. I'd say that qualifies as a yes. You?"

He gave her a *get real* look and glanced at the space between them, watching as her gaze dropped down his torso, lower, then stopped. "Does that look like a yes?"

"That looks..." She bit her lip. "Better than my fantasies."

"You've had fantasies, huh?" Using the towel around her, he tugged her out of the bathroom. "Tell me one."

He expected a joke, a typical Cassie wisecrack, but her face was utterly serious. "This. You." She swallowed and reached up to kiss him, locking her hands around his neck and pressing against him. "Us."

He dragged the towel up her back and used it to squeeze some water out of her hair. "I don't think I've ever known you to be at a loss for words."

"Color me speechless." She closed her eyes and let her head fall back as he dried her hair, then he pressed the towel on her shoulders, her back, her breasts. Everything was so…dear. Feminine. Soft. Perfect.

Cassie was *perfect*.

He knelt down to dry her stomach and hips and thighs, admiring every inch of her and planting kisses in the wake of the towel, pulling delicious whimpers of pleasure when he hit a particularly sweet spot.

"Yes, that." She closed her fingers over his head and guided his mouth all over her. "Definitely fantasized about that."

His tongue found curves and angles, sweet skin, and one incredibly cute innie. He eased her onto the bed, patted his own body dry, and dropped the towel, staring at her while his heart clobbered his chest.

"Do you ever have any fantasies?" she asked, scooting up to put her head on the pillow, but never taking her gaze from him. "About me?"

"Do I ever *not* have any is a better question." He bracketed her legs with his, straddling her as he laid his body over hers. "At the most inopportune times, too."

276

She laughed softly. "Sunday dinner?"

"Always at Sunday dinner." Leaning down, he kissed her lightly, knowing it was just a prelude to a thousand more that would only get deeper and more desperate. "I was jealous of every bite of bread pudding that went into this...delicious...mouth."

She moaned into each kiss. "You wanted to sleep with me?"

Every single night.

He bit back the declaration and forced a few drops of blood to stay in his brain and protect him from blurting out something stupid.

"I wanted to..." No, he couldn't tell her that he knew from the moment he laid eyes on her that she was so much *more* than any woman he'd ever met. More fun. More exciting. More attractive, inside and out. He knew, deep down, that she would rock his soul and make him question his decisions and threaten his stability and *change* him. Maybe he'd never put it into words, but now, tonight, like this, with her...now he knew. And he knew better than to tell her.

So this night would be fun and sexy and perfect, but it wasn't going to be easy.

After a moment, she pressed on his chest, pushing him up so she could see his eyes, so he closed them, knowing he was so damn transparent where she was concerned. "You wanted to what?" she urged.

Wanted to think about words like *forever* and *always* and *permanent* and...*love*.

"That dirty, huh?" she teased.

"Not dirty at all." Stupid, useless, and a little bit terrifying. But not dirty. "Unless you think this is dirty." He inched down her body, pausing at her breasts, tasting one, caressing the other, adoring her body, kind of the way he adored her heart and head.

"Mmm." She arched and sighed noisily, fingers digging into his hair. "I think it's...*oh*. Not dirty at all. Sweet, actually. Sexy. Nice."

With each kiss and suckle, a new wave of delight rolled over her, making her mew like a kitten and moan with unapologetic delight.

"I want you." She squeezed his shoulders and dragged him back to kiss her mouth. "I want you, Einstein."

He gave her that kiss, long and deep. "Einstein can't think straight right now."

That brought a victorious gleam to her eyes. "You don't have to think." She touched his lips with her fingertips. "When your mouth is this clever."

Holding her gaze, he moved against her, wincing as pleasure and need collided and made him a little desperate. "And to think I'm not even Greek," he teased.

"I know." She branded his neck and chest with kisses, digging her nails into him, then lightly scraping them all the way down his back, sending sparks and blood and a gnawing hunger all to one place. "And you can tell that's such an...issue." She slid her hand around to the front, closing her fingers over him with a little groan of delight. "A huge, *huge*...issue."

He wanted to laugh, but all he could do was give in to the unbelievable tsunami of pleasure rolling over him with each stroke of her hands.

He tried to slow down, tried to make every second stretch to infinity, but the more they found the staccato rhythm of their bodies, the more need muscled past any shot at leisurely getting there.

Reluctantly pausing to seek a condom from the nightstand drawer, he sat up enough to get a full view of her body, everything pink from the rush of blood and maybe the brush of his whiskers.

Her hips rose and fell as if beckoning him back, her eyes shuttered, strands of wet inky-black hair splayed on his pillow. She looked like the prophetess she'd been named for, elusive and beautiful and...*his*.

Except she wasn't his.

"Any day now," she teased without opening her eyes.

"Sorry. Took a detour."

Her eyes flashed open in surprise. "To where?"

To...feelings. Futures. Forever places he had no right to go. "Safety drawer," he said, holding up the packet as proof. "Stay with me now, Cass," he murmured around the packet he tore open with his teeth.

Reaching up, she put both hands on his shoulders and curled her legs around him. "Don't worry. I'm not leaving these beauties anytime soon." She squeezed hard, pulling him down, placing a kiss on one shoulder, then the other.

It was stupid to cling to that promise, but he did anyway. Held on to the words and the hope and the possibility that she really wasn't leaving with the same strength he held on to her as he finally found his way home, as close to Cassie as he could be, but even that wasn't close enough. He'd always want more.

Not leaving...anytime soon.

He held her, soaking up her ragged breaths, riding every rise and fall, letting the build to ecstasy take over every single thought but *Cassie*. He said her name over and over, and she whispered his, and for one long, exquisite, insane moment, they were joined in body and heart and soul, both of them lost and out of control and completely connected.

After the last tremor shook them, he dropped onto the pillow, buried his face in her wet hair, and managed to keep his mouth shut and not pour out his feelings.

He couldn't keep her. But he'd had this moment, this release, this memory. And that would have to be enough.

Except he already knew it wouldn't be.

Chapter Twenty-One

Cassie woke to a predawn silver sky, shaking off a dream of someone holding her down.

Not someone. That was the weight of Braden's arm wrapped around her, pinning her to one spot. Against her bare body, he still slept deeply, breathing steady and slow into her hair.

She frowned into the darkness, pulling at wisps and threads of the dream, working to get something more than a vague feeling of...longing. Whatever she'd dreamed, it left her...no, not longing. Frustrated. Stymied. Humming with that old familiar need to get a job done.

But what? Squeezing her eyes shut, she dug deep into her filmy dream memory and came up with...her father?

She sucked in a soft breath, which made Braden stir against her. "You okay, Cass?" he muttered.

"I'm not sure." Who dreamed about her father when in bed with her lover?

Instantly, he tightened his grip on her. "What's wrong?"

She turned slowly to face him, shocked for one second at how close and warm and real he was. "Nothing." She curled her leg over his, settling into the shape of the two of them that had become achingly familiar overnight.

"Liar." He searched her face. "Something's wrong."

"I think I dreamed of my dad."

"Bad dream?"

"Just…what's he doing here?" she asked on a laugh, then flicked her hand in the air. "Go away and let me be an adult, Daddy."

"Did you call him Daddy?"

"Sometimes," she admitted. "Like I call my mother Mommy at times. Just for a call back to childhood."

"Maybe he appeared in your dream to tell you what he thinks of…" He glanced down to their entwined bodies.

She studied his face for a minute, letting herself fall back a few years, remembering her father before he was sick, when he was strong, healthy, vibrant. Cooking hard in the back of Santorini's, dispensing life lessons like dollops of tzatziki.

"He'd have liked you," she said quietly.

He lifted a dubious brow. "An Irish dude?"

"He didn't care about being Greek or not. That's all Yiayia. Remember, he married my mother." She touched his cheek, scraping her nail against his scruffy whiskers. "He liked a man who was passionate about things. He respected people who are all in and maybe go a little overboard. You're like that."

"Overboard?" His eyes flashed with something that hovered between guilt and worry. "Like…how?"

"Like refusing to give up on Jelly Bean."

With a soft grunt, he shut his eyes. "Yeah, I forgot about that."

"Give it this week, Braden," she urged him. "Let Daniel and Liam work with him."

"I will, but…" He swallowed. "I want to work with Jazz. I'm going to see how she and I do together."

She drew back, her eyes wide. "Really?"

"Yeah. I'm going to start ADC handler training with her this week."

For some reason, that disappointed her. "You're giving up on Jelly Bean?"

He blew out a long, sad sigh. "Look, he's everything I ever wanted in a dog and he's mine forever, but after last night? I know that this town, this whole area, needs an ADC more than I need to have my dream dog doing the job." He lifted his head. "Where is Jazz, by the way?"

"Probably waiting by the kitchen door to go out, like the angel she is."

He rolled his eyes. "Yep, she's flawless. I should take her outside." He started to push away immediately, but she grabbed his arm. "She's fine. It's not even six o'clock in the morning, and I walked her before you got home. I can't believe you've changed your mind about Jelly Bean."

"I have to do what's right," he said. "Not just what feels right, or what I want to be right, or what should be right. It's small and stupid of me to cling to the dog who doesn't have the most important attribute for the job. Jasmine will probably make a top-level scent-detection dog, just like my uncle said." He gave a dry laugh. "Which, if I know Daniel Kilcannon, is probably the reason he had me take Jazz 'temporarily.'"

"So what do you want to do about Jelly Bean?"

"I'll let him finish the tests at Waterford this week. And while he does, we can work with Jazz and complete the stops for the scavenger hunt."

Cassie narrowed her eyes. "Which you don't need to even have anymore, if you're not sending Jelly Bean to ten grand worth of higher education."

"We can still have a scavenger hunt, but give any proceeds to a worthy cause."

"Oh." She shifted a little. "Okay."

"You sound disappointed, Cass." He tipped her chin up to look into her eyes.

"I am disappointed," she admitted. "But only because I had such high hopes for Jelly Bean."

"He's a great dog and can do a lot of other jobs. Anything that doesn't require scent discernment. I'm not giving him up or letting someone else have him. If I can't get permission to take them both to the station when I'm on duty, I'll leave one at Waterford or at my mom's house. It'll work out."

"Okay," she said. "What kind of hours do you work this week?"

"Three ten-hour days. I'm off the whole weekend, then a bunch of twenty-fours." He gave her a quick kiss and rolled away. "Let me check on Jazz. Don't move. Don't even think about moving."

"Brush my teeth?"

"You brought a toothbrush?" He looked pleasantly surprised.

"Clean clothes, too."

"Ooh. A premeditated sleepover. What changed your mind?"

"I'm not sure," she whispered. "But I knew I had

to be here last night." She gave him a light poke in the arm. "Go take Jazz out. We can talk when you get back."

It pained her to lose his warmth and strength, but she still needed time to know exactly what to say. Because she honestly didn't know what changed her mind, only that it had. Was that temporary insanity or a change of heart?

Ten minutes later, Braden was back, with Jazz, who settled on the floor and laid her head on the dirty T-shirt he'd dropped last night. Since he'd even taken time to brush his teeth, too, he smelled too minty fresh not to kiss.

She started there without talking, lingering over his lips, delaying the conversation she didn't want to have. The kiss led to more, but Braden showed remarkable restraint, finally easing her away to look into her eyes.

"You still didn't answer my question, Cass. What changed your mind?"

"What changed your mind about Jelly Bean?" she replied. "Sometimes you realize it's—what did you call it? Small and stupid? I was just clinging to a preconceived notion that was wrong." She rocked into him with an unabashed invitation. "Turns out I was right."

But he didn't rock back. "Does that mean you changed your mind about leaving?"

She heard the hope in his voice, just like she'd seen the struggle to keep things light when they made love last night.

"You can't change a mind that's not made up yet," she said. "And you're putting the cart before the horse or, in this case, the job before the offer. No one has officially asked me to move anywhere yet."

"Yet."

"Yes, yet." She snaked closer. "But we have now."

But he was having none of it. "Then we're back to where we were. Temporary."

"Jasmine was going to be temporary," she said. "And look how fast you were able to slide into permanent with her."

He shook his head. "Dogs are not people, so don't conflate the two."

"I don't know what conflate means, Einstein, but the idea is this: You think you don't want someone to come home to, but I know that you do. That's not the case with moving. I've wanted to live and work in a big city my whole life." She squinted as something occurred to her. "Maybe that's why I dreamed about my dad. He's the only person who knew that and took me seriously."

He relaxed a little, coming closer, the way he always did when he wanted to know more about her. "How?"

"He knew what we were all meant to be before we did. He always knew the twins would take over Santorini's and that Theo would go off to find his way in the military, and Nick was born to be a doctor. He called me his 'little lady executive' because I used to sit behind his desk in the back of the restaurant and pretend to be on the phone bossing people around."

That made him laugh. "You are bossy, but in the sexiest possible way."

"He'd come into his office, and I'd have his phone to my ear, pretending to take notes, telling people they had to have the spinach delivered by tomorrow at ten or I'd take my business elsewhere!" She pretended to slam a phone almost as hard as the memory slammed her. "Dad would say, 'That's my little lady executive. You'll be running Wall Street someday.'"

"Ahhh."

She inched back. "What 'ahhh'? What does that mean?"

"It means now I understand what's motivating this desperation to move to a big city."

"It's not desperation, Braden. It's a goal, a dream. Same as handling an arson-investigation dog. Nothing has to motivate it."

"My dad died in a fire that was deliberately set. My motivation is pretty straightforward. And if you want to run a business, which I get and applaud, you can do that here. We have businesses in Bitter Bark. And not a single dedicated event-planning company, to my knowledge."

She just sighed, because the argument made sense, but so did that big-city dream—to her, at least.

"True. It's not Wall Street," he added. "It's Ambrose Avenue, and that might be a disappointment to your father."

She started to argue, then stopped because the dream came back to her. At least, a piece of it. She had been in the den of their old house in Chestnut Creek. Dad was around the corner in the kitchen, talking to Mom. About her.

She couldn't remember what he was saying, but she wildly disagreed and kept trying to get up and tell him that. She kept calling out, "Daddy, Daddy!" but someone was holding her back from getting off the sofa and marching into the kitchen to defend herself.

Alex? Nick?

No, it wasn't one of her brothers. "It was you."

"Excuse me?"

"In my dream. I was trying to tell my father something, but you had my arm and wouldn't let me go."

His brow lifted with interest. "Symbolism. One of my favorite things in literature."

"Well, I was trapped under your arm before I woke up, so it wasn't that symbolic."

"Yes it was," he said softly. "I'm holding you back."

She searched his face. "But you don't want a permanent relationship, remember?"

He didn't answer, but he didn't have to. She could read it on his face.

"You change your mind?"

"You changed my mind," he said gruffly. "And who knows, Cass? You could change my mind about a lot of things. Like…where I live."

She blinked, stunned by that. "Braden."

"In the meantime…" He eased her into him and dragged his hand down her arm and over her hip. "I'm going to do everything I can…" He kissed her and slowly began to move against her. "To help us…" Sliding her onto her back and under him, he started feathering kisses on her lips and jaw and throat. "Enjoy every minute we have."

Her response melted into a sigh as his hands moved over her with that slow, confident touch that turned her into a pool of liquid from the waist down.

"I need a new name for you, Einstein. Tell me a

great lover in literature. You know, like Romeo or Tristan. Rick in *Casablanca*. I know. I'll call you Heathcliff."

He stopped the kiss he'd been planting on the rise of her breasts. "Another of my favorite things in literature. Irony. And you just delivered some."

"How?"

He lifted his head to look into her eyes, his gaze a little sad. "You just picked nicknames of heroes who each and every one ended up dead or alone."

"Oh." She pressed a hand to his cheek. "I don't want you to be dead or alone, Braden."

"I'm not...now." He lowered his head and continued a trail of kisses down her body and did everything he possibly could to make it impossible to give him up.

Bushrod Square was packed Friday afternoon, with an atmosphere of festivity permeating the square mile in the center of Bitter Bark. From end to end, there were tourists, food and craft vendors, musicians, jugglers, families enjoying picnics, and so many dogs.

None of that distracted Jasmine as she trotted between Cassie and Braden, the three of them heading to the bleachers to watch today's main event, the Waterford Farm Dog Show.

"I can't believe how long it's been since Waterford held one of these," Braden said, scanning the crowd and nodding to a dozen familiar faces.

"Waterford has had dog shows before?" Cassie asked. "I never heard that."

"Not since my uncle opened the actual training and rescue facility," he said. "But when Aunt Annie was alive, she used to wrangle up a bunch of foster dogs and rescues and friends, and it was a big party day at Waterford Farm. Not a real dog show like Westminster, mind you. Just a way to blow off steam and laugh at the antics. You know, Best Kisser and Fastest Tail Chaser. Nothing too serious."

"It should be fun," she said, reaching over to squeeze his hand. "You're not nervous, are you?"

He threw her a smile, loving that she always got his undercurrent of feelings. He'd noticed that in this past week when they'd been virtually inseparable, except when he was at work.

"Just really excited about seeing JB again," he said. "After my conversation with Uncle Daniel last night, I couldn't be more convinced I've made the right decision."

Yes, it had hurt a little when his uncle called with the news that Jelly Bean's olfactory problems were still evident, and his scent detection was hit or miss. Mostly miss. There could be no "miss" for an arson-investigating dog.

"And I'm excited to tell my uncle that we have at least one Accelerant Detection Canine ready to get trained for certification." He pulled their joined hands to give Jasmine a head rub, the way they did whenever Jazz found her target scent, which was...always. "Right, Jazzy?"

The regal Lab didn't so much as lose a beat of her beautiful walk, her ebony head high, her long curve of a tail swishing side to side, her keen blue eyes scanning the crowds.

"Will Jelly Bean sit with us?" Cassie asked. "I'm dying to see how these two get along."

"Of course. We'll hang with the whole family over there." He notched his chin to the massive white tent, already seeing many of his cousins, siblings, and the family dogs. "Look, your mom is checking people in."

Cassie slowed her step and held them back, and of course, Jazz did the same. "Look at her, Braden. She's so happy."

He studied her mother, seeing so much of Cassie in her gestures and expressions and the way she tilted her head back and gazed up at Uncle Daniel, who stood behind her with his hands on her shoulders.

Yes, he'd seen Cassie look at him like that. And that alone gave him hope.

"They're great together," Braden mused. "I never dreamed my uncle could be so happy again."

"Right?" She shook her head and blinked as if her eyes were tearing up. "There was a time when I never thought my mother would laugh like that again, and now she's downright joyous." She sighed and looked up at him. "They belong together."

So do we.

But Braden just squeezed her hand and nodded. He'd become an expert at not saying what he was thinking, at least when he was thinking the things he knew she wasn't ready to talk about. Might never be, to be honest. But they'd made an agreement to live in the now, and right now—with sunshine pouring over Bushrod Square, almost all of the people he loved gathered under one tent, and a reunion with Jelly Bean just moments away—this now was great.

"There he is!" she squealed, excited enough to elicit a bark from Jazz.

Jelly Bean rested contentedly under another table filled with programs and brochures. A kick of happiness Braden honestly didn't expect hit him right in the solar plexus as Jelly Bean sat up, looked right at him, and barked.

"JBeee!" Braden called, letting go of Cassie's hand to jog closer to his dog. Jelly Bean stood, shook off, and barked at him, then poked his head out from under the table. When he spotted Braden, he set off, loping full speed across the grass, rounding two people, and jumping so they both went right down to the ground for a good wrestle.

Behind him, he heard Jasmine bark, then, seconds later, she reached the two of them, pulling a little more than she usually would at the leash Cassie held.

"Whoa, somebody's jealous of you rolling around with that dog," Cassie teased. "Jasmine's not happy, either."

Laughing, he got his arm around Jasmine's head and Jelly Bean's, too. "Get along, you two."

Uncle Daniel arrived, too, grinning at the three of them on the ground. "He's been ready to see you for a few days," he said, giving Cassie a quick hug as Braden hopped to his feet.

"I've been ready to see him."

"How's our Jasmine doing?" his uncle asked.

"Great." He looked the other man directly in the eyes. "She's going to make an unparalleled ADC, Uncle Daniel. Your instincts are dead-on. She could smell two kinds of dirt on a fly's ear in the next county. All we need is for you and Liam to run her through the paces and sign the affidavit. I've already arranged for a little time off to take her to the ATF for certification training." Damn, it felt good to say that.

Uncle Daniel looked down at Jelly Bean. "Shhh. He understands English, you know."

"Oh, I know." Braden put a hand on Jelly Bean's head. "But the truth is, when a decision is right, you just know it."

His uncle beamed at him, silent for a moment, then he gave Braden an emotional bear hug. "Good call, son."

"Thanks," he said softly. "And thanks for steering me in the right direction. Can I take Jelly Bean now?"

"Uh, no."

Braden jerked back. "Why not?"

"Because he's our best dog in the show." He thumbed toward the massive ring set up in the center of the square. "The way that dog takes orders? He's a shoo-in for Best Dancer, Wiggliest Butt, and by far the Fastest Hot Dog Eater. And just forget the Binky Bob."

"The what?"

"He broke the practice record for finding the pacifier at the bottom of the baby pool."

Next to him, Cassie wrapped her arm around Braden's waist and looked up at him. "That's our boy."

He looked from one face to the other, then down at the dogs, almost crumbling when Jelly Bean sat up straight with a glimmer of pride in his eyes.

"So, go get a beer and join the family in the VIP section right here." Uncle Daniel nudged them toward the tent. "I think Jelly Bean is going to win the day."

"He already has," Braden muttered as he crouched down in front of the dog. "Right, JB?"

He barked once and wagged his tail ferociously.

"And you don't even snarl at my girlfriend anymore."

Cassie bent over to whisper in his ear, "That's because the pressure's off him. I've never seen him happier, Braden."

He turned to her, overcome with that same relief he imagined Jelly Bean had. It was just enough to say what he was thinking. "I've never been happier, Cassie." He leaned forward and kissed her. "I just want you to know that."

"Oh, Braden. I—"

"Cassie, there you are!" A man's voice broke through the noise of the square, deep and unfamiliar. Not a brother, cousin, or friend, Braden sensed as he slowly stood, turned, and came face-to-face with Jace Demakos.

"Hey, Braden, how are you?" He reached out to shake Braden's hand like it was the most natural thing in the world. Like he wasn't here to wreck the day, kill the moment, and suck the joy out of Braden's life.

"Jace. Good to see you." Braden shook his hand, but the man's attention was already on Cassie, who brushed her hair back and slayed the guy with a smile.

"How are you, Jace?" she asked.

"You tell me." He reached into his back pocket and pulled out a white business envelope. "Don't look so shocked. I told you I'd bring it back from Chicago."

"Oh...wow." She took it and glanced at Braden, a war zone of emotion in her eyes. "That's, well...yeah. Thank you."

"Thank the head of Human Resources. I was able to get some sweet perks into that deal. They're letting me build a great team, Cassie, and I really hope you'll be on it." He threw a look at Braden to add, "If you're willing."

"It's not my decision," Braden said simply.

"Yeah, yeah." Jace nodded as if he had a clue what Braden was going through. "I know it's a big change, but..." He nodded to the letter. "It's a solid offer, Cassie. Take some time to look over the details, but I'm afraid you don't have too much time."

"I don't?"

He let out a breath. "Minor change in timing means you'd have to start next week. The company has an apartment right on the lake that you can have for one month until you find your own place, if you don't mind living on the twenty-sixth floor. But we hit the ground running on Monday, so I'd really appreciate it if you could give me your answer tomorrow."

"Tomorrow?" She barely breathed the word, sounding as shell-shocked as Braden felt. "That's the Kibbles for Kindness event, and after that—"

"After that, we need you to pack up and go straight to Chicago on Sunday. HR is expecting you on Monday for a quick training program, then we'll meet with the agency on Tuesday for the event on July fourth. You should be kicking ass and taking names by the end of the week as Family First's brand-new manager of special events."

"Oh, Jace, I..."

Can't. Say it, Cassie. Say you cannot leave that soon.

"I can't..."

Yes. Braden literally held his breath.

"I can't believe this," she finished, stabbing Braden's heart with a nine-inch nail.

"Believe it," Jace said, stepping back as if he had something way more important to do than stand here and kick Braden in the metaphorical teeth. "I gotta find the mayor. You..." He pointed at her. "Make the right decision and make it fast."

He added a wink, nodded goodbye to Braden, and jogged off to go make someone else's life hell.

Cassie stood stone-still, holding the envelope to her chest, looking down at Jelly Bean as if she couldn't bear to look at Braden.

"Congratulations, Cassie," he said softly.

When she looked up at him, her eyes were swimming with tears. "It's everything I ever wanted," she whispered, cracking his heart in two.

"I know."

"But you just said when a decision is absolutely right, you know it."

He reached for her, pulled her into his chest, and planted a kiss on her head, with one simple thought: There was still hope.

"Come on, babe." He slid his arm around her. "Let's go watch Jelly Bean slay the competition."

Because one of them had to.

Chapter Twenty-Two

As night fell, the sparkling white lights in the trees all over Bushrod Square started flickering, casting a golden glow on the last of the cleanup campaign. Perched on the bottom row of the empty bleachers, Cassie finally opened the envelope that had been burning a hole in her handbag all day long.

She'd refused to look, even though Braden urged her to. The moment she did, the very second it all became real, everything would change. The magical time with Braden would be over. The thrilling, precarious free fall into something that felt a lot like love would end with a sudden crash to the ground. The hours of sweet sex and hearty laughs and shared histories and bougatsa in bed would turn into... goodbye.

Not for the first time that day, Cassie's eyes welled up as she looked out at the square where Braden, Connor, and a few of their cousins were breaking down the last of the obstacle course and dog show equipment. She could hear the teases they flung, the jokes they shared, the undercurrent of family and unconditional love that seemed to surround the Mahoneys and Kilcannons and, now, the Santorinis, since Alex and John were in there, too.

They'd all worked together to take down the giant tent and pack everything into various trucks and the Waterford Jeep. A few dogs wandered around, but most slept, worn out and waiting to get into one of those trucks and head home.

Every once in a while, Braden glanced over at her, but he was giving her space and time, and she appreciated that. Didn't mean she wouldn't love to have him next to her right now, but he knew—and she did—that this had to be done alone.

Taking a breath, she slid her finger under the back of the envelope and pulled out the folded pages, about three of them. No surprise, her hand trembled a little as she opened the letter and read the first line.

…excited to offer you the position of…

She blinked and skimmed.

…starting salary of…

"Oh." She stared at the number, which exceeded what she'd expected. That much money would get her that dreamy high-rise apartment, and—

A dog bark pulled her attention, making her look up to see Jelly Bean coming toward her. His Best of Show gold medal swung from his collar as he trotted toward the bleachers.

"Hey, JB," she called to him, reaching out her hand. "Nice work today."

But he walked right by her, barking at something behind the bleachers.

"I'll say you're the best of show!" Simone London's soft Southern accent floated between the bleachers, and then she came around the side to greet Jelly Bean. As she bent over to give him some love, she glanced at Cassie. "Hello," she said softly. "I heard Jelly Belly was amazing in the dog show."

For one crazy minute, Cassie wondered if Braden had called her or texted her, and the thought cut right through her chest.

"It was on the Bitter Bark website," she said quickly, making Cassie know her face had given away her thoughts.

"Yes," Cassie said. "He stole a lot of hearts today."

"Good boy!" Simone said, rubbing his head. She straightened slowly and glanced at the open field, no doubt looking for Braden.

Cassie quietly closed the letter she held and waited, sensing the other woman had something to say. Like...*can I have him now?*

"So, I just came over to congratulate Jelly Bean and..."

"You can go talk to Braden," Cassie said, using the letter to gesture toward him. "He's right over there."

She shook her head. "Actually, it was Jelly Bean I wanted to say goodbye to."

"Goodbye?"

"I gave notice at the college, and I'm moving back to California tomorrow."

Cassie blinked, not quite processing that. "Really? That's a big move."

"I have friends in LA and a good lead on a job in admissions at USC, which makes Vestal Valley College look like a grade school."

"I bet." Cassie looked past the edge of the square to the red brick buildings at the edge of a campus she always thought was quaint and inviting. "Wow. Los Angeles. That's..." Like the queen of big cities. Cassie waited for a little punch of jealousy, but all she felt was a twinge of sadness. For Simone.

"Yeah, there's really nothing to keep me in Bitter Bark anymore," Simone said. "I'm ready for a place with real shopping and a concert hall and maybe more than one hair salon that isn't called a beauty shop."

But Bitter Bark Beauty did a great job on Cassie's hair. "I get that," she said, but the words felt...false.

Simone shifted from one foot to the other, sighing. "Braden seems happy," she said, brushing back some blond hair.

Cassie nodded, swallowing the fact that his happiness was probably going to end the minute she told him what was in this letter. "He was really proud of Jelly Bean today," she said, remembering how he'd cheered for the dog until he almost lost his voice.

"Well, I feel kinda dumb."

Cassie drew back at Simone's admission, which sounded like it came from the heart. "Why?"

"You know." Her pretty features fixed in an expression of embarrassment, and she gave a dry, self-deprecating laugh. "Trying to get him back and all."

Cassie just smiled. "Can't say I blame you, though."

"Yeah." Simone rubbed Jelly Bean's head. "But a girl's gotta know when to hold 'em and when to fold 'em, right, Jelly Bells?"

He barked once and rolled over, shamelessly begging for a belly rub.

Crouching down, Simone ran her nails over his stomach, but looked up at Cassie. "I always knew that he'd change his mind about that 'living alone because he's a firefighter thing' if he met the right person."

Cassie took a slow breath, her fingers pressing into the folded paper she held.

"I just wanted to be the right person," Simone finished. "But it looks like you are."

What could she say to that? *I'm dumping him for a job and a high-rise?* "He's really a good guy," Cassie said softly.

"The best." Simone stood and pulled her hair back in a makeshift ponytail. "Take care of him," she whispered. "He deserves so much love."

Cassie stared at her, trying to swallow, but the lump in her throat prevented even air from getting through. "Yeah." It came out like a croak. "He does."

With one more nod, Simone turned and went back the way she'd come, making Jelly Bean flip onto his feet, stand up, and watch her leave.

"Don't cry," Cassie said to him. "Please don't whine like your heart is broken. I don't think I could take it."

He looked into the empty space for a long time, then walked straight to Cassie, climbed onto the bottom bleacher, and laid his head on her sneaker.

"Damn, dog. You really can speak English." She reached down and flipped his ear between two fingers, the way she'd seen Braden do it a million times. "Then would you please give me some idea what I should do with this problem of mine?"

Jelly Bean lifted his head, licked her ankle once, and dropped his head back down.

"Does that mean stay or go?"

But the dog was silent, and weirdly content, and somehow that just made the decision harder.

Braden refused to open his eyes even though his inner body clock said it was past six and time to get up for his twenty-four-hour shift that started at seven. He didn't want to see the slivers of early morning light between the slats of his blinds. Didn't want to put his feet on the floor and instantly see Jelly Bean's dusty-gray head pop up with a look that said he knew it was a workday. Didn't want to leave Cassie asleep in this bed next to him.

Because the minute this day started, this night—this blissful, satisfying, comforting night that had been spent entwined with each other—would be over. Everything would be over.

Temporary would slip into *long-distance* and that would soon become *sporadic* until it all ended up as...*what used to be.*

He swallowed noisily against a lump in his throat, and immediately Jelly Bean stirred from his bed on the floor, then lifted his head with an expectant look. He knew what rising at six a.m. meant—twenty-four hours at the fire station.

Except, shouldn't Braden take Jazz with him, to work on handling between calls? Of course he should; he was way behind in working with the dog. So he'd have to leave early and swing by Waterford to board Jelly Bean.

He slid his legs out from the covers and put his foot on the ground, but it landed on something slippery and cool. Bending over, he saw a spiral notebook that one of the dogs must have nudged out from under the bed.

Lifting it up, he recognized the handwriting of a numbered list...of to-do items before the scavenger hunt. He turned the page, inching back when he saw the word *Braden* at the top in purple ink with little scribbly doodles around it. On the first line, there was a numeral one and the words *figure out what to do.* Damn, girl. She really did write everything down.

Next to him, the sheets rustled. "You're awake."

He let the paper fall back to cover that page and show her list. "I found a to-do list on the floor."

"Oh." She turned and pushed some hair out of her face. "I've been looking for that notebook." She took it and put it on the nightstand on her side of the bed. "Where are you going?"

"Work." He let his gaze travel over the part of her body where the sheet dropped, automatically sliding back in to touch her. "In a minute."

Without a second's hesitation, Cassie slid even closer, her silky thigh ribboning over his bare leg, her tender fingers traveling across his chest. "You okay?"

"Bracing myself for what's ahead."

"A twenty-four-hour shift?"

He blew out a breath. "If only that were all."

"Braden. I've been thinking."

He stared at her, silent. Here it came. Here came...*long-distance.*

"We could still make this work if I'm in Chicago."

"Or if I am," he whispered.

Her eyes shuttered closed. "Your family would never forgive me. Worse, you'd never forgive me.

That's not even an option on the table." She shook her head. "You can visit, though."

"It won't be enough." He pulled her closer, deeper into his chest. "So you're taking the job?"

She sank back down on his shoulder, quiet. Long enough for him to know the answer.

"That's good," he said before she could formulate an answer that would just be BS anyway. She was going. "That's the right thing to do."

"Are you sure? Because I'm not. Not at all." She traced one finger over his chest, circling the heart that was breaking inside. "There's a lot to love in this town," she whispered. "A lot."

For a long moment, he didn't move or breathe or dare to hope. "Cassie, if you don't take this job, every time you got called into Santorini's when they're short-staffed, you'd think about how that wouldn't happen if you were in Chicago. Every time you step out of your apartment in Bitter Bark, you'd think about how it's so sadly on the second floor. Every time we're together, you'd blame me for your lost opportunities and dreams."

"And then you'd kiss that right out of me, put me on this bed, and do that...that..." She bit her lip. "You know, what you did last night when I kind of scared the dogs with a scream? That."

He almost smiled, but what was so much fun in bed last night had already become a bittersweet memory. "What happens when the sex isn't enough?"

"Oh, since that'll probably be sometime after the next decade, I'm not worried."

He turned his head to look at her, lost as always in the very depths of her impossibly dark eyes. "I don't know what's going to happen over time, but I do know this: you should take that job."

Very slowly, she nodded, and his heart cracked a little bit more.

"And I hate to say goodbye, but…" He managed to slide away from her. "I have to take care of the dogs and get ready for my shift."

She held on a little tighter. "Braden. We need to figure this out."

Long term, long-distance wouldn't work. He knew that like he knew his name. One of them would be in a constant state of disappointment. "Tomorrow."

"I'm supposed to leave tomorrow."

He tamped down a very dark curse and climbed out of bed, grabbing sweats he'd left on the floor. "I don't have a ton of time this morning," he said, signaling to Jelly Bean to head to the door, and Jazz followed, too. "I have to take Jelly Bean to board at Waterford until my shift is over."

"I'll take him," she said without a nanosecond's hesitation.

He slowed in the doorway and looked back at her, trying not to moan at the sight of her naked in bed with her hair cascading like a black veil over her shoulders. "Jelly Bean," he repeated. "I'm taking Jazz to work on handling training between calls. Until chief gives permission, I can only take one at a time."

"I know the difference between the dogs." She sat up, pulling the sheet up and denying him a view of her breasts. Didn't matter. They were burned into his memory forever. "Jelly Bean and I are making progress, Braden, and I can take him to the square today for the bake-off. He'll love it much more than a kennel at Waterford."

"That's not exactly a clean break, Cass."

She tossed the sheets down with a little frustration. "I don't want a clean break, Braden." Sliding out of bed, she walked right to him, completely, breathtakingly, astonishingly naked. "I don't want a break at all."

He stared at her for a minute, letting his gaze fall over her, which just made his brain go numb and the rest of him go...not numb. If he didn't move, he was never going to make it to his shift on time. "I'm taking the dogs out," he said, his voice like sandpaper as he headed toward the kitchen.

No surprise, she was waiting for him in the kitchen when he came back in, dressed in a T-shirt of his that reached her thighs. She handed him a cup of coffee and nodded to the two food bowls. "I got them some food and water."

"Thanks." He took the cup and held her gaze. "And of course you should take Jelly Bean today. He'd love that."

"Okay." She stepped closer. "When should I get him back to you?"

"My shift ends at seven Sunday morning. I usually sleep for a while, then go to Waterford in the afternoon. Will you be there?"

She made a little face and looked away. "Not if I take a two o'clock flight out of Charlotte."

Then he wouldn't be there either, because sitting at that table with the whole family knowing she was gone—

"I'll bring him over here in the morning when you get home. Then we can…"

"Say goodbye," he finished, lifting his cup and giving her a wry smile. "That'll be fun."

"Braden." She slid her arms around his waist and pulled him into a hug. "Why can't we make this work?"

Setting the cup on the counter, he returned the hug, pressing her against him and planting a kiss on her hair. "Because you changed me, Cass. I went from having walls to wanting someone in those walls with me."

She leaned back. "Simone…might not have left yet."

He grunted, knowing she was not serious. "Scratch that. I went from having walls to wanting *you* in those walls with me. In my life and my bed and my arms. Every day."

"What happened to worrying about coming home every night?"

He searched her face, and his heart, for the most honest answer he had. "That was just self-preservation and fear. That was not knowing a woman strong enough to handle whatever life threw at her. That was BC. And my life will never be the same since you infiltrated it. But I sure as hell don't want to be the man who stomped all over your dreams and made you give up everything you ever wanted because I was another life situation that got in the way."

"You're not a life situation, Braden."

"Then what am I?"

She grasped him a little bit harder, agony all over her expression. "I don't know," she admitted.

"Okay, I'll tell you." He took her face in his hands, holding her creamy skin and delicate features like she was a precious possession. "I am the man who loves you, Cassandra Santorini. And you're the woman who made me want to throw away the old hang-ups and give life and love and forever a chance. The one who made me think about...about the whole enchilada. Marriage, babies, and growing old on rocking chairs." He closed his eyes, shocked by his own admission. "I'm pretty sure I started thinking about that the first time I saw you. And I only got more sure every day."

"Braden." She stepped back, just as shocked.

Of course she was. This wasn't what Cassie wanted, no matter what she said. And he wasn't going to beg her, guilt her, or compromise his feelings into something that fit her plans.

"I hope you find everything you ever wanted in Chicago, Cass. I hope you stand up on the twenty-sixth floor and look down at all the people you don't know and wonder about them. I hope you are the powerhouse your dad thought you should be. I hope you have a thousand notebooks with things to do and are successful and..." He closed his eyes. "And in love. Whoever he is, he'll be the luckiest guy on earth."

She stood there, staring at him, her hands over her mouth as if she had to hold in her response. But he didn't wait for it. He didn't need to.

He took a step back, went to his room to dress, and when he came out, she and Jelly Bean were on the patio. He walked toward the door, seeing her with her head down, writing furiously in that notebook he'd found under the bed.

On second thought, it was better not to let JB know he was leaving with the other dog. One broken heart was enough in this house.

So he slipped out the front door, climbed into the truck, and sat for a minute, composing himself while Jazz settled into the passenger seat like she'd made this trip a hundred times. Or maybe he was just waiting for her to come running out here to profess her love and her decision to stay.

When that didn't happen, he pulled out and drove away, without saying goodbye to the woman and dog he loved most in the whole world.

Chapter Twenty-Three

Cassie and Jelly Bean arrived early to set up the Kibbles for Kindness fundraiser, so she was surprised to see Jace already in the square, already surrounded by contestants, cameras, and at least a dozen different dogs.

Yikes. She shifted the pile of notebooks, a laptop, a fancy camera, and her phone from one arm to the other. Maybe she'd done too good a job of raising awareness for this event. Was that a TV station from Charlotte?

Before he saw her, Cassie took a deep breath, not fully prepared for the conversation he, of course, would want to have. But in the middle of that mayhem, she couldn't talk about his job offer, so she confidently powered forward and called Jace's name.

"Cassie. Thank God." He managed to break away from one of the women who was waving a dog treat under his nose, jogging to Cassie to escape the crowd. "Please tell me the judges are going to be here soon," he said under his breath. "Because these bakers actually think *I'm* going to taste their treats."

"I have a judge right here." Turning to the

bleachers, she carefully set her pile of work stuff down and tugged on Jelly Bean's leash. "Darcy is bringing the others. She and Ella will manage them onstage, and you don't have to do a thing except sit in on the interviews with the five finalists." She glanced around. "Why is everyone so early?"

"Anxious," he said. "These ladies want to win. They're trying to bribe me. Someone named Linda May tried to stuff something called a raspberry *croi-treat* down my throat. Newest thing, she said, croissants for dogs."

She snorted. "Best baker in Bitter Bark, or so her name tag says. Is Ella here yet?"

"I haven't seen her, but I need some help unrolling the Family First banner."

"I'm on it," she assured him. "And let's get you somewhere protected and peaceful."

"I knew you'd know what to do." He added an expectant tilt of his head. "And I hope you've made your decision."

She inhaled and looked up at him. "I have, Jace, I—"

"Cassie!" She turned at the sound of Ella running toward her, being pulled by three large dogs. "I got the judges! There are two more back there with Darcy and—whoa!" One of the dogs jerked his leash and made Ella stumble just as she reached them.

"Whoa is right." Jace practically scooped her into his arms, saving her from a face-plant. "Easy, girl."

Ella froze for a moment, then righted herself, her eyes flashing in a way that Cassie knew meant the wrong thing was going to come out of her mouth. "*Girl?*"

Oh…boy.

"I need your help," Cassie interjected, taking the leash of a jumpy retriever. "Let's get someone to watch these guys in the judges' area, and then we'll hang the banner and you…" She nodded to Jace. "There's coffee and shade in the media tent, right near the Thad statue. Go relax, and I'll be over when you're needed."

His shoulders dropped as tension eased. "I knew hiring you was the smartest thing I ever did."

"*What?*" Ella choked the word. "You *hired* her?"

He cringed, knowing he shouldn't have said that. "Not officially yet, but—"

"You're taking her away from Bitter Bark? From our family? From my—"

Cassie stepped right in front of her. "Ella. We have a job to do right now. A big one. Let's focus on that so Jace doesn't have to worry about anything."

It was enough to quiet her, but only until he was out of earshot.

"You're moving away?" The question was loaded with the same agony that had plagued Cassie all night, but had finally eased with this morning's decision, which Braden had a right to know before anyone else.

"Ella, I promise I'll…" Her voice faded as her gaze moved across the judging area and landed on Gramma Finnie and Yiayia, both laden with baskets and bags, moving slowly, with Pyggie and Gala trotting behind them. "We have to help them."

Ella turned and didn't hesitate even one second as they both hustled toward the older women who, even at nine in the morning, looked overheated.

"Here, let us take those," Cassie said, grabbing the basket that seemed to drag Gramma Finnie down.

"Thank ye, lass. We had to park a mile away. There are more people here than yesterday for the dog show."

Ella elbowed Cassie. "That's because Superwoman was in charge of publicity."

"Everyone wants their recipe to win a national contest," Cassie said, taking a few bags from Yiayia. "Look how much trouble you two went to."

"Too much," Gramma said, using her free hand to pat Yiayia's cheek. "Poor Agnes can't even speak."

Cassie turned to her grandmother in time to catch a flash of fury in her eyes, but it immediately disappeared. "I'm fine, Finnie," she said. "Just a little winded."

But a closer look at Yiayia told Cassie she didn't look fine at all. "You should sit down, Yiayia."

"I don't need to..." Yiayia closed her eyes and seemed to sway a little. "Let's just get our stuff set up."

"I will not," Gramma Finnie said, crossing her arms and looking like she was digging her little rubber soles into the grass, "until you get off your feet and rest. I heard you working to catch your breath this morning."

"Yiayia!" Cassie exclaimed, searching her grandmother's face for clues to her health. "You shouldn't be out here in the sun all day."

"I'm fine," she insisted, taking a step, but then closing her eyes and putting her hand over her chest. "It's just warm."

"And only going to get warmer," Cassie said, already making a decision she knew would be fought tooth and nail. "I'm taking you home."

"What? Like hell you…" She stopped, swallowed, and took a breath. "I don't want to go home, Cassie. Dear."

The singsong voice had no effect on Cassie, who was already digging for keys from the purse hanging on her shoulder. "Ella, you have to step in and do my job while I get Yiayia home."

"I got it, Cass," Ella agreed. "Darcy is already over there, and my mom just texted that she's parking and on her way, too. We got this. I'm going to score Gramma Finnie some shade and a seat for her table."

"Oh, Finnie gets to stay, but I don't? What kind of treatment is that?" Yiayia sounded very much like, well, Yiayia, with her hackles up and her back against the wall—the place she hated most in life.

"Gramma Finnie doesn't look like she's about to keel over."

"I'm *younger* than she is."

Finnie stepped forward and once again put her hand on Yiayia's cheek. "Sweet friend, if anything happened to ye, I'd be lost. Do this old lass a favor and get a wee bit o' rest at home. Then come back and join me for the judgin' and celebratin' our new fame and fortune when our Dogmother Delights are the best-selling line for Family First."

Cassie watched Yiayia surrender right before her very eyes. "I guess I could use a little nap after last night." She gave Cassie a sheepish look. "We were up until two baking."

"Good heavens," Cassie said, sliding an arm around Yiayia. Then she turned and snapped her fingers for Jelly Bean, who was taste-testing a treat. "Let's go, JB." Instantly, he broke away from the lady giving him the treat and came over, the leash he really didn't need dragging in the grass. "My car's right on Ambrose Avenue," Cassie said. "Let's go."

With a halfhearted wave to the others, Yiayia acquiesced and walked next to Cassie. "This isn't going to help you impress that Jace Demakos," she muttered.

"I'm not trying to impress him," Cassie said. "I'm worried about you."

When Yiayia didn't argue with that, but put a hand on her chest again, Cassie knew she'd made the right decision.

In the car, Yiayia sighed as if she was finally relieved. "I feel better."

"We're still going home."

"That's fine. I want to get some more oregano to sprinkle on some of the treats. Finnie really made me go light."

"Yiayia." Cassie shot her a look. "You're not going home, getting oregano, then coming back until I know you're okay."

She didn't answer, but looked out the window, strangely silent. Cassie figured she was saving up for an argument, but none came, even after they pulled into the driveway of the Victorian on Dogwood Lane.

When she turned the ignition off, Yiayia's expression softened as if she really was happy to be home. "Thank you, *koukla*."

Cassie's heart folded in half. "It's fine. I'm going to stay with you for a while to make sure you're okay."

"No, you are not. I'm going straight to my bed, and you have so much work to do at that event."

Cassie lifted one dubious brow. "If you do

something like get that oregano and Uber back to the square—"

She laughed. "That's what *you* would do, Cassie."

She knew better than to argue with the truth.

"And maybe, a long time ago, I would have, too." Yiayia let out a long, slow sigh. "But I know my limits, and I promise I'll go to bed."

"Okay, but I'm calling Mom to come over and sit with you. I'll stay until she gets here."

"Please." Yiayia narrowed her eyes and squeezed Cassie's arm. "You have an important job to do over there. Ella's up to her eyeballs and in over her ditzy little head. Go back before she completely screws the whole thing up."

Cassie half smiled. "You sounded a lot like that old Yiayia I knew and mostly loved."

She gave a frustrated grunt. "That old meanie does rear her ugly head every once in a while. Truth is, Ella is a sweet girl, and her flightiness is endearing. But they need you there. Please."

She was right about that. They did need her there, and fast. "Okay."

Yiayia gave her a quick peck on the cheek and got out of the car, having enough pep in her step for Cassie to feel comfortable letting her go in alone. After the door closed, Cassie pulled out and reached for her phone to call her mother.

She was halfway out of the driveway and still digging through her purse before she remembered the phone was on the bleachers in Bushrod Square.

"Damn it." She hit the brakes and pulled back in, opened the door, and instantly, Jelly Bean scrambled out of the back to come with her.

"Oh, JB," she said on a laugh. "Now you're my best friend. It's like you know exactly what I'm thinking. Don't tell me you can read, too, and saw what I wrote today. Come on. In the house to use Yiayia's phone."

He followed her and stopped when she pulled the screen door open, only to find the house door locked.

She knocked and called out, keeping one hand on Jelly Bean's head. When Yiayia didn't answer in thirty seconds, Cassie banged a little harder. "I forgot my phone, Yiayia!" she called out.

Still nothing.

"That's weird. She's barely had time to get to her room." She smacked her hand on the wood again, hollering her grandmother's name. Next to her, Jelly Bean barked, then paced the porch and barked again.

"Right?" Cassie mumbled, feeling as frustrated as the dog. "What the heck? Yiayia!" She peered through the kitchen window, squinting at the...open door to the basement. "She went down there? For oregano? Oh, that woman!" That was Yiayia—manipulating as always.

Furious, Cassie shifted from one foot to the other, huffing out a breath as she waited for her to come back upstairs, cupping her hands at the window to see into the kitchen. And waited some more. And waited long enough that her usual buzz to take action mixed with a low-grade worry that something was wrong down there.

She looked around, digging back to her childhood, to Yiayia and Papu's house and...where they'd kept the spare key.

"Please, God. Please." She stood on her tiptoes and

patted the top of the windowsill, already spinning through plan B. She'd go to a neighbor's house and call—

Something metal hit the porch.

"A pain in the butt, but a creature of habit," she said to Jelly Bean as she scooped up the key. He grew even more anxious as she unlocked the door, giving a growl as he nosed his way between Cassie and the door. "Hang on, hang on. We'll get in."

But she barely had the door open before the dog forced his way in, barking hard, and headed straight for the basement door. He stopped at the top, pawing the floor.

"Jelly Bean!" She followed him, looking down into the darkness, patting the wall for a light switch she couldn't find. Why wasn't the pantry light on? Was her grandmother down there? "Yiayia? Are you there?"

All she heard was a moan, barely audible, but that was enough to make Jelly Bean lunge forward, and in that split second, Cassie realized she was standing on his leash. Time stood still as her foot went flying off the top step.

There was no second step. No third step. And no soft landing as her legs buckled under her, and her body went tumbling. Her head hit the handrail, and her hands smashed the steps before her face did, bringing her to a sudden, vicious stop that sent her foot through the open riser, where it lodged as she fought for balance and control.

The crack of a bone in her foot was loud enough to hear over the barking, and violent enough to make her instantly nauseated.

White-hot sparks of misery exploded in her head, making her cry out in a voice that didn't even sound like her own, and for a few frightening seconds, she couldn't even remember her name.

She stayed perfectly still then, trying to get her bearings in the dark and trying not to howl as pain licked through her entire body.

"Oh God." The fact that she could actually moan was good. She wasn't dead. She wasn't dead, but the pain made her wish she were.

Jelly Bean's barks were loud and out of control, but they stopped when he came right to where she was sprawled over three steps. He licked her face, whined, and licked her again.

"Yeah," she grunted. "I need help. Yiayia?" Her words were barely a whisper as the searing pain sliced through her. "Are you there?"

From the dark pantry, another groan. "I think…I'm having…another one."

Another what? Blinded by tears and choked by a sob, Cassie attempted to push herself up to get to the pantry. "I'm coming," she said. But it would be slow.

"My heart." A reedy voice floated out. "It's stopping again."

An injection of adrenaline spiked through her veins, making Cassie push through the pain and force her foot out from between the stairs. Holy mother of God, it hurt.

But she was free and able to crawl down the rest of the stairs to the pantry. Sharp, hot stabs of agony jabbed at her calf and ankle, but she ground her teeth together and ignored them.

She had to save Yiayia. She *had* to.

At the pantry door, she could make out her grandmother's body slumped on the floor.

"Yiayia." Cassie dragged herself closer, willing her eyes to adjust to the darkness. "Are you having a heart attack?"

"I think so," she mouthed, her eyes closed. "This one is worse than the last one."

The last one? She reached for her with hands pulsing with bruises. "I'll help you." But how? She had no phone and could barely crawl. By the time she got back upstairs and got help, Yiayia could be dead.

Yiayia moaned and moved, starting to become visible in the dark. "This is my fault."

Yeah, it was. But Cassie had no will to fight. She had to *act*.

"I have to get back up those stairs and get help." She put her hand on the floor, and it smashed into something that felt like dirt, but from the smell that hit her nose, she knew exactly what it was. She'd come down for that stupid oregano!

Using the anger to help her push, Cassie tried to right herself, but the pain was too intense as another wave of nausea hit, and her head suddenly felt disconnected from her body. "I can't get up."

Yiayia sobbed quietly. "I wanted to change. I did. I tried. I don't want to die, *koukla*."

"You're not going to." Although, even as she said the words, she couldn't be sure that wasn't true. "Not if I can do anything about it."

But she couldn't.

"I don't want to go to the…other place."

"We're not going anywhere at the moment."

"I was there. They sent me back."

How could they get out of here? How could they get help? Who'd hear her yelling, even if she could in all this pain? "What are you talking about?"

"When I died...the first time."

Cassie blinked, surprised by the news and encouraged that her night vision was starting to work. She could see...a little. At the same time, she tried to make sense of what Yiayia was saying, but failed miserably. "You...died?"

"And now I've changed. I feel...love. I care. I want you to love, too. All you kids. Even...Katie." Her voice cracked. "But I lied to you and came down here, because I'm not changed." She choked on the next sob. "And now I'm going...to...*hell.*"

"No, no." Cassie shook her head, trying to will the adrenaline not to disappear until she could do something to save them. "You're not going to hell, and we're not stuck here because..."

With her eyes adjusting, she looked around in desperation, able to see Jelly Bean taking it all in, barking and growling and occasionally sticking his nose in the spice on the floor.

"Because...we have the world's smartest dog."

Yiayia whimpered, but Jelly Bean looked up as if he knew exactly what that meant.

"That's right. You're going to get help." But how? If he went back to the square, would anyone even notice him with all those other dogs? Would Ella or Darcy or Gramma Finnie wonder why he was there and Cassie wasn't? By the time they figured it out...it could be too late.

"We need to call 911," Cassie muttered as the thread of an idea formed. "We need to get the EMTs here. We need…" Her gaze fell to the half-empty bottle of oregano. "We need to send a message to the fire station."

He barked.

"Fire station? You know what that means?"

He barked again, and she almost cried with hope.

"I think you do. And I think you're going to pull a full-on Lassie and go there. With…" She snagged the small glass bottle marked *rigani*. "A sign to our favorite firefighter." Fighting through the pain, she pulled Jelly Bean closer and tied the leash that had almost killed her around the bottle, securing it with a knot, then wrapping the remainder of the strap around his neck and tucking it all into his collar.

It took forever, and every move hurt, but it was her only shot.

Once it was secure, she got both hands on his head and forced his gaze on hers, just the way Braden did when he wanted to be sure the dog understood.

"Go get Braden. At the fire station. Understand? Braden. Fire station. Help." She gave him a nudge toward the stairs and heard his paws as he ran up them, thanking God that she'd left the kitchen door open and that the crappy screen door didn't latch.

Then she dropped her head on Yiayia's lap in utter exhaustion and pain.

"You think that dog speaks English?" Yiayia whispered.

"I know he does."

Yiayia's hand settled on Cassie's head, moving slowly over her hair. The gesture was so comforting and welcome, Cassie didn't bother to fight the tears that rolled down her cheeks.

The tears didn't stop while Yiayia managed to talk. They didn't stop as she finally learned Yiayia's secret. They didn't stop when the old woman begged forgiveness from Cassie and the God she believed had sent her back with a purpose and a second chance.

The tears stopped only when the blinding pain became so unbearable, Cassie blacked out.

"You gonna train that dog all day, or do some paperwork?"

Braden looked up from where he crouched in front of Jazz, squinting at Declan as he crossed the grassy area in front of the station. "I'll get it done," he said. "I'm behind on handler training with her."

As Declan got closer, he eyed Braden. "You okay?"

Define *okay*. Living, breathing, going through the motions? Yeah. "I'm good," he said with a shrug.

Declan came closer, wearing a face Braden knew all too well. "You've been better," he said. "Like for a few weeks, you've been great. And now..."

He stood with a huff of breath, knowing better than to dodge his oldest brother who, for twenty years, had decided he needed to be Braden's father when he could. "Cassie's moving to Chicago. Dream job. Need I say more?"

Declan stared for a moment, then snorted. "Man, do I know about women and their dream jobs."

Braden had a good idea who he was talking about. Evangeline Hewitt, Declan's closest friend since Braden could remember, had settled into Raleigh as a veterinary neurologist who rarely returned to Bitter Bark. Although his brother didn't talk about it, he was always a little sullen when one of those infrequent visits ended. Long distance *sucked*.

Of course, Declan and Evie were childhood friends and had been glued together in high school and college, but suddenly that friendship looked different to Braden. Maybe Declan *could* help him.

"Makes you wonder about someone's priorities, doesn't it?" Braden asked, stepping away from Jazz. "I mean, what's more important than..." *Love.* "Family?"

Declan gave a sad smile. "Sometimes, work is. When it's a purpose, a drive, a reason for getting up every day, who are we to say a woman can't have that when we..." He gestured toward the truck in the driveway. "Do this."

"But we save lives, and she..." *Does events.*

"She gets to do what she wants to do," Declan said. "And if I know Cassie, she's probably ridiculously good at it and can rise to the top in any situation."

Braden just stared at him. This wasn't exactly the advice he wanted.

"Give her time, give her space, give her a chance to pursue what she wants," Declan said. "Family's here, and there's always a chance she'll come back."

A chance. "And I'll just wait?"

Declan's smile was sad and knowing. "Pretty sure you could get a job in Chicago, bro."

"I know I could, but..." But this town and these counties needed the services that Braden and Jazz could offer. *Really* needed them. There were probably a hundred arson dogs in Chicago.

Behind him, Jazz barked, then darted toward the street.

"No," Braden called, but Jazz ignored the order, taking a few steps onto the sidewalk, staring into the distance, barking furiously at something or…someone.

Braden's heart catapulted to his throat. It was Cassie. It had to be. She'd come to tell him…

What the hell?

"Jelly Bean?" he and Declan said at the exact same time, with matching shock at the sight of the dog tearing down the street toward the station.

They both ran toward the dog, along with Jazz, meeting him on the sidewalk, where Braden nearly fell to the ground to get at eye level.

"What are you doing here?" He looked past Jelly Bean's head, scanning the entire street and parking lot for any sign of Cassie. "Where's Cassie? What are you doing?"

"He's not going to answer," Declan said dryly.

"But…" Yes, he was. "What the hell is this?" His leash was wrapped purposefully around his neck, with something stuck between it and his fur. "A bottle?"

"She sent you a message in a bottle?" Declan suggested.

As Braden pulled out the bottle and stared at the word and the tiny Greek flag, he didn't know whether to laugh or cry. "It's Greek oregano," he said.

"Mmm. Romantic."

Braden looked up at his brother, a hundred explanations running through his head, all punctuated by Jelly Bean's insistent, furious bark.

"Maybe it's something to do with the scavenger hunt you're setting up."

"Maybe, but..." He looked at the bottle, remembering her telling him she'd dropped the bottle in the basement pantry. Squeezing his eyes shut, he tried to think, but JB would not stop barking, like he really was trying to answer.

Braden looked into the green eyes he knew so well, trying to decipher what the dog was communicating, but seeing only...wild and intense concern.

"Something's wrong," Braden muttered, standing slowly. "Something's very wrong."

"Call Cassie."

Braden grabbed his phone, corralling the two dogs closer, and only more frustrated by voice mail. "She should be at the square with Ella for an event today." He jabbed the red button, ended the message, and tapped Ella's name.

"Very busy right now." Ella's frustration came through louder than her actual voice. "Very, very—"

"Where's Cassie?" Braden demanded.

"Good question. She took her grandmother home ages ago, and I thought she'd be back by now. If you talk to her, please tell her we need her so flipping bad right now."

Braden didn't answer, but sliced his brother with a look. "This came from a basement pantry at the bottom of stairs that I would bet my life aren't to code."

Declan's eyes widened. "Let's go. I'll get the crew."

As they ran into the station and Declan sounded the call, Braden didn't bother to ask his brother if they could bring Jelly Bean. He was as important on this call as the two other EMTs that piled into the truck.

It wasn't until the sirens screamed and they went careening toward Dogwood Lane that Jelly Bean finally quieted, satisfied that he'd done his job. And Braden had never loved him more.

Chapter Twenty-Four

B raden drove straight to Waterford Farm when his shift was over, having gotten the text that both Cassie and Yiayia had been released from Vestal Valley Hospital the night before while he was working.

At eight in the morning on a Sunday, Waterford would normally be deserted, hours away from the weekly dinner that would bring everyone together. Today, the driveway was filled with every car and truck he recognized from all three families.

In times of trouble, the Kilcannons and Mahoneys—and now the Santorinis—gathered, no planning necessary. He wasn't the least bit surprised to see them all in the big kitchen, spilling out to the den and even the central hall when he walked in with Jazz and Jelly Bean.

But he was surprised as hell to see Jace Demakos sitting at the island counter sipping coffee like he *belonged* there.

Braden swallowed his emotions and braced for the resounding greeting he expected from the family. And he got it—loud, exuberant, and joyous...for Jelly

Bean. Amid the hoots and cheering, the exclamations came fast and furious. Even Jazz barked, as if she knew her pal was the star of the day.

"There's our hero!"

"All hail King Bean!"

"Hands down the best dog ever!"

"Move over, all other dogs!"

Barking, circling, and wagging his tail so hard he hit a few people, JB reveled in the attention, accepting treats and rubs and praise from everyone. Once they were done, Braden was finally acknowledged with hugs and high fives from the guys, kisses from the girls and Gramma, and one bone-cracking embrace from his uncle.

"Thank you for training him like that," he said to Braden. "Thank you for believing in that dog."

Braden gave a solid pat of gratitude to his uncle, then leaned back to ask, "How are they? I heard Yiayia did not have a heart attack, which we kind of figured based on her vitals in the ambulance."

Katie came up to him and added her own squeeze and a kiss of gratitude, tears spilling from her dark eyes. "Yiayia has costochondritis." She said the word like she'd just learned it and still was getting comfortable with the pronunciation. "The doctors think she must have injured cartilage in her ribs from lifting something too heavy. The symptoms feel exactly like a heart attack, especially familiar for someone who's *had one before*, which..." Katie wrinkled her nose to show her displeasure. "She never told us she had. Can you believe that?"

Braden shook his head. "And only one broken bone in Cassie's foot?"

"Yes, thank God. A slight concussion, but nothing…" Katie closed her eyes and hugged him, overcome with emotion. "It could have been so much worse, Braden."

He blew out a breath, remembering the moment he'd found her and Yiayia and pieced together what had happened. This gathering could be for a far darker reason, which was why the mood in the kitchen was celebratory.

"Six weeks in a cast," Uncle Daniel said. "Six weeks in a boot."

"But she'll dance at our wedding," Katie added, wiping a tear. "All thanks to Jelly Bean."

He glanced at the dog, licking peanut butter directly out of Ella's hand. "Cassie and Jelly Bean might be the two most resourceful creatures on earth."

"Weimaraners are action dogs," Uncle Daniel said.

"Which makes JB a perfect match for Cassie," Braden joked, his gaze shifting past Katie to the man at the counter. When their eyes met, Braden gave a nod, and Jace lifted a coffee cup in greeting.

"I just came over to check on her and let her know the job will wait for her," the other man said.

That was met with a rousing, massive dead silence.

Jace gave an embarrassed laugh. "And that, due to unforeseen circumstances, no winner was chosen for the Family First treat contest."

From across the kitchen, Gramma Finnie raised her fist like a warrior. "Watch out for us next year!"

That brought the levity back, but Braden couldn't laugh with his family. He was still thinking about that job. If Cassie didn't take the offer, he knew it would be because she'd been injured and her dreams had been derailed. Not because she'd chosen Braden and Bitter Bark over the job.

"Can I see her?" he asked Katie.

"Of course." She slid her arm around his and guided him out of the kitchen. "We've set her up in the downstairs guest room, where she'll be staying since there's a flight of stairs up to her apartment. Yiayia is resting in Pru's old room right now, but she's going to be fine and will head back home tomorrow."

"And when do we start building a set of stairs to code in that house?"

Katie snorted. "Josh has already volunteered one of his construction crews."

"That's great. I'm glad to hear that."

As they walked through the center hall to the other side of the house, Katie squeezed his arm. "Cassie's a little loopy from the painkillers," she warned him. "The concussion is slight, but she did get her bell rung. Not sure she'll even remember later what she says to you."

In other words, declarations and promises should be taken with a boulder of salt. "Got it." He nodded as she opened the door and stepped back, letting him enter the dimly lit room alone.

"Hey, cuz," he whispered, going to the bed where her foot was raised and covered in a cast.

She fluttered her eyes open. "Einstein."

For some reason, that just broke his heart into a million pieces. "I brought your favorite dog. He's in the kitchen, being showered with love."

"Well deserved," she said with a smile that looked like it took all her strength to give him. "C'mere, honey. I miss you."

He approached the bed and propped on the side, careful not to disrupt her peaceful position. But he couldn't help reaching out and stroking her hair and cheek. She'd been in and out of consciousness when they'd arrived, and he had no idea if she even remembered him talking to her as they carried her stretcher, or holding her hand in the ambulance when tears of pain rolled down her pretty cheeks.

"How you feeling, gorgeous?" he asked.

She made a face. "Like I tripped on a leash and went flying down basement stairs."

He flinched at a vivid, horrific mental image.

"Totally my fault, not his. Jelly Bean is... unbelievable."

"Pretty sure he's been named the King of All Dogs forevermore."

"Mmm. And I live to serve my king. Remind me if I ever think he doesn't like me again that he's big on grand gestures and that whole 'showing and not licking' thing."

He gave a quick laugh, amazed that she never lost her sense of humor, even when her one-liners were slurred.

He caressed her face again, which made her eyes grow heavy. "You want to sleep?"

"I want to tell you...something." She took a deep breath, wincing.

"It hurts to breathe?" he asked.

"Every cell in my body hurts," she said. "Especially..." She pressed her hand against her heart. "This one." Then she moved that hand to slip it around his. "Braden, I wasn't going to leave," she managed to say. "I swear I wasn't. I didn't get a chance to tell you...or Jace."

Oh, how he wanted to believe that. With every fiber in his body, he wanted to believe that. But something deep inside wouldn't let him, because he'd seen the look on her face, he knew what she wanted from life, and he had no doubt that when he'd left the house twenty-five hours ago, she'd been scribbling her Chicago To-Do List.

And then, in an instant, life changed. A brush with death, a mild concussion, and no doubt a little shock from the fall might make her think she wanted to stay now, but in a few weeks? When her head cleared and Jace was still waving management positions in a big city?

"Well, he's out there with his offer."

"He's here?" She tried to roll her eyes. "Send him in, and I'll tell him right in front of you."

"Cassie, listen, this accident doesn't have to change what—"

"Braden." She tried to sit up a little, but he put his hand on her shoulder to keep her still. "I made this decision before I fell." She frowned. "I know I did, but the whole day is...fuzzy." She tried again to push up. "But I know I did."

"Shhh. Just rest."

"You don't believe me." The frustration came through her weak voice.

Did he? Was *wanting* to believe the same as believing? "I...I think that it's hard for a person like you who likes to make things go her way and then the universe or fate or God—*whatever*—throws a monkey wrench into your plans."

"So you think I'm just saying I was going to stay because I have to?" Her voice cracked, and instantly he shook his head and quieted her. "But that's not—"

"Babe, what happened happened. And it throws you off your plans, but you're not going to change your whole life because you fell down the steps."

"I'm going to change my whole life because..." She lifted her lids and looked into his eyes. "Because I love you."

The words were so airy and soft, he barely heard them, but they had the same impact on his heart as if she'd screamed them from the top of a mountain.

"I don't want to live without you," she said, her eyes welling. "I don't want Chicago or a high-rise or a job if there's no Einstein by my side."

For a whole lot of heartbeats, he just looked at her. Held the words against his heart and reveled in the peace and hope and completion they gave him.

And then he remembered that these were the very promises and declarations Katie had warned him not to trust. They were fueled by sedatives and numbed by a mild concussion. The fact was, Cassie might not ever remember these words had come out of her mouth.

But he would. Forever.

And it would be so easy to say the same three words back to her. Because he did. He loved her with everything he could and some he hadn't known he had. Which meant he had to say something else completely.

"Cassie, you'll never forgive me or yourself if you give up your dreams."

"I have other dreams now," she said, her voice cracking and her words slurred. "I can prove it. I swear I can. I just can't...remember how."

He wasn't sure what she meant, but he understood why she'd say it. "You took a bad fall. You're on some strong drugs. Your mind and memory and even your emotions are out of whack."

She winced, not liking any of that, but he just rubbed his thumb over her knuckles for a minute. "I'm going to give you some time to think and..." He gave a smile. "Make your action plan."

"Time, I got. The woman of action is sidelined for a while."

"Not for long. Not if I know her." He patted her hand, knowing she wasn't going to love what he was about to say. "And you're going to be pampered like a queen here."

"Mom will pounce on my every need," she agreed. "Think she'll mind if you sleep here?"

He swallowed. "I'm not going to sleep here."

She stuck out her lower lip and glowered at her foot. "Hate this cast, but then you better plan nice long visits."

"I'm not going to be in Bitter Bark for a while."

She blinked, her eyes clear for a second as that sank in. "Where are you going?"

"I got a call today that the North Carolina ATF arson squad has an opening for three weeks of ADC and handler certification training. I'll board there with Jazz and complete the course."

"Oh...three weeks? Is it far?"

"Too far to come home during the training, which is intense and you cannot miss a day, but when it's over, Jazz and I will be fully certified for accelerant-detection training."

She sighed and nodded. "Wow. That's what you want. That's your dream. I'm happy… What about Jelly Bean?"

"JB will revel in his hero status and board here at Waterford."

"Board schmoard. He's never leaving my side." She managed a loopy smile. "I bet I could train him to bring me my crutches."

That made him smile. "Sure. He's yours while I'm gone."

"And…what about me?" She found his hand and tried to squeeze. "Am I yours while you're gone?"

Searching her face, he was very quiet for a moment, not wanting to share all the thoughts that had tormented him that day. Like the fact that he'd almost lost another person he loved, almost missed another last goodbye, almost had to go through unimaginable grief all over again, and he wasn't at all sure he could stand that.

So, the reality was, it wasn't his life he was worried about, but the person he loved the most. Love meant…loss. Hadn't he learned that at thirteen?

"I need time, too," he said honestly. "I think a complete break is good for us."

She let her eyes close as that hit. "I wasn't going to take the job," she whispered. "And you'll never believe that now."

He wanted to tell her she was wrong, but he couldn't. "You just get better. Heal that foot. Figure things out."

"I already figured them out, Braden." Her voice

rose and so did her shoulders, the pain flashing in her eyes along with determination to make her point. "I love you. I realized it yesterday and…and…"

"Shhh, Cass."

She fell back on the bed, tears escaping. The problem was, he'd never really know if she would have made that declaration twenty-four hours and one catastrophe ago.

"I'll be back in a few weeks." He smoothed her hair again. "You'll have time to get better, and I'll…"

She closed her eyes and let out a ragged sigh. "It hurts."

"I know, babe." He closed his eyes and leaned close to her. "It could have been so much worse," he whispered as the harsh reality punched him for the twentieth time that day. "You literally could have died. And I honestly do not think I could have…" His voice cracked, making her look up at him, searching his face and waiting for him to finish. "I know life is fragile," he said in a rough whisper. "I see lives lost way too often. But when it's someone who is your very reason for…for *breathing*." He blinked back the moisture in his eyes. "Cassie, I don't know. I just don't know."

"I'm your reason for breathing?"

He didn't answer, but held her gaze long enough that she had to see the truth in his eyes. Finally, she bit her lip and nodded. "Then you come back to me."

"I will," he promised.

"I'll be here…" Her voice started fading, and she couldn't keep her eyes open. "I'll never leave…" Her breath grew steady and deep. "I'll stay…forever… Einsteiiii…"

He watched her sink into sleep, wondering if she'd wake and think she'd dreamed this conversation. Maybe she wouldn't remember it at all.

But he'd replay it a thousand times.

After a few minutes, he tucked the comforter under her chin and leaned close to her ear.

"I love you, *agapi mou*." That was probably redundant, and bad Greek, but he didn't care. It was true.

Chapter Twenty-five

P ru came flying into the back office of Bone Appetit, her eyes as bright as her smile. "Done with station seven!" she announced with a clap. "Beggin' for a Slide is scavenger hunt perfection!"

"How did it come out?" Cassie asked, shifting her ideas notebook to the side to reveal her fundraising list notebook, homing in on the name of the organization she'd chosen to get money for tomorrow's event. Since they'd lowered the entry fee to ten dollars and made it far more fun than serious, close to a hundred dog-and-people teams were now signed up to participate in Lost and Hound. "Because we need this money."

"The Beggin' Strips are buried by the playground with one of Gramma Finnie's cute little paw signs cleverly hidden on the rock-climbing wall," Pru said, throwing a grateful look at the two grandmothers side by side on the sofa in front of a card table covered with poster board and colored markers. "And once they find the Beggin' Strips, they'll locate the clue to 'climb every mountain.'" She sang the last three words in her best *Sound of Music* imitation, making them all laugh.

"The mountain is the slide?" Cassie guessed.

"Bingo. But they have to take a video of going down the slide with their dog and then find the next clue, which will send them to station eight." She took a breath and dropped into the chair. "Which I hope Ella and Darcy are setting up right now outside of Bushrod's and not sitting *inside* Bushrod's day drinking."

"I used to love day drinking," Yiayia muttered to Gramma Finnie. "Bad habit, I know, but it sure helps improve a game of canasta."

Gramma's little shoulders shook under her cardigan. "Oh, Agnes. I know my daughter keeps a wee bit of Jameson's in here." She gave her best friend a sly smile. "Might make the poster art a tad more interestin'."

"And it might make us miss the deadline of this scavenger hunt," Cassie warned. "And we cannot let down the fine people at Anything's Pawsible." She tapped the page covered with notes and ideas she'd written one morning about two and a half weeks ago when she'd come out of her fog and started to...buzz.

The first thing she'd done was gather a crew of family and friends to help her breathe new life into the scavenger hunt, then she started researching potential nonprofits to reap the benefits. When Daniel mentioned an organization dedicated to training dogs who had failed service school, but still needed a purpose in life, she knew where the funds should go.

"You've done excellent work, Pru." Cassie leaned over the desk, careful not to move her casted foot from the small stool where it stayed propped up under the careful eye of Jelly Bean. For three weeks, he'd followed her around no matter how slowly she hobbled, constantly watching the cast like it was his reason for living.

"What's next?" Pru asked.

"Well, Aunt Colleen and my mother are setting up station nine, but…" She glanced at the sofa. "No genius ideas, Dogmothers? We need something amazing for the last station."

"I used all my genius for station four, Sneak a Peek at a Greek." Yiayia grinned. "Poor Alex will have to have his picture taken a hundred times tomorrow when all our contestants visit Santorini's."

"It's a brilliant scavenger hunt station, Yiayia," Cassie told her.

"It's the least I can do, *koukla*." Yiayia gave her the same look she'd worn for almost three weeks. A mix of sorrow, regret, guilt, and shame—and some Botox beginning to wear off. "Since I ruined your life."

All three of them looked at Cassie, who just let out a sigh. "You didn't ruin it, Yiayia. I just wish I'd told Braden how I feel before he left."

"Well, he'll be back very soon," Gramma assured her.

But what would have changed? He'd still think she hadn't gone to Chicago because of the accident, not because…

"You just have to tell him again," Yiayia insisted.

"We'll back you up," Gramma added.

"We need a plan," Pru said, leaning forward and propping her elbows on the table. "You and I are very good at that."

She smiled at the teenager who, along with Gramma Finnie and Yiayia, had made it their mission to keep

Cassie's spirits high during these long weeks of recovery and loneliness. The recovery was steady, if uncomfortable. Loneliness, however, was deep, profound, and left her a little breathless in the middle of the night.

Braden had been gone for twenty days—not that she was counting—and she hadn't heard a word from him.

"I can plan all I want, but convincing him is another matter. I should have told him." She swallowed a familiar lump that formed every time she remembered bits and pieces of their last conversation. All she could clearly recall was him shushing her and feeling frustrated because she couldn't prove *when* she'd made the decision to stay, only that she had.

And she'd told him she loved him, but he hadn't said it back. Or had he? Maybe she'd dreamed he'd called her *agapi mou*.

"Now, lass. You know you can't start the next chapter of your life if you keep rereadin' the last one." Gramma Finnie pushed up from the sofa with remarkable ease considering her age, coming over to put a knotted but tender hand on Cassie's shoulder.

Cassie reached up and covered that hand, closing her eyes for a moment as the words of comfort settled on her heart. "I am rereading…" Suddenly, she sat up a little straighter, her eyes widening. "Reading. Reading. Writing!" She tried to launch up, but of course, the cast kept her in place, and Jelly Bean barked from under the desk at the sudden movement.

"What is it, Cassie?" Pru asked.

"I remember!" She smacked her hands on the notebooks in front of her as a memory flashed in her brain, bright white like it was lit by lightning. That's how all of the memories from that day came back, when they finally appeared at all.

For three weeks, minutes had come back in little trickles…the conversation with Yiayia in the car, finding the key above the door, the moment she'd come in from the patio and realized Braden had left without saying goodbye.

But right now, something big and beautiful exploded from the depths of a concussion. "I wrote it all down!"

"Of course you did," Yiayia said. "Your father taught you as a child that if it's not on paper, it won't happen." She lifted her brows, a move she could barely make a few weeks ago. "His father, my dearly departed husband, was the same way."

But Cassie wasn't listening to Yiayia's musings. Instead, she closed her eyes and saw her pen moving across a page that said *Braden* at the top.

"But after that, I wrote something. I wrote…" She pressed her fingers to her temples as if she could squeeze her brain back into perfect working order. "I wrote him a letter." She breathed the words in a sigh of disbelief. "How could I forget that?"

"Because you fell down seven steps, clocked your head, and broke your foot, lass."

"All to save me."

Instantly, Pru slid into the seat next to Yiayia. "You need to stop being so hard on yourself, Yiayia. Cassie's forgiven you a thousand times."

"I have," Cassie agreed, looking with love at the young girl who'd never known Agnes Santorini as anything but a sweet, if dry-witted and slightly

343

impatient, old lady. "But now I have to figure out how to get Braden to believe me."

"Show him the letter," Gramma Finnie said.

She turned to stare at her. "I have no idea where I put it," she whispered.

"Think!" Yiayia ordered.

"Be strategic," Pru added. "Where might you put it right now if you had to?"

She squeezed her eyes shut and tried to imagine. "Somewhere he'd go…a long time from now." She looked up, holding Pru's intense gaze. "I kind of remember that I didn't want to show it to him right then. But in the future. It was more of a time capsule than a love letter, if you know what I mean."

Pru shook her head. "No clue."

"Where would he go in the future?" Gramma Finnie asked.

Cassie plumbed the depths of her concussed brain and came up with… "A tale."

"A dog's tail?" Pru asked.

"No." Threads wove together, and a picture emerged. "A book tale. Something he'd read on Easter when he was nine and stayed home with his dad."

Gramma Finnie bit her lip. "I do remember an Easter without Joe and young Braden. How sweet that he remembers, too."

"Oh, he does," Cassie said, the whole morning's writing coming back to her. Not exactly what she'd said, but the general idea. Lots of love and promises…all made before she fell. "You know what I wish? I wish he'd find that letter on his own. That would be perfect. That would make everything right."

"Well, where is it?" Gramma asked. "What book?"

Cassie shrugged and let them think she didn't remember because the secret she shared with Braden was too precious, too personal.

"You know what *I* wish?" Yiayia asked, tapping the poster board in front of her. "That we could be given the instructions for station ten so we can finish up and squeeze in a game of canasta this afternoon." She gave Gramma Finnie a very serious—even harsh—look, making Gramma's eyes widen just a bit.

"I would very much like to beat you again, Agnes."

"Not without me, you don't." Pru stood up and looked from one to the other, a conspiratorial smile on her face. "I know *exactly* how to do that."

But Cassie barely heard the exchange, still digging through her memory banks to try to unearth exactly what she'd said on that piece of paper she'd folded and put into *A Tale of Two Cities*.

"Are you in, Cassie?" Gramma Finnie asked. "We can finish this up and play all afternoon."

"I think I'll rest," she said. "If you don't mind."

"Oh, we don't mind at all, lass." Gramma Finnie pressed her hand into Cassie's shoulder, emphasizing the last words, and Cassie knew they were just trying to make her feel better for not playing.

But nothing could make her feel better until Braden was home and holding her...forever. Was that even possible?

She reached down and gave Jelly Bean a scratch, her gaze falling on her fundraising notes.

"Yes," she whispered to the dog. "Anything's *Pawsible*, right, Mr. Bean?"

"Right," Yiayia said. "Now let's get to work, Dogmothers."

She heard Pru giggle and whisper something to Yiayia, but Cassie just forced herself to focus on the job at hand, not the hole in her heart.

As soon as he reached Ambrose Avenue after the three-hour drive home from training, Braden knew something was up. When he stopped at the light and saw a neon poster board that proclaimed *Lost and Hound Scavenger Hunt Sign-Up* with an arrow toward Bushrod Square, he hit his brakes and stared at it.

Hadn't that been canceled?

Would Cassie be there? In the square? Running things on crutches, Jelly Bean at her side? Or had she given the whole thing up to someone else to do?

As it had for three solid weeks during training, his chest tightened at the thought of her. What would happen when he saw her? Where would her heart be now that they'd been apart for three weeks?

All he knew was that he didn't want to win Cassie by accident—literally. In his mind, he'd lost her the last morning they were together, and her decision was made.

So when the light changed, he forced himself to turn north, away from the square and toward his house. Whatever she was doing out there—if she was even there—didn't concern him anymore. Jelly Bean didn't need ten grand worth of training.

Jazz had aced the certification, of course, and together, they were ready to start arson investigations. In fact, they already had a call out in Simon's Run tomorrow morning, since there had been another fire while he was gone. Not as serious, but deliberately set. He and Jazz were needed there.

A few minutes later, he pulled into his driveway, which looked painfully empty without that little red Ford Escape parked there.

"New normal, Jazzer," he said to the dog in the back.

They climbed out together, and he hadn't even gotten his bag out when Jazz gave a sharp bark and started toward the front door.

"Anxious to get home, are you?"

But her bark was one he'd come to recognize well in the last few weeks. It marked a target found. Not necessarily an accelerant. For that, she would bark twice and stand perfectly still, staring straight ahead so she didn't disturb anything, waiting for her reward.

But for food that had been used as a reward, she'd bark like that, wag her tail, and head right toward it. At the moment, she was nosing the welcome mat at his front door.

As he got closer, he could see a tiny yellow square, like a Post-it Note, stuck to his door. A package attempted to be delivered, he thought as he grabbed his duffel bag and started walking. Or...or...

A note from Cassie.

Stopped by to see you...

He shook that nonsense right out of his head. The only reason Cassie wasn't waking up in her high-rise in Chicago right now was because she damn near killed herself when JB's leash tripped her.

He reached the door and squinted at the words.

Lost and Hound Starts Here.

"It does?" He glanced left and right, hoping like

hell some other scavenger hunters weren't lurking. Of course, no one was around.

He pulled the sticky note off and stared at the five words in an unfamiliar combination of print and cursive. He'd seen Cassie's handwriting many times. This wasn't hers.

He flipped the paper over to find an arrow pointing down, where Jazz was doing her level best to get her nose under the faded doormat.

Still uncertain of what the heck was going on, Braden bent over to lift the mat and found a flattened, slightly torn Miller Lite label. Which was not like him at all, since he didn't generally live like this was a frat house, but he'd probably had a beer out here sometime in the last year. Maybe the label...

Or was that a clue?

He lifted it for a closer examination, and as he did, he smelled something sweet. Not like beer, but...peanut butter? Sure enough, on the back was a little smear, the rest of which was on the ground and being licked up by Jazz.

So, not trash, but something someone knew a dog would be able to find.

His heart lifted for the first time in days. But how could she have done this? And why?

And where would this "clue" lead him?

He opened the door, half hoping, half dreaming Cassie would be on the other side, but the house was as cool and quiet and empty as when he'd left three weeks ago. Studying the beer bottle label again, he went on instinct to the fridge, opening it to spy a six-pack in a cardboard case that had been there for weeks, since Cassie had brought it over. Four of the slots were empty, but he leaned over and peered in, and sure enough, there was another sticky note.

This one said 6L, 4R, 3L, 1R.

A combination lock? A riddle? No...those were dog handling instructions for pacing. Six paces left, four right, three left, and one more to the right. He followed them, unable to wipe the smile that threatened. How would she know that?

He stopped in the middle of the spare bedroom that he used as an office and reading room. Turning, he looked around for another clue, weirdly excited about it, but...there was nothing. Everything looked the same and as untouched as the last time he'd been in here.

He took a step, and his foot tapped something that went rolling across the floor. Looking down, he saw a small plastic...was that an Easter egg? Like the ones they used at Waterford for the kids' egg hunt last year?

He picked it up, shook it to hear something rattle inside, and realized that by now, he was not just smiling, but grinning ear to ear. No one else could have done this. No one else could be so clever and...

But she could hardly walk, he reminded himself as he snapped open the egg. Inside was a tiny, travel-sized case of baby aspirin.

Baby aspirin? What the...

"A sick kid at Easter!" He spun around, his gaze on the bookshelf that covered one wall. She was the only one still on earth who knew that story, with the possible exception of his mother, and she sure as heck hadn't done this. He went right to the shelf, and his gaze landed on the worn spine of a book that was about twenty-five years old.

A Tale of Two Cities, Children's Classic Version

No one but Cassie could have even known he owned this book, let alone that he'd read it on Easter as a kid. No one. But how had she done this? And why?

Very slowly, he pulled it out, opening to the first page, ready to read the famous first line of a classic. But that page was covered by a piece of lined paper folded in half. Another clue?

As soon as he opened it, he recognized a page of notebook paper he'd seen before. His name was scribbled at the top in what was now very familiar handwriting. Under that, he saw the numeral one and the words *figure out what to do* and knew this page was torn from the very notebook he'd found under the bed. The one she had been writing in the morning he left.

The morning everything changed.

Taking a breath, he walked to the couch, perched on the edge, and immediately Jazz came over, taking up her position at his feet.

"She wrote this before she left my house," he said to the dog, knowing that she didn't understand. Hey, they couldn't all be Jelly Bean. "So that means…"

Whatever it said had been in her heart before the accident.

Finally, he let himself read what she'd written as point number two.

2. Tell him tonight.

3. Hide this letter in the book.

4. Wait 10 years for him to find it. Maybe 11. Or 12. Whatever it takes.

What was she talking about? And if she hadn't

wanted him to find it for ten years, why set up this scavenger hunt?

He let his gaze shift down a few lines to read the rest.

Dear Braden,

Someday, when you read this book to your son or daughter, you'll find this page from one of my zillions of notebooks. I hope it makes you smile. At me.

Because when you open this book to read it to a little nine-year-old, I want to be on the other side of the bed, with a couple of dogs, and maybe another baby in my arms. That's the future I want, Braden.

In my tale of my two cities, this is the one I choose. Bitter Bark, not Chicago. Where you are, surrounded by our complicated, wonderful, beautiful families. I want a small town and a sweet life, with a view from the mountains, and one absolutely perfect firefighter.

And when you read this letter, you'll look over the little head of the child between us and know I made the right choice. That temporary can become forever. That dreams can change. And that no job, no city, no view from above is worth losing what I believe we have right here on earth.

I love you, Einstein. I loved you when I wrote this, and I'll still love you when you finally read it.

It was the best of times...and who knows? It might keep getting better.

xo
Cass

He sat perfectly still for what had to be five minutes, staring at the words, blinking back the tears, and imagining that bed and this book and those kids and his...wife.

Finally, he folded the letter carefully and headed out to make it all come true.

Cassie made it to the top row of the bleachers, but it took a good five minutes to hobble up there on crutches with Pru behind her and Jelly Bean leading the way.

"There," she said as she settled into a seat. "Now we can see everything. It was genius of you to make sure almost all of the stations are visible from here."

"And look at all the people down there." Pru gestured to the dozens and dozens of "hunters" and their dogs, an air of excitement buzzing all around. "Makes you wonder about them all, doesn't it?"

She smiled at her, seeing so much of herself in young Pru. But then, sometimes Cassie thought that was this girl's secret power. People of all types connected with her—from grandmas to children.

"I used to wonder about things like that," Cassie said. "But then I realized that the people I know best are the ones that matter, not all those strangers out there."

"Mmm." Pru tapped her phone and stood, peering out toward Ambrose Avenue, squinting into the bright sun, then texting something on her phone that she angled away from Cassie. When the phone buzzed, she read it and giggled. "Yiayia's worried you're going to fall."

Cassie snorted. "With good reason. Tell her to relax

and keep giving out the free Santorini's samples."

"And Grandma Finnie says we just made our first thousand dollars on entry fees."

"That's awesome. Are you group-texting those two?"

Pru giggled. "I'm an official Dogmother now."

"Really."

"They needed a little youth on the bench, if you get my drift. But I had to pass a test to take it from 'honorary' to 'official.'" She leaned closer. "Gramma would have let me, of course, but Yiayia isn't quite so easy to wrap around my finger, you know?"

"Oh, I know. I was fourteen and trying to wrap her once. So, what did she make you do? Roll a dozen melomakarona in under a minute?"

"Nah, just break into a house."

Cassie choked. "What business are these Dogmothers in, exactly?"

"The business of happiness, lass," she said in a dead-on Gramma Finnie brogue. "And no worries. I was able to get in using this." She tapped her temple. "Just like you found Yiayia's key."

"And who's happy about you breaking into their house, if I might ask?"

"It's all part of the scavenger hunt." She gave a big smile, showing off perfect teeth that she often bragged had been in the hands of a good orthodontist. "We call it station zero. Oh!" Pru stood and peered in the direction of Ambrose Avenue, then texted with the super-thumbs of a teenager. "I gotta go."

Cassie blinked at her and tried to grab her wrist. "Oh no you don't. I don't want to be up here alone with one foot in a cast, Pru, even with Wonder Dog."

"You won't be alone." She turned and planted a kiss on her cheek. "Just stay still for…" She looked out to the square. "One minute. See ya!"

With that, she scrambled away, her long, dark hair flying as she darted to the bottom of the steps.

"But…" Cassie curled her fingers around the metal bench, watching with dismay as Pru stopped at the bottom of the bleachers, talking to someone around the side but blocked by the last few rows. She pointed up to Cassie, then disappeared behind the seats. And then she saw…

Shoulders.

A pair of big, strong, crazy-hot *shoulders* in a blue T-shirt that surely matched the color of his eyes. She couldn't see them behind mirrored sunglasses, but when Braden looked up at her and slid those glasses off, everything in Cassie melted like chocolate in the sun.

"Braden," she whispered.

Instantly, Jelly Bean's head popped up, and he barked, slapping his paws on the bleachers, then throwing a look to Cassie. "You can go," she whispered. "Run and kiss him just like I wish I could."

Released, Jelly Bean tore down the steps, and Jazz, who stood at attention at Braden's side, barked in greeting, and in a second the three of them were all but rolling on the grass in a happy reunion.

After a minute, Braden extracted himself from the two dogs and slid his sunglasses into the collar of his shirt, looking right up at Cassie.

"Glad to see you're not afraid of heights, cuz."

"I am a little dizzy," she admitted. "Might need an EMT."

He climbed the bleachers two at a time, reaching her before she could exhale the breath she'd been holding since the second she saw him. He loomed over her for a moment, then dropped down on the bleacher in front of her, putting a very gentle hand on the cast that had been signed by half of Bitter Bark.

"How's my girl?"

My girl. She managed a shaky smile. "Better now."

He leaned in and put his hand on her cheek. "I missed you."

"Oh." She closed her eyes and angled her head into his touch. "Same."

"I can't believe you're still having the scavenger hunt."

"All proceeds to Anything's Pawsible, a nonprofit dedicated to retraining service dogs who haven't quite found their calling yet."

He frowned. "All failed serv—"

"But be careful. We don't use the term 'failed service dog' around Jelly Bean. He understands English, you know."

He laughed, and the sound rolled over her as warm as the sun. "You look good, Cass."

"Crutches make me sexy."

"Sexi*er*." He slid his hand over her shoulder and down her arm, leaving a wake of chills despite the summer sun. "So, I won."

"The training? Was it a competition?"

He shook his head. "But Jazz did graduate at the top of her class."

"Why am I not surprised? And her valedictorian bark?"

"Standing ovation."

She laughed from her belly, maybe for the first time in weeks. "So, what did you win?"

"The scavenger hunt."

She drew back. "Then get down there so they can ring the bell and give you a trophy. You and Jazz?"

He shook his head. "I have a feeling my portion of the scavenger hunt doesn't count in today's competition."

"I'm confused," she admitted.

"I was, too, until I found this." He reached into his back pocket and pulled something out, pressing it between his hands. "The grand prize." He revealed the folded, lined paper to her with the stubs from a spiral notebook feathered down the side.

Cassie stared at the familiar piece of paper as a thousand different emotions welled up and made her eyes sting. "You found it."

"Of course. Clever clues." He added a smile. "The Easter egg with baby aspirin? That was brilliant."

"The Easter..." She couldn't finish the sentence as so many possibilities swirled. But then she looked over his shoulder and spotted Gramma Finnie and Yiayia looking up at the bleachers. "I think we had some help from professionals," she said.

"We needed it," he said, leaning closer and pulling her attention back to his face. "You wrote this before I left."

"Are you sure about that, Einstein?"

He nodded. "I saw you writing on the patio that morning, and I saw the page when it was blank not an hour before. And even if I didn't know those things, Cass, I believe you. I believe everything you wrote in that letter."

Except… "Um, can I read the letter?"

He inched back. "You wrote it."

"I don't remember exactly what I said. Something about finding it in the future and that I wanted to be there, but…"

"You can read it, but before you do, can I say something?"

"Anything."

He reached both hands under her hair, tunneling his fingers and pulling her closer. "I love you with all my heart and all my soul and every brain cell I have."

She smiled. "That's a lot."

"And if you want to go anywhere, to any city, at any time, I'll go with you."

She shook her head. "Not leaving Bitter Bark."

"Cassie, wait a second. You've wanted this your whole life. You can't just give up your dreams."

She looked at him for the longest time, her heart beating steady with certainty. "I've wanted *this* my whole life," she whispered. "The love of a man like you and this big, wonderful family of ours. We'll visit the cities, but this is home. This is where I—*you and I*—belong."

After a moment, his eyes shuttered closed and he leaned his forehead against hers. "That's perfect, but I want you to know, I'd go anywhere for you."

"But I want to stay here *with* you. Anyway, I've already started setting up my event-planning business, and I'm thinking I'll do a little PR on the side. Jace agreed to let me consult, so I got a client in Chicago, and I'm going to pitch Anything's Pawsible. I'm going to suggest they make Jelly Bean their national spokesdog."

He leaned back. "You should call your company Woman of Action, Incorporated."

"I like that, Einstein. You can be my business partner."

"How about I be..." He eased her closer. "Your everything partner?"

"Oh." She breathed the word, almost kissing him. "I think we could do great things together."

"Mmm." He pressed his lips to hers. "We could make a home and a family and a life together."

She sank into the kiss, and the promise, and the complete and total confidence that she was absolutely where she belonged. "We could make all our dreams come true."

"Like the ones in your letter."

"I better read that." Opening it, she smiled as she skimmed the top list and then took her time on the part she'd written, each word coming back to her. After a moment, she closed it, put it next to her, and looked at him. "My father said when you write things down, you make them happen."

"Smart man." He pulled her into him. "And like my father, I'm not going to spend one minute worrying about life or death. I love you, and I will come home to you every day and every night." He sealed that promise with a kiss.

"Braden. I love you, too. So much." She deepened the kiss, feeling nothing but bliss and joy for the first time in three weeks. Nothing but certainty and love. So much love.

All of a sudden, a bell started ringing and dogs started barking and a cheer went up over Bushrod Square. They parted less than an inch.

"Is everyone watching us?" she asked in mock horror.

"Let's find out." Very slowly, they broke apart and turned toward the main tent, where crowds were surrounding a small group all wearing the same red shirts and a black and white dog in a red bandanna. One of the people held a trophy in the air.

"Oh, they won the scavenger hunt," Cassie said. "That's what all the cheering is."

"Not all." He nodded to two little old ladies off to the side, beaming up at Cassie and Braden, clapping with their own victory.

Cassie lifted the letter and waved it at them, making them laugh and high-five each other.

"Oh, I love them," she said.

Braden settled next to her on the bleacher, putting his arm around her and pulling her against his amazing shoulder and good heart. "We should name our first daughter Agnes Finola."

"No. I don't love them that much."

He laughed and pulled her closer, and at that moment, Cassie knew what her mother meant by feeling alive and secure and grounded, all at the same time. It felt exactly like this.

Epilogue

"Finn, my friend. We are off our game."

Finnie lifted her shot glass and eyed the golden liquid she hadn't had a sip of yet. "It's a long wedding, lass. Katie hasn't even thrown her bouquet yet. Best take it slow."

"I don't mean drinking." Agnes jabbed her with a friendly elbow, then lifted the glass of ouzo in front of her. "Although you Irish do give us a run for our money at these events."

"Sláinte." Finnie tapped the other glass.

"Yamas," Agnes responded, but didn't take a drink, instead getting closer to look through Finnie's bifocals like she was peering right into her soul.

"What?" Finnie asked when the stare became uncomfortable.

"It's October," Agnes said. "We are one-for-one and zero for trying."

"Not zero," Finnie argued. "We've worked on Connor."

"Who hasn't in this town?"

Finnie smiled. "He can't help it. The ladies love him. And we tried Declan."

"Look up confirmed bachelor and find his picture." Agnes rolled her eyes. "We might have to go to plan B for Ella."

"Oh no," Finnie gasped. "Jace will be back. Cassie's got him as a client for her new company, and he's always finding excuses to have meetings here instead of Chicago. Maybe you should start to lay the groundwork for Alex or John, since Nick and Theo are not local."

"They are at the moment." Finnie launched a brow and pointed across the winery terrace where a hundred friends and family had gathered on a glorious autumn afternoon to celebrate Katie and Daniel's wedding. Just off to the side, those two Santorini men stood talking to each other, both tall, dark, and Greek. Well, Theo was Greek. But Agnes seemed to have stopped seething about that, probably because she knew anger caused stress, and stress could cause trouble for her.

"Nick doesn't seem too happy in Africa," Agnes mused. "Too bad he's only here for a few more days."

"And he has a girlfriend," Finnie reminded her.

"Does he?" Agnes snorted softly. "A real girlfriend would have flown here to meet the family. And Theo's only on leave until tomorrow. We need to get cracking, missy."

"We've been busy," Finnie replied. "This is our third wedding in three months, and is it my fault that Cassie caught the bouquet at Darcy's *and* Beck's weddings?"

"She'll probably catch it again today, since it is her mother doing the throwing."

"I think that would seal the deal for a Christmas engagement," Finnie said.

"Which means we better get to work on the next couple," Agnes insisted. "What are we waiting for?"

Finnie sighed. "I have been distracted," she admitted. "Molly had her little lad, and Chloe had her sweet lass. Look at them." She pointed to the small gathering of Kilcannons on the side of the dance floor, many of them fussing over the babes both born two months ago. Molly's little Danny boy was the spittin' image of his father, Trace, who couldn't seem to go ten minutes without holding the child.

And Shane and Chloe's wee Annabelle was Kilcannon through and through, looking so much like Finnie's firstborn, Liam, that she'd spent a few too many days out by the tiny gravestone, remembering those dark days when they'd lost him.

"The new wee ones have had my attention, and all that construction in the house, Agnes." Finnie threw her hands up just thinking about the noise. "I might be too tired for much more matchmakin' this year."

Agnes slapped her hand on the table, making the little shot glasses tremble. "Finola Kilcannon, we made a deal. Don't go crapping out on me now."

Finnie gave her a wry smile. "I don't think the Big Man likes when you talk to me that way."

Agnes closed her eyes. "I should never have confessed all that."

"'Tis a good thing to be honest." She patted the other woman's hand. "It'll keep you nice and, well, nice, lass."

"But what about our purpose?"

"Our—"

"If you don't mind, sir, I have this under control." The woman's voice coming from behind them was tight and sounded like it had been ground out from between tightly gritted teeth.

Finnie and Agnes turned toward the door that led to the winery kitchen, where Alex stood about two feet from a blond woman they both recognized as Grace Donovan, the owner of Overlook Glen.

"I'm sorry, but the Pinot Noir won't work," Alex said.

The woman was a few inches shorter than Alex, with a narrow frame, but she lifted her chin as if she meant business. "The Pinot Noir is perfect for this meal."

"It's lifeless."

She gasped and drew back. "I will have you know that that wine was made using the latest viticulture and enology, with a measured amount of sulfur dioxide and genetically modified grapes."

"Exactly." He shoved the bottle at her. "Cork your science experiment and give us something with a soul."

"Cork it? Shows how much you know about wines. No one 'corks' anymore."

"Then use it to water your plants and call someone to bring us wine that deserves to be served at my mother's wedding. Preferably a Shiraz for this course, but we could settle for a Merlot."

"*Settle?*" She grasped the bottle with both hands like she was squeezing the life out of the poor thing. Or maybe imagining it was Alex's neck. "There is nothing wrong with this wine, Mr. Santorini." She stood on her tiptoes and got right into his face. "Maybe there's something wrong with your mouth."

Even from where they sat, they could see that very

mouth kick in an almost smile. "Are you serious? I'm a chef."

"You're a pain in my butt and have been since you first showed up at my winery." She lifted the bottle high over his head. "First pour, sir?"

"You wouldn't dare."

Grace stared him down, tipping the bottle a centimeter. "It would give me so...much...*pleasure*."

Alex returned the glare, but it sure looked like his head inched a wee bit closer, like the woman was a magnet and he was steel.

For the space of three whole heartbeats, they stayed riveted like that, the only movement the rising and falling of their chests with each strained breath.

"Oh my," Finnie muttered.

"I think he's going to kiss her," Yiayia whispered.

They both waited, watching, wondering what would happen next.

"I have a Shiraz," Grace finally said, lowering the bottle.

Alex rubbed a knuckle under his lower lip, still holding her gaze. "I'd like a...taste."

Yiayia sucked in a breath. Finnie gripped her chair cushion.

"I'll have a server bring you a bottle." With one more slow breath, Grace backed away and headed down a stone hallway, while Alex watched until she disappeared. He finally turned back to the wedding, closing his eyes and adjusting the jacket of his tuxedo.

"Every time," he murmured. "Every damn time."

Finnie turned slowly and stared at Agnes, silent as they picked up the glasses.

"To frenemies!" they whispered in unison, tapping the rims. Then they threw back the shots, ready for round two.

Pour a nice glass of wine, bring your appetite for love, and stay tuned for more romance with Grace, Alex, and a trio of precious pups in THREE DOG NIGHT, up next in the Dogmothers series!

Want to know the minute it's available? Sign up for the newsletter.

www.roxannestclaire.com/newsletter-2/

Or get daily updates, sneak peeks, and insider information at the Dogfather Reader Facebook Group!

www.facebook.com/groups/roxannestclairereaders/

The Dogmothers is a spinoff series of
The Dogfather

Available Now

SIT…STAY…BEG (Book 1)

NEW LEASH ON LIFE (Book 2)

LEADER OF THE PACK (Book 3)

SANTA PAWS IS COMING TO TOWN (Book 4)
(A Holiday Novella)

BAD TO THE BONE (Book 5)

RUFF AROUND THE EDGES (Book 6)

DOUBLE DOG DARE (Book 7)

BARK! THE HERALD ANGELS SING (Book 8)
(A Holiday Novella)

OLD DOG NEW TRICKS (Book 9)

Join the private Dogfather Reader Facebook Group!

www.facebook.com/groups/roxannestclairereaders/

When you join, you'll find inside info on all the books and characters, sneak peeks, and a place to share the love of tails and tales!

About The Author

Published since 2003, Roxanne St. Claire is a *New York Times* and *USA Today* bestselling author of more than fifty romance and suspense novels. She has written several popular series, including The Dogfather, Barefoot Bay, the Guardian Angelinos, and the Bullet Catchers.

In addition to being a ten-time nominee and one-time winner of the prestigious RITA™ Award for the best in romance writing, Roxanne's novels have won the National Readers' Choice Award for best romantic suspense three times, as well as the Maggie, the Daphne du Maurier Award, the HOLT Medallion, Booksellers Best, Book Buyers Best, the Award of Excellence, and many others.

She lives in Florida with her husband, and still attempts to run the lives of her young adult children. She loves dogs, books, chocolate, and wine, especially all at the same time.

www.roxannestclaire.com
www.twitter.com/roxannestclaire
www.facebook.com/roxannestclaire
www.roxannestclaire.com/newsletter/